Green Flash

L.M. Lawson

This is a work of fiction. The characters and events in it are inventions of the author and do not depict any real persons or events. Any resemblance to actual people or incidents is entirely coincidental.

Printed in the United States of America
First Edition
2nd Printing, Feb. 2001

ISBN 0-939837-36-6

Published by
Paradise Cay Publications
P.O. Box 29
Arcata, California, 95521
800-736-4509
707-822-9163 fax
www.paracay.com

ACKNOWLEDGMENTS

Thanks to Carl, Anne, Paul and Tom for their help, support and encouragement, and to my parents who instilled in me a sense of commitment.

ABOUT THE AUTHOR

After selling their business, Lori and husband Carl, left Dana Point, California aboard their 28-foot Bristol Channel Cutter, *Bijou*. Their intention was to spend the summer cruising the islands off the Southern California coast, then return home to start another business. However, nine years and over 20,000 nautical miles later, they've sailed from the west coast of the U.S. through the tropical regions of Mexico and Central America to the colder latitudes of England and Norway. They continue to live aboard, *Bijou*, as they journey the canals of Holland, Belgium and France to the Mediterranean.

1

It happened in the sliver of time between radio transmissions.

"Break. Break. Break." Staccato, rushed and emphatic, the words punched across the airwaves. As if timing an entrance to a revolving door, the sender had waited for an opportunity to jump in, but missed it by a beat and clipped into Zulu Zulu Tango.

Jed Caldwell straightened his back and stared at the microphone. An otherwise routine morning was shattered. The triple "break" was only meant to be used in an emergency. He assumed the hundreds of listeners extending from Southern California and Arizona to the southern boundaries of Mexico had stopped what they were doing and turned to their radios. Unaware of the interruption, Zulu Zulu Tango continued, and as she neared the end of her call, Jed readjusted his glasses and felt his heartbeat quicken.

When Caldwell retired as a dispatcher from the Cincinnati Police Department, he had merely traded his professional microphone for one in amateur radio. From the powerful station in his home on the west coast of Mexico, he coordinated a handful of other land-based hams, and together they helped connect maritime mobile operators cruising the waters north and south of the border. Some days radio waves enabled signals to soar and on other days they buried them in static. In either case, Jed's small network of volunteers extended his reach by relaying information to and from him when he couldn't hear.

As soon as the frequency was clear, his southern relay jumped in. "Jed, we have a breaker, did you copy?"

"Roger, roger. Zulu Zulu Tango, please stand by, we have a

breaker. Breaker, I copy you, how can we help?" Jed turned to a clean page in his log and gripped his pencil.

"My wife's gone . . . I was off watch and just got up . . . I don't know what happened . . . she's just gone . . . I've looked . . . she's not anywhere . . . ."

The male voice shook and sounded frantic, but not hysterical. Jed's long practiced ear assessed the distress without the benefit of a face and conjured up a vision based on the few broken phrases. This wasn't a bogus call. He pictured the man waking, carefree and with thoughts only on the journey.

That pleasure quickly soured once the man went on deck, maybe he called out to his wife and she didn't answer. With the Pacific Ocean surrounding him, he searched, and then searched again. Each moment more frantic than the last, more filled with dread. Finally, the horror of the inevitable would have dropped like a shroud. Of all the thoughts and feelings this man had before turning on the radio to call for help, Jed believed guilt would override them all. In spite of all the present day talk of equality, this man probably considered himself the captain, and thus responsible for his missing wife, almost as much as if he'd pushed her in.

Background noise scratched and crackled from the speaker on Jed's set. The anxious husband hadn't released the transmit button.

Caldwell waited. The tip of his pencil slipped into his mouth and he bit down. Listeners changed every season, and what little they knew of him they picked up during an hour of radio chat with their morning coffee. Still, they counted on him to know what to do. Although he didn't wish for disaster, Jed lived for these moments. It was what helped him get over the gap left after retiring from the force.

In a wink, the background noise disappeared, the normal hiss of dead air taking its place. Everyone expected him to speak. As Jed took charge, his warm, liquid voice began to soothe the breach left by the morning's interruption. It was a talent on which, over the years, he'd come to rely.

"Roger, breaker, I understand. All stations listen up; I've got reasonable copy, but I don't want to miss anything. Breaker, can you give us your lat and lon?"

It took a moment before a subdued voice answered him. First

came the call sign, then the name and then the latitude and longitude. Jed heard resignation in the man's voice, but it was too soon to abandon hope.

"Roger, Eric, good copy. For those of us who don't have a chart right in front of us, where is that approximately?"

"That puts us . . . I mean . . . I'm about a hundred and fifteen miles west northwest of Zihuatanejo."

Jeannie, Jed's Southern California relay, jumped in with her call sign.

"Go ahead, Jeannie," said Jed.

"I'll get on the phone to the Coast Guard and find out what else they need to know; I'll be back."

"Thanks, Jeannie. Okay, Eric, we've got things going on this end. Don't give up hope yet. I know it's tough, but we need you to hang in there. We'll need your help. To keep the airways free for when Jeannie comes back, make responses brief. Say 'roger' if you understand."

"Roger."

"What's your wife's name?"

"Jennifer. Jennifer Stover."

"What time did you last see Jennifer?"

"At four a.m. That's when we changed watches."

"Good, Eric. Do you run navigation lights at night?"

"Of course."

"Were they on or off when you got up?"

The pause was longer this time. "She must have been okay for most of the time because our nav lights were out when I got up. She would have turned them off after dawn. I noticed something else, too; our video camera is gone. Maybe she was taping something and . . . ." Background noise took over for Eric's voice. Seconds passed before he released the transmit button.

Jed waited and when he heard the familiar sound of a clear frequency, he began again. "Roger, Eric, I copied all of that. You're doing great; this information will be very helpful. What are your current speed and course, and have you changed course since you realized Jennifer was missing?"

"Well, I'm drifting now. All the sails are down. According to her last entry into the log, we had maintained a course of 113 degrees and when I got up we were going just over two knots."

"Good, Eric, I got all that. Are you injured or ill?" Jed grimaced as the words disappeared down the microphone. Grief aside, he needed to know if Eric was all right, but the question still sounded ridiculous.

After a brief pause, a pinched voice responded, "Not in the normal sense."

2

Jessie Fox ducked her head to catch a glimpse of the ship's clock on the wall in the cabin below. Bright, relentless sunlight let in by the portholes washed out the usual richness of the wood, and she could hear the whirl of fans in their endless struggle to circulate and cool the hot air. Another half hour to wait.

She exhaled with enough force to lift the dark brown bangs that clung to her forehead, but the cooling effect was gone in an instant. As her hand fluffed the rest of her soggy locks, she wondered how people with long hair stood it. A quick fan of her face, then another fluff, and she gave up the effort. Her hand paused at the scopolamine patch behind her ear, stuck there to prevent seasickness, but moved on without touching it. In these wilting conditions, the itch it caused had become persistent.

She studied the slack, ineffective sails and thought again of the clock. Neal, her husband, usually remained optimistic that the wind would come up if they just gave it enough time. But after hours of drifting on a flat sea in the baking heat, even he set a limit. Nature had a half hour to come through with a breeze, or the solitude surrounding them would vanish, to be replaced with engine noise.

She watched him pick his way back from the bow, his bare feet scarcely touching the hot deck. He ducked under the awning and draped his agile skier's body on the seat opposite her. After slipping the cap off his shaggy, sun-bleached hair, he used the sleeve of his T-shirt to wipe the sweat from his forehead. He had been crabbing about a haircut for days, but Jessie had put him off. Now, as much as she liked this rough and tumble look, she would relent and clip it, if he still wanted it cut.

She diverted her hand as it, once again, made its way to the itch at the nape of her neck, and instead used it to adjust her large-brimmed straw hat. Her gaze went forward along the deck and she watched as wavy lines of hot air rose off *Dana's* topsides. Neal's voice drew her attention back to the cockpit.

"Man, the deck is hot. We need something for our feet. Grab your shoes; we may have another bet coming up."

His comment pulled her to a stand and she cursed when her hat made contact with the awning overhead and slid down over her eyes. She grabbed the brim and pulled it off to follow Neal's point. In the distance she saw an interruption in the glassy water.

A new contest. On this trip, the game was to correctly identify any interesting flotsam or jetsam that floated across their path. The loser had to make the first dinner they had on board once they reached port. After going back and forth, she was again ahead and could taste the chicken enchiladas that Neal said he would make.

Minutes later, clad in hats and rubber-soled deck slippers, they left the shade of the cockpit. Jessie slung their binoculars around her neck and moved forward, sliding one hand along the stout, shoulder-high safety line that stretched from boomgallows to forward shroud. Gripping it now and then, she kept her balance as *Dana* wallowed in the calm sea.

On the bow, the jib and staysail hung like limp hankies and Jessie pushed them aside to clear the view. She peered through the glasses and studied the water. "I think it's wood, probably from a boat, with a piece of it sticking up," she said as she passed the binoculars to Neal.

Her mate adjusted the focus and held steady for a moment. He lowered the glasses, then put them back up to his eyes. "I'm going to say it's a seal sunning himself."

A wrinkle formed across Jessie's forehead, and she took the binoculars back for another look. "It's too big; you're on."

With the half-hour wait finally over, and still no promising breeze, they lowered and secured the sails. Jessie turned the key to the engine and it sputtered to life. Neal took the helm, and she stood forward on the cabin top to get a better view.

Long before they got there, she knew her bet was lost, but at the same time, what floated in front of her wasn't a seal. It never would have allowed them to get so close without swimming away. She felt the tingle of excitement when it became clear what they were approaching and waved at Neal to reduce speed. He put *Dana* in neutral and joined her as the inertia from their forward glide died.

A few feet off the bow, the round, leathery body of a sunfish glistened beneath the surface. Its size reminded Jessie of the top to her mother's patio table. Basking in the limitless, rich blue water, it stretched a fin skyward as if collecting the abundant warmth. Sunlight plunged beneath the water's surface and framed the huge fish in a fan of angled rays.

They drifted past, transfixed by their chance rendezvous. A good reach might have allowed them to touch it, but they didn't try. Indifferent to their presence, the large aquatic creature lazed where it was as they floated away.

"Well, we didn't seem to disturb his sunbathing much," said Jessie just above a whisper.

"Mmm . . . With the engine on, I'm surprised at that."

"Man, I heard they were big, but I had no idea . . . Randy and Gail will be green when we talk to them at noon; they can't possibly top this."

For a long time, Jessie glanced back along their path and caught sight of the elevated fin. There were no winners in this round, but the close encounter with one of nature's elusive sea dwellers kept her restless with excitement.

Once the fin dropped below the horizon, her attention went back to the path ahead. A hard, crisp line encircled them where the blue overhead met the blue water. No landmarks, no interruptions. Engine noise became as relentless as the sun. She leaned over the companionway steps and reached down to grab a pouch secured in a teak box affixed to the cabin's aft bulkhead. The pouch held a navigation unit about the size of a cellular phone. After pushing a couple of buttons, she waited as the GPS gathered information from unseen satellites orbiting the earth. Seconds later the unit beeped and displayed *Dana's* position across its small screen. This trick of technology still amazed her.

Armed with their position and the sunfish story, she climbed down the four companionway steps to the cabin below. Though calm, the sea's constant pulse influenced *Dana* enough to send rounds of sunlight, let in by the portholes, jumping around her interior. Jessie flipped the switch to the ham radio, checked the frequency, then made a call to Randy and Gail, who were also at sea a few hundred miles away.

It had been in California two years ago that a friendship began to develop when the couples met and discovered they shared similar cruising plans. When not in the same port, they kept in touch by radio through the morning ham net. But, if both were at sea, they liked to set up their own schedule and talk every day, for entertainment as much as for anything else.

Jessie didn't have to wait long for Randy to respond. After the normal formalities of weather conditions and positions, the friends chatted about progress and plans, then Jessie gloated about the sunfish. With one hand gripping the microphone and the other gesturing as if she could make the image clearer, Jessie described their experience.

Randy's full nasal sound came back loud and clear. "I saw one once off San Diego. I acted like an idiot, tripping over things to get pictures, all of which were disappointing. They are something all right. Well, nothing that exciting going on here. Say, speaking of unusual things floating at sea, did you hear whether or not they found the woman who fell overboard?"

"No, but then we haven't had the radio on except to talk to you. I figured since she was lost before we left port, there wasn't much hope."

"That's probably true. Oh, well, I meant to ask you yesterday and forgot, so we've been keeping an eye out just in case. It's not like we have a lot of other things to do."

She watched Neal step down the companionway ladder and she smiled at the thought of their contest. "I guess you could say we've been keeping a lookout, too." Her husband winked at her, then turned, opened the lid to the refrigerator and began rummaging around.

Randy's response brought her back to the conversation. "We should be in Melaque tonight, when do you two expect to get into

Zihuatanejo?"

"It looks like we'll make port sometime tomorrow. I guess it depends on whether we get any wind. If it stays like this, we may be doing a lot of motoring. How long do you think it'll be before you join us?"

"It's going to be a couple of weeks at least," said her friend. "You have company coming soon, right?"

With a laugh, she said, "Yeah, Sonny arrives in a couple of days. He's been on board for a weekend here and there, but this will be his first long stay. It will be good to see him, but he's used to things happening a little faster than they do around us, so it should be interesting. Well, unless there's more from your side, I can't think of anything else. Will we talk tomorrow at this time?"

"You bet. Even if we go ashore, we'll be back by noon. There's not much left from this side either, Jessie, so until tomorrow, fair winds."

After good-byes, they finished the transmission with call signs, then announced the frequency was clear. Jessie paused to make sure no other listener was waiting to connect with her or Randy and snapped the radio off when no one jumped in.

Neal's head reappeared from the fridge one last time, holding another bottle of Fanta orange soda that he added to the collection of drinks and food containers. A few minutes later, plates piled high with chopped raw vegetables and tuna fish salad, they climbed the companionway steps to the shady cockpit.

"Talking with Randy has made me think more about Sonny's visit. He was all right for a weekend because he didn't have a chance to get bored. But two weeks . . . ." Jessie's voice trailed off as she conjured up a vision of Sonny pacing the full length of *Dana.* She bit into a sweet Mexican carrot as her focus sharpened. Easygoing was the first error most people made in their impressions of Sonny. He was an artist at connecting socially and that, along with his unrelenting drive, had made him a successful, wealthy man. Those attributes wrapped up in a modest build, a casual manner and a bright smile made it understandable how those first impressions went awry. She didn't know why, exactly, but the three of them had clicked. Even with that, their friend's upcoming visit concerned her.

"He knows what he's getting into. If it doesn't work, there are places he can stay in town."

"But then we'll miss the conversation that goes with morning coffee and a late night drink. I like that part."

Neal stopped eating and looked at her. "Are we remembering the same guy? The guy who claims to have before and after midnight friends, and who frequently makes back-to-back dates in one evening because he's just getting started when date 'one' wants to call it a night? The guy with two ex-wives who claim living with him is impossible without uppers? If you have those conversations, they'll happen regardless of whether he stays on the boat. What we wouldn't have are peace and quiet when we're tired and he's not."

"Okay, okay, you're right."

"Sonny will be fine. We don't need to worry about him. I think it'll be great seeing him again."

"Oh, me, too. I just hope there's enough going on to keep him interested. Our pace was slower than his before; now that we're cruising, it'll be positively dull. Are you done?"

Neal scooped up the last bite of salad and waited for Jessie to descend the companionway ladder, then handed her his plate. He checked the autopilot and compass, and when satisfied they were still on course, he stepped out of the cockpit into the sun. Absorbing *Dana's* motion with his knees, he readjusted his cap and worked his way to the bow.

The open space of sky and sea added to his sense of freedom; it felt good to have nothing weighing on his mind. Benign weather, a sturdy boat and no bottom line. He had enjoyed owning a ski store, but now he preferred the challenges he faced with life aboard a boat. Only one ruffle creased his carefree thinking and it had arrived in a recent letter from his ex-wife Sally.

Everything was fine, she said. "Jeremy and Kim miss you, of course. Jeremy loves college and Kim is involved with school and friends. They are both so busy they barely have enough time or patience for Larry and me. I know you're disappointed that they aren't making any plans to come down for a visit, but they are teenagers and it's always a guess as to what motivates them. Remember, they were never as interested in sailing as you were." The letter went on to explain the routine things going on in her life. He was glad that she seemed satisfied with her second marriage. Sally deserved a normal, stable life, which he realized long ago he could never have happily shared with her. She was right though; he was disappointed that his kids kept coming up with excuses about a visit. He had expected it, even understood it, but that didn't soften the sting.

He sidestepped the bundle of dowsed sail on the deck and leaned against the staysail stay. His eyes searched as far as he could see on the path ahead and then scanned the area around him. At that moment, he and Jessie were the only living things visible in this portion of the Pacific. He let that thought steep as his eyes slowly swept the horizon again. His scan stalled, as if slowed by a speed bump, when he caught sight of something he must have missed before. Pigeonholing the thoughts about his kids and the enormity of the Pacific, he noted the object's position and made his way back to the cockpit for the binoculars.

* * *

A few minutes later, Jessie found him sitting on the forward hatch, adjusting the focus on the glasses. As she sat next to him, she gazed at the path of glitter that sparkled its way across the water toward the sun and danced with the sea's constant motion. It was so peaceful. *Dana's* engine wasn't as intrusive as it had been in the cockpit, so she could almost forget it was running. She felt a tug at her hair and pretended that nature, not their motoring, produced the breeze. When Neal passed her the lenses, she raised them to her eyes.

After studying the knot that shared their water, she said, "What do you think?"

"There are a few birds flocking around it. I'm going to say it's a log."

"With birds flying around it, maybe it's an animal. Sure is high out of the water for that though, huh?" When she brought the binoculars down and looked at Neal, he was smiling at her. "What?"

"Well, my thoughts exactly," he said.

"Okay, so maybe it's not an animal." She raised the lenses to her eyes again and for an instant saw a splash of color. When she lowered the binoculars, she smiled, then turned to him. "I think it's an abandoned buoy."

He lost his smile and took back the glasses she offered. He held them in place for several seconds, but when he lowered them, the creases around his eyes and mouth suggested pity. "You're imagining things; bets are on."

They walked back to the cockpit and the relief of the shade. Neal disappeared below and resurfaced with two Fanta *naranjas*. She took a swallow of the cool, sweet orange drink and watched as they narrowed the distance to the object of their game.

* * *

"Can you tell what it is yet?" Irritated that she had left her hat in the cockpit, Jessie used a hand to shade her eyes from the water's glare.

Dana's engine rumbled on.

Near her on the bow, Neal held steady as he peered through the binoculars. Even though the shape was high out of the water, the birds swarming around it made it obvious that there was, or used to be, some kind of animal there, too. "No, not yet; it's too hard to tell." He lowered the binoculars and handed them to her.

"I'm not all that sure I want to find out. It would be just our luck that out of the tens of thousands of square miles possible, we'd pick the one with that woman in it. I'll tell you what, it sort of looks like a log. I'll just give this one to you . . . the score's even." She tentatively held the glasses to her eyes and turned the focus knobs. It was no use; they'd need to get on top of whatever it was to solve the mystery. She must have imagined the color she saw before. It didn't matter, the irregular shape made a buoy impossible. After one last glance, she lowered the glasses, but caught something just as they left her eyes. She raised them back into position to confirm what she saw.

"Whatever it is, it's wearing a lovely shade of red."

"Here, let me see." Neal stretched his arm out and took the binoculars. He refocused. "Right, I see it now. Well, sorry, babe. I was going to let you concede, but now I want to know what it is." He lowered the lenses and blew her a kiss.

"Thanks a whole lot. I saw some color before, but since I didn't see it again, I thought I imagined it. Now, even with the color, I know it's not a buoy. How about if you look, I'll drive."

Dana closed the gap, then Jessie disengaged the self-steering to take over the helm. The propeller drew a circle of foam in the water as she steered around the floating debris. Birds lifted, hovered and flew away once the intrusion proved persistent. Some drifted back, but kept their distance. She maneuvered until sunlight angled in from behind and spotlighted the focus of everyone's attention. She pulled the throttle into neutral while Neal walked forward to study their find.

He called to her from the bow. "Jess, I'd like you to take a look at this, see what you think."

It was never a good sign when he called her Jess. She wrinkled her nose and called back, "Neal, I don't need to look. I'll believe you, I know it's not a buoy. Just tell me what it is . . . or was."

He joined her in the cockpit and glanced from her to the object. "I can't tell for sure, but I'd like you to have a look to confirm what I think it is." His smile was gone. This was not a tease.

"That's very confusing and you're scaring me. What difference does it make what I think?" She reluctantly stepped out of the cockpit and moved forward. Neal got *Dana* back into position.

Jessie studied the tangle, then kneeled on deck and leaned out over the water for a closer look. She rocked back and sat on her heels, her eyes fixed on the water. When she pulled them away and settled them on Neal, they grew wide with realization. "It looks like a red jacket or something. It looks like it's on a body."

3

"Neal, did you hear me?" Jessie raised her voice and pointed to the water.

"Yup," he said and left the tiller to join her on the bow. Leaning into the rigging to balance himself, he peered over the side.

Jessie untucked her legs to sit on the deck just as *Dana* lurched in reaction to an errant wave. Water slapped the hull and the boat rolled, forcing Neal to tighten his grip on the shrouds that supported him. They both stared at the clump floating nearby.

"That's what it looked like to me, too. I wanted you to tell me I was wrong."

"I was only kidding before; it never occurred to me that we'd really find . . . Neal, tell me this isn't happening. What are we going to do with . . . ?" Jessie's voice trailed off. The red jacket was clearly visible in the tangle of drifting wood.

Dana's rolling calmed to a gentle rock.

"There's been a lot of debris floating around; it must have snagged the branch after it was in the water for a while. I don't see any . . ." Neal cleared his throat and adjusted his cap, ". . . appendages."

"That's probably why there's still something left. I mean, I would think that something would have . . . you know . . . eaten it. God, Neal, what if it *is* that woman?"

"That's my first guess." Neal's thoughts tiptoed around whether or not to put the engine in gear and get back on course. Could he live with that?

Several minutes passed while they watched the gap widen between them and the tangle of body and branches.

Jessie broke the silence. "I'd like to just put *Dana* in gear and keep going, but I'm afraid I wouldn't think much of myself tomorrow. What about you?"

Implications exploded as his earlier carefree thoughts vanished. He suddenly felt laden with unwanted responsibility. "Damn it," he said, hitting the wire that sent a vibration through the rigging.

Overcome by his own sense of morality, he turned abruptly, catching himself on the shoulder-high line to regain his balance. He pounded his heels into the deck as he stomped back to the cockpit and put *Dana's* engine in gear. He jerked at the tiller and began to drive.

As Jessie made her way aft, he felt her eyes on him. When ready, he leaned over and put the engine back in neutral. The tangle regained its position a few yards off to starboard.

"We'll have to tether it to us until we decide what to do."

"After that," she said, "I'll get on the radio. Maybe we can find out if they've found that woman."

On its downward slide, the sun began to cast shadows across *Dana's* deck. They sat in silence.

Neal did a mental inventory, stepped down into the cabin, pulled open a locker and grabbed a coil of three-eighths-inch line. He began to unwind it as he returned to the cockpit and Jessie. "Do you want to drive or tie?"

She looked at him and chewed her lower lip as she always did when she was trying to make up her mind. "Mmm. Drive."

He smiled and when she smiled back, the burden seemed lighter.

"Chicken," he said. "Just take it slow. I'm going for the jacket rather than the branches in case the whole thing decides to come apart when I start messing with it. Once you put the engine in neutral and I have a hold of the thing, be ready with the boat hook if I need it, okay?"

She nodded and moved to the bow to get the long pole from the deck bag, then walked back to the cockpit.

"Ready?" Said Neal.

"Yeah. I'll circle and come in again." Jessie laid the hook aside, took over the tiller and put the engine in gear.

Neal moved to the side deck and using a bucket, sloshed water to cool the area of the deck he needed. Beneath the temporary, shoulder-high safety line, *Dana* had a permanent, thigh-high safety wire that circled her perimeter, supported every four to five feet with a stainless steel stanchion bolted through the deck. Along the aft quarter, the safety wire that stretched between two stanchions had a clip that could be released to create a gap. At sea, this gate was closed and locked, but in port they unclipped it to make it easier to get on and off the boat. To have more freedom of movement, Neal opened the gate and waited as Jessie turned the boat away from the tangle and circled around. When his target came back into view, he lay over the side, resting his chest across the wooden bulwark. An inch thick and eight inches high, the bulwark edged the deck and before he even started his salvage work, it was digging into his ribs. Glancing down nearly three additional feet of shiny fiberglass to the sea, Neal knew this exercise would leave a few bruises. He watched as they closed in on the collection of twigs and human remains; they slowed to a stop.

Out of the corner of his eye, he saw the boat hook poised and ready for action. He lowered his torso toward the water until his hands could work at getting a grip on the red cloth. Gravity pulled at him. The pressure across his chest turned to pain and his muscles began to complain. Every movement forced a groan or grunt from the effort. The tip of the boat hook dropped into his work area, snagged a wrinkle in the jacket and helped hold the collection of flotsam near Neal's hands.

"That's it . . . hold it right there . . . that's great."

Neal could feel the blood rushing to his head. It throbbed as he felt around on the jacket for a place to attach the line. He had to compensate for the up and down motion of the boat and as gentle as it was, the job still became a test in determination. When he couldn't find anything substantial, he decided to thread the line through holes worn in the jacket. As he threaded, his hand bumped against something hard that was a few inches below the surface.

"What's this?" His voice was raspy from exertion.

"What is it?"

"Just a sec." Neal finished the tying, then patted the body in search of the hard object. When he found it, he yanked and it came to the surface. "It looks like a video camera. Hang on a minute, it's attached by . . . looks like the strap is secured by Velcro. Jessie, can you get the boat hook on this strap?"

"Sure, " she said, looping the hook at the end of the six-foot pole around the strap he held for her.

"Okay, let's see where this goes." Feeling his pain escalate to agony, Neal's hand fumbled with the strap until he felt the Velcro. The familiar parting rip of hook and loop filled the air as he pulled. He untangled the camera's strap and then freed it from Jessie's boat hook, but with muscles shaking from fatigue, he found it impossible to move without the use of his hands.

"Neal, let me put the boat hook down and I'll take that from you."

It seemed an eternity before she pressed in next to him. He felt her hand on his and her voice in his ear said, "Got it." He let go and grabbed for a stanchion.

* * *

While Jessie cradled their treasure, she heard Neal grunting as he pulled himself back aboard. Satisfied he would make it and that there wasn't much she could do to help, she secured the camera and returned the boat hook to its deck bag. On her way back to the shady cockpit, she saw him sprawled on his back like a sunbather, panting.

She called out to him, "You okay?"

"Yeah, but I need to just lie here for a minute."

While *Dana* rocked the weariness from Neal, Jessie studied their find. The effects of the sea had worked on the metal. White aluminum oxide and a green tinge she couldn't identify covered the once shiny case. Algae and slime coated the nylon strap.

She called out to Neal, "It's one of those splash-proof cameras; I wonder if any water got inside."

She shifted the camera in all directions to see if there were any cracks or chips in the case.

"How's it look?" Neal called to her.

"It looks reasonable except for corrosion on the metal parts and some growth on the housing and strap. We probably shouldn't open it until we know what we're supposed to do with it."

Neal groaned and rubbed his chest as he settled opposite her.

She handed the camera to him and he turned it all around to inspect it. The knobs he gently tested were frozen. He set it down on the cockpit bench and they both stared at it.

"It'd be interesting to know if it recorded anything," said Jessie.

"Wouldn't it. But let's see if we can find out first what we're dealing with. What kind of questions do we want to ask if you get someone on the radio?"

They spent several minutes putting together a script before Jessie stepped over the camera and disappeared down the companionway. "Do you remember seeing that list of maritime nets someone gave us a while ago?"

Neal leaned onto his knees and cupped his chin with one hand. "Try the bag with the information on Mexico." From the cockpit, he watched her open a locker and pull out a watertight bag filled with papers.

She thumbed through tourist leaflets and clipped articles, then stopped. "Found it. It would be great if there was a net going on right now." Both were quiet as she studied the paper. Neal took a walk around *Dana's* deck, checked their cargo and its tether, then joined Jessie in the cabin. While she read, he snapped the radio on. They were still tuned to the frequency on which they had talked with Randy and Gail. It hissed and spat at him, but there were no voices.

"We just missed the Pacific Maritime Net and I don't see any others until later. The best thing to do is get on the dial and call." Jessie flipped the page over again and frowned as she studied the times and frequencies of the maritime nets listed. She knew that all of this was academic to Neal. He hated talking on the radio and wouldn't make the call anyway. Whatever she decided would be fine.

"Whatever you're comfortable with," said Neal as he pushed buttons and turned the dial.

Static spit and hissed at them with varying intensities as he passed over the increasing numbers on the LCD read out. When he arrived at a quiet spot, he stopped. Jessie leaned in to look at the frequency and compared it with a chart she kept by the radio; it seemed all right.

She felt hot and her heart beat faster as she silently rehearsed the script that was scribbled on the paper in front of her. She felt ridiculous. No matter how many times she used the radio, her mind took her through a period of stage fright. Calls to Randy and Gail were the only radio experiences that didn't make her sweat. Before her courage wilted completely, she reached for the microphone and pressed the transmit button.

"CQ, CQ, CQ. This is Kilo Charlie Six Charlie Bravo Quebec calling any station." No response. She tried again. Still, no response. As she began to regain composure, she improvised. "CQ, CQ, CQ. This is Kilo Charlie Six Charlie Bravo Quebec maritime mobile calling any station . . . anybody out there?"

Both Jessie and Neal jerked away from the radio when a voice reached out to them loud and clear. "CBQ this is KC6-CCB, Wayne, in Tempe, Arizona. Where are you maritime mobile?"

Jessie and Neal exchanged a look. She brought the mike to her mouth and pressed the transmit button. "We're thirty miles off the coast of Mexico, south bound to Zihuatanejo, a port north of Acapulco. We have good copy on you, how do you copy me?"

"You're a little light, but I can hear you. Mexico, huh? That's great. What kind of radio and antenna are you operating?"

Jessie looked at the front of their set, then realized the man at the other end of the wave could keep her talking about the world of radio for hours. She decided to ignore his question and turned back to her script. "Nice to meet to you, Wayne. We have a situation here that might require some help from U.S. officials. We're in international waters and have found a body floating at sea. We know that a search was in progress some days ago for a person who fell overboard off a sailboat near here. This could be that woman and if not, we've found . . . somebody. Can you call someone . . . the Coast Guard, I guess, and find out?"

The bold, clear voice became hesitant, and they could hear disbelief in the tone that issued from the radio. "I want to confirm you've found a body . . . a human body?"

"Roger, roger." Jessie released the transmit button and waited.

Seconds of dead air passed before Wayne responded. "Okay . . . I understand. Now what is it you want me to find out and who's 'we?'"

Jessie no longer needed the script; she repeated her information and told him who was on board. When he confirmed that he had heard and understood their situation, she continued.

"Roger, Wayne, that's correct. I'm going to give you our position, boat documentation number and description. We are drifting right now, not sure yet in which direction." She transmitted the information and waited for him to repeat it. "Sounds like you got it all, Wayne, thanks."

"Roger; I'll give the Coast Guard a shout and find out what else they need. You sure you want to stand by?"

"Roger; we're on a thirty-two-foot sailboat miles from shore, we're not going anywhere. We won't keep the frequency clear, so you may have to wait or break in when you're ready. Will that be okay?"

"That'll be fine, Jessie. You two take care and I'll be back as soon as I can. This is KC6-CCB clear."

Jessie repeated her call sign and cleared, then was contacted by another station who wanted all the details repeated. When Jessie asked if the station was in a position to help contact officials, the answer was no. He was calling from his boat anchored in a cove along the coast of Mexico. She watched as Neal disappeared up the steps to the deck, then thanked the operator, but begged off, claiming low batteries. Another station jumped in to fill in the details and the two new stations volunteered to take on the responsibility of keeping the frequency occupied until Wayne got back. Within minutes, there were three or four stations exchanging salutations and information. All were cruisers stretched along the Mexican coast.

"I guess that's one way to spend the cocktail hour," Jessie said as she stared at the radio and listened to the voices. She got up and checked the battery power reserve, then followed Neal topside.

Longer shadows stretched across the deck and her shoulders slumped when she checked the tether; it was still secure. *Dana* bobbed and Jessie gripped the rigging to steady herself. She looked to the horizon and thought the calm conditions and the sharp, clear line where sky met sea made the evening perfect for a Green Flash.

She heard Neal behind her and glanced over her shoulder. He checked the tether and when he looked up, she recognized the expression. "Yeah, I was hoping the knot had slipped, too." He smiled and made his way toward her.

"Neal, do you remember what conditions are right for a Green

Flash?"

He gripped the rigging just above her hand and wrapped his other arm around her waist. They pressed against the wires as he looked around. "I think this looks pretty good, based on what I've read."

"The flash happens right as the sun goes down, right?"

"It's supposed to happen just as the top rim drops below the horizon."

"Is it a big flash like fireworks or do we just see green?"

"I don't know. I've never talked to anyone who's seen it."

They rocked with the boat. The voices and crackle from the radio added to the mix of water splashing against *Dana's* hull and halyards clanking against the mast. The deep, rich blue of the water at midday flattened to black in the low-slung sun of dusk.

Jessie tried to put thoughts of their last entanglement with some of life's ugliness on hold, but they bubbled up again, and she decided to let them come. Along with them came thoughts of her family. This time she would be more careful how she explained all this in a letter home. Eighteen months ago, her older brother Daniel had taken problems she and Neal had in Cabo San Lucas to catastrophic proportions that had rumbled for months. He meant well, but he disapproved of what she was doing. Her father had still been alive then and helped temper Daniel, but her mom was alone now. Tears welled and added to the salt already making her face taut. She cleared her throat, leaned more heavily into Neal and decided to indulge in a fresh water rinse once the sun went down. She said, "We're tangled up in circumstances again, aren't we?"

As if he knew she needed it, he tightened his arm around her. His lips only inches from her ear, he said quietly, "I'd say so."

"Would you say the ideal situation would be that they are still out searching and they could catch up to us and take . . . this . . . off our hands?"

"If they're close, that's all right, but I don't want to hang around here for a couple of days, waiting for someone."

From below the call was repeated. "KC6-Charlie Bravo Quebec; KC6, Charlie Bravo Quebec; KC6-Charlie Bravo Quebec, this is KC6-Charlie Charlie Bravo; are you there, Jessie?"

Jessie didn't make it to the radio in time to jump in at the pause, so sat through the call again and then responded. "KC6-Charlie Charlie Bravo, this is KC6-CBQ."

"Oh, great, still reasonable copy. I've got some news for you. Based on your location, you may have the person you were talking about, a woman named Jennifer Stover. The man from the U.S. Coast Guard that I spoke to is checking to see if there's still a ship out searching. If so, they may try to connect with you. He said he'd let me know as soon as he could, but he thought it would take about an hour to get confirmation. He wanted your weather conditions, wind speed and direction, plus sea conditions. Oh, and also the condition of the body, just in general terms. If you can give me those, I'll pass that on. I'll contact you again when I hear from him, but I'll call in an hour regardless, just to stay in touch. If for some reason we don't connect, I'll try every hour on the hour to reach you, how does that sound?"

"Like we're putting you out, Wayne, but we appreciate the help."

"Glad to. Other than this, you two doing all right?"

"Yeah, we're fine. We've got plenty of supplies and the weather's great. Let me give you the specifics." She relayed everything to Wayne and finished by telling him about the camera and the deteriorated condition of the body.

"Okay, got it. You guys hang in there; I'll talk to you as soon as I hear from him, or in an hour, whichever comes first." Wayne signed off.

"This is KC6-CBQ maritime mobile. I'd like to thank the other stations who have been keeping the frequency occupied. I know you can't keep this up indefinitely." Jessie released the transmit button and hung up the mike.

The other voices chimed in their thanks for the acknowledgment and encouraged Jessie and Neal with their support, then continued bantering. Jessie rejoined Neal on deck. With one arm wrapped around the mast, he balanced on the boom several feet above the cabin top and looked toward the pending sunset. Jessie sat on deck below him and secured herself for the show.

"You know, legend states if you see the flash, you'll never again be deceived in matters of the heart. That you'll be able to see clearly into your own thoughts as well as others. What do you think, babe?"

"I think you remember strange things."

"I know, but secretly you're impressed." He looked down at her and kidded her with his grin, which she tolerated with a shake of her head.

They both clung to their perches as the flame-red ball hit the water line.

"I'm always surprised by how fast it goes." Jessie grabbed glances at the horizon until it swallowed the sun and the upper rim dropped out of sight.

"Did you see it? Did you see the green?"

Jessie looked up at Neal. "You're serious. You saw something?"

"Yeah, didn't you? I mean it wasn't a big flash or anything, but I saw green." He looked down at her. "You didn't see any green." It was more a statement than a question.

She shook her head and looked back at the glow left on the horizon. "Are you sure?" When he didn't answer, she looked back up at him and caught his eye.

"Can't help it, babe, I know green when I see it and that was it."

She turned back to the horizon and said, "I think you imagined it."

Above his laughter, they heard the call. Jessie moved quickly to the cabin. Neal was right behind her.

After they exchanged greetings, Wayne relayed his information.

"Well, the news isn't so good this time. The search was suspended two days ago. To get a ship out to where you are could take as long as two days. I told him I'd call you and find out what you wanted to do, then let him know. So, I guess I'm asking, what do you want to do?"

"Stand by, Wayne." The transmit button snapped as she released it.

"I know what I want to do, how about you?" Neal faced her and waited.

"I know I don't want to wait here for a ship, but after that, I'm not sure."

"We can at least tell him that."

"Right." Jessie raised the mike. "Wayne, we don't want to wait for a ship. Not sure what we will do, but that's a certainty."

"Okay. He said if you decided against waiting, he needs to know where you're headed so they can have someone there when you arrive. Authorities want to see you, the body and the video camera. Of course, he stressed the importance of getting to shore as soon as possible."

"You can tell him we're heading for Zihuatanejo, which is a few miles from Ixtapa and about a hundred-and-twenty miles north of Acapulco. If everything goes as planned, and I stress the word 'if,' we should be there tomorrow evening or the next morning. I can't be more specific than that."

"Fine, I'll let them know. I guess that's it for now, Jessie. I'd like to get back to you in case there's a question or they need more information. When can we talk again?"

She and Neal looked at the clock and both agreed. "Three hours from the top of the hour and we show that as nine minutes from now. Would that be okay?"

"Sounds fine; we'll meet right here in three hours, nine minutes. Take care you two and I'll let you take us off. This is KC6-CCB, clear until later."

Neal disappeared topside while Jessie said good-bye to Wayne. Before closing down, she spent a few minutes chatting with the other stations that had maintained vigilance throughout. She heard them signing off as she flipped the switch to her radio and the cabin fell silent.

Neal was taking down the cockpit awning as she climbed the companionway. In shiny, silver-coin splender, the moon lit the night like a porch light, dulling the radiance from the stars that filled the sky.

As he folded the awning, Neal looked at the moon. "Now what?" he said.

"I guess we have a body to deliver."

4

To make the delivery, they needed their eight-foot fiberglass dinghy, which was stowed on the cabin top while underway. After taking down the shoulder-high safety line, Jessie and Neal lifted *Pointer* off her storage chocks and righted her. They clipped a bridle to her, then snapshackled the bridle to the mainsail halyard, which transformed *Dana* into a makeshift crane. When they began winching, *Pointer* inched upwards until high enough to swing free. Suspended from the load end of the mainsail halyard, their small tender was ready to launch. Neal pushed and pulled the dinghy into position over the water and braced himself.

"Okay, I'm ready."

Jessie had wrapped her end of the mainsail halyard three times around the winch that was affixed to the mast. By controlling her end, she could control the speed of their dinghy's drop. She eased the line slowly through her fingers and watched it slide around the winch. *Pointer* descended while Neal fended and steered, protecting the two boats from each other.

Once the line went limp, Jessie tied it off. *Pointer* was in the water. She worked her way to the side deck, instinctively checking her safety harness to make sure she was still clipped to the boat. It was secure.

She knelt on the deck beside Neal. "Everything okay?"

"I guess so." His body angled down over the side while his hands positioned two round white fenders to act as a buffer between the two boats. His voice sounded flat.

"We still all right to do this now?"

Her partner pulled back to a kneel, looked at the full moon and then up at the lights shining down on them from the mast. "I'd rather be doing this during the day, but it's calm and we can manage with the light we've got. How do you feel about it?"

"I'm not nervous, if that's what you mean," she said, "but hoisting a dead body into *Pointer* and towing it back to shore has my imagination going. I can't help but think how this would play out in a Stephen King or Hitchcock movie."

"There's always the alternative."

"We've already had that discussion. You want to cut it loose, the deck knife is right there in the cockpit, but I can't. To me it's the wrong thing to do."

"Right." The word had a slight edge to it.

"Hey, Neal, what's going on? I thought we agreed to this."

Neal balanced on *Dana's* bulwark, then eased into the bobbing dinghy. He secured *Pointer,* unclipped the hoisting gear and passed it up to Jessie. Gripping the stainless steel stanchions, he stood in the dinghy and looked up at her. "I'm not saying I don't agree, I'm saying I don't like it. As long as it's not jeopardizing us or the boat, I'm for doing what we can. I keep thinking we have a long way to go, though, and if the situation changes, I might change my mind. C'mon, let's get our suits on." He climbed aboard *Dana* and she followed him to the cockpit.

She could go along with that. If the situation changed and it came down to choosing between themselves and a lump of unidentifiable flesh, the moral decision would be easier to make. But under the circumstances, she knew she would regret it if they didn't at least try to return this woman's remains to her family.

Putting aside his comments, she sat and untangled the bridle used to lower the dinghy. Next to her lay an old square awning she had hunted down earlier, and after clipping the bridle to the awning's grommets, she said, "I think this will work great as a sling. With the bridle shackled to the main halyard, we can hoist the body just like we do *Pointer.*" The way it came out, it sounded to her as though she had been talking about a package not the remains of another human being. She looked at Neal, but he was busy rummaging around in the snorkeling gear and hadn't noticed. The moment of guilt passed and she held up the makeshift sling to show it to him.

He paused in his search, and after pulling and stretching it he said, "This is good . . . it should be fine."

Once the equipment was sorted and organized, they grabbed their wetsuits and pulled them on.

"Gloves, I definitely want gloves," said Jessie as she rummaged to find them. When fully suited up, she wrestled with pulling on her safety harness. "It's going be awkward working in this thing."

"I know," said Neal, "but better that than getting separated from the boat. You have the light?"

"Yep," she said as she snapped the light on and off to test it.

"Bring the knife, too." He slipped on his harness, then slung the straps to his mask and fins around one wrist. Grabbing the sling, he stepped onto the side deck.

Jessie followed. She heard the snap of his clip on the lifeline and remembered as a kid the neighbor's dog running back and forth over the yard, its leash sliding the length of the clothesline. With the five feet between the two stanchions and the dozen feet Neal rigged on his harness tether, they figured he would have enough freedom to get Jennifer Stover set up for hoisting.

She watched him attach the sling to the mainsail halyard then stare down at the clump that floated inches in front of the dinghy's bow.

"You wondering why we're doing this?" Her clip snapped in next to his.

"Yep."

"Neal . . ." She stopped when he raised both his hands in front of his chest, fingers spread, in a plea for her not to go on.

She exhaled the rest of her thought, because she agreed. They had made a decision and all this extra discussion was beginning to confuse the issue. He put his arm over her shoulder and pulled her close enough to kiss her hair. She melted into his side and laid her head on his shoulder.

"With the full moon and water lapping at *Pointer,* this should be romantic." He tightened his grip and she felt his lips again on her hair, then the weight of his head rested against hers. Passion pulled at her, but the decomposing body that floated in front of her eyes chased it away, and she wondered how many more times this woman would come between them.

She said quietly from the safety of his arms, "I want to go over again what we're going to do."

Snuggled together, they reviewed their plan.

When the discussion finished, they silently stared at their burden for a moment, then Jessie said, "Okay, let's get on with it," and stepped aside to give Neal room to ease into the dinghy. Once he was settled, she took a deep breath and followed.

Two lights mounted halfway up the mast bathed them in a low-watt glow, casting shadows as they got ready. *Pointer* bobbed in the inky black sea as Neal donned his mask and fins. Within seconds he was in the water.

Jessie snugged the lanyard to the underwater light around her wrist and turned it on. Leaning over the dinghy's side, she submerged it and, without getting too close to what the branches had snared on their journey, turned the light's beam on the snarl.

A few feet away, her husband went to work. All but the crown of his head dropped out of sight in the dark water and Jessie could hear his puffing, amplified through the snorkel.

He surfaced. "I need the light where my hands are. Something's snagged and I can't get it free." He clamped his teeth again on the breathing tube and dropped his face in the water.

Jessie directed the light and a moment later Neal's head resurfaced. "I'll need the deck knife."

After a pause, she groaned to herself. "Hang on; I left it in the cockpit."

His curses filled her ears as she climbed aboard *Dana* and reached into the cockpit for the knife. A flash of light caught the corner of her eye. In reaction, she looked up and studied the water, but blackness stretched out in front her. Must be my imagination, she thought, and struggled to suppress scenes from *Jaws* that began to feature in her thoughts.

She eased back into *Pointer* and Neal said, "What took you so long?"

"Nothing, but let's hurry. All of a sudden, I want this to be over."

"You and me both. You got the knife?"

"Yeah, here." She passed the knife to him and they resumed their labors.

Minutes later he surfaced again. "Okay, there it goes." He pulled the branch free and set it loose.

When he passed the knife back to Jessie, a shadow made the distance deceiving and the handle clipped *Pointer's* side, deflecting it away from her hand. The "plunk" was followed by Neal's walrus-size splash as he dove after it. Jessie's beam sprayed light across the area and glinted off a piece of metal making a rapid descent beneath them.

Neal surfaced in an explosion. "Goddamn it." He swept his hand across the surface of the water and sent up a spray that reached *Dana's* deck.

Jessie sat in silence; words wouldn't help.

Off the bow of the dinghy, Neal treaded water, panting and spitting with the effort. He snatched the sling and jerked it into place. His teeth clamped on the snorkel and his face disappeared beneath the surface.

Trying to forget the fact that losing the knife might be an omen, Jessie grabbed the tether that held the body and pulled it toward her. She leaned over *Pointer's* side and maneuvered their albatross into the pyramid of bridle lines until it hovered over the sling. Neal steadied the bundle while she tied the two together. Once everything was secured, she waved an "okay" signal with her thumb and pointer finger in front of Neal's mask.

He surfaced and in one sweep of his fins was alongside the little boat. "Let's go over again how we're going to hoist this thing into *Pointer*." He gave a strong kick and surged out of the water. Jessie leaned as a counterweight to balance the dinghy while Neal pulled himself aboard.

In silence they checked that everything was secure for the moment, then climbed onto *Dana*. In the cockpit, Neal snapped open one of the bottles of orange soda they had left for themselves and handed it to Jessie. He opened another for himself and took a swallow. "I'm sorry for blowing up like that over the knife. It's just losing it that way was such a waste. We should have known better and either tethered it or used something we could afford to lose." He sat and water oozed out of his black wetsuit as if it were being squeezed from a sponge.

Jessie sat opposite him and after a few moments of silence said, "I know; I'm sorry we lost it."

"I'm struggling with all this, Jess. Intellectually, I know taking the woman with us is the right thing to do, but something keeps pulling me the other way. It's nothing I can put my finger on, but I know I don't want to get involved. Somewhere down the line we'll regret taking on the responsibility."

They both tipped their bottles for another drink.

The tug was light, but unmistakable. The couple exchanged a glance. As if on cue, they both spun around onto their knees and looked over the side at their cargo. It still floated among the lines of the hoisting bridle.

Neal's eyes snapped to attention on a patch of dark water that had for a second glowed a phosphorescent green. He looked up at the spreader lights, then leaned into the cabin and snapped them off. The full moon continued to glow like a night-light. On their knees, peering down at the water, they saw another lightning flash of green in the water.

"We've got someone's attention," said Neal.

"I don't like this," said Jessie, feeling a chill cross the back of her neck.

Another green flash lit the water on a T-bone course to *Dana*. They felt the tug and then were bounced off their knees onto the deck when something hit *Dana's* hull. The two soda bottles crashed, unbroken, and rolled around, spilling the rest of their contents. When Jessie and Neal scrambled back to where they could see the water, another green flash streaked toward them. They braced for the hit. Neal reached into the canvas pocket that hung off the cabin side next to him and fumbled with the knifeless sheath.

"Damn it, the knife."

Green flashes exploded all around them, and the once quiet water seethed with bubbles. Light and the splashes of powerful, muscular bodies broke the surface.

"Hang on, " Jessie yelled as she wedged herself down the companionway steps. The next hit catapulted her against the stove, branding her with a bruise. Pain spread and forced her to howl. *Dana* heeled with a sudden yank, blocks squealing under the strain of the tightened lines.

"Goddamn it," Jessie shrieked, clenching her teeth and gripping the stainless safety bar that ran along the galley counter. Her home shuddered as the predator shook its quarry back and forth, trying to rip it free. Slippery with sweat, she struggled to keep her hands on the bar until the motion stopped. With a groan, *Dana* bobbed upright and before the violence could begin again, Jessie snatched a stout galley knife and yelled to her mate. "Neal, try this."

He appeared in the companionway and reached down for the knife, then pulled himself into position. Leaning out over the water, he slid the knife into place and sliced through the tether that secured Jennifer Stover. In the same moment, the water surrounding them erupted in day-glo green and something struck the boat with such force, it felt as though the fathoms of water beneath them had vanished, dropping them onto solid ground.

5

The familiar sound of her friend's voice chirped through the radio. "I can't believe it. Stumbling across Jennifer Stover was probably one chance in a million." Jessie pictured Gail sitting in *Carmen's* spacious cabin, gripping the microphone. The ever-present baseball cap, with the black ponytail pulled through the gap at the back, would cover her head. To Jessie, the ordinary scene provided some comfort.

"You should've been there," she told her friend. "Come to think of it, you *should* have been there, it was your husband who reminded us about her. Tell him it's all his fault. I even joked about it. Imagine my surprise when I found out the joke was on me." She paused, but didn't release the transmit button. "Just kidding, Gail, this is still too bizarre to believe."

Jessie flipped through the memories from the night before as she talked. In one hand she held the microphone, the fingers of the other worked at combing her hair. More than anything, she wanted to back up twenty-fours hours and relive them, leaving out the bit about Jennifer Stover. She exhaled and rested her forehead on the palm of her hand.

Gail's voice came quietly from the radio. "Hey, I know. You just don't think things like that will happen." With more strength in her tone, she said, "What we can be grateful for in all this is that *Dana* wasn't seriously damaged. If your visitors *were* sharks, things could be looking a lot worse this morning."

Jessie rubbed her eyes and gave a weak chuckle at the comment. "You're right about that. I had visions of them punching a hole in the hull. Right now, we could be madly bailing or floating in a life raft."

"Or worse."

"Yeah . . . or worse. They shredded our dinghy bridle, so that's another 'fix-it' project that joins the list. But, except for the players and where it took place, the light and water show they put on was pretty spectacular." She looked at the companionway and saw Neal working with the jib sheet.

"So what's going to happen now?"

"I thought we might be off the hook after our visit from the body snatchers, but Wayne said officials still wanted the video. He got a name and number for us, and we're to call them when we get into Zihuatanejo. I guess we'll start there." Jessie felt gravity pull at her body as *Dana* heeled. Wind filled the sails and she heard the rush of water on the hull next to her ear. They were making good time.

"Have you looked at the video?"

"With what? We're not aboard *Carmen*, Gail."

Her friend's response began with a laugh. "Well, see there. We've finally found a practical reason for this entertainment center that Randy insisted we build for our main cabin." She paused. "This is a serious question now. How are you two doing?"

Jessie pulled at her bangs and stared at the camera that rocked gently in the cubbyhole where they had temporarily stowed it. "I wish it hadn't happened. I don't want to get tangled up with the authorities again. We had enough of that in Cabo a year-and-a-half ago."

The laughter in Gail's voice disappeared. "Jessie, forget Simon and his crew. They stole a boat and murdered a couple of people. They got what was coming to them. You shouldn't feel responsible, they killed themselves."

"Thanks, Gail, and I know that." She looked up at the cabin head liner and pressed a finger against her upper lip. The tears that threatened to form retreated.

"Would you like us there? We could sail down in a couple of days."

Jessie wiped her eyes. "Absolutely not. I've had too much time to think about this and I'm feeling sorry for myself. Sonny's coming in a couple of days, he'll provide more distraction than we need. He'll eat this up. I laugh when I remember how concerned I was that things would be too quiet. Not anymore. We want to catch up with you guys again, but not like this."

"All right, I believe you, but if you change your mind let us know. When does it look like you'll pull into Zihuatanejo?"

"We think late this afternoon. Apparently a guy by the name of Satch, a non-ham operator anchored there, has been listening in and passed the word around that we're on our way. We got a message earlier telling us people are expecting us and will help however they can."

"That's good to know. You're going to be pretty busy the next couple of days. When do you want to connect again?"

Jessie's thoughts required a few seconds of silence. "Let's pick up on our normal day next week, and if something comes up, we'll give you a call on the net. You still listen most days, don't you?"

"You bet. That's fine. Unless you have anything else, take care and good luck with all this. We'll be thinking about you."

The two friends said their good-byes, and Jessie joined Neal in the cockpit. Stretched out opposite him under the awning, she watched *Dana's* frothy wake trail off behind them. Sunlight glinted off the rudder varnish, and the white paddle to the wind vane leaned with the breeze, keeping them on course. She felt her tension ease.

The first time she and Neal spotted *Dana,* with her classic lines and sparkling brightwork, they had wanted her. Interested in upgrading from a day sailor to an ocean-going vessel, they had looked at other boats, but none captured their passion as much as the one now whisking them along the Mexican coast. Even before the old boat sold, they had begun the negotiations to make *Dana* theirs. Since that day, she and Neal had not seen another boat that challenged their decision.

Water whooshed and lines squeaked around winches, replacing the monotonous drone of the engine. *Dana's* dance with the wind lay the world at a slant, but Jessie knew this speed drove them more quickly to their destination and whatever awaited them there. Heat penetrated the awning, but not the burning rays, so she and Neal wedged themselves in and watched the miles slowly drop away.

* * *

Ever since they began sailing, their typical on board shower meant using soap and salt water to scrub clean, followed by a lavish final rinse of fresh water from their modified three-gallon insect sprayer. Watching her fluff her hair dry, Neal knew that family and friends back in the States remained skeptical of the method no matter how much reassurance they were given that it worked. Dressed in clean clothes, he felt fresh, even if a little reluctant to tackle their upcoming landfall. A rosy color tinged the sky and washed the high, thin clouds in sunset pink.

"That must be our guy," Jessie called out from her perch on the cabin top.

Neal spotted the grey, inflatable dinghy creating a path of foam and spray as it moved toward them. Once in range, radio contacts had switched from ham to VHF, to include Satch Jurgeon, the contact in Zihuatanejo. Looming up behind him, headlands marked the entrance to the bay fronting the modest fishing village.

"Why is he doing this?"

"He wants to help, Neal."

"The body's gone. What kind of help do we need?" Neal gripped the tiller and felt the vibration of the engine through the soles of his feet. The sails were stowed and lines coiled, but not secured. That would come after they anchored. That thought made him remember something. "Is the anchor ready?"

"Nope, but it will be." Jessie gave one last look at the approaching dinghy and disappeared below. Seconds later she reappeared. "All set."

As she took a position amidship, the dinghy sped astern of them, rounded up and cruised alongside. Its pilot waved and smiled, then pointed. Jessie followed the point; ahead of them was a cluster of dinghies floating beyond the harbor entrance.

"Neal, there's a whole fleet of them." She glanced over her shoulder at him.

He dreaded it. The idea of dinghies swarming around them, making a big deal over nothing, pulled his eyes to the sky. He tugged at his cap and readjusted his grip on the tiller.

Once past the entrance, Zihuatanejo's horseshoe bay came into view. Even in the dusky light the white, sandy beach glowed. A variety of vegetation, including palms, backed the beach, and beyond them the town spread for blocks. Long, flat, white houses roofed in red tile or grey corrugated iron joined the palms and scrub that marched up the slopes and overlooked the bay. Rocky cliffs interrupted the sand in a couple of places, dividing the beach into sections.

Neal navigated the channel and smiled, knowing most of what he saw matched his year-old memory of the place. Deep inside and to the left of the bay was the main beach, Playa Municipal. It stretched in front of the village and was still lined with the sturdy, open, wooden *pangas* used as both water taxis and fishing boats. Only a few steps to the right was Playa Madera, where Neal had spent some memorable moments attempting to play beach volleyball. The net was still there, and although not highly skilled, two teams in bathing suits seemed deeply involved in a game. His eyes moved farther around the bay, past a rocky promontory, to Playa la Ropa. Popular for its line of palms and thatched roofed *palapas*, the beach was, even so late in the day, busy with people. Finally he took in Playa Las Gatos. Across the bay from town, it was the most remote and most pristine of the group. Memories of a lazy day with suntan lotion and their snorkeling gear flooded back. This was why it was their favorite port, and in spite of the cargo they were carrying and the fuss about to be made over them, he was glad they were back.

The crews of the dinghy flotilla waved and yelled "welcome" as Jessie and Neal approached. The cluster appeared connected, and when Neal focused on them with the binoculars, he saw the occupants passing plates and containers.

"They're rafted up, it looks like a potluck." He lowered the glasses and let them dangle around his neck. He laughed now that he could erase the vision of a dozen dinghies buzzing around them, trying to help, and he felt even more lighthearted about their return.

"So that's what they're doing," said his mate and she gave the group a big wave as they passed.

Their escort moved in closer with a hand cupped around his mouth. Neal bent and put the engine in neutral.

"Welcome. The name's Satch. We thought you'd like some food when you got in. Any reason's good enough for a potluck, you know. There's plenty, and we'll drop some off once you get settled. It's kind of tight in here so if you want, I can show you a couple of places that opened up today."

"Thanks." Neal yelled above the engine noise and gave the man a wave and thumbs up. When he glanced at Jessie, she lifted her eyebrows at him. "Well, we can't say, don't bother."

"I'm not sure. There are times when I think *you* could." She smiled at him and pulled playfully on the bill of his cap.

He bent to engage the engine. "I'm not that bad. I just didn't see the need to make a big deal out of this, and I'm happy they felt the same way."

The dinghies in the gathering belonged to larger vessels that dotted the harbor. Satch guided them through the maze, pointing out two open areas where they could anchor. Once the mission was accomplished, he waved and left them to make their decision. They watched his dinghy thread back through the anchorage and return to the raft-up. After they chose a spot, it was like centering a picture. They judged distance to the surrounding boats and how the wind blew, then dropped their anchor.

* * *

As the sun set, one by one the portholes of the fleet began to glow and the lights from Zihuatanejo created a luminous ring around the harbor. Boats bobbed and halyards clanked against their masts in an even beat. The same note hit over and over again, like a drip from a leaky faucet. Dinghies and *pangas* traveled back and forth on business and pleasure. In the distance, laughter erupted from a cockpit, then died away.

Once settled, Jessie and Neal felt like members of a reception line. As the dinghy raft-up splintered off, visitors trickled over to see them and drop off food. Each guest came aboard with a slightly different version of what happened to Jennifer Stover.

"I can tell you that the thought of watching my boat sail away from me after going over the side is enough to keep me up nights," said Mae Larssen. The crisp clothes she and her husband Anders had worn when they first met Jessie and Neal in Cabo were now limp and faded from sun and soap. "Almost makes me ask myself what the hell I'm doing out here."

"I think the most frightening thing is that they couldn't find her," said Jessie. "It's been so calm the last few days. If they couldn't find her in such ideal conditions, what chance would there be if conditions were worse?"

The group nodded in unison as they sat shoulder to shoulder in *Dana's* cockpit. Satch, their earlier escort, and his wife Claire rounded out the circle and brought the number to six.

Satch said, "I was listening to the radio when someone asked the rescue guys what the chances were of finding someone in these circumstances, and I swore the guy said there was close to a 90 percent chance they wouldn't find her. I would have asked again, but without a radio license I can only lurk. I can tell you, that woke me up."

Anders adjusted his position. "Course the fact that Eric can't say for sure when she went over made it harder to figure out where to start looking. But still, we don't move that damn fast. You wouldn't think a couple of hours would make that much difference."

"We heard they guessed she went over after dawn because the nav lights were off," said Neal.

"Yeah, that's right. Eric's pretty sure that if the light switches had been on when he got up, he would have been irked at his wife for forgetting to turn them off. All he remembers is feeling grateful for some extra minutes of sleep. It was after he realized what happened that things blurred."

Neal helped himself to another brownie and said, "Have you talked with Eric Stover then, Anders?"

"Hell, yes. He's right here in Zhuat. In fact . . . ." As he said *Z-wat,* the older man stood and ducked back and forth under the boom, then pointed. "That's his boat right over there. Blue canvas, about forty-feet, name's *Osprey,* you know, like the bird. I'm surprised he hasn't been over here already. I'm sure he'd want to talk to you."

Jessie and Neal exchanged a glance. It seemed impossible, but no one had mentioned it.

Mae hinted at scandal when she leaned in toward the middle of the circle and quickly glanced around the group. "At the raft-up, someone told me that he was spending the evening with Sonia Sieverson. Do you know them?"

"Yes, we met them in Cabo." Neal remembered Hal Sieverson plucking them out of the water the night an errant *panga*, sent by a killer named Simon, swamped *Pointer* as they rowed home. Everyone knew the rumors of Hal's abusive behavior, but that night in the water he had been a saint.

"Supposedly, Sonia and Eric were consoling each other. Hal's in the States on some business thing and Sonia's upset about being abandoned on *Koror.* One of the people anchored next to them said there was an unholy row the night before he left. He was screaming at her because she wanted to go back with him, but he was against it. Clear as a bell through the night, he said that his going home wasn't a vacation, he had business to attend to. That, instead of whining, she should be grateful for the opportunity to relax and enjoy the time on the boat. Since she didn't run out and buy her own ticket, he must have threatened to cut her money off or something. It's a nasty, explosive situation and in Eric's fragile state, he'd better be careful or he'll find himself trapped in the middle of it." To emphasize her point, the older woman retracted from the center of the circle with a gentle, "Hmph."

Anders shook his head. "Mae, Eric and Sonia are good friends. It's right that they spend time together now. Don't start spreading rumors where there are none," and before his wife could protest, he turned toward Neal. "Eric's been walking around like a wounded animal. We all kept our hopes up for Jennifer's return until we started getting information from you two. Today especially, Sonia's insulated Eric from all the talk."

"Anders, I'm not gossiping. Eric seemed devoted to Jennifer. It's that Sonia I wouldn't trust. She's insulating him all right, she's looking for a way out. Hal's a fossil compared to her, you know she's with him because of his money. I heard Jennifer is from a comfortable family, and I suppose Eric will inherit her portion. Sonia must know that."

Jessie noticed Claire drop her glance at the mention of Eric's devotion. When she looked up again, she focused on Jessie.

"Satch tells me you found the video camera she was using. Was there anything on the tape?" Her voice was soft and breathy. As she spoke, she rounded up the wisps of hair that had escaped her hat and were batting her in the face. When she curled them around her ear, Jessie noticed the nails. Pastel peach acrylic.

"Yes, we did find a camera," said Jessie, putting out of mind her own work-worn nails. "In fact," she reached down into the cabin and retrieved the corroded black box from the galley counter right by the steps, "it's the only thing we managed to salvage. Some of the people who came over tonight wanted to see it, and I'd run down so many times to grab it out of my shower locker, that last time, I just left it out." She handed it to Claire, who looked closely at it before passing it to her husband. "We don't have a TV or VCR, and even if we did, I don't think we would have tampered with it. Not sure what kind of damage that might cause."

"You don't have a TV?" said Claire.

"Ah . . . no we don't. Never felt the need for one."

"Oh, you must read a lot then."

Jessie wondered what one had to do with the other, but said, "Yes, we both love to read."

The camera had made the rounds and ended up again in Jessie's lap. She reached below and placed it on the galley counter, promising herself she'd put it away once everyone left.

"I love to read, too," said Claire, stretching her foot to a point as she crossed her leg.

Satch laughed and said, "Claire always has a book in her hand. Can't go anywhere without one, just in case she has a few minutes to spare. I'd bet money there's one in her bag. If we sink, it'll be because of the weight of her books."

The corners of Claire's mouth twitched; her eyes remained expressionless, but never left her husband's face.

Neal chuckled and said, "I'm afraid we suffer from the same problem. If you have some you've read, would you be interested in an exchange?"

Their guest's glance lingered a moment longer on her husband before turning to Neal. Her shoulders pinched together much like the purse around her lips and she said, "Oh, I don't think so, I usually find most people don't share my taste in books."

"Claire, why not?" Satch stretched his arm and encircled his wife's shoulder. "For the postage to ship those hardbound books home after you've read them, you could buy them all over again."

It was barely noticeable, not a big gesture at all, but Claire leaned away from him as if his closeness was unwelcome. "I'm sure they don't care to hear about that, Satch."

His hand firmed its grip on her shoulder and his eyes darted out to the anchorage. Like water dowsing a fire, the exchange put out the flow of conversation.

An engine sputtered to life in the distance and was the only sound to fill the seconds that passed. Anders shuffled his feet and Mae picked at imaginary lint on her shirt. Jessie felt her shoulders bunch up.

Neal finally broke the brittle silence. "Claire, you may be right, but if you ever change your mind, let us know."

Another twitch that might have been a smile worked the corners of her mouth, but Claire said nothing.

"Well, I think we ought to let these people get settled. Neal, Jessie, if you need help with any of this, you know where to find us. We aren't leaving for a couple of weeks." Anders stood and shook Neal's hand.

"Thanks, Anders. Good to see you again. Thanks for the food." Neal left the cockpit to help with the dinghies.

When Claire rose, Jessie stood and said, "It was nice meeting you. Thanks, Satch, knowing that someone was here and willing to help made it easier out there."

Satch met Jessie's outstretched hand and shook it with the same enthusiasm that spread across his face. "That's okay, Jessie. I was glad to help, although all I did was lurk on the radio a bit. I'm surprised, though, that Eric hasn't been over to collect the camera. I'm sure he wants to know what's on the film. Well, if you need anything, let us know."

Jessie stumbled over the words, not quite sure what to say. "That's all right, Satch, the U.S. authorities want to see it, so we couldn't give it to him right now anyway."

"The authorities? What do the authorities have to do with it. It's Eric's camera, it belongs to him."

"I wish it were that simple. The thing is, they are expecting us to deliver it."

"I can't believe what I'm hearing. Eric's one of us. You make it simple. You just give it to him."

"Satch, I really must go." Claire's mouth twitched again briefly as her eyes met Jessie's. The nails corralled the hair one more time around her ear before she gently pushed her husband toward the gate.

Satch glared at his hostess for several seconds before he allowed himself to be prodded along.

Jessie felt the heat from a blush as she fell in behind them and joined Neal on the bow. They watched the two couples climb into their dinghies and cast off. A final wave good night and they were alone.

"Can you imagine having hardbound books on a boat?" Neal led Jessie back to the cockpit.

"I'm still trying to figure out how she keeps those nails. She didn't look too happy did she?"

"No kidding. Interesting combination those two."

"He certainly squawked when I told him we weren't giving the camera to Eric right away. We didn't even consider that option when we thought about this, maybe we should have."

"Jessie, we've already made a decision, and nothing I've heard so far has changed my mind," said Neal as he surveyed the party leftovers in the cockpit.

When she began to help Neal clean up the glasses, plates and silverware, Jessie momentarily forgot the camera and turned her thoughts to the person who went into the water with it. "First Mac in Cabo . . . and now Jennifer Stover. God, that's creepy. Flat calm and you fall overboard . . . you're gone. I can't imagine what it must be like to be in the water and watch the boat sail away from you with no hope of ever catching it or of anyone even knowing you're gone until it's too late."

Neal draped his arm over the boom and turned to her. "Jessie, stop."

She looked at him and said, "Not until you promise that when you're on watch and I'm asleep, you'll be careful and wear your harness."

"I promise, now you."

"The same."

Once the signs of company had disappeared, they settled in the cockpit with a glass of El Presidente brandy and surveyed their neighborhood. The *zocolo*, or town square, sat on the waterfront and was the focal point for the community. A brightly lit basketball court dominated the area, and they had seen players running back and forth all evening. They reminisced about last year's Miss Guererro parade that had filled the square to capacity and of the rock concerts that turned the court into an amphitheater. Every time they had gone ashore, they had wandered the shady *Malecón* to the square to see what was going on. They agreed it was going to be fun getting reacquainted with their favorite port.

"I didn't expect so much activity when we got here. Man, I'm beat." Jessie took a sip of the auburn liquid.

"Me, too." Neal stood and stretched, then picked up his drink. "Here's to another safe, albeit interesting, passage."

After they clinked glasses, he leaned over her, cradled her head with one hand and kissed her. The kiss kindled a heat in Neal that made him linger, savoring the taste of her brandied lips. "Mmm, that's nice," she said, setting down her drink and reaching up to him.

A dinghy engine cut off and drew their attention away from each other. It drifted in toward *Dana.*

Jessie stood abruptly and clipped her head on the aluminum boom with a "plink."

"Damn it," she said as she rubbed at the pain.

Neal gathered her in his arms and continued to watch the dinghy.

"It's okay, Neal, I'm fine." Jessie gave two more rubs then moved away to greet their guest.

"Not another one, " said Neal under his breath. As far as he was concerned, it was too late for the curious to be out. He sat abruptly, hoping his body language would say what would be impolite to say out loud.

The dinghy came in close and its pilot leaned in to grip *Dana's* side. He had dark, curly hair that looked squarish from a bad cut, and his light skin, deeply tanned, looked even more so set against the turquoise shirt and white shorts. A solemn face with dark eyes met

Jessie as she walked to the sidedeck gate to greet him.

Her crouch brought her to his level. "Hi, what can I do for you?"

The dinghy driver cleared his throat and said, "Hi. I know it's late, but I've been debating all evening on whether I really wanted to come over here." His deep voice was strong and yet not arrogant. "Obviously you know what I decided. Please forgive my intrusion. I'm Eric Stover."

6

An even flame from an oil lamp reflected off the teak and bathed the cabin in a golden honeyed glow. To Neal, the color gave their home afloat a warm, friendly feel. The only thing missing was the music of Vivaldi or Mozart. Instead, a persistent tap drew his attention back to their guest, and he watched as Eric Stover's left hand worked a paper clip up and down on their galley table.

Neal knew Jessie had felt obligated to invite Eric aboard, but he had still groaned inwardly when Eric accepted. He had willed the man to refuse; the man hadn't. The tapping continued. Neal fought the urge to snatch the paper clip away, but then Jessie would have a legitimate reason to grouse at him for his behavior.

"I've been watching from *Koror*. I didn't want to get tangled up in a discussion with a lot of people, so I waited until things were quiet over here. Sonia . . . I think you know her . . . she says Hal met you in Cabo." Jessie and Neal nodded and he went on. "She's the one who convinced me to come over tonight. I guess I'm supposed to want to know what you saw, but I don't. That probably doesn't make much sense." Eric took a swallow from the beer he had brought with him and continued to tap.

"It's okay, Eric, I wish we had better news for you." In the cozy cabin, Jessie sat across from him, their knees separated by less than two feet. Neal stood at a distance, one elbow resting on the companionway steps.

"You said you saw a red jacket; her windbreaker was red. It doesn't ever get really cold, you know, but she usually put it on for that dawn watch. She hated getting up, but once she was over that trauma, she liked to watch the sky lighten just before sunrise. It was her favorite time of the day." His glance bounced between Neal and Jessie, then down at the table. His eyes squinted as he shoved the paper clip away and scratched his forehead.

"Christ, I'm a mess."

With her legs together and her hands clasped, Jessie leaned forward, resting her elbows on her knees. "We can't know what you're going through, but it doesn't take much imagination to realize it must be agonizing."

Eric went on. "Lots of people wear red jackets. You had to be able to tell if it was a woman . . . in her late-twenties with long, light brown hair, almost blond?"

Jessie looked at Neal and then back at Eric. "Eric, I'm sorry, but no, . . . we just couldn't tell for sure."

Neal heard a tug in her voice and knew the vision the words conjured. It would have required closer scrutiny of the blob of flesh they had found to determine the sex, and the hair . . . there hadn't been enough left to tell, especially in the water and with the failing light. He shook the thought from his mind. Checking the body over more closely was not something he would have done willingly.

Eric cupped one hand over his mouth and blinked a couple of times. It took a second for him to regain his composure.

"Someone told me you got in the water with the . . . ah . . . whomever you found." He cleared his throat and his left hand reached for the paper clip. Before the tapping began, he tossed it aside. "Did you find anything . . . I mean was there anything on the . . . ah . . . person . . . like maybe a video camera?" His eyes locked on Jessie's.

Neal's elbow came off the companionway steps and he shoved his hands in his pockets. Word of finding the camera had spread. They made no secret of it, even pulled it out when requested, to show some of their earlier guests. Eric knew about everything else, why not the camera? Neal contributed nothing. He decided to watch and listen.

"I'm surprised you didn't hear, Eric, but yes, we did. It was secured by a strip of Velcro. Since we were outside Mexico's territorial water, we've been dealing with U.S. officials and they want to see it, but we can show it to you if you like." Jessie stood and disappeared from the main cabin to a small area up forward.

Eric bit at his lips and rubbed his hands over the top of his thighs. The cabin went quiet and Neal imagined he could almost hear their guest's heartbeat. Eric's attention focused on Jessie, his whole body leaned to watch what she was doing.

"When I first got here a couple of days ago," he said, his eyes never leaving her, "I had people coming over all the time. It wasn't so bad at first, you know, but it was all the time, always wondering how I was doing. They meant well, but I couldn't stand it any more, so I started spending time on *Koror.* Hal's gone back to the States on business and Sonia is still pretty upset about being left behind. She needed a few things fixed, too, so I guess you could say we've been helping each other. Satch found me there last night."

He relaxed a little, took a swallow of beer and chuckled as he continued. "I think he regretted it at first. Sonia screamed at him as he approached, and she was locked in the head by the time he pulled alongside. It must have been the light, she thought Hal had come back unexpectedly. I don't know, I guess there are similarities in their looks. Anyway, once we convinced her it wasn't Hal, Satch told us about you finding someone. He didn't want to get my hopes up, but he wanted me to know you were headed here. I had to press him, but when he finally said the person you found was dead, it was more than I wanted to know. I went below and Sonia talked to him. I've avoided everyone else since then. If she knew about the camera, she didn't mention it."

Before he finished, Jessie had returned with a blue nylon bag and sat next to him. His eyes had trained on it, watching as she slid the lock toggle along the line that secured it and pulled the camera out.

Eric's eyes dropped shut and he bit down on his lower lip. He didn't need to speak; it was obvious he recognized it.

"God, we're sorry, Eric. This has to be terrible for you," Jessie quickly rebagged the camera and pulled the toggle closed.

Eric reached for the bag and Jessie responded automatically by lifting it toward him. They froze when Neal spoke.

"Sorry we can't let you take it, Eric, but officials are expecting us to hand it over to them."

The moment felt suspended. Jessie and Eric looked at him; Jessie's arm drooped under the weight of the camera and dropped back into her lap.

"Neal, I'm not so sure . . . ," Jessie said, fumbling for words.

"This isn't a moral issue, Jessie, it's a legal one. We've told them we have the camera and that we'll bring it to them. I intend to do that. Nothing personal, Eric, but I don't want us to get tangled in a legal hassle that might complicate our involvement. If we hadn't taken on this responsibility, I'd gladly give the camera back to you, but as it stands, we can't."

"It's Jennifer's family," he began quietly, looking down at his hands, "they were against this cruise from the beginning. They think that if she's dead, then it's my fault. I've had some conversations with them since this whole thing started that frankly scare me a little." He looked up at them, his smile was weary. "I guess I should have figured they'd blame me emotionally, but I get the impression that they're trying to find a way to blame me legally."

Heat began to burn in Neal. His pulse raced at the possibility of a confrontation. He willed himself to remain leaning against the steps with his arms crossed, to remain calm. "Hearing that concerns me even more, Eric. I sympathize with your situation and believe me when I say that what happened to you and Jennifer has haunted me from the first time I heard about it, but I'd like you to understand our position. Under the circumstances, if we give you the camera, our involvement will definitely get more complicated."

Urgency began to tinge their guest's words. "But I need answers about what happened. I keep having these nightmares. I have to know. If you give me the camera, I'll tell the authorities whatever you want. That I forced you or coerced you in some way. Surely we can work something out?"

Neal watched his wife chew on her lower lip. Before he had a chance to speak, she made a suggestion.

"Neal, what about just watching the tape. We would be right there, Eric's mind would be eased and we could keep our commitment. They would understand that wouldn't they?"

Eric's earlier animation stilled and he went quiet.

Neal stood upright, shoved his hands in his pockets. He ignored their guest's sudden departure from the conversation and directed his words at Jessie. "The people who want the camera aren't required to have compassion or to understand. Obviously there's a question about this whole thing and they're looking for answers. They know we might have one. What would we tell them when they come to collect it?" He sounded brittle and his voice snapped like a frozen wooden dock underfoot.

"We would tell them the truth. The owner of the camera wanted to see the tape, and we saw no harm in showing it to him."

By the tone and deliberate calm of her voice, Neal knew she was seething, but this was one time he wouldn't relent.

"Don't oversimplify the consequences, Jessica. We'll do what we both agreed to do, and what we told them we'd do. It keeps our involvement straightforward and uncomplicated."

For the first time Neal felt *Dana's* cabin closing in on him, but he resisted the temptation to climb the steps to the deck. Eric's misfortune filled the small space with heavy desperation. Remove Eric and the cramped feeling in the cabin would disappear.

"Eric, give Neal and me a chance to talk more about this."

Neal shook his head and leaned toward her, his voice quiet. "Jessie, no amount of talking will change my mind about this, and Eric has a right to know that."

With both hands up in surrender, Eric said, "It's okay, Jessie, I understand. It was thoughtless of me to push the issue. Thanks, at least, for letting me see the camera. As much as I didn't want it to be true, seeing it has settled one thing in my mind. Jennifer is not floating around on another boat. She won't be coming back." Eric looked down at his hands, then stood. "I'm sorry, Neal, for coming on so strong. I hope that you can understand my position. I want answers, too, and we both know how agonizingly slow bureaucrats can be."

Neal looked down at the hand Eric extended to him. He looked back up into the other man's face and noticed the lines and shadows around the eyes. Neal's resistance wavered. He reached for the hand and slowly shook it. "Yeah, Eric, I probably would have done the same."

Out on deck, Jessie helped with dinghy lines and once Eric cast off, she waved good-bye. Neal leaned against the boom, one arm draped over it and watched the dinghy make its way home.

Jessie turned away from their departing guest and walked the few steps back to the cockpit. She locked her husband in a stare and hissed, "You were an absolute shit. The man just lost his wife for God's sake. How could you be so cruel? And you know how much I hate being called Jessica, especially when you're mad."

It wasn't that he hadn't expected it, but the intensity was stronger than he had anticipated. "Jessica's your name, and when you exasperate me, it slips out. Getting back to the issue, what happened to our decision to keep our distance on this? To deliver the camera and move on?"

"That was before there was anyone else to consider. Why can't he take things from here? It's between him, the family and the police. As far as I'm concerned, he can have the camera and give it to the police himself."

Neal's face fell in disbelief. "Do you know Eric Stover?"

"Of course not," Jessie snapped at him as she descended the steps to the cabin.

Neal followed, feeling his anger continue to rise. "Have you somehow gotten information on Jennifer's disappearance that I don't know about?"

Jessie rubbed her forehead, the volume in her voice increased to match his. "Neal . . . ."

"Then how do you know there isn't a question about how she went over?"

"I can't believe this. Based on what you just sa[illegible], how can you say that man pushed his wife overboard?"

"That's not what I'm saying. But I also can't say for sure that he was sound asleep in his bunk."

"Neal, what are you talking about?"

"Maybe it was an accident. Maybe they were changing sails or putting up a spinnaker pole and she slipped or maybe they were just reckless."

"But then he would have picked her up."

"Maybe he did and she was dead."

The statement stretched the tension between them to the snapping point, but Neal pressed ahead before Jessie had a chance to object to his speculations.

"If so, his story is a graceful way to cover up the mistake. He'll be able to walk away from all this with his character intact. The point I'm trying to make is that there are a lot of possibilities. If there's some speculation about what happened, we want to steer clear. I don't know Eric Stover, and for selfish reasons, I don't want to get to know him."

She shook her head, then looked around and sat abruptly. "I'm beginning to think we're involved whether we want to be or not. I thought it would be a simple matter of dropping the camera off, but meeting him has clouded the issue for me. This all just seems so melodramatic."

Neal didn't respond right away. The fact that she thought he was overreacting to the situation rekindled his anger. His focus dropped from her face to the cabin sole, lamp light flickered across the floor boards. He calmed his breathing and lowered his voice. "Jessie, you thought getting that body back here was the right thing to do. I didn't like it, but I agreed. This is different; I can't explain it, but I've got a strong feeling about this, and if you believe the right thing to do here is give the camera to Eric, we're going to have problems."

His eyes met hers, but hers escaped to the refuge of the lamp's flame. The pause was a long one.

Finally, she said quietly. "Once we turn that camera over, Eric will probably never see it again or if he does, so much time will have passed, it won't matter any longer. He's hurting now. Project us into this situation. If I were the one who went overboard and someone put you through all this, I know you'd be furious, and I know I'd come back from the dead to haunt them."

Neal studied his wife's profile, silhouetted by lamplight. Somehow he had to find the words that would better explain his position. "Jessie, this man is a complete unknown and we have no idea what their relationship was like. We've got Eric's story, but others could be credible. How can we possibly know for sure that what he's saying is the truth?"

A few seconds passed before she took a deep breath. Her voice reminded him of flat soda, the effervescence and passion of anger were gone. "Okay, Neal, we'll keep the camera and give it to officials ourselves. But I have a condition."

He hadn't convinced her, she was compromising.

"We get up early to do our port check-in, and then we call about the camera. The faster we get rid of it, the faster Eric gets it back. Deal?"

The lamp brushed the high points on her face with golden light. The safe harbor he usually found in his wife's eyes and smile was gone, her face slack. After a moment he said, "Deal."

7

"Look, Mr. Johnson, this puts us in an awkward position. Eric Stover is, after all, the woman's husband, and he wants to know what's on this tape. Isn't there some way we can speed this along? . . . thanks, I'd appreciate that."

As she held the line, a rhythmic beat drew her attention away from the phone. Jessie turned and watched a stocky girl in a red, makeshift uniform dribble a basketball across the cement court, weaving a path through her green-clad opponents. The player's dark ponytail swished in time to the beat.

People wandered the square; some settled to watch the game while others stopped briefly to chat or gaze at the harbor. Benches huddled around the base of the few trees that shaded the expanse of uneven brick, and as the sun crossed the sky, their popularity peaked or dropped away, depending on the shadows. Weeds grew in neglected corners, but the typical collection of plastic soda bottles, chip and candy wrappers were pleasantly absent.

Knee-high children with coal-black hair, each clutching a box of Chiclet gum, approached everyone, raised the box and their melancholy brown eyes in hopes of making a sale. Jessie smiled but shook her head at the little girl who walked toward her, and without skipping a beat, the young peddler changed course toward the next customer. From a distance they looked clean and neatly dressed. Up close, the matted hair, runny noses and dirt smudges matched the frayed edges and dulled colors of their clothes. In some places, serious life begins at a young age, Jessie thought sadly.

Sweat broke out on her forehead and worked its way down her

face. Why were phones always out in the sun, she wondered as she swiped the trickle away. Neal caught her eye as he rounded the corner and joined her, a soft briefcase containing their official boat papers tucked under his arm.

The atmosphere on *Dana* while getting ready to come to town had been cool and filled with efficiency. Jessie went with Neal to the harbor master's and immigration offices, then left him to handle customs and the rest of the check-in while she called the number Wayne had relayed to them over the radio. The thump of the basketball and the squeak of sneakers dropped to background noise when the voice at the other end of the line returned.

Jessie listened, then said, "Well, that's a possibility I suppose." When she saw the wrinkle form between Neal's eyes, she said, "Can you hang on a second? Thanks." She covered the mouthpiece and explained to Neal that there was a delay, then mentioned the alternative suggestion.

"Sonny's coming tomorrow. How can we take off for Mexico City. Besides he lands there. We can't expect him to come all the way here and then turn right around and go back."

She tightened her hand over the phone. "When we call him today to confirm his plans, we can ask him."

Jessie noted the curt shrug and when her partner turned his attention to the game without another word, she put the phone back to her ear. "You said the man in charge of this is a Desi who? . . . Swainyo. When did you say he'd be there? Okay, I'll call back, thanks again."

"So, what's going on?" Irritation mingled with the words. They walked side by side toward the cement basketball court and sat on a bench to watch the activity.

Since they had a problem to solve, Jessie pushed aside the animosity and muzzled her own urge to snap. "The number we got from Wayne is for an office in Mexico City connected with the U.S. State Department. I got the impression it's not actually at the U.S. embassy, but still a part of it. Mr. Johnson, the man I talked to, is an assistant to a Desi Swainyo, who is the man in charge of looking into Jennifer's disappearance. Swainyo won't be in his office for a while, so this guy talked to me. I think Eric's right about her family digging into this. Johnson seemed too eager to accommodate us for it to be routine."

"So what's the holdup then about getting someone down here?"

"It's a small office and there's a conference in Mexico City that has everyone pretty busy this week. Bigwigs are coming in from all over, I guess. Johnson kept going off and talking to people, but the bottom line was they can't free anyone to come down here until next week. If we still had the body, he told me they would have coordinated with Mexican officials to help out, but not just to pick up and deliver a camera. I don't think the people Wayne talked to the other night really discussed the arrangements they promised us with the people in this office. The guy's voice tensed up when he talked about it."

"So he suggested we bring it to them."

She nodded. "The last time he came back, his voice sounded excited, like they'd come up with an idea. His exact words were, 'We'd work something out if you'd consider bringing it to us.' Swainyo will be involved with this conference for a couple of days, but he'd be able to get together with us once everything got underway. That means we could see him before the end of the week and at least shave off a couple of days. God, what do we tell Eric? He'll go nuts having to wait. Do you think Sonny would consider going?"

Neal leaned forward and propped his elbows on his knees. His glance fell to the uneven brick between his feet, then flicked to the court. From his actions, Jessie could tell the last thing he wanted to do was take a plane or bus to the big city, but they had made a deal, and if need be, she intended to remind him of it.

"If we make it sound like an adventure to Sonny, he'd probably go along with it. We can't call him for awhile yet. Do you want to start shopping or go back to the boat?"

The combative tone in his voice rankled, but she chose not to challenge it.

"We may have to get a few more things tomorrow, but I grabbed our list before we came in. Let's get that stuff now and see where we are when we're done." Jessie's eyes left the activity on the court and focused on Neal. She took a tentative step toward peace. "I know it would be easier to just wait until next week, so I appreciate your going along with this."

Neal's gaze stayed on the court. "We made a deal, Jessie, which I'm sure you'd be quick to mention if I didn't go along with it. Ready?" He stood without looking at her or waiting for a response.

Heat rose in waves from the pavement as they walked in stony silence along the narrow lanes lined with T-shirt and souvenir shops. The area bustled with tourists. They worked from memory through the "pedestrians only" streets until finally car horns and racing engines chased away the holiday atmosphere and mixed with the heat. Darting between the cars that sped by, they crossed busy Ave. Benito Juárez and entered the Zihuatanejo market.

Plump, ripe fruits and vegetables displayed by several vendors pulled them from stall to stall, and the pungent smell of fish and freshly butchered meat drifted out from the market's core. Scrawny dogs, buzzing flies and dirt floors were an accepted part of the spectacle. Clumps of consumers negotiated the tight aisles as sellers chatted, haggled, bagged and collected. Laughter, sprinkled throughout, created a carnival-like atmosphere. The couple wandered, getting a feel for what was available and checking prices.

"This stuff looks great," said Jessie, pausing at one stall and inspecting the brightly colored, hearty looking produce. Behind the counter, made by a board stretched across two crates, a young girl eyed all the activity with quiet curiosity as she hung on the arm of a woman not yet out of her teens. When Jessie smiled at her, the girl dropped her glance with a smile and buried her face into the woman's shoulder. In basic Spanish, Jessie asked for the prices of a few items, nodded when it sounded fair and selected what she wanted. To her, bargaining for produce was for the hardened hagglers. The woman weighed it, wrapped it and announced the total. Jessie passed over the *pesos,* smiled at the girl who had stared at her during the transaction and moved on.

She joined Neal, who was discussing tomatoes with a boy not yet in double digits. Neal's few key Spanish phrases, delivered with no embellishments, got the point across that they wanted green tomatoes. The boy nodded vigorously and shouted at an older man across the stall, who shouted something back. Their young clerk raised a finger to suggest they wait a moment and disappeared behind a curtain. Seconds later, he reappeared with a basket of rounded green tomatoes. Neal nodded and asked the price, nodded again and pulled out what he wanted of the green fruit. With a flourish, their young attendant put them into a plastic bag, spun it to twist the top and handed it to Neal in exchange for the meager amount.

Weaving through the commercial throng, they wandered from one stall to the next until their mesh shopping bags were full. Although not a word was exchanged, détente settled over the pair. One purchase even warmed the chill between them, and they worked carefully to balance the rare find of strawberries and kiwis on top of their other purchases.

When they returned to the *zocolo*, a large crowd had gathered to watch a new set of teams battle for points on the basketball court. They settled their packages on a bench and Neal sat with them while Jessie made calls to Sonny and Desi Swainyo. She was gone only a few minutes.

"Sonny got called into a meeting, wants us to call back at four," she said as she sat on the bench next to their packages and kneaded the muscles in her shoulders that complained of the load they were carrying.

Neal looked at his watch. "What did Swainyo say?"

"I explained the situation to him, and he said they would put us in a hotel for a couple of days if we'd consider bringing it there."

"Sonny, too?"

"I didn't exactly tell him about Sonny. All I said was that we had a complication in getting to Mexico City and that we'd like someone to come here. His response to that was to add a couple of meals to the deal."

Neal sat in silence for a moment, then with what seemed like the effort needed to push a boulder uphill he said, "That's probably still cheaper than sending someone down here for a couple of days. What did you tell him?"

"I said we had to discuss it some more and that we'd call him either later today or tomorrow. He prefers today because tomorrow that conference starts and he'll be unavailable."

"Why not call him back now and tell him we're coming. We'll sort something out with Sonny, and I'll come back in at four and give him a call. I should be able to figure out something to say to convince him it's an opportunity he wouldn't want to miss."

Jessie looked at him. "Did I just hear you say you'll make the call?"

"Yeah, do you object?"

It was sarcasm in the tone that sparked the embers into flame.

"Don't get all indignant with me. You hate using the phone. I'd be the one calling your mom if she were dying. What makes this so special and why the change of heart?"

"Look, I thought you'd be busy on the boat, and I was just trying to save you a trip. If you want to come back in and make the call, go ahead."

Jessie's glance darted out to the players running the length of the court and saw the goal that pulled a cheer from the crowd. Rather than react to Neal's remark, she got up and stalked to the phone to call Desi Swainyo. She worked at smoothing the furrow developing between her brows as she thought about her recent discord with Neal. It felt like one wheel had derailed and was ready to pull the whole train off the track.

Mr. Desi Swainyo confirmed his offer and told her Mr. Corbin Johnson would coordinate her arrangements when she knew them. She walked back to the bench and began assembling her packages.

The white flag now fully withdrawn, she snapped at Neal. "You make the call to Sonny. It's time to get back to the boat. This meat should get in the fridge."

Fully-laden, they trekked along the shady *Malecón* to where the dinghies were beached. In contrast to their frosty silence, bright, tropical sunlight danced on the water in the harbor where *pangas* and dinghies bounced over each other's wakes.

When they got close, Jessie noticed *Pointer* had been pulled away from the rest of the dinghies. She frowned and slowed. Neal stopped in front of her and she followed suit when she saw what had happened. This, on top of everything else, brought her close to tears and she erupted.

"Goddammit, what the hell is this?"

Sand, from the patch surrounding *Pointer,* had been dug up and dumped into their tender up to the gunwales. It reminded Jessie of a measuring cup packed with brown sugar. A quick glance around proved none of the other dinghies had been touched.

She stared, trying to make sense of the scene, until the ache in her arms grew intolerable. Neal had already stacked his packages out of the way a few feet from *Pointer,* and Jessie placed hers next to his. Her anger sizzled as she thought about the random selection that had singled them out for the prank.

"Why the hell didn't someone stop the kids and chase them off?"

Neal grunted agreement, but added nothing. Instead, he began the process of cleaning up and Jessie resigned herself to helping. They removed their two-horsepower engine and propped it up against a nearby dinghy, speaking only when necessary and then with few words. Toiling and sweating, they rolled *Pointer* over, then pounded on her keel until the sand dropped out. After brushing the inside, they righted her and remounted the engine. In spite of the tensions between them, they got the job done, and standing a few feet away was a crumbling sand replica of their dinghy. The incident hadn't been catastrophic, just an incredible annoyance.

Once they got *Pointer* in the water and loaded the groceries, they waited for a lull in the surf before they launched. Settling next to the engine, Neal gave one pull on the starter cord and brought it to life. Facing each other, but avoiding eye contact, they headed home. Jessie watched *Pointer's* replica blend in with the rest of the sand as they pulled away from the beach. She asked herself what it was going to take to heal the rift separating her from the man who sat across from her, the man she loved.

Once back aboard *Dana,* they kept one eye on the time as they mixed a weak bleach solution to sterilize the tomatoes and other unpeelable produce they had bought at the market. They also spent time rearranging things in anticipation of Sonny's arrival.

After one glance at the clock, Neal stopped what he was doing and said, "I guess I'd better head in. We need anything else while I'm there?" Neal checked his daypack, then slung it over his shoulder.

"It probably would be a good idea to get some more water. The jug is on deck."

"Okay then, I'll see you later."

Jessie watched him climb the companionway steps, missing the kiss she usually got when he left. She listened to the sounds of his departure and felt irritation rise again. She didn't understand how it could be so black and white for him. In her frustration, she banged the can of Green Giant corn in her hand on the table. He could at least try to understand that it wasn't that clear-cut for her. She sat, tapped her foot and shoved the can around the table to help her think. It reminded her of Eric's paper clip tapping. When she stopped, she heard the louder tap of someone rapping on the hull. It pulled her out of her thoughts and drew her topside to answer the knock.

* * *

Remembering the phone call to Sonny made Neal smile as he dragged *Pointer* back into the water. Their friend's enthusiasm for his upcoming visit was infectious and Neal was almost suspicious of the burst of excitement that traveled down the wire when he mentioned a trip to Mexico City. In fact, it got more mysterious when Sonny quickly dismissed the suggestion that the couple meet him in the capital. Even though he would land there and change planes, he insisted he would travel on to Zihuatanejo as planned. Just as quickly dismissed was the idea of heading back to the big city by bus, so Jessie's guess was right, they would fly. Neal grinned and accepted it. That was typical of Sonny and it was his vacation.

With that decided, they confirmed his arrival time and discussed plans to meet at the main *zocolo* near the basketball court. He reassured Neal that he was perfectly capable of grabbing a taxi at the airport and getting to town on his own. If the basketball court was as popular as Neal suggested, he'd find it. Neal told him they'd be waiting.

Standing at the stern in water past his knees, Neal maneuvered *Pointer's* nose into the waves and waited for a lull. Once launched and underway, he detoured around the anchorage, slowly working his way home. When he remembered the water jug, forgotten on *Dana's* deck, he altered course and headed straight back. With the atmosphere so chilly on the boat, he'd grab the jug and make another trip to shore. It would give them both extra time on their own.

Lost in these thoughts, it took Neal several seconds to notice the dinghy attached to *Dana's* stern. When he recognized it, his heart began to pound and the red heat of anger tinged the tip of his ears. The dinghy belonged to Eric Stover.

Neal pushed the throttle on *Pointer's* engine to full and readjusted his cap. Speculation about the why's for Stover's visit led to only one answer. He hated himself for thinking Jessie could renege on her promise, but he had rarely seen her so torn over an issue, and this stranger was in a position to take advantage of it.

As he approached, the two people enjoying the shade of the cockpit awning stood as if one were preparing to leave. Neal cruised in quickly, cut the engine and pulled along *Dana's* port side. After securing *Pointer*, he boarded and joined the other two. Jessie was pulling her guest's dinghy along the starboard side for boarding.

"Just leaving, Eric?"

Neal's eyes searched, but saw nothing large enough to be the camera. The departing visitor gripped the deck stanchions and lowered himself into his tender. He glanced up at Neal, wearing a tired smile.

"Afternoon, Neal. Yes, I'm off." Then turned to Jessie. "Thank you, Jessie. I'll think about your offer."

Neal studied first one then the other. He was an eye blink faster at relieving Jessie of Eric's dinghy painter and had no intention of letting go until he found out what offer Jessie had made. "What offer is that?" He directed the question at his wife.

She looked at him, then at their guest, then back at him. She took a deep breath as if summoning self-control.

"I've suggested that if Eric intends to go to Mexico City to stake his claim for the camera, he might consider flying at the same time we do."

The answer was so unexpected it stunned him. He felt theatrical standing with one hand gripping a limp dinghy painter and his mouth agape. Nothing came to mind except, "Why?"

"Because . . . Neal." Petulance frosted her reply and didn't provide answers to the crowd of questions he had.

Recovering some of his composure, Neal turned to Eric and, with no attempt to hide the sarcasm, said, "Sorry I missed your visit."

"Neal, if by that you're implying that I waited for you to leave before I came over, you credit me with more dramatic motives than are at work here. There's nothing sinister about this. I was alone, got overwhelmed and decided to try my luck about the camera one more time. The fact that you weren't here was a coincidence. Jessie explained your position again and we talked. All I'm trying to do is quiet the roar that's going on in my head. I don't want to upset your lives, I just want to know what happened. If you believe that's being . . . devious, I'm sorry, it's not meant to be."

Dana's deck went quiet. Neal watched his wife avert her eyes to the boats in the harbor. They did a tour and when Neal saw her pause and straighten her back, he followed her glance. The woman in the cockpit of a nearby boat removed her glasses as she set down her book and leaned forward. Claire Jurgeon, Neal guessed, was an intelligent woman, and she could infer a lot from what she saw. He looked back at Jessie, but her gaze had moved to the sky, then it dropped to their guest.

"I'm sorry, Eric. I just want you to know I understand if you're angry with us. Just in case you're interested, I'll come over and tell you the flight times when we know them." She turned from him and made her way back to the cockpit.

"Yeah, sure. Okay."

Eric's glare challenged Neal to possession of the dinghy painter. Flying to Mexico City together was an unwelcome development, but if restricted to that, and Neal would make sure that it was, it was better than more complications over the camera. He handed the painter back to its owner, forced the tension from his face and nodded good-bye. As if in comment to the gesture, Eric turned his back on Neal, settled in his dinghy and sped away.

Neal watched the foamy wake for a second, then bent under the awning and sat heavily onto the cockpit bench. Issuing up from the cabin were angry noises of things being banged around. This situation was going from bad to worse. Neal felt helpless. He didn't want to be the heavy in this, but it was all so clear to him. Why was turning over to authorities what might be evidence in a suspicious death causing such an uproar? The excitement over Sonny's visit disappeared. What enjoyment could the three of them share in their small boat under such explosive conditions?

He swept an irritated glance down the length of *Dana.* The water jug sat within easy reach. He grabbed it and dropped it into *Pointer* with a bang. For the time being, he preferred the heat ashore to the heat at home.

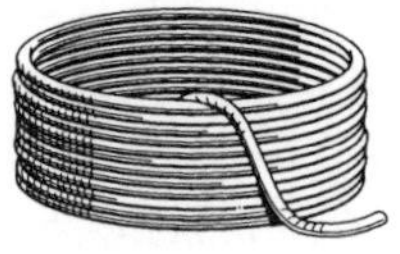

8

Jessie heard the familiar bang of an empty water jug landing in *Pointer* and held her breath. When the engine started and moved away, tears formed as she turned away from the pan she had thrown angrily onto the stove. She pulled on a pair of rubber gloves, climbed out into the cockpit and began hauling tomatoes out of the bleach bath. Seldom in their ten-year relationship had they fallen so far out of harmony with each other. Sonny would be able to tell instantly. She arranged the produce on a towel in the bright sunshine and sorted through her thoughts. Adding a third person to the mix would be like adding heat to a container already under a lot of pressure. Something was bound to give. Tossing the gloves down next to the tomatoes, she returned to the cabin, troubled over the upcoming visit.

She sat, rested her elbows on her knees and cupped her chin in her hands. The trip to Mexico City might be the best answer. Her head came up. Neal hadn't told her how Sonny felt about the trip. Even in his anger, he would have mentioned it if Sonny had objected. She dropped her chin back onto her hands. Then again, maybe not. She ached inside from battle fatigue. The chasm between them kept widening and Eric's latest visit hadn't helped, especially her suggestion that he fly to Mexico City with them. But what harm could there be in that? Since she was bound by her agreement with Neal not to give the man his damn camera, the least they could do was offer him a little moral support. After all, it was just a quick flight from here to there, not a commitment to tour the city.

She stood abruptly, then moved to the forward cabin and her shower locker. Yanking open the door, she grabbed the nylon bag that held the camera and pulled it out. It felt heavy in her hands, and rotating it, she went over again the aggravations it had added to her life. An overwhelming temptation to pitch it over the side possessed her, but she resisted and was about to put it back in its place next to her shower bag when she paused.

They had decided that while in port, they would make room for Sonny by stowing some of their own things in the cavity left by the anchor chain. Instead of putting the nylon bag next to her shower things, Jessie changed course for the chain locker and shoved the bag with the vexing camera deep into the jumble that had found temporary residence there. It felt symbolic. If she could bury it and close the door, maybe she could think about something else for a couple of days.

* * *

The next morning, Jessie gently spun the metal display of postcards and chose two more to add to the ones she'd already selected. Tension still existed between Neal and her, but Sonny's arrival later in the day had brought them ashore early to do errands. She flashed through the assortment in her hands and then was aware of someone's approach. Assuming it was Neal, she said, "Well, none of these are great, but I think this is the best of what's here."

Her head snapped up when the voice responding was female.

"I had a difficult time choosing, too. With so much beauty around, you'd think they could produce a better postcard." Claire Jurgeon's pastel peach nails glowed in beautiful contrast as she curled the flyaway strand of auburn hair around her ear.

"Oh, Claire, hello. Sorry, I thought you were Neal."

"Hope I didn't startle you, but . . . ." She looked around and Jessie noticed her glance stopped at Neal. He was thumbing through a book. She stepped in closer. "I wanted to talk to you alone."

They fell in step and walked to the other side of the stall.

"It's about Jennifer. I don't usually like to talk about other people, but I sense you're in a peculiar situation and you ought to know." Her voice sounded as pastel as her nails. Her matching peach rayon dress draped over her, and she reminded Jessie of the women in those gauzy photographs surrounded by flowers and greenery next to a glittering brook. She looked so cool in spite of the sultry air that Jessie felt even more limp and rumpled.

"What about Jennifer?"

"I am naturally horrified by what happened and I'm haunted by some things she told me. Most people think they were a happy couple, but I'm not so sure. Jennifer was the kind of person who worked at keeping up appearances. She started talking to me after I broke down on her boat about a year ago. You see, I find cruising awfully tiresome, but I endure it because Satch doesn't seriously quarrel about spending the money needed to make things comfortable. I also know he has a short attention span. Rock climbing, racing, whatever delivers an adrenaline rush has made an appearance at some point in our marriage. One day a switch will flip, and he'll require something new to spike his heart rate. Planning amusements for himself is what he does best. Normally, my part is on the sidelines as cheerleader and that suits me, but cruising has required more immersion from me than I like, and that day on Jennifer's boat, I'd had enough. Jennifer graciously listened and remained discreet, as I hope will you."

She looked out at the street and readjusted her Raybans. "Shortly after that, she mentioned a few things about her situation, and from then on whenever we shared an anchorage or a harbor we enjoyed long conversations. I haven't discussed any of this with Satch; I believe he rather likes Eric and, frankly, I don't. Jennifer and he originally planned to cruise for two years. She had come into some money from her parent's estate, and Eric persuaded her a cruise could be sort of a last hurrah before they settled down to start a family and serious careers. Apparently, six months ago he began campaigning to extend it and head for Costa Rica this season."

"And she wasn't enthused about the idea."

"She was torn really. She loved Eric and Eric loves all this. In high school, he spent time in Mexico as a foreign exchange student, so speaks fluent Spanish and he loves boats. This cruising dream was his, not hers. She mistakenly believed she would enjoy it because she enjoyed sailing around Southern California with her father when she was a child. It didn't take long for water concerns, bargaining every time you turn around, and all the rest to wear thin. She longed for the convenience of home."

Claire looked around, stepped aside to let someone pass, then moved back.

"That sounds like a story that could apply to a lot of people we've met. Why is that important for me to know?"

"This accident is very convenient for Eric. There's obviously no evidence of any wrongdoing, nothing convincing, just a feeling I have. I saw all of you on your boat yesterday. No one looked very happy, so I assumed it had something to do with the camera. He wants it back, doesn't he?"

"Yes, and it's an awkward situation for us because we're already committed to turning it over to the authorities. He says he's obsessed with the idea that the tape may show what happened and feels an urgency to see it. Are you suggesting it might be more than that?"

Jessie watched Claire as she considered an answer. "I know you have to do what you think is right and I know people are talking, saying you're wrong in not giving it back to Eric, but I think you should give the camera to the authorities."

"Claire, I'd say Satch would be in the group that believes our decision wrong."

"I know; don't worry about him. I disagree with him." She smiled as if the notion caused her no complications.

"I don't understand. Why are you telling me this?"

"Well, it's kind of a moral issue, isn't it? There will always be two sides. It's my understanding you have an obligation, and I believe I possess information that might help illuminate the path ahead for you. I also felt I somehow owed it to Jennifer. Don't misunderstand me, Satch is my life and I'm committed to him, but sometimes he gets these ideas in his head. It should be obvious that I don't share the same commitment to Eric."

"If you're implying what I think you are, it seems like a pretty desperate act for Eric to commit. It would have been simpler and less risky to divorce her. I mean, even now the authorities are questioning her disappearance. How could he hope to get away with it?"

"Well, they have no proof, do they? Unless there's something on the tape, there's no way to tell what actually happened. It's Eric's word against whose? Also, there was nothing simple or risk-free for

Eric in divorcing her. She comes from a family that retains a full-time lawyer. Being free of her was one thing, but being free of her and keeping the money was quite another. I think this 'accidental' death was very timely. There's one more thing."

Out of all the words tumbling out of Claire's mouth, Jessie latched onto the phrases, "two sides," "owed it to Jennifer," "keeping the money," and "Eric's word against whose?" Her brows knit together and she struggled to concentrate. The woman opposite her looked down and then took a breath before she continued.

"She swore me to secrecy and I haven't yet said anything to anyone. She wanted to tell Eric in her own way in her own time. I'm not sure she ever did." She looked around and then leaned in closer. "She was pregnant . . . ."

Jessie barely heard the last bit of news and although Claire announced it with some drama, its effect was lost on Jessie. She was still struggling with those phrases, and when she thought back to what Neal had been saying two nights ago, she felt a mist begin to thin. Claire's mouth was moving, but Jessie's thoughts overrode any words coming out of it. For the first time in days, her view was clearing. It took seconds to tune back in.

" . . . I'm just not sure . . . Jessie, are you all right?"

"Hi, Claire, how's it going? You changed your mind yet about exchanging some books?" Neal's approach interrupted the conversation like a tripped circuit breaker.

Realization filled Jessie with clarity and she wanted to talk to Neal, alone. "Claire was just telling me how difficult it was for her to choose cards, too. With so much beauty around, you'd think they could come up with better postcards. Right, Claire?"

Claire didn't skip a beat. "Yes. It seems a pity that this is the best of the lot, and I quite agree with your choices. I'm also quite set in not exchanging any of my books. Well, I must be off, I hope I helped a little." Her gaze lingered on Jessie for several seconds, the corners of her mouth lifted before she turned and in a cloud of peach rayon drifted to the next stall.

"You two were talking about more than postcards. What's up?"

"C'mon, we need to talk." Jessie counted out the *pesos* for the cards and led Neal to a bench in the main *zocolo.* Sonny wasn't due for a couple of hours. Maybe that was enough time to ease some of the tension between them.

Jessie sat and swept her gaze over the harbor. Boats housing dozens of fellow cruisers filled the anchorage. Some boat names she recognized from past harbors and anchorages, some were new to her, but like any community, whether she knew them or not, there was a bond that connected them. A disturbance had ruffled this community, and she and Neal were a part of the disturbance. It shouldn't be a surprise that an issue that set up sides between her and her husband would do the same to the people out there. She also finally understood the point Neal was trying to make the night they met Eric.

She raked her fingers through her short hair, took a breath and began. "You were right, Claire wasn't talking to me about postcards. It seems she and Jennifer Stover had become pretty good friends over the last year and they talked."

She turned and faced Neal. He gave her no reprieve. He remained set, expectant, and for the next several minutes she relayed what Claire had told her about Eric, Jennifer, the family lawyer and the baby.

"To me," said Jessie as she finished, "Claire comes across as a little dramatic so I'm not sure how much to believe. If it's true, I'm a little surprised to hear that Jennifer was pregnant. News like that in this kind of situation would have exploded by now. Do you think it's possible Eric doesn't know?"

Neal didn't answer right away, so she carried on.

"I assume you would agree that unless he does say something about it, we know nothing."

That brought an instant reply from her mate. "Absolutely."

She nodded at his emphatic response and continued. "Anyway, while Claire talked, it hit home that I haven't even thought about Jennifer in all this. You were right the other night, there are other credible stories. Even though she's not here to tell it, Jennifer has a story. It's embarrassing to admit that, but now it's so obvious. It never occurred to me to doubt Eric's story. I just assumed it was true and felt it was cruel, at such an awful time, to accuse him of lying. I'm not saying I think he's guilty of anything, but my need to carry the banner for him has been blown away like a puff of smoke."

Neal moved his gaze out to the water. His arms folded across his chest and the fingers of one hand stroked his lower lip. It was a long time before he spoke.

"I'm not sure if we're on the same side now or not, but if what you just said means I don't have to like the idea of going to Mexico City, especially on an errand for him, it helps a little."

It wasn't what she wanted to hear. "I know you don't like it, but it's done and I'll try to make it up to you. Did what I say make any sense?"

He moved closer and put his arm around her. "To me it made enough sense to lighten the burden that's been bogging us down."

She leaned into him and when she felt tears well up and burn her eyes, she buried her face in the nape of his neck. They may still differ on details, but she felt they had crossed the top. This issue would no longer tear them apart.

They faced the street and eyed every taxi that slowed. One of them would deposit Sonny. When one finally did, Neal wasn't surprised to see their trim friend emerge, confident as ever, and wearing a lightweight, wrinkle-free suit with a pastel tropical shirt and deck-soled leather loafers. Neal knew the modest luggage would be filled with equally appropriate clothing for his stay on the boat. Sonny, a seasoned traveler, researched the weather and customs of his destinations and spared no expense to arrive ready for the experience.

They hurried their steps, reaching him as he thanked the driver in Spanish and handed over the folded bills he pulled from his pocket. When he turned to scan the *zocolo,* his tanned face lit up as he caught sight of them.

"Man, don't you look dapper. You'll put us both to shame," said Neal, reaching out his right hand with a smile he couldn't control. Sonny shook it and both men wrapped their left arms around each other. After a few slaps on the back and a laugh, they separated.

"It's great to see you, Sonny." Jessie squeezed past and looped her arms around his neck. She pecked him on the cheek and laughed merrily when he lifted her off the ground in a bear hug.

"Ahh, and it's great to see the two of you," he said, beaming from the welcome. "You won't believe what they get for these dapper duds. Some blended thing that can be twisted into a Ziploc bag until you need it. Then you shake it out, spritz it and presto, dignity. What can I say, I had to have it." He slung one bag over his shoulder and readjusted his sunglasses while Neal grabbed the other bag. "You're both looking good. I was hoping for a little more fray around the edges to justify my work existence, but you disappoint me."

"There is life after work, Sonny," Jessie assured him as they all fell into step. "Do you want to tell us about your trip over lunch or a drink before we head back to the boat?"

"An ice-cold Mexican *cerveza* would go down well, and about staying on the boat – the more I've thought about it, the more convinced I am about staying ashore."

Jessie stopped and stared at their visitor. "Sonny, it's okay. We've made room for you, it'll be fine."

Neal kept walking. He felt liberated and decided this discussion could carry on without him. He didn't want to be close enough for Jessie to call on him for comment.

"Jessie, look at me and tell me you haven't thought how tight *Dana* will be with the three of us on board. Well, actually with me on board. You know me, I'm up at dawn and not in bed until after midnight. I'd drive you crazy and the situation would drive me crazy. Enough said. I've thought it over and there are several places nearby that have vacancies. I know because I had the cab driver show me. After a drink, you can help me pick one, and please don't go on about it, it doesn't suit you."

"You've made your point, but I want to make one, too. *Dana* is as good as she gets right now. She's clean and tidy, and if you don't come aboard now, you'll miss that window where she's at her best. Just so you know."

"I've been aboard her enough to know how beautiful she is. A little dust and disarray won't change that. Take me for a sail and I'll be happy."

"You're impossible."

"Exactly. That's what my ex-wives and kids tell me."

They made their way to an open air *cantina* and stepped beneath the thatched roof. Compared to the hot streets, it felt like a cooler. Most of the tables were occupied by other travelers, some Neal recognized as people off boats in the harbor. They sat at a table next to a group of five, who looked up and stared in his direction, then huddled in toward each other as if engaged in a serious discussion. Not on our side, he thought.

"Please tell me my fly isn't down. I know I checked it before I got out of the cab," said Sonny, shuffling his chair to get squared with the table.

"It's not you, Sonny," said Neal, ordering three beers from the young boy who came with a notepad. "I'm sure it's our tangle with this video I was telling you about on the phone."

"Ah, yes, the reason for our journey to Mexico City. I would say that those folks gathered around that table are not praising your integrity. I think maybe it's time you told me what I'm involved in here."

Once three frosty bottles were delivered with a large plate of sliced limes on the side, Neal and Jessie filled Sonny in on as much as they knew. When Neal noticed Sonny's attention wandering, he closed the discussion with, "So that's why in a couple of days, we're going to Mexico City."

"Sounds like fun to me. With Eric along, it should add an interesting dimension. Well done, Jessie! When was it that you needed to be there?"

"You don't have to rub it in. I've already scored high points with my husband for extending that invitation. Mr. Swainyo said he would have time on Friday afternoon." She tapped her fingers to count out the days. "That's what, three days from now?"

Sonny checked his watch and squinted as if calculating something.

From behind him, Neal heard a familiar voice call out to them.

"Hi, you guys. How's it going?" Anders and Mae Larrsen crossed the *cantina* and let their sunglasses fall on the lanyards around their necks. "You get anywhere with that situation that got dumped in your lap?"

Obviously on our side, Neal thought, as he smiled at them and said, "Well, I'm not sure. What do you two hear about what's going on?"

They looked limp from the heat and whatever else they had been doing and took the offer from Neal to pull over two more chairs and join them.

Mae patted at her hair and wiped the sweat from the bridge of her nose. "Opinions seem to run two ways. Either you're incredibly brave for dealing with all that's happened, or you're a traitor and not one of 'us.' I think that's about the way things fall right now, wouldn't you say, Anders?"

"I think most people don't give a damn, but you know, there will always be a few who have to butt into things that don't concern them. I don't envy your position, and I'm not sure what I'd do in your place." He ordered for them and then noticed there was another person at the table. "A person with real clothes on, who's this?"

Jessie did the introductions. "Anders, Mae, this is Sonny, a friend of ours from the States. He's just arrived and will keep us company for a couple of weeks. We met Anders and Mae in Cabo San Lucas and have crossed paths a couple of times since."

"An interesting time to visit these two. Have they told you what you've stepped into?"

"I've just been briefed."

"It'll all blow over. People love a good tale, especially when it's gruesome. Anyway, welcome to Paradise." Anders's chair squealed as he shuffled it to a better position at the table.

For a couple of rounds, conversation and laughter flowed freely until their neighbors began loudly commenting on their merrymaking. It was the threat of teaching a lesson to those who didn't understand the idea of community that sent a glance around Neal's table.

Anders was the first to twist in his chair and challenge them. "What's put the bee in your bonnet, Clyde?"

The fact that Anders knew his name shut the man up, but it didn't have the same effect on his wife. "Under the circumstances, it's unseemly that those two should enjoy such gaiety. A man is suffering because of what they're doing, and that doesn't sit well with a lot of us."

Clyde stood and urged his wife to follow him.

Anders said, "Now, Ivy, I know for a fact that Jessie and Neal have agonized over this, but they could be in a bit of trouble themselves if they didn't consider the commitments they made. Come on and join us for another beer."

Clyde had Ivy on her feet. "Not on your life. What about the commitment to us, the people who share that anchorage out there?" She squinted and pointed her finger at Jessie and Neal. "You two just take care or there will be more to deal with than a little sand in your dinghy."

Neal snatched a glance at Jessie, her eyebrows arched and her mouth gaped in surprise. Probably not so much by the threat as by the admission.

Ivy spun around and stomped out the door. Husband Clyde and the rest of their table followed in her wake.

Anders yelled at their backs. "Hey, your running away isn't going to solve anything."

Neal leaned over and touched the older man's arm. "It's all right, Anders. No need for you to get tangled up in this." He sipped his beer and watched the group raise a cloud of dust as they pounded their way down the dirt street.

"The atmosphere seems a little tense," Sonny said with a chuckle as he squeezed the juice from a lime into the narrow neck of his beer bottle.

Anders squared himself to the table. "What's this about sand and a dinghy?"

Jessie's glance at Neal told him to take the floor. "It's nothing really. We thought it was a bunch of kids. Well . . . maybe it was, but they're a little older than we pictured." Neal went on to describe the incident with *Pointer.*

Mae tutted when she said, "People just get so silly sometimes. What business is it of theirs anyway? Believe me, not everyone feels that way. You two okay?"

Neal had noticed the strain in Jessie's eyes and he wondered if that's what had prompted Mae's concern.

Regardless of how she felt, his wife managed a smile and said, "Anyone touches my little dinghy again, and I'll personally rip out their spark plugs."

Laughter erupted and before anyone could respond, Anders'

voice jumped in. "Say, there's a group of us getting together for dinner tonight at El Carne, why not join us? None of that lot will be there, I guarantee it. It's only a little better than a street stall, but the food's great and easy . . . ." Mae's glare stopped him short. "What? . . . What did I say?"

"Oh, for heavens' sake, Anders, you're such a klutz." Mae turned to Jessie as if to find some understanding in another women's face. "Well, it certainly is no problem for us, but you might want to know that Eric and Sonia will be there. That's not meant to discourage you, and I feel foolish mentioning it, but I thought you should know that. If it matters, we'd like it if you came."

Jessie fidgeted and Neal was about to respond when she answered.

"Thanks, Mae. And, yes, it matters that you don't mind. What do you think?" Jessie's glance shifted from Neal to Sonny.

Neal said to Jessie, "If our guest is up to it, it's fine by me."

"A chance to meet the other side. Should be interesting," said Sonny.

9

The dinner group stretched down the lane as one or another of its members got sidetracked by the souvenir shops. When the earliest arrivals entered El Carne, they greeted the young man at the door and pointed out those bringing up the rear. He nodded, made a quick count, then led them under the peaked thatched roof to a place at the back. His shout brought out another young boy, and together they strung three wooden tables together and arranged plastic chairs, pulled from neighboring tables, around the new table for fifteen.

Bare wood poles hand-hewn by machete supported the thatch overhead. Eyelid shutters suspended from the edge of the roof were propped up with sturdy sticks, and the opening they left allowed an uninterrupted breeze to drift through. Interspersed throughout the restaurant, brown-tinged banana palms struggled to grow in clay pots brightly glazed in red and orange.

Chairs squeaked and scraped across the cement floor as the group jostled for position and settled. Neal sat across from Jessie at one end of the table, with Sonny beside her and Anders and Mae next to him. There was an empty chair next to Neal and another one farther down the table. As Jessie scanned the group, people laughed, moved around and called out greetings and introductions. Much to her relief, no one mentioned Jennifer Stover or the video.

Several in the party she recognized, but hadn't met before, others she knew too well. Claire Jurgeon gave a small wave as she sat at the other end of the table next to her husband Satch. His eyes met Jessie's and a twitch crossed his face that she took as a tolerant smile. Claire must have taught him that, she thought, smiling and waving back at them.

A light breeze drifted in through the open shutter. When it brushed across her, Jessie fluffed her short hair, still damp from a recent shower. That had been a true luxury.

She hadn't argued any more with Sonny about staying on the boat. He was right. With no easy access to shore, the situation would have soon driven them all crazy. They had found him a spacious bungalow in a small hotel close to the water near Playa Madera, only a few minutes by foot from town. As it turned out, there was one big advantage to the new arrangements, and she and Neal had jumped at the chance when Sonny offered them the use of the room's shower before dinner. She let her eyes close briefly and again enjoyed the cool, drying breeze.

When she sensed a drop in the level of conversation, she opened her eyes and glanced down the table. Eric and Sonia had arrived.

People had moved over to give the new arrivals two chairs together, and by the embarrassed glances that flew around the table, it hadn't been intentional, but the two chairs left empty were next to Neal. With a possible clash pending, conversations limped along as eyes stole quick looks at Jessie's end of the table. She joined their uneasiness. The earlier cool, drying breeze grew hot and sultry, perspiration broke out on her upper lip. What would Eric say?

Jessie watched them work down the table, greeting people. When they got to their places and Sonia caught sight of Neal, she suddenly reversed course and nearly collided with Eric, who followed closely behind. Conversations round the table stopped mid-sentence.

Satch, seeing the calamity, tried to shoo those nearest the empty chairs into sitting in them, but Eric calmed everyone by saying, "No, don't be silly, this is fine."

The couple whispered back and forth, then Eric nudged his friend toward the empty chairs and they settled, with Sonia next to Neal. His companion never made eye contact, but Eric smiled and greeted Jessie's end of the table as warmly as he had the rest of it. In doing so, he resolved the intensity of the moment much like a symphony resolves a discordant note.

Chatter resumed as the long, bare table quickly filled with baskets of chips, bowls of salsa, plates of limes, and almost two dozen bottles of beer. Freestanding plastic frames, placed along the table, displayed the handwritten menu.

"I've heard this place has really good shrimp tacos," said Sonia Sieverson, flipping her long blond hair back over her shoulder. Her glance dismissed Jessie and Neal, but lingered as it landed on Sonny. The light touch of makeup accentuated the right parts of her face and her eyes danced.

That kind of beauty comes naturally, Jessie thought, and at the same time, gave up on the idea of an evening free from the effects of Jennifer Stover's death. Sonia's snub made that obvious.

Sonny studied the beauty across from him for a moment before asking his friend, "Shrimp tacos sound great to me, unless you have any other suggestions, Neal?" His smile slid over to Neal, who was studying the menu, then slid back to the beauty.

That beauty flicked an assessing glance between the two men, and took less than a second to decide that despite his friends, this man across from her was too interesting to ignore.

The exchange registered with Eric, too. His arm made a protective drape over the back of his companion's chair, his other arm rested on the table. He said, "I'll pass. You know me, just one puts my body in full revolt."

But Sonia was preoccupied and it took a second for her friend's comment to register. When it finally did, she pulled her eyes away from the stranger to look at Eric. "Oh God, I'm sorry. I completely forgot." Her hand came to rest on the arm Eric lay on the table, her gaze returned to the man across from her. "I was there once when he scooped a chip into an innocent looking dip. Shrimp dip, as it turned out. It was awful, he got so sick, it spun everyone around for a couple of hours." With a warm smile at her friend she said, "You did get over it, but, man, you sure gave us a scare."

"What an inconvenient allergy to have in these parts," said Sonny with sympathy. "But since I particularly like shrimp, I'll take the lady's recommendation."

"Yeah, they should be good," said Neal as he passed the menu on. "Oh, Sonia, Eric, this is Sonny Jackson, a friend of ours from the States. He's here to torment us for a couple of weeks."

Sonia extended her hand. "Hi, real pleasure to meet you. As a kid my friends started to call me Sonny, you know, a nickname for Sonia, but for some reason it never stuck."

Sonny stood and took the outstretched hand, "The pleasure's mine, and I'm glad it didn't stick, Sonia suits you."

"Thank you, that's very nice of you to say."

A lady used to compliments, Jessie thought.

"This is Eric Stover, a dear friend." The men's hands met across the table. "Hal . . . that's my husband . . . abandoned me on that barge he calls a boat while he went back to the States on some business thing. Eric's been my escort and all-around lifesaver since he pulled into port a couple of days ago."

As Sonny gripped Eric's hand, he said seriously, "Hope this isn't bad form, but my sympathies for your loss . . . very tragic."

Jessie stole a glance at Neal. His eyebrows went up and he nudged her under the table.

Eric hesitated. His glance darted to their end of the table before returning to Sonny. "Thanks, I appreciate the sentiments."

Sonny went on, smiling at Sonia as he eased down into his chair. "I envy you your task, Eric. Hal must have a great faith and trust in your friendship."

Eric's face relaxed almost to a grin. He rested one elbow on the table and returned his other arm to the back of Sonia's chair. "Yeah, well, she needed some help and I think he knows she's pretty safe with me."

"Just being a friend of these two," the visitor waved his hand toward Jessie and Neal, "I know that a boat requires a lot of work. I'm here for a couple of weeks with nothing but time on my hands; if there's anything I can do, please let me know."

Sonia said, "Do you have a boat?"

Sonny laughed and shook his head. "No, too much effort, too little space. I admire anyone who can put up with them. Jessie and Neal are willing to deal with the hassles and allow me to come and visit whenever I crave a dose of adventure."

Sonia smiled, folded her forearms on the table and leaned onto them. The low neck of her loose cotton top gaped, and her tanned, rounded breasts bulged from the pressure. Sonny's gaze dropped to the cleavage and lingered.

Jessie knew by looking at Eric that he had noticed the obvious flirting, and she found it curious that he actually looked amused.

Sonia made no attempt to shy away from Sonny's gaze. Including no one else in the conversation, her eyes and attention remained solely on this interesting newcomer. "Makes perfect sense to me. I wish Hal felt that way. The man could do anything he wanted, but this romantic notion of his to sail off into the sunset has been one hell of a ride. One I can't wait to get off."

From beside her, Eric said, "Sonia, you told me to rein you in if you got too scathing."

"You're right, I'm pissed because he left me behind." She leaned back again and flipped her hair. "What are you vacationing from, if you don't mind my asking?"

"No, not at all. I work for an advertising company. The hours are awful and the pressure tantamount to torture, so I dangle these getaways like carrots to get me up in the morning."

Jessie almost turned away, afraid the expression on her face would show the groan she stifled. Sonny loved his work and never needed any excuse to get up in the morning, a fact about which his two ex-wives and three children constantly reminded him. There would be no stopping Sonny if Sonia became the object of his attention, and Jessie could already hear the gossip fly if that became too obvious to others at the table.

She thought back to when she and Neal had first experienced Sonny's unflagging personality. As a new skier, he decided to come along on one of the week-long ski packages they offered through their store. His energy was boundless, and his need for only a few hours of sleep with constant activity the rest of the time meant he kept a rugged pace for most normal people. He wasn't a nervous person to be around; in fact, he could enjoy a quiet evening of discussion over wine with friends as much as a night on the town. Most nights he did both. She thought of him as a human chameleon, always getting along and adapting to those around him. He was fun company, but she and Neal often wondered if they knew the real Sonny. Was that even possible?

The food arrived and conversation ran freely and easily, touching several topics. Sonny acted as a grounding wire for an otherwise charged situation and it soon became clear to Jessie that his attentions were turned on Eric as much as Sonia, with both responding warmly to his attention. Maybe the trip to Mexico City wouldn't be that bad.

"I know what we should do," said Sonny when he'd finished his third taco. "Sonia, since your escort and all-around lifesaver is deserting you for Mexico City for a few days, why not come along? Sounds like you could use a break from the boat and I know we'd love your company. I say we rent a car and all go together at least one way. It would be a great chance to see the countryside and if we share the cost, it might work out cheaper than flying and would avoid the horror of taking a bus." Sonny, excited by his own proposal, swept the group expecting to gather support for the idea.

Stunned, the small group at the end of the table paused.

Jessie could have cuffed him. There had been no discussion of this between them. In fact, based on discussions so far, Sonny should have known better than to suggest it. Traveling together on a plane or even a bus was one thing, but sharing the tight confines of a car? Neal would never go for it.

Another second and her husband came through, true to form. "Ah, Sonny, I don't think that's such a good idea."

Sonia's elbows backed off the table and her hands took refuge in her lap. She stared at Eric, and the two looked as though they were attempting telepathic communication. His arm returned to the back of Sonia's chair, and Jessie watched his thumb begin to stroke her shoulder.

He leaned toward her slightly and spoke. "It's up to you, but you could use a few days away, and I sure wouldn't complain about your company. If you explain that to Hal, I'll bet he'd go along with it. What do you say?"

Sonia looked down and then back at him, "I don't know, Eric, you know how Hal gets. It sounds great to me, but . . . well . . . I don't think I should."

Jessie found the sudden change in Sonia's behavior uncomfortable. The coquettish, flippant attitude of a few minutes ago had vanished and was replaced by slumped shoulders and nervous glances. Although the silence in real time was brief, it felt eternal. Eric tried again to reassure his companion, and Sonia's eyes made a quick trip around the group until they finally settled on Jessie. The eyes made the struggle apparent.

Sonia took a big breath, "Oh, what the hell, why not?"

Jessie didn't think the woman was as confident as her words implied.

Eric said in a quiet voice, "It'll be all right, I'll talk to Hal, too. I'll get him to understand the situation."

Sonny ignored the personal turmoil going on across from him and unleashed his enthusiasm on the group. "That's great. It'll be fun. I've heard about a place just over the mountains between here and Mexico City that's supposed to have a fantastic art gallery. Since we can't talk to Mr. . . . I can't remember his name . . . until Friday, we could stop there on the way. That is, if no one objects."

For Jessie, the words sparked a revelation. So that's the reason behind the enthusiasm for a trip to the capital so soon after his arrival, she thought. Laughter bubbled to the surface as she realized how he had manipulated everything to arrive at this point. It seemed that Neal hit on the same revelation. Accompanying a slight shake of his head, the corners of his eyes crinkled with a smile.

The plan had pulled Anders, Sonny's other neighbor, away from the conversation going on at the other end of the table. "You're talking about taking the road that crosses the mountains from here?"

Sonny shifted to answer the question. "That's the one. When I mentioned my travel plans, a good friend of mine told me about this place. It's called Tampu and is just far enough out of Mexico City to discourage casual traffic. It's not far off the road that goes from here to the capital, so I thought it would be a perfect stop for a night. The gallery shows pieces from expats who fled from the U.S., Canada and Europe for one reason or another, and it's gaining quite a reputation for quality stuff. According to this friend of mine, it brings in buyers from all over the world."

"Not that I want to squash your plans, my friend, but there are stories about that road. We had friends who went that way to Mexico City by bus, and the thing crashed, ran head-on into a car. Everybody ran. These friends tried to help those who got hurt, but people kept pulling at their clothes, telling them to move on, to get out of there. The drivers disappeared and the whole scene was chaos. Before the police arrived, these friends got bundled up into a car and whisked away. Scared the pants off 'em. Apparently you don't hang around at the scene of an accident unless you're prepared to go to jail until the police sort it out. And not only is the road torture to drive, but drugs are a problem and it's notorious for bandits. It's supposedly faster and safer to go by way of Acapulco."

Neal set his taco down and slowed his chewing as he listened to Anders, then said, "Sonny, I think it would be better if we checked into flying or taking the dreaded bus through Acapulco."

Sonny ignored Neal's comment, "But that road doesn't get close to Tampu. I feel for your friends, but accidents can happen anywhere, and there would be five of us, a daunting number for a bandit, don't you think?"

Anders chuckled. "A bandit, maybe, but not for bandits. But hey, it may be just my old-age caution talking."

Jessie studied Eric's face for signs of distress at the cavalier attitude over this otherwise somber journey. His eyes remained on the beer in front of him. The thumb and middle finger of his left hand gently rotated the bottle round and round as if delicately unscrewing it from the table. It seemed he had retreated from the conversation and she wondered what he was thinking. Her attention went back to the discussion.

"Well, if you agree to drive and take the hit if we wreck the car, I'll consider it. You're a man out to age me before my time. Just don't come up with any ideas that require a boat unless you own it." Neal lifted a beer bottle to his mouth and drained the dregs.

"Sounds fair. I'll do some checking around and let you know what I come up with. We can decide then." Sonny looked down at his empty plate and then made a quick tour of the plates in front of the group. "If everyone's finished, can I suggest an after dinner drink at the Pension del Mar? . . . beautifully appointed hotel near Playa Madera?"

Jessie hesitated along with everyone else.

"Don't all rush in with an answer. Sonia, how about you?"

Sonia looked at Eric and when he nodded, she turned to Sonny and said, "Yes, that would be nice." Her eyes landed on Jessie as if looking for both forgiveness and permission.

Jessie, feeling the situation speed past her, forgot Sonia's earlier snub and returned her smile. "Thanks, Sonny, sounds great." She heard Neal sigh and mumble something that could be taken as resigned agreement and everyone stood to leave.

"I'm so glad you three decided to come. I think it went all right, don't you?" Mae had edged her way through the crowd to stand next to Jessie.

As she replied to Mae's comments, Jessie noticed Eric pull Sonny aside for a moment and the two walked away together, heads bent in conversation. "Yes, Mae, I'm glad we came, too. I hope everything will work out. Are you coming over to Sonny's room?"

"Oh, I don't think so. We'll head back to the boat. I think Anders already told Sonny that. Just in case we don't see you again before you go, have a safe journey however you decide to do it. We'll keep an eye on *Dana* for you."

Instead of Eric leaving with Sonia as expected, Jessie noticed him pass through the door with Satch. Was there a change of plans? With a head shake, she dismissed the speculation. She figured she would know soon enough and leaned toward Mae as if passing on a secret. "Thanks, Mae. If nothing else, it'll be interesting."

Mae glanced around. "I think you might be right."

* * *

Jessie and Neal waved good night to Sonny as they quietly closed the door to his bungalow. A few people still remained in tight discussions that would carry on for hours yet. The night air was warm and still with a softer humidity than at the height of the day. Surf gently pounded the beach as they made their way along the lighted cement and sand walkway that joined Zihuatanejo and Playa Madera.

Neal's instinct was to search the anchor lights until he found the one that belonged to *Dana.* It was always reassuring to find it in the spot where it ought to be. Jessie's arm was around his waist and his around her shoulder. The warmth and affection that flowed between them again made him smile, and he cast another glance out at the anchorage as he thought about their evening.

The dinner had been nothing special, but the gathering at Sonny's afterward had been fun. Sonny might be impossible to take in large doses, but he was an inspiration otherwise.

Neal laughed at his friend's antics and said, "No wonder Sonny does so well. Not only did he get me to agree to go on this crazy trip, I think I might enjoy it. I like Sonia, and if Eric weren't going, it could actually be fun."

They stopped to look at the harbor and Neal pointed out *Dana's* anchor light.

"Speaking of Sonia, did you warn Sonny about Hal?" said Jessie.

"As a matter of fact I did, but Eric had already mentioned it. When he told Sonny he couldn't join us back at the room for drinks, he brought it up. From what Sonny said, Eric encouraged him to work on Sonia, get her to feel more comfortable about this trip. As far as I could tell that's like asking the lion to comfort the lamb. Anyway, Eric thinks Sonia could use a break and he'll take care of Hal. Wonder what he's up to?"

"You know, Eric could be a nice guy. Ever think of that?" she said as she picked up a stone and tossed it into the water. "It's Sonny's brazen attitude that staggers me. Most people would be more sensitive to the reason for this trip to Mexico City, but he's turned it into his personal tour and getting away with it."

"He's on vacation, Jessie. Except for the fact that we have Eric tagging along, I like the idea . . . that's funny."

"What is?"

"Was that a flashlight on *Dana?*" Neal moved a couple of steps to get a better view. He didn't want it to be true. Who would be out there at this hour? When he stared, he saw nothing.

"I can't tell . . . ." Her voice faded.

They both studied the anchorage.

"Well, I'm with you," said Jessie from beside him. "But if Sonia gives Sonny any encouragement, he won't let a little thing like her marriage to an abusive man stop him. At least Eric will be there to act as her conscience."

Neal saw the light again, and Jessie must have seen it, too.

"Yes . . . yes, I see a light. It looks like it's in the cockpit. We weren't expecting anyone, were we?" she said, joining him at a brisk walk along the path.

He wasn't even sure he answered her, but the thought made him think of their padlock and the altercation with Ivy and her gang at the *cantina* earlier that afternoon. Not many months ago, they were locking up tight whenever they headed ashore. The reason, three men on a boat had tormented them in Cabo San Lucas and those men were now dead. Even if only in a small way, he and Jessie had contributed to their fate. Her nightmares over the incident had finally stopped and time had dulled the recollection. They had become more casual about security, and earlier, when they left for a shower and dinner, they only looped the lock through the clasp without actually snapping it shut.

Those thoughts spurred Neal from a fast walk to a run. They still had to get to the other end of the beach where the dinghies were kept and then across the harbor to *Dana*. If it were someone carrying out the threats made at the cantina, that someone had plenty of time.

Pounding the bricks along the *Malecón*, Neal ran. Sweat drenched him and his chest heaved in the moist, humid air that a few minutes before had been soft and romantic. Jessie was somewhere behind him, but he couldn't wait. He didn't even bother looking out at the harbor. One thing possessed him and drove him on, he wanted to get to *Dana* as quickly as possible.

Neal pounded on until he reached the dinghies. Breathless and with legs weak and shaking from the effort, he gripped *Pointer's* gunwale and pulled. His hands slipped as he dragged. Once he ended up flat on his back and another time on his knees. He was covered in sand.

When Jessie arrived moments later, she grabbed the gunwale opposite him and they pulled together. Neal finally felt the beach let go and *Pointer* floated.

"Hop in," he said quickly to Jessie as he looked to the water.

With little surf, he didn't pause. He pushed, clambered in and started the engine.

"Neal, have you been able to see anything?"

"No, there are too many other boats in the way. We won't be able to tell what's going on until we get farther out."

Jessie twisted to watch ahead. When they finally got past the boats that blocked their view, their floating home lay in front of them.

Neal shut *Pointer's* engine down and they floated twenty yards off *Dana's* stern.

Jessie turned back to face him. Just above a whisper she said, "There's no dinghy there. She looks okay."

"I'm going around once, keep your eyes open."

She nodded and twisted to face forward again.

Dark and seemingly alone, their boat drifted on her anchor, her night beacon gently swinging from the constant motion of the sea. Without the wind to set the boats in a uniform pattern, the stillness allowed currents and eddies to influence the floating hulls. The result was a scattered formation with no order or reason; they called it the harbor waltz. In fact, *Aurora,* their neighbor, lay at ninety degrees to *Dana.*

Neal readied the oars and rowed once around their home. When they saw nothing, he eased *Pointer* alongside.

He put a hand on Jessie's shoulder when she got ready to disembark and pleaded with his eyes for her to stay put until he could check things out. She glowered at him, but nodded. Even though no one else seemed to be around, he felt the need to be cautious.

Neal eased himself aboard and tiptoed to the cockpit. His efforts on the beach shouted at him from every muscle in his legs. Was he in any shape to meet someone now, he thought, as he made an unsteady duck under the awning and took a quick look. No one lay hidden in the cockpit. He sat and almost stopped breathing while he listened, no unusual sound or motion.

From shore, could they have confused where the light had come from? He glanced at *Aurora* and admitted it wasn't impossible. *Dana's* drop boards were in place and the lock was looped through the clasp, but not snapped shut. Light glinted off it and made Neal pause as his right hand reached for it. There was a difference. He thought back to their departure. Were they in such a rush that he threaded the lock through the clasp backwards?

Jessie, standing in *Pointer,* drifted back to where she could see him. Without a word, he showed her he was going to take the boards out and look inside. She nodded and secured her grip on one of *Dana's* deck stanchions.

Neal unlooped the lock, snatched out the top drop board and quickly slid back the companionway hatch. He leaned in to search the darkness of the cabin. Not knowing what he was looking for, he searched for anything that didn't seem right. All he heard was the tap of sand hitting the deck as it fell from his clothing and skin. Their flashlight hung inside on a hook, an easy reach from where he leaned. He grabbed it, snapped it on and flashed its beam quickly around the cabin. Nothing seemed out of place, no obvious signs of anyone having been there. He breathed more easily as he removed the bottom drop board and climbed down the steps, turning a light on as he went. Outside, he knew Jessie waited for a report.

After taking a quick tour, which included a check to make sure the camera was still in the chain locker, he returned to the deck where she was tying off *Pointer.*

"Well, I don't know," he said slapping at the sand that covered his body. He told her everything was fine, including the news of the camera and lock. "I suppose I could have threaded the lock backwards, we were in a hurry."

Jessie helped dust him off and laughed in spite of the possible seriousness of the situation. She ruffled his hair and said, "You're a real sight," then added more soberly, "You think we both imagined the light?"

"Maybe they were using a flashlight on *Aurora?*"

She looked over at their neighbor and shrugged, her voice filled with doubt. "It's possible, but I would have sworn it came from here."

His sigh was audible. "Yeah, me, too."

"That threat from Ivy this afternoon might have affected us more than we thought."

They studied each other. Neal wondered what they would do even if someone *had* come aboard. Who would they report it to and what would they say, especially if they found nothing missing. "Maybe," he said finally.

Neal was first down the companionway steps and he reached his hand up to help her down. Below in *Dana's* cabin, they performed the usual dance around each other while they looked more closely for signs of intrusion. With each reassurance that their home had not been violated, their mood lifted and they began getting ready for bed. Almost convinced that they had placed the light in the wrong cockpit, Neal grabbed the shower kit he'd taken ashore and made his way forward to put it away.

When he pulled the door open to the shower locker, he froze.

"Jess, come here a minute."

He felt her lean in behind him and both saw that the contents of her side of the locker had toppled over, mixing in with his.

"Hey, don't lay that mess on me. When we went ashore, I was sitting in *Pointer* waiting for you, remember? You came back for toothpaste."

He remembered all too well. Jessie squeezed his shoulder at the same time the back of his neck bristled and fury swept through him.

10

"Yeah, this happened last night. I'd like to think we were just in a hurry to get ashore, but I don't think so. When Neal and I first got to Zhuat, we had lots of people on board and we made no secret that we stowed the video in our shower locker. Up until yesterday that didn't seem to be a problem. Whoever came last night, though, went away disappointed. By sheer luck I had gotten so disgusted with the situation that I moved it, stuffed it away so I wouldn't have to look at it. Of course, in Neal's mind, Eric is the only guilty person, but I'm not as convinced."

Jessie paused but still pressed the microphone's transmit button. With her other hand, she kneaded out the tension that pulled at the muscles between her eyes. It was good talking with her friend, but it would have been nicer to have Gail there in person.

Jessie continued. "I want to believe this guy, Gail. He's nice, and sane people, besides me, like him. It's just too bizarre to think he's capable of killing his wife, especially in such a coldhearted way, and because of that, I can't picture him as the one prowling around on our boat last night."

"What are you going to do?" Gail's steady voice sailed out of the radio as if she were next door, not hundreds of miles away.

"There's not much *to* do. We'll just carry on. I think the faster we get rid of the damn camera, the faster all this antagonism will die down."

"Have you talked with Eric?"

"Not about what happened on the boat last night. Naturally, he's miserable about what happened to Jennifer and was unhappy, at first, about our decision. Now, I think he's accepted it. At dinner last night he was actually charming and didn't seem to be holding a grudge. But I can't say the same thing for some of the people in this anchorage. When it comes to matters concerning Jennifer Stover's death, I worry more about them than Eric. I can understand the division of allegiance, but some seem to be taking their loyalty to extremes. Getting away for a few days will be good for everyone, I think, and for Eric's sake, this trip to Mexico City better result in him seeing the tape. At least it would ease his mind about what happened."

"I can't imagine seeing what happened would ease anyone's mind."

"Well, maybe for him it's better to know than not know."

"I suppose," said Gail, with some doubt in her voice. "But don't let the rest of this get you down. You and Neal have decided what you're going to do, so trust yourselves and do it. Screw the rest."

"Right, ma'am, will do. I'd like it to be that easy." Jessie tapped her pencil and then wrote "screw the rest" in her radio log as she listened to Gail's response.

"Don't we all! Well, good luck. I wish we were down there, but it doesn't look like we'll be leaving here for another week at least. Will you give me a shout on the net when you get back from the big city? I'd like to know how it went."

"Sure thing. I wish you were here, too, but we'll be fine. I just needed to bend a trusted ear. Give Randy a hug and we'll talk to you when we get back." They both transmitted the usual sign-offs and Jessie snapped off the radio.

Overhead she heard deck noises. Neal was working on something and she grabbed her mug of cold coffee to join him.

Her foot was on the first step of the companionway when she heard. "Ahoy, *Dana.*" She poked her head out and watched as a *panga* pulled alongside. Sonny stood in the bow, dressed in shorts and a light breezy shirt. Neal was there to help him aboard, and the skipper of the stout, open fishing boat waved as he maneuvered his vessel away.

She called out, "Sonny, what a surprise! It shouldn't be, I suppose, but it is. Want a coffee?"

"Love one, " he said, snatching the white baseball cap from his head as he ducked under the awning and dropped onto the cockpit bench. Neal followed and settled opposite him.

"Neal, how about you?"

"Yeah, thanks."

She took his cup. "Did it take more than *pesos* to get that guy to give you a lift out here?" She dispensed three mugs of steaming coffee from the thermal airpot, passed them to Neal and joined them in the cockpit.

"I saw him working in his boat on the big wharf, the *muella*, right?" His lips and tongue worked to pronounce "moy-yea" and they nodded. "So I asked him for a ride. We negotiated a price and he ran me out here. I know we made plans to meet later, but Jessie made me feel so guilty yesterday about not staying on the boat that I thought I'd come out early and join you for coffee."

"I don't believe a word of it. The guilty part, I mean. What have you found out, Sonny?" Jessie laughed and sipped at her mug.

"Jessie, your insinuation wounds me, but I have to admit I've been out getting information about the road and a car, and I have some good news."

"Even after sleeping on it, you still want to do this?" Neal blew at the steam that curled up from his cup.

"Why not? It's supposed to be beautiful country and it isn't really all that far. It'll be fun."

Neal said, "I don't think you got my message last night. Eric and I didn't hit it off. I don't think bumping for hours over the mountains of Mexico confined in a car with him will be fun."

"You don't have to worry about that."

"I'm not worried about it. I'm just saying that fun might not be the appropriate word to describe this adventure you're arranging."

"I mean you don't have to worry about Eric; he's not coming with us."

Jessie joined her partner in a simultaneous, "What?"

She saw the smile pull at Sonny's mouth. Their response was what he wanted and expected.

Neal said, "Okay, Sonny, what's the story?"

"Well, as I was running around this morning, I ran into Eric. He was in town making some calls and he told me then. Apparently he has the same opinion of your relationship as you do and felt it would be better to meet us there. He also added that he still feels a little lost and having to be social with people is often difficult. Being conf*iii*ned . . ." he leaned forward toward Neal to emphasize the word, ". . . to a car for hours sounded like torture. He thought you'd understand. He'd rather fly."

"Smart man. I like him better already."

"That'll throw a blanket over Sonia's plans," said Jessie.

"Oh, she's still coming. I just came from there."

"Ah-ha, I was right about the guilt." She pointed an index finger at her friend then laid it across her lips. "Now how is she going to explain that to Hal?" She mused over the speculation.

"One of the calls Eric made was to Hal."

Jessie's finger dropped as she said, "And he's going along with this?"

Sonny shrugged. "Jessie, I'm on vacation, I don't care whether Eric is leveling with me or not. It just takes too much energy trying to figure the angles. He wanted to talk so I let him. Over a Coke, he essentially told me he thinks Hal's too abusive and Sonia deserves better. He and Jennifer witnessed a couple of episodes, and he's decided if Sonia wants to go to Mexico City, he'll cover for her. He told Hal he was coming with us."

"But why doesn't she go with him? That would make more sense," said Neal.

Sonny shrugged his shoulders. "I don't know. He didn't say and I didn't ask."

Jessie set her cup down. "But, Sonny, Hal will find out. People here will notice Sonia gone and see Eric walking around. It won't take much for them to figure out what's happening, and someone will let it drop in Hal's ear. I can't believe she'd go along with it. Especially after the hesitation she had last night."

Neal said, "Sonia knows that Eric's changed his mind?"

Sonny nodded, then shook his head at Jessie's offer of another cup of coffee. "Eric stopped by her boat on his way to shore and told her. When the news made her nervous about going, he suggested he make the call as planned and she could decide later. He actually encouraged me to go out and talk to her, let her know that she'd still be welcome to come along."

Jessie leaned in toward Sonny. "So, in spite of the nervousness she feels toward her husband, she decides to throw caution to the wind and drive up into the mountains with you. What magic did you work?"

"With us. There's three of us, Jessie."

Jessie's eyes went skyward and then returned to her friend. "Somehow, if Hal finds out, I don't think that fact will count for much."

"Hey, there's no pressure here from me and nothing's going on between us. I'm not going to lie and say I wouldn't want it, but it's up to her. She's a striking woman and even though I haven't met the man, my sentiments regarding Hal run pretty close to Eric's. When she came for drinks with you guys last night, she was looking over her shoulder, but at least she came. I think she had fun even though 'Eric the Escort' begged off. All I did was go over there this morning and tell her that we'd still like her to come if that's what she wants to do. If she has reservations, she didn't mention them. All she told me was yes. I think she's used to having fun and cruising isn't fun for her. It's made Hal unrecognizable from the way she tells it and she wants him to quit and go home, but he's not ready. Makes me wonder why she doesn't go home without him."

Neal leaned in toward their friend as if he wanted to make sure Sonny heard, "He's got the money."

Neal knew Sonny's looks appealed to women, but he also knew that the cut and style of his clothes were not lost on Sonia. She would know their value and would know what kind of bankroll it took to wear them. He hoped his friend wasn't that naive, but then Sonia was in store for a few surprises of her own, so Neal dropped the subject. He felt the burden of the next several days lighten with Sonny's news. Having only Sonia along would be easy.

Neal's thoughts went back to the trip and he asked, "You said you had good news about the trip. Was Eric's decision the good news, or is there more?"

Sonny grinned and snapped his finger. "Oh, yeah, I almost forgot I hadn't told you. I've got a car. The owner of my hotel has a brother-in-law who rents cars. He took me over there this morning and we set it up, pending your approval. Insurance, detailed instructions to Tampu and a reasonable rate. We can go back anytime today and settle it."

"Did they say anything about us going over the mountains with it?" If Neal hadn't watched for a reaction, the slight purse Sonny made with his lips would have gone unnoticed. Neal believed he was hoping not to have to address that question.

"Well, not really."

Neal watched him squirm and pressed for more. "What does . . . 'not really' mean?"

"Okay, so they did agree there's been some trouble, but not recently and not with *gringo* tourists. You can ask them when we go back. I got the impression it was no big deal, but to be cautious they recommended that we fill up with gas at the bottom and not stop until we get to Tampu. I mean people use the road every day to go back and forth, so it can't be that bad."

Neal shifted his glance to Jessie, and her eyebrows arched before she turned to Sonny and said, "I know you want to see this place, but I hope you don't mind if I reserve my decision until we go in and talk to these guys again."

Neal said, "I guess we've been in other places where one incident gets told and retold until it sounds as though there's something disagreeable going on all the time. This rumor could be one or two incidents that occurred years ago and gets retold so often that people believe that it happens all the time."

"Exactly, that could be it." Sonny grinned and bounced his glance back and forth between the couple.

His friend's efforts already that morning left Neal weary. "Jessie, does it seem to you that at . . ." Neal leaned and looked at the clock in the cabin, ". . . 9 a.m., we've missed out on half the day?"

Sonny laughed at the dig, but bridled his merriment when, through the course of discussion, Jessie and Neal told him the news about their nighttime visitor. The mood in *Dana's* cockpit turned serious and over the rest of the coffee the three friends discussed possibilities. When the pot was empty and their speculations had still brought no answers, they left for shore to see a man about a car.

* * *

"Ahoy, *Osprey,*" yelled Jessie as she cut the engine and drifted in.

Eric's wet head appeared in the companionway and he smiled. He brought the towel draped over his bare shoulders up to his head and rubbed. "Hi, Jessie, coming aboard?"

"Yeah, just for a sec if that's all right."

"Sure, c'mon." He came on deck and helped with *Pointer's* line, then led her to the cockpit and indicated a place for her to sit.

"Sonny told us about your decision. I was sorry to hear it, but I understand. I wanted to come over and give you our final plans so you could get organized. It looks like we're leaving this afternoon." She settled in the cockpit and noticed her comment stopped him cold.

"That was quick." He stood looking down at her, then slowly dropped onto the cockpit bench opposite her.

"I know. I'm still catching my breath." Her frantic morning crowded her thoughts.

When she and Neal had returned to town with Sonny, they had discovered the deal was already signed and their only input was in approving the car. Irked by their friend's steamroller tactics, Jessie and Neal still felt obliged to listen as the rental man explained, in his abbreviated English, the attributes of the car. In the course of the explanation, it became clear there was more to this than a rental agreement.

Neal pressed for an explanation, and Sonny admitted that the only way he could use the car over the mountains was to buy it. He then turned to the rental man and said, *"Banditos?"*

The rental man laughed and shook his head. *"No, no banditos,"* and with a mix of English and Spanish confirmed it was the potholes and other drivers that worried him.

Sonny continued to explain that the sale wasn't yet legal; he'd just put up the money to cover the cost of the car should he not bring it back. Once returned in good condition, the man would refund the money minus the normal rental costs. Throughout the explanation, the small, lean rental man grinned and nodded.

Noting the doubt in their faces, Sonny had said, "Humor me, you guys. Don't worry about the deal. I've decided that since this was my idea, I'll take care of the money part. I just want to know if you'll go to Tampu in this car."

Jessie saw Neal gear himself up for an argument, but then realizing the futility of it, he changed tacks. "I get the feeling you'll go with or without us, am I right?"

"Weeeell," Sonny said, then shrugged and nodded, " . . . Yes."

Neal turned to her and said, "What do you want to do?"

"What have we got to lose? We'll go with him."

They thought that was that until Sonny pushed one last hurdle in front of them. "Ah . . . about leaving, how about this afternoon?"

Jessie felt Neal tense and waited for the explosion, but Neal let out a laugh and whooped like he'd just stepped off a roller coaster. "And you're here for two weeks!"

With a major victory in his pocket, Sonny drove them back to the waterfront and told them not to worry about Sonia. He'd take a *panga* out to her boat and help her get ready so that his friends could spend the time getting themselves organized. The *panga* would stop by *Dana* in two hours to pick them up.

On the way home they noticed Eric's dinghy bobbing next to *Osprey*, and Jessie suggested they relay their plans. Neal agreed to get off at *Dana* and start closing the boat up if she would do the relaying.

Now on *Osprey*, sitting in the shade of the cockpit awning, she felt the light sea breeze brush her face, and the heat she'd gathered from their wanderings in town began to cool. "Oh, this feels great," she said as she slipped one hand through her sweat-damp hair.

"I suppose you have to get going, but I poured myself some fruit juice, join me?" Eric said over his shoulder as he descended the companionway steps.

Jessie said she would and watched him move around below. He was barefoot and wore a pair of florescent pink shorts that set off his dark tan. A nice looking man, she decided. A glass filled with pale yellow pineapple juice sat on the galley counter, and he lifted it, took a swallow and gazed out a porthole. He stood for several seconds, as if lost in thought.

Jessie wondered if he had forgotten she was there. "The juice looks great, yes, please."

The comment jostled him out of the trance. A glance in her direction seemed to remind him of his offer and he filled a second glass.

He handed it up to her, then wrapped the towel around his head and vigorously rubbed to finish drying his hair. "Jessie, I'm sorry, but I just remembered I'm supposed to be somewhere shortly." He slung the towel over his shoulder and shook his head to loosen the curls, then grabbed his glass and joined her in the cockpit.

"That's all right, I shouldn't stay long anyway, we have quite a bit to do before we leave." She took a sip of the sweet, tangy juice. "Mmm . . . this tastes great. Thanks. Eric, I'm really sorry you and Neal didn't hit it off. I hope you know this has nothing to do with you personally. He's just concerned about getting tangled up in something that will stop us from leaving here."

"Jessie, believe me I appreciate the feeling. I just want to know what happened and somehow I don't think he understands how insane this all seems to me." Eric sipped some juice. "Now, tell me about your plans."

His eagerness pigeonholed any comment she felt obligated to make in Neal's defense. "As you know, Sonny still insists on driving. We just came from settling with a guy for a car. It might be a crazy thing to do, but Sonny is sometimes hard to dissuade."

Eric glanced out at the harbor. "Yes, I get that impression. You're still stopping at Tampu?"

She nodded and took a longer sip from her glass. It wasn't an easy conversation. One day meant nothing to them, but everything to Eric. At least if he came with them, he'd have the group as a distraction. "I know this must seem whimsical to you, but Sonny really does take his art collecting seriously, and this is something I'm sure he planned from the beginning before he knew anything about Jennifer. Our suggestion of a trip to Mexico City made it easier for him to convince us to go to Tampu. He probably couldn't believe his luck and I expect he's determined to find something. The trip alone will make any piece more valuable to him, particularly with the notion of bandits thrown into the mix." They both smiled, but Eric's was sad and he remained silent. "It's not too late. Are you sure you won't change your mind about coming with us?"

"Jessie, it's better this way. I'm not up for a lot of socializing, and no offense, but especially with that group." He looked down at his glass and swirled the juice before lifting his eyes back to hers.

Jessie resisted the temptation to reach out and comfort him. From his comment a spector of Hal appeared in her thoughts.

It was as if he read her mind. "Hal understands, I made sure of that. I won't say anything more to him, and even though I personally don't blame Sonia for wanting the company of a man who has a more generous approach to women, I like Hal enough that the situation could get uncomfortable for me."

"I understand, Eric, you don't need to explain. I'm curious, of course, but that part has nothing to do with us. I'm just concerned for you over the next couple of days." Their eyes locked and Jessie could feel the heat from a blush creep up into her cheeks. She looked down at the piece of paper she pulled from her short's pocket. "Ahh . . . We should be at Mr. Swainyo's office at noon, Friday. I called to confirm our arrival day and that you'll be with us. His assistant suggested the time. Here's the address."

Jessie handed him the paper. Eric studied it, smiled as he said thanks, then drained his glass.

She continued. "I just hope we get to Mexico City. The road has lots of hairpin turns and potholes, not to mention crazy drivers. Add bandits to that and I don't know . . . . " She shrugged and they both laughed. ". . .You may be smarter than you think about not coming along."

Eric's face stilled and he said in a voice quiet, but flint hard, "Just make sure you get that camera to Mexico City."

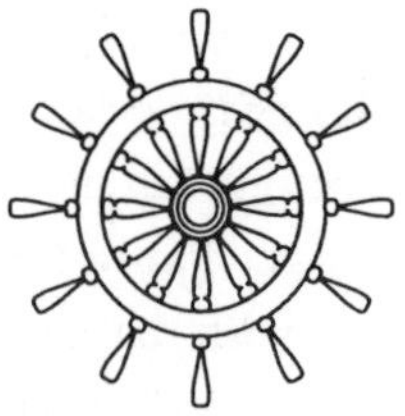

11

Keeping their possible intruder in mind, Jessie and Neal spent time securing *Dana* before rowing over to say good-bye to Mae and Anders. With promises of vigilance from the older couple, they felt better as they showered and put the final touches on their packing, only minutes before the *panga* arrived.

All four of them looked flushed from the rush of getting ready and few words were exchanged as the *panga* whisked them to the *muella* and the notorious vehicle.

Jessie's jangled nerves began to relax once the car was in motion. They stopped for gas at the recommended place and drove on. Settled in the back next to Neal, she rested her head on the seat back and let air from the open window blow on her face. The rhythm of the wheels on the road coaxed her eyes closed as the slogan, "Leave the driving to us," floated through her thoughts. She woke with a start when the car began bouncing in and out of potholes. They had begun their ascent to Tampu.

The lightly traveled route was a narrow ribbon of broken asphalt and eroded dirt that wound around and through the mountains. Pine and oak trees, with boulders and thick undergrowth, covered the slopes. It wasn't unusual for vehicles coming from the opposite direction to sway uncomfortably wide of their lane as they negotiated the curves, forcing Sonny to the edge of the blacktop. A steep ditch ran along both sides and with no shoulder, the road's potholes seemed the easiest feature to tame, or so they thought.

Sonny gripped the wheel and concentrated on the road. He was quiet for minutes at a time, which on any other occasion would have concerned Jessie, but not on this one. She was glad he took his job seriously.

One time he burst out, "Can you believe this . . . Isn't it great?" then hunched nearer the wheel to negotiate around another crater.

Sonia was the unlucky person to occupy the passenger side of the front seat. On one occasion, Jessie saw her tense up when a vehicle flew around a curve and headed straight for them. To avoid impact, Sonny had to veer close to the sheer drop-off at the edge of the road. In the back seat, Jessie felt her own foot jam against the floor on the imaginary brake. Once the danger had passed, Sonny's hand left the wheel for a moment and stroked Sonia's hair. They exchanged a few quiet words and he went back to his driving. No one paid much attention to scenery.

The finalé was a dust-covered yellow bus coasting downhill toward them, bursting with too many people. To ease the outward pull around the corner, it cut into the center of the road and headed straight for them. Jessie's breath caught in her throat and her eyes widened. Sonny veered, and her muscles braced as she felt the seat under her drop. The jarring shook her insides as the belly of the car hit the lip of a hole at least a foot-and-a-half deep. They knew because their curiosity made them walk back later to inspect it. The car scraped, then crunched, then clanked until yards up the road they found a slightly wider spot to pull over. Her ears rang from the screams forced out of everyone by the jolt.

* * *

"Sonny, I'm not a mechanic. I have no idea what's wrong with the car. But I'd say that if fluid runs out of it like that, it's pretty serious." Neal lay on his back in the dirt next to his friend, surveying a large dark puddle forming under their car.

"I think you may be right. What do you suggest?"

"Are you up for pushing it the rest of the way?"

Sonny rolled his head toward Neal. No words were necessary; the look said surely you jest.

After the pitch into the pothole, the four of them had poked, prodded and made suggestions, but the vehicle hadn't responded.

While the men continued to deliberate mechanics, Jessie and Sonia leaned against a tree a few feet off the road and discussed the events of the last week. One among them was Sonia's apology for her attitude toward them the night before.

"God, what happened to Jennifer is so awful, and I feel so for Eric, you know? Like I said last night at Sonny's, I didn't know you were having dinner with us and it was such a shock to see you. He's a good friend and I was pissed at you for putting him through this. But he doesn't seem mad. He knows you're torn up about it and says he understands the spot you're in. I decided, since he feels that way, then so can I."

"It's been difficult, so I'm glad to hear he doesn't necessarily hold this against us, and I wish more people thought like you. No need to apologize again, I think I would feel the same way. Loyalty to friends and all that."

"You know, " said Sonia, pushing off the tree and pulling at her shirt to straighten it. "I just can't believe that Eric is capable of doing anything to intentionally hurt Jennifer. Whenever we got together, they seemed so close. I'm not saying that they didn't have disagreements, but who doesn't?"

"Did it seem to you that she wanted to quit and go home?"

"I liked Jennifer, so don't get me wrong when I say this, but I think she was a little spoiled. Her family indulged her, and she was used to getting her own way all the time. I did hear her say once that their cruising time was almost up and that they would be heading home. You could have knocked Eric over with a feather, but instead of arguing he seemed very understanding. He's a great sailor, everyone says so, and he belongs here, doing this. Not like Hal. Hal belongs in a boardroom. He scares me to death sometimes. We always have way too many sails up and it seems wherever we go, the anchor drags at least once or twice. Hal blames the bottom, then the anchor and eventually it's all my fault. I could be on the other side of the world and if a 'this' broke or a 'that' got stuck, it would somehow be my fault. At first I argued with him all the time, but . . ." she looked down at the ground and kicked at a small stone, "I usually don't anymore. It's just easier not to."

Jessie's mind raced to find something appropriate to say, but couldn't. This beautiful woman could have had her pick of men and she chose a man like Hal. Jessie was about to mumble something, anything, when Sonia continued.

"I don't want to talk about Hal. I just wanted to tell you that Eric is a nice guy and that he loved his wife. She didn't talk about their relationship that much, but all the times we saw them, they seemed happy together. I'm so sad she's dead, but Eric is numb. I've never lost anyone that close to me, but I know it's been a nightmare for him, and he says the ache from it is more than he can stand sometimes."

"Yeah, that's what he says. I guess it'll take a lot of time." Jessie waited for a few words about the baby, but none came.

"I know it will," Sonia said and wiped her eyes. "Enough of this or I'll start bawling. We seem to have a problem of our own to solve this afternoon."

The opportunity passed. She either doesn't know about the baby or isn't talking about it, thought Jessie. Grateful for the change in topics, she said, "I hope you've managed to keep your hat on today with Sonny's energy exploding all over the place."

The blond laughed and said, "What an interesting man. Is he always like this?"

"I have to say that, yes, he is."

She left Sonia to walk across the road and gaze into the tangle of trees and underbrush. She looked at her watch and shook her head. They'd been stuck for almost an hour. At first, not knowing their situation, they had let a couple of trucks and buses pass by without flagging them down. It was beginning to look as though they might regret that. She estimated at least twenty minutes had passed since the last vehicle, a loaded bus, ground uphill past them. Enough time to make them all edgy about the immediate future. It was getting late and maybe the sparse traffic meant something.

The spit of gravel got her attention and she looked down the road. A small, white compact car with something fluttering from the antenna sharply turned around and accelerated back down the mountain, around the curve and out of sight.

She glanced across the road and saw the legs of two men studying the underside of a car with an attractive blond crouched nearby watching them. The picture her husband and two friends created didn't look threatening, but she brought the number to four, which might arouse suspicion. More as a joke, she called out, "Looks like we scared somebody off."

Sonny's voice spilled out from under the car. "Yeah, we look like bandits all right."

Jessie paced the road, stopping occasionally to kick a stone into the ditch. Discussion from under the car started and stopped as the men exchanged ideas. Finally, Sonny left Neal on the ground and walked to the front of the car.

"Sonia, could you get in and pop the hood?" When the ping of the locking mechanism released the hood, he raised it and spent several more minutes poking and prodding.

Sonia moved in beside him, ducked her head under the hood and rested her elbows on the frame. "What do you think ails it?"

Sonny shook his head. "I have no idea." He looked at the woman next to him and they both laughed.

From her place across the road, Jessie saw their laughter fade.

Sonny leaned slowly toward Sonia, hovered closely for a breath or two, then eased in until his lips found hers.

Unable to pull her eyes away, Jessie remained riveted to the scene until the rev of an engine grew too loud to ignore. A truck labored around the corner and up the hill toward them. A flood of relief moved her to action and she called out, "Hey, look, there's a truck coming."

Sonny and Sonia emerged from under the hood and Neal scrambled out from under the car. Everyone's attention went to the truck. At first Jessie felt joy at being rescued, but then another feeling took its place. She crossed the road and moved in next to Neal and whispered, "We should probably flag him down, but at the same time . . . ."

Neal put his hands on his hips and watched the truck, then his eyes swept the surrounding trees and undergrowth. "I don't think there's anything to worry about. I only see the driver, but it wouldn't hurt, I suppose, to have the pepper spray handy."

"Right." Jessie knew where it was, ducked her head in the backseat of the car and grabbed it. In all their travels through Mexico, aggression by locals had been the least of their worries. Because of that, she felt overly dramatic as she tucked the spray into her short's pocket, her finger on the trigger. She knew it was all due to the hype about the road, but a sudden realization hit her that if anything were to happen, she would have to do something about it. Had the truck been farther away, the spray and responsibility would have found its way into Neal's pocket. Instead, as the truck approached, she flexed her knees into a ready position.

Sonny said from the front of the car. "What do you think?"

"It's probably a guy trying to get home. He'll be as nervous of us as we are of him. Just keep your eyes and ears open," said Neal.

"Do you think we should ask him for help?"

"Unless you think any of us are going to get this thing started, yes. We may get lucky. If he travels this road a lot, there's a chance he's good at jury-rigging things like this. I say we at least try. You know a lot of Spanish, here's your chance to shine."

"I don't know a lot of Spanish."

Neal did a half turn toward his friend, "What about all that wheeling and dealing that was going on in Zhuat?"

"Hey, I know a few phrases to get me by. If I need more, I hire a kid." Sonny looked around. "But they seem to be in short supply here."

Jessie said, "I can't believe it. If I didn't know any better, I'd say you were just being modest." She looked away and then turned back to him again. "I don't believe it."

"Believe it, I fake it. You've been down here for months, don't you know any?"

"Well, let's hope between us we know enough."

The truck crept up the incline toward them. Jessie could hear Neal mumbling in Spanish. Probably rehearsing the few phrases he could pull together from memory. Their dictionary was in the car, but she didn't know exactly where, and rummaging around in it might scare the man away. It was getting late and the idea of spending the night in a disabled vehicle on a remote mountainside wasn't appealing.

The truck pulled up to them and stopped. A broad smile led the stout, Hispanic man out of his truck and across the road. "*Buenos dias. ¿Tienen Uds. problemas con su carro?"*

* * *

After introductions, Neal and the other three watched with growing concern while Fernando tinkered, then made several unsuccessful attempts to start the car. Neal felt shackled by his inadequate command of the language, and renewed promises to himself about practicing it more diligently. Even with the dictionary that Jessie unearthed, it took many hand signals and time to communicate with their good Samaritan.

Fernando finally got out from under the car, shrugged his shoulders and shook his head. The string of words that followed sent Jessie and Sonny thumbing through the dictionary again.

"What do you think, Sonny? I get that he's offering us a ride to Tampu, but that we'll have to leave the car here."

"I think so, too" said Sonny. "The word *pesado* probably means that the car's too heavy for him to tow uphill." Sonny went into the dramatics of acting that assumption out and got a vigorous nod and several *sí*'s to confirm it.

Fernando smiled with his hands on his hips as he waited for them to finish their discussion.

Sonny closed the dictionary with a snap. "I think we ought to take him up on his offer, don't you?"

"What about the car, Sonny? You know if we leave it, there's not much chance it will be here tomorrow."

"Jessie, it's just a car. Leave it, we'll let tomorrow take care of itself. I say we go."

It made sense to Neal, so he was glad when everyone else agreed.

Fernando began helping stow bags as they gathered their things together, asking if they wanted any bags to ride in the cab. His gestures suggested that the back of the truck would get bouncy and dusty, and when Jessie mentioned to Neal the bag with the camera, Fernando nodded and said, *"Sí, está bien,"* and found a spot inside where it could ride.

When their driver motioned for the women to sit up front with him and the two men to ride in the bed, Neal caught Jessie's eye.

"We'll be fine, enjoy your ride in the back."

Jessie settled in next to Fernando while Sonia, clutching her purse, sat by the window. Neal pictured the driver's hand on the gear shift next to his wife's vulnerable bare leg, but shook his head and brushed it aside. With a giant step onto the wheel, he swung his leg over the side and into the bed. After grabbing a couple of empty gunnysacks strewn around the back, he and Sonny attempted to cushion the area on which they planned to sit. They leaned against the cab, wedged their bags around them and braced for the upcoming bumpy ride.

"Having a good time, Sonny?" he said, letting the sarcasm seep through.

"The best, and you know it."

That made him smile, "Yes, I'm afraid I do."

Neal wasn't sure exactly why, but ever since they had arrived in Zihuatanejo, he felt he was struggling against a current going too fast the wrong way. The camera, the trip, all seemed wrong, and he couldn't get rid of the feeling.

It had become more obvious when Sonny began planning the trip to Tampu. Normally, Neal would have leapt at the chance to see the country. Instead, all he had seen was a mountain of problems form in front of him. Angry with himself for this seemingly sudden attack of sensibility, he had disregarded the alarms going off in his head and took Sonny's lead. With the latest developments he began to question that decision. Only, now wasn't a good time to dwell on it.

The truck burst into sound, and the engine raced before it groaned, then lurched into first gear. The two friends knocked shoulders and bounced as their forested surroundings began to move. From the back of the truck, they watched Sonny's damaged car recede and finally disappear around a corner.

* * *

Neal's misgivings began to fade again as they bumped along. The engine's grind polluted the solitude of the rugged terrain much the same as a dinghy engine pollutes a peaceful, quiet anchorage, but at least they were moving toward Tampu. If Sonny had been more concerned about his car, Neal would have willingly joined in on the worry, but his friend seemed almost indifferent about it. They shouted back and forth over the noise, joked about the road, Fernando, and their current mode of transportation. Neal knew Sonny was bursting with excitement over their adventure.

At first, the movement he caught out of the corner of his eye meant nothing to Neal, but it grabbed his attention. He looked toward where he thought it had been, and a man in dark trousers and a dirty white T-shirt emerged from behind a rock and began running in their wake. When the truck slowed, he and Sonny exchanged a look of disquiet.

Neal pulled himself to a stand and pivoted around to look forward. In front of the truck, several more men in dark trousers and tatty shirts of varied colors spanned the width of the asphalt. More appeared from behind rocks and trees to join the road block. Feet wide apart and hands on hips, the men stood their ground aggressively. Rocks hurled from the side of the road hit the truck and clipped Neal on the shoulder. A drop to his knees brought him eye level with the window that separated him from the inhabitants of the cab.

His heart began to pound and an invisible band squeezed his chest as he worked at breathing. He banged on the window, but the women were too busy gesturing and yelling at Fernando to hear. The truck lost power and rolled to a stop. The grind of the starter motor told Neal that Fernando was trying to get the truck going again. When the smell of gasoline filled the air around them, he knew that in the panic, their driver had flooded the engine.

"I see at least eight," Sonny bellowed from his crouched position in the corner where the cab and bed panel met on the driver's side.

Neal shuffled to the opposite corner on the passenger side and peered over.

Even though the rush was expected, it came before either of them had time to set up a defense. Within seconds, the bed of the truck was overrun with men carrying sticks. Neal's head rang with noise. He heard his own voice join the shouts and above it all he heard a familiar yell from Jessie.

Facing the enemy, he felt a rush of power and grasped at the first thing his hand touched. He gripped the shoulder strap of one of their daypacks and swung it at the first man who closed in. The force of the impact knocked the assailant off his feet and into the man behind him.

Neal felt a stinging pain across his bare legs as a stick found its mark, then another on his shoulder and across his right cheek. Arms, legs and bodies wrangled in confusion as Neal swung the daypack again. A wail from a man, not in the truck bed, momentarily stalled the offensive action of the men around him, and Neal took the opportunity to swing again, smashing the face of his closest adversary. The momentum of the swing threw them both into the side of the bed and the adversary fell backwards, over the edge and onto the ground.

A shrill cry followed by another voice shouting a string of incomprehensible Spanish rose above the melee. All the shouts, both male and female, added impetus to Neal's swing. Over the crescendo of confusion and noise came the roar of their truck's engine. It lurched forward, knocking all the men near him, including Neal, off their feet like bowling pins.

The fallen knot of men shoved, kicked and scratched to get upright. Neal felt his head explode with stars when a foot connected with his jaw. Falling back, he had the wind knocked out of him when another foot used his chest as a springboard. Men's shouts and foreign words grew faint. Flat on his back on the metal floor, he heard the beautiful drone of the truck's engine and felt every pebble in the road as they jounced forward at full speed.

His next conscious thought was the noise he made when he breathed. It sounded like a groan. He felt pain in several places, but nothing screamed at him, so he began to test arms, legs and, finally, torso. Once satisfied nothing was seriously wrong, he rolled onto his side.

Sonny lay next to him, both hands rubbing his temples.

"Sonny, you all right?"

"Neal . . . Neal?" The calls drowned out Sonny's response and Neal rolled over more until he could see the window to the cab. It framed Jessie and Sonia's concerned faces. Their fingers spread across the glass as if trying to reach him. All he could think to do was wave, then a ferocious bump shot pain through him and he rolled onto his back again. In spite of his battle wounds, he felt a growing sense of calm. Everyone seemed all right.

"Sonny, . . . now are you having a good time?"

Silence followed and widened.

Just before Neal summoned the energy to roll over again, he heard Sonny clear his throat and rasp out a response.

"The best, and you know it."

"God, I was afraid you'd say that."

12

They stopped at the first *pueblo* they came to. Fernando's gestures and apologies told them he was afraid to stop any sooner. Crumbling stucco made the small community look shabby, and its residents seemed suspicious of a truck carrying bleeding *gringos.* The streets quickly became deserted and Fernando abandoned his attempts to get help. After reassuring hugs and nonstop chatter about what happened, all five of them took stock of the injuries to themselves and their belongings.

Two bags had gone with the attackers, which meant Sonia and Neal would have a limited wardrobe for the rest of the trip. Her purse almost went, too, and as that registered, Sonia stood silently for a moment and struggled between tears and a smile. She clutched tighter at the bag that carried her credit card and defiantly admitted to hearing the shopping was great in Mexico City, and this gave her an excuse to take advantage of it.

Fernando caressed his truck and although the four friends wondered how he could differentiate old from new, he pointed to a couple of dents and scratches while he shook his head.

Grinning with relief until his damaged cheek hurt, Neal listened as Jessie reassured him she was all right and told what she knew of the battle.

To her, most of the men had run to the back to get at Neal, Sonny and their bags. She saw only two men assault the cab, and after they ripped open the front doors, they pulled Sonia and Fernando clear of the truck. When they reached in again, one went for the daypack, the other for the purse, but Jessie was ready for them. With can poised for action, she hit both attackers with a blast of pepper spray.

It got instant results. They abandoned their efforts, screaming and clawing at their faces as they backed out of the cab.

Residue mist from the spray spattered on her own face, but not before Jessie had grabbed and clamped her arms tightly around the daypack. When the burning finally forced her eyes shut, she gripped the pack more firmly, determined not to give it up. Although she couldn't see, she heard Sonia scream, then felt weight on the seat on either side of her. No one pulled at her or the daypack again, but she remained huddled until the burning eased and the truck was well underway. Their identification papers and the precious, saltwater-soaked video camera had come through without a bump or a wrinkle.

Sonia took over the story from there. She confessed to paralysis as she was jerked from the cab. Everything ran in slow motion, but she remembered Fernando looking dazed on the other side of the truck and their two assailants rushing back, presumably for Jessie.

The man who had deserted her for another go at the truck suddenly shot back out of the cab, screaming. Frantically wiping at his eyes, he dropped Sonia's purse, staggered around, then tripped and fell. When she realized no one else was coming at her, she screamed at Fernando to get back into the truck and go. Even though she used English, she must have gotten through to him because he shouted a long string of what she guessed were Mexican expletives, jumped behind the wheel and turned the key. Remarkably the old road warrior started. No longer threatened by her attacker, she kicked his leg out of the way to snatch her purse off the ground and scrambled back onto the seat next to Jessie. As they bounced away from the scene, she looked back and saw the two men who attacked the cab trying to stand with the help of one or two others. The rest were running into the woods. Neal and Sonny lay in the bed of the truck, motionless, the remainder of their bags scattered around them.

Once the story had been told and they were all reassured that no one needed emergency care, they climbed back into the truck, bruised and bleeding, to continue their journey. The road took them through more dense forest and more shabby *pueblos*. They had been lucky, Neal thought. Although the odds had been against the *gringos,* their opponents hadn't scored much.

* * *

"What a dismal place. They cut down all the trees," Sonny shouted. A blue bruise topped with a gash and dried blood held a prominent position on Sonny's forehead. Like Neal, he complained of aches and pains, but otherwise was in good spirits. From their position behind the cab, they watched the road disappear behind them.

Neal's head throbbed with pain and his cheek ached where the stick had split the skin, but he resisted the urge to touch it. Last time his curiosity had started the bleeding again. In response to Sonny's comment, he raised himself enough to look around and then eased back against the cab. The potholed dirt road had brought them into another *pueblo.*

Faded stucco walls lined both sides. Weeds and rubbish left to collect in the corners made the road appear neglected, and the occupants of the houses that lined it, on the edge of poverty. Limited clearance on either side required pedestrians to walk with caution, and two women reemerged from a recess where they had scooted as the truck passed. In many of the closed doorways, men leaned and watched as if that was all they had to do. Neal peered through two or three of the open doors and was surprised to see neatly arranged courtyards with greenery and flowers bordered in expensive, elaborate black wrought iron. As bleak and unkempt as it looked on the outside, this pueblo had a few residents with money.

The view from the back of the truck opened up and presented what looked like a town center. Potholes and debris acted like natural speed bumps to the dented, unwashed trucks that roared through. People on foot kept a more sedate pace, no one bustled.

Sonny's voice seemed unreal as he pitched it over the engine noise, "Looks like a park."

Trees, hedges and statues set along winding pathways radiated out from a large, central fountain, forming an oasis in the dust. Small groups of people occupied the plentiful benches that dotted the shade under the greenery. Neal leaned closer to his friend to lessen the need to shout.

"That's probably the *zocolo* or main square. Pretty impressive."

They both turned when they heard knuckles on the window behind their heads. Sonia moved her pointer finger down and nodded.

Neal slid his glance to Sonny. "I think she's trying to tell us this is the place."

They both looked back at Sonia and she made a circle with her thumb and pointer finger in an "okay" sign.

The truck stopped without pulling over and Fernando called out to a man across the road. A small, white car with something fluttering from the aerial sped up from behind and split the distance between them and the man, burying him in a cloud of dust. He waited for it to settle before he pointed down the road and swept his arm to the left. Fernando yelled a response; the truck ground into gear and continued.

Sonia batted at the thick air then yelled out her window back at them, "This is the place."

Neal watched Sonny glance around with renewed enthusiasm, but none of the buildings they could see would pass for a gallery. Dust lifted and swirled around their heads as the truck bumped through and away from the center of activity.

Minutes later the road was swallowed by a thick tangle of trees and underbrush. The truck slowed and turned. Neal leaned over the side of the bed and looked forward. The new road was little more than a trail. Two worn, dirt tire paths disappeared into the foliage ahead. Branches snapped at the top of the truck's cab and the engine groaned as it crept forward. They could have walked faster.

Neal twisted around again and knocked on the window. Jessie struggled to turn to the sound, but the confined space in the truck's front seat allowed for only a half turn of her head. When she caught Neal's glance, she nodded and flashed him an "okay" sign again.

Sonia, seeing Neal's concern, turned to hang out the passenger window to say something, but ducked back inside and rolled the window up when a branch slapped at her.

He wanted to know where they were going, but before he could shout the question at them, the truck bumped out of the dark, dense foliage into the light and stopped. Hedges, brightly colored flowers and evergreens surrounded a low, white stucco house that sprawled in both directions from a large wooden door. A gable with two windows rose in a peak over the door. Like the bill on a cap, a verandah shaded the entire ground floor. Patches of white showing through the foliage at the edge of the clearing suggested the existence of other smaller buildings. Neal saw people sitting on benches on the verandah and a man kneeling over a bed of flowers.

Feminine laughter burst out of the truck as the doors opened.

"I guess this means we can get out," said Sonny. He slowly unrolled to a stand and kneaded his back as he stretched. The dust that had settled on him rose and drifted away as he slapped at his shorts. Bruises dotted his legs.

Neal eased out of the back to the ground. He watched Fernando walk across the clearing and talk to the man tending the flower bed. Every muscle in Neal's body groaned, but in spite of that, it felt good to be moving around.

With laughter still on their faces, Jessie and Sonia joined Neal. "You guys do okay back here?"

"My ass will never be the same, someone is pounding a sledgehammer in my head, my legs wouldn't make it up a small set of stairs, and I'm wearing a coat of dust, but hey, I'm not complaining. Where are we anyway?" said Sonny, still standing in the back of the truck looking war torn from his recent battle.

"I think it's called Alta Linda," said Jessie. "Fernando kept telling us how beautiful Alta Linda was and that when we got here everything would be all right. As we pulled in, he pointed and said, 'Alta Linda.' We were lucky, in spite of everything, he's been very nice."

Jessie lifted the bag she carried from the cab, opened it, checked inside, then closed it and slung it over her shoulder. Seeing her again, whole and undamaged after their recent combat, prompted Neal to wrap his arm around her shoulder.

Sonia pulled at her blouse and shorts to straighten the wrinkles brought on from their journey. "I think so, too. He's got the biggest smile, and he's kind of handsome. He was dragged into all this because of us, but he doesn't seem to blame us."

She rubbed at a smudge and continued. "I could sure use a shower . . . wish I had some clean clothes."

Neal slipped his other arm around Sonia and pulled her toward him. She blinked away a tear and rested her head on his shoulder.

With a woman on either side of him he said, "We might be missing some clothes and carrying around a few bruises, but thanks to the two of you, it wasn't worse."

"Hear, hear," said Sonny. He seemed to creak as he slung his leg over the side of the truck and, with considerable effort, eased himself to the ground. "Looks like a *pension* or something."

Neal said, "Yeah, nice setting. Fernando's alerted someone to our arrival."

The four friends watched a couple emerge from the wooden door and walk toward them. They weren't Hispanic and looked tall, even from a distance, but when Fernando stood almost childlike next to them as they exchanged a few words, Neal guessed they were inches above six feet. When they pointed to a place beyond the house, Fernando nodded and walked away. Their faces seemed comfortable with smiles and their hair was tinged with grey. The giant couple strode tall as they approached the four travelers. The woman extended her hand and spoke first.

"Welcome to Tampu and Alta Linda. My name is Sage Weaver, and this is my husband Peter. We're so sorry to hear about your difficulties." Her straight, once blond hair fell loose to her waist and was held off her face by a colorful tie-died band.

Expat Americans, Neal thought, as he took the hands offered. More years showed on their faces up close than showed from a distance. "Thanks very much. I'm Neal, this is Jessie, Sonia and Sonny." They all nodded their greetings as they shook hands.

Peter's soft voice seemed incongruous to his size. "Fernando told us a little about what happened. Come inside and use what you need to get cleaned up. We've got bandages and such. There's no doctor here, but the *pueblo* has a pretty good medic. We could get him for you."

Neal looked at the group and when no one came forward he said, "I don't think we're in need of a medic as much as clean water and some Band-Aids. Thanks."

With no urgency in his step or speech, Peter led the way to the house. "We haven't had trouble on that road for some time and we haven't heard any news that would particularly prompt it today. I know it's hard to believe after what happened, but we live in a pretty lazy, trouble-free spot." They mounted the steps to the shade of the verandah. "Fernando went to talk with our handyman about your car. If Tomy thinks he can get it back here, it might be worth your while to talk to him about it."

"That'll be great." Looking around, Neal said, "You have a beautiful place."

Sage's voice reminded him of a delicate sea breeze, warm and soothing. "Thank you, we like it. Come inside. I'll show you around, point out the restrooms and get the first aid kit for you. Then you'll be better able to decide what else you need. From the look of those bruises and cuts, you have some mending to do. And again, if you decide you want to see James, he's the medic, it's no trouble."

Sonny moved in next to Sage. "Thanks, Mrs. Weaver, that's very kind. On the way in, I looked for the Outpost Gallery, but didn't see it. Is it far from here?"

Sage laughed lightly. "Through it all he has the strength to ask about art. Andre will be pleased. It's not far at all. Most people who stay with us, even if they have a car, prefer to walk. For one thing, the trail to the village is lovely and the Outpost is on the way, but also because it's actually closer. We've got a map inside, I can show you, and please, call me Sage."

"I'll leave Sage to show you around, and I'll go find out Tomy's opinion of your car situation. I think these battered and weary travelers could use a sherry when they're ready, what do you think, Sage?"

"Agreed; you'll find us in the lounge."

Peter disappeared around the corner of the house as Sage led them through the front door.

They walked into light and space. The peaked gable they had seen from outside towered over their heads and late afternoon light streamed in through the two windows at the top.

A small, compact woman with thick, shoulder-length, jet black hair scooted across a wide arch at the other end of the large entrance hall. She glanced their way and disappeared, then as if doing a double take, she reappeared in the arch.

"Mareya, we have four guests who have had some trouble. *Banditos* on the mountain road. I'm going to show them where they can clean up and get the first aid kit for them. Tomy's sorting out what he can do for their car."

Mareya bounded into the room with an energy level that seemed impossible so late in the day. Her smile battled with the wrinkle of concern that creased her delicate, black eyebrows. She shook everyone's hand as Sage introduced them. "So sorry you had to come to us under such circumstances. You're in good hands, though. Sage will get you comfortable and if anything can be done with your car, Tomy will do it. I'll get the first aid kit." English was not her native language, but years of practice had rounded the sharp edges of her accent and she sounded comfortable using it. With comments about bringing the kit right away, she disappeared.

Wide arches moved the guests from the foyer to a large sitting room. Big cushioned furniture dressed in green, leafy patterned upholstery accentuated the pale green painted walls. Areas empty of furniture displayed various forms of art, all contributing to the feel of being outside, while remaining inside.

Large, spacious restrooms angled off the big room. Mareya arrived with the first aid kit and while battle wounds were assessed and dressed, they took turns explaining the assault to the two innkeepers.

Mareya sat on the arm of Sage's chair as they listened to the accounts. "Sticks and rocks instead of weapons, at least it's not as organized as some in the past. Not that it makes it any better. These men are still common criminals, but with no weapons, maybe they needed money for something. Why men think they can get it like this . . . ." Mareya shook her head.

Neal felt himself melting into one of the overstuffed chairs. "They didn't get much if that was their intention."

Sage stood. "That, probably more than anything, says they were new at this. Maybe with a face full of pepper spray, they'll think twice about doing it again. How about a drink and some food? It's on the house."

Although Neal struggled to climb out of the chair, the thought of food reminded him that he was hungry. Others groaned as they moved their battle weary bodies to follow Sage. Mareya disappeared through an arch ahead of them.

Sage pointed out a few pieces by local artists and grouped the rest as things that had always been there. "The previous owner's wife, now ex-wife, liked to putter with a blow torch. She welded all this from things she found around here. When we bought his half of the business, he left them here."

Neal said, "You share the business then?"

"Yes. I'm not sure if it's true everywhere in Mexico, but here foreigners need a Mexican National as a partner. Mareya's husband Lano was the one who built this place with an American friend, oh gosh, it has to be twenty years ago now. We actually began vacationing here while they both ran it. When Lano died of a heart attack, things began to fall apart. Mareya did what she could, but the American partner was having a rough time and relied on her to do the day-to-day running of the place. He wasn't very supportive and got really nervous about her business approach. The bottom line, he wanted out. Peter and I had some trials in our own lives that year and we found refuge here for several months. We got to know the situation and Mareya. We liked what we saw, so we put a deal together. The man jumped at it and we've never been sorry."

"It's beautiful. Was it always like this or have you made changes?" Jessie walked next to Sage, wondering if producing this feeling of space was their idea.

"Peter loves to hammer, so a few walls have been removed to give it more of an open feel. Regular doorways replaced by the wider arches. Mareya was all for it and I guess those things seemed natural to us with our size and all. The one factor that got us to stay here the first time though was the gable. That's always been open to the roof. We thought it was beautiful and so unusual for here. We gather it was the American partner's idea."

Sage guided them through another arch, and a bright green wall of jungle appeared in front of them beyond a series of large windows. Wood crackled as it burned in a big stone fireplace at one end of the room and a small bar decorated the other end. Chairs, with the same green, leafy upholstery, sat around tables and filled the floor space in between.

"Oh, good, someone's laid a fire. Up at this elevation the cool weather is almost at an end, but we keep the fireplace active as long as we can. It adds to the atmosphere in here, I think."

"It feels as if we're in a tree house," said Sonia as she wandered over to the windows.

"This room is Peter's masterpiece. We have always liked hiking and camping and being outdoors, so we wanted a place that got everyone close to nature year round. You know, open air in the summer and yet cozy in winter. I think his biggest success was finding someone to make the windows. It's not like we need a lot of insulation here in winter, it doesn't get that cold; however, the damp and chill requires some protection to be comfortable." Sage joined Sonia at the windows and pointed out the clasps that secured the glass. When unsnapped, the glass windows could be replaced by screens.

A young boy wearing a crisp, white shirt and black trousers appeared through a door near the bar and laid a tray of small glasses filled with a dark amber liquid on one of the tables. Next to it someone had already placed plates of sandwiches, sliced carrots, tortilla chips and salsa. He flashed a toothy smile at everyone and left.

"Thank you, Angel," said Sage, pronouncing it Ahng-hell. She turned back to her guests. "Mareya's nephew. Nice boy, and still young enough to want to be useful. Please help yourself. There's more sherry if you want it. I wish it were under better circumstances, but welcome to Tampu and Alta Linda." They all raised their glasses to Sage's toast and took a sip.

Sonny said, "Madam Weaver, you have salvaged the wreckage of our day with your hospitality. I think I speak for everyone when I say, thank you."

Everyone raised their glasses again. Sage blushed and dipped her head to acknowledge the compliment. The glasses were drained and replaced on the table. She walked to the bar and came back carrying a bottle to refill them.

Sonny picked up a sandwich and before he took a bite said, "Outside you mentioned a map?"

"Oh, yes, it's over here." She led them to a wall next to the bar and traced the road to the *pueblo*. "You see the road makes a wide bend and enters the *pueblo* at this end, then goes through the town and around to get to the gallery." Her finger drew a U-shaped journey from the *pension* to the gallery. "But if you take the path, it leaves Alta Linda right outside, cuts through the trees straight across, enters the *pueblo* from the other side and goes right by the gallery, which is right there." The footpath cut across the top of the two legs of the U and slightly down one side.

"It can't be that far then," said Sonny.

"It's about a fifteen minute walk if you don't stop. A couple of regular guests have, over the years, donated benches to put along the way. We maintain them and I find it tempting to stop and just soak it all in. I love it and take any opportunity to walk it. If you have no other place to stay tonight, we have a couple of rooms available. Under the circumstances, we'd be willing to negotiate the price as sort of compensation for what you've gone through. That's not meant to pressure you. I just wanted you to know."

"Thank you, Sage, we might take you up on that." Neal was curious about the gardens he had seen behind the walls as they entered Tampu. "I noticed some nice places behind the stucco walls when we came into town. It looks like the pueblo, despite the dust, is doing pretty well."

A knot of wrinkles formed between her eyes then disappeared, much like a strong wind blows a dark cloud briefly over the sun. "Yes, the demographics of Tampu are curious. The hills are filled with beautiful homes tucked away among the pines. If you walk the trail to the pueblo, you'll see some examples. Most are inhabited by Americans, Canadians and Europeans. Very private people, many are writers and artists, which contributes to the Outpost's success. They want this area to remain remote, but at the same time they want their little luxuries, for which they are quite willing to pay. The local people who were enterprising enough cashed in on that and have done quite well."

"Has this caused problems?" Interested by her brief scowl, Neal couldn't resist asking.

"Well, no, not really. In fact, the post office-slash-bank is one of the best I've seen in Mexico. It's tiny, but you'll be surprised when you walk in there. The Deli is just what it implies. It imports from all over and has cheeses that are out of this world. Then a couple from Switzerland moved in a few years back. She paints and he bakes. He got together with the local baker and began making things that the hill people liked and . . . well . . . if you stay for dinner tonight, you'll taste some of their bread. It's unlike any bakery you'll find anywhere around here."

"Sounds like there's a 'but' that follows all that," said Jessie.

Sage shook her head and laughed. "There's no doubt that those of us in business would like to see the place spruced up a bit, but our efforts don't get us very far. Apart from the few luxuries I just mentioned, and the *zocolo*, the artistic community wants Tampu to stay the bleak dust bowl you saw when you came in, but I don't think they alone oppose us. There are a couple of estates owned by wealthy and powerful Mexican families in these hills. I've never seen them, but I know what roads go to them. If those families like Tampu the way it is, it will stay the way it is. As outsiders, Peter and I will never know the real reasons for why things don't happen here, and Mareya is Indian. It's safer for her to stay out of the politics and not meddle. I don't think there's anything sinister about it; I just think it's the same anywhere the rich have decided to live."

Sage paused. Her remarks hadn't explained the storm cloud that passed over her face, and Neal knew more would follow. He suspected the others sensed it, too, when no one jumped into the pause. But the moment vaporized when the door opened. Angel peeked through and called to Sage.

"I'm sorry, I've probably bored you silly. Excuse me. Please make yourselves at home and let us know if you need anything. I'm sure Peter will join you shortly."

Sonny said, "Don't apologize, I found it all very interesting." They all nodded in agreement. "Don't let us keep you. We'll find you if we need anything."

They watched Sage, carrying her glass, disappear through the door.

"That was enlightening, I wonder what came next?" Sonny grinned and watched Sonia drift to the fireplace. He followed. His arm went around her shoulder and pulled her toward him. A brief smile tugged at the corners of her mouth, but it quickly disappeared and her attention went back to the fire.

"This is all probably better than he hoped for." Jessie joined Neal at the big windows and swept the outside vista with her eyes. "What a neat place."

Neal remembered Sonia's earlier comment and agreed with her, the dense forest with an abundance of green and brown gave him a sense of being in a tree house. Birds chased each other around the foliage and their songs carried through the glass.

He took a sip of sherry. "Isn't it . . . I'm not a big fan of sherry, but it's a nice touch."

"Sonny is loving all this. We get ambushed, the two of you come out of it with cuts and bruises, and to top it off, he might lose thousands of dollars on a car he only used for a few hours. How much money do you have to have to get that blasé about it?"

"Don't start trying to figure Sonny out, it's gotten us nowhere in the past. These people seem honest. If the car can be salvaged and is still there tomorrow, it might be fixable. You know the mileage Sonny will get out of this story. It's worth every penny to him."

"Yeah, but if he's going to throw it away like that, it would be nice if some of it landed on us."

"His money comes at too high a price. Look at the way he lives. No thanks, I like things the way they are."

Jessie stole a glance at the twosome by the fire. "Sonia seems a little nervous. I wonder if she's beginning to feel guilty about being here with . . . ," she leaned in trying to be discreet, ". . . another man. I got the idea from talk in the truck that Eric's decision not to come with us took away any pretense of innocence she felt about accepting Sonny's offer."

Neal wrapped his wife in a hug. "Maybe, but let's not worry about them. This place is a luxury for us. I say we splurge. Let's book a room and enjoy ourselves."

Jessie leaned her head against his. "Sure. I can't tell how Sonia feels, but I think Sonny would go for it."

"Well, even if they don't. We can. I like it and I like the people. It's peaceful and just what we need after all we've been through today."

"Don't remind me. It makes my body ache just thinking about it. Was it only this morning that Sonny dropped all this on us?"

Neal felt pain and stiffness in his own body. He stroked his partner's back and gazed out at the paradise that surrounded them. "The realization that he arrived only yesterday tires me even more. I'm not sure I'm in good enough shape to have him around for two weeks."

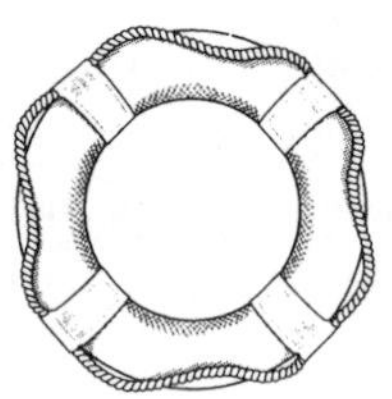

13

Leaves and twigs crunched under her feet as, the next morning, Jessie walked the dirt trail a dozen steps behind Neal. Somewhere in back of them, out of sight, Sonny and Sonia followed. Neal paused at a bench and looked over his shoulder beyond his mate to the empty path, then sat.

Solid wooden planks, carved and fitted together, created the comfortable-looking seat and when Jessie caught up, she eased in next to him. A bronze plaque fixed on the wood between them read, "Savor the beauty of this valley; you are in Paradise. The L.W. Walds. 1979."

Jessie ran her fingers over the raised lettering and wondered if the Walds still came to sit on this bench. Overhead a dense canopy allowed slivers of sunlight to break through its cover and cut the air diagonally. The shafts lit small areas of rambling growth close to the ground.

Jessie leaned back and glanced at the empty trail. "They must have stopped at the last bench. Hormones are running high between those two. I'm not sure we should wait."

Neal laughed and stretched his bare legs out in front of him. Purple bruises darkened the skin in a few places and after touching one, he laced his fingers behind his head. "Well, it couldn't happen in a nicer place. I can understand why Peter and Sage kept coming back."

Jessie matched Neal's stretch and relished the peaceful surroundings. Noticing Neal's bruises, she thought of their frantic experiences from the day before and felt grateful again for the lazy, uneventful morning.

"Yeah, it's beautiful. I like the way they found it. What a kick to strike out from your hotel in Mexico City to do a little exploring and stumble onto a place like this. It would have to make a pretty big impression to change vacation plans and then, eventually, life plans, too. I know they mentioned how many years they came back before they bought the place, but I don't remember."

"Ten, I think they said." Neal brought his hands down and rested his head on the back of the bench.

"That's right, ten years. It's interesting, I think."

Jessie felt cool and dry even after the exertion from their walk. Probably the altitude, she thought to herself. A bird song broke out above them and she looked up to search the branches for the origin of the music. "I'm glad Fernando brought us here. I hope his experience with us hasn't soured him on helping anyone else he might come across on that road."

"I don't know. He seemed okay about the money we gave him for the ride and the scratches to his truck. What happened could give him stories to tell for a long time."

Jessie laughed. "It's going to give *us* stories to tell for a long time. After dinner last night, it seemed to me Peter was pretty sure that he and Tomy would find the car in reasonable shape."

"I got that impression, too. They left early enough this morning. Maybe they'll get to it before too many other people do."

"If it's fixable, it won't be soon enough for Sonia. I noticed she twisted her nose when Peter suggested taking the bus on to Mexico City." Jessie smiled at the thought of their companion's reaction to the suggestion they ride public transport to make the rendezvous with Mr. Swainyo and Eric. According to Tomy, if the problems weren't serious, the car would be fixed by the time they headed back to Zihuatanejo.

"You're right, it doesn't sound as though she's traveled on too many Mexican buses, but then I think she's done a few things in the last couple of days that she's not used to doing."

"I'm surprised she's been such a good sport about losing her clothes. Of course, Sonny's promise to take her shopping in Mexico City probably helped, but she really didn't seem to mind going to dinner wearing that mixture we threw together for her last night. I think she looked great and at least the clothes were clean."

Neal laughed. "Speaking of clean clothes, how did we end up with that pile Angel dropped off this morning?"

"Mareya came for them while you were in the shower last night. Said she would run them through with some sheets and towels they were doing. I gave her everything we had on."

"Sometimes things work out."

Jessie felt dreamy as she responded to his comment. "It has this time. I can still taste that meal from last night. I think even Sonny was impressed. Sage was right about the bread . . . hot and soft . . . it makes my mouth water just thinking about it. Pesto and sun-dried tomato, who would have guessed?"

"She did say the hill people liked their luxuries."

Their heads rested on the back of the bench and when they heard a noise on the trail, they rolled them in the direction of the sound.

When no one appeared, Jessie said, "Do you think it's worth waiting?"

"No, they know where we're going. They can meet us there."

After they had a stretch and shared a lingering kiss, Jessie followed him onto the trail. Her thoughts slipped back to the night before and the conversation that took place around the fire. Sage and Peter had remarked that this valley was unusual in that it had escaped the slash and burn of many other areas, plus the vegetation was slightly more tropical, with acacias and ferns. It was a big influence in their decision to buy Alta Linda.

In her own mind, Jessie had questioned whether the gentry in the hills could really make it worthwhile for the local residents to willingly live with inconveniences that would discourage tourism. According to their hosts, Alta Linda and most of the hill people invested in private water, electricity and septic systems, while the general population still worked with primitive plumbing and a generator that shut down at 8:00 p.m. Was that a natural difference between those with money and those without, or were other pressures brought on to camouflage Tampu from a world of people looking for just this kind of retreat? To her, tourism was a tenacious industry. It had found Taxco, nearby. Why not here? Granted, Tampu had no silversmiths like Taxco, but there was plenty of beauty. She wondered as she looked around if a deliberate effort were being made to insulate Tampu, and if so, why?

She came out of her reverie when Neal abruptly stopped in front of her. She halted and said, "What's up?"

"I guess this must be the Outpost."

A structure of natural wood, glass and angles, set in a small clearing peeked through the trees. The building would have been expected in the forests of Big Sur on the west coast of the United States, but its contemporary contours and elegance came as a surprise in the remote mountains of Mexico. The well-crafted, wooden monument near the entrance faced away from them, but Jessie made a bet with herself that "Outpost" would be worked into the wood across the front.

The trail wound through a small depression and then brought the walkers into the clearing. Sculptures placed throughout created a balance with the building, and Jessie recognized a few pieces as those done by the ex-wife who was so handy with a blow torch. Another small clearing set apart from the building but joined by a path held a handful of cars. No other signs of civilization existed, so she guessed the road into the place must be on the other side of the cars.

They walked between the various metal and stone sculptures, studying the plaques next to each piece. The plaques listed the title, material, date and artist. Those without a price said in bold capital letters, NOT FOR SALE.

By the time Jessie reached the door to the gallery, laughter drifted in from the trail behind them. She stopped and waited. Neal finished his study of the outside pieces and joined her.

Sonny and Sonia emerged from the trees, spotted them and took a couple of steps in their direction. Jessie saw Sonny hesitate when he noticed the outdoor sculptures and she called out, "We'll see you guys inside, okay?"

"Yeah, we'll be there in a minute."

Jessie pulled the door open and stepped inside, Neal followed. The gallery was small, so the building's large size had other uses. Works of art hung on the white walls, and spaced throughout, sculptures sat, poised atop pedestals. Simple, hunter green, upholstered seats were positioned for long, lingering looks at the exhibits. Temperature and humidity gauges suggested a controlled atmosphere, and strategic lighting brought out the shine on the highly polished tile floor and instilled a reverent silence.

"Well, this is something," said Neal, one notch above a whisper.

"Isn't it?"

They heard a whoosh and then a muted thud. A man had come through a swinging door at the other end of the gallery. He was thin, perfectly proportioned and wearing a wheat-colored three-piece suit that would have been a common sight in the summertime heat of New York. As he walked toward them, his expression was serious, but not unfriendly. Neal had always told Jessie she looked pretty in the tropical print rayon dress she often wore while sightseeing. But as she watched this stranger approach, she felt grossly underdressed. The man didn't seem to notice. His hands pressed together, prayer-like, in front of his chest and showed long, slender fingers with clean, well-trimmed nails.

"Welcome to the Outpost. Please help yourselves to a glass of wine," with a slight bow, he waved one hand in the direction of a small, round table that glistened with glasses of white and red wine, ". . . and feel free to browse. We have many other pieces not on display that are catalogued in the book on that counter. If there's anything in there you wish to see, it would be my pleasure to show you. My name is Andre, I am the proprietor."

Jessie felt herself dip her head in response to his bow, "Thank you, Andre. You have quite an extraordinary gallery." Her comment had the same effect as a scratch behind a cat's ear.

A satisfied smile creased his serious face. "Thank you, you're very kind. Please enjoy." Andre repeated the slight bow and moved away to take up a position near the door. Jessie assumed he hovered there to repeat his greetings to Sonny and Sonia.

She moved alongside Neal. "Can you believe this?"

"I'm working on it, but the rest of the pueblo doesn't prepare you for it."

"Do you think he was born Andre?"

Neal smiled and gave a slight shrug.

A burst of sound at the door announced Sonny's arrival. The

atmosphere that had subdued them had the opposite affect on their friend. They heard laughter and a rush of verbal exchanges at the gallery entrance. Neal handed her a glass of wine and they began browsing. She couldn't distinguish her friend's words, but when Sonny began asking questions, Andre picked up wine for the newcomers, and they moved their animated conversation to the catalogue. The proprietor had sensed a live one.

* * *

"I'm glad you found it so interesting. It's been around for so long, I don't think much about it any more. I forget that it comes on so strong. Compared to the rest of Tampu, I guess the Outpost is . . . well . . . unique." Sage unconsciously wiped the bar as she talked.

After towing the car as far as Tampu, Peter's value in the operation had disappeared. He had left Tomy in the *pueblo* and hiked the trail back to Alta Linda, arriving only minutes after Jessie and Neal. Whether it would ever run again was still in question, but the news of its recovery was cause enough for a celebration. Since, for Neal, part of the fun of being in a foreign country was trying the various brews and spirits, he had nodded when Peter offered him a glass of *pulque* to propose the toast for the four of them. Made from the fermented sap of the maguey plant, the nut-like flavor and oily texture had suited the ceremony, but one glass was enough, and once empty, Neal had replaced it with a Dos Equis.

Peter swiveled on the stool next to him and said, "The gallery has gone through several changes. Andre is a clever and ambitious man. When we first arrived, he had only a small wooden building, more in tune with the rest of the pueblo. *Avanzada* he called it then, which means 'outpost' in Spanish and maybe that's how he felt about it. It's out of the way now, but then, every time it rained he worried about being stranded. He managed to cajole the local artists into allowing him to show some of their work. To their amazement, he would sell it and continues to do so. He never advertises. The place is never mentioned in anything produced by the Mexican tourist board and yet there always seems to be buyers, and more all the time. One guest from Britain showed me a write-up in a travel book they brought from home, and it gave Tampu a lousy review, but mentioned the Outpost as worth an hour on the way to or from somewhere else."

Neal rotated the Dos Equis bottle in front of him with one hand. "What does that kind of review do to business?"

"We get a lot of repeats and they spread the word. Andre frequently recommends us, too. We do some advertising, of course, but unless someone wants solitude or has a particular interest in expensive art, there's not really much to bring a person here. Naturally, that kind of review doesn't help, but I can't say we've suffered too much from it and the small hotels in the pueblo aren't affected at all. They're all family-run and mainly attract people from Mexico City."

"Hi, all." The rumpled khaki suit was the first thing Neal noticed, then his eyes slipped up to the hair. It looked as if the man had stood in front of a fan. He yawned as he slid onto a stool, dropped his elbow on the bar and brought his hand up to support his head.

"James Darling, you look a fright. What have you been doing?"

"Maria Garcia finally delivered. I've been there since yesterday. An orange juice please, Sage."

"You need more than that." Sage poured the juice and placed the glass in front of him. "I thought she was going to Iguala to have her baby."

"Well, she didn't. When I came here, I had no idea I would be spending my time like this."

"Silly woman, you've been telling her for weeks she should get ready to go there. What was her excuse?"

"I don't have the energy to go into it all, but the bottom line is, she changed her mind."

"Oh . . . Jessie, Neal, this is James Darling. He's the . . . well, he brings God to the people, right, James?"

"Very humorous, innkeeper." He raised his glass and pronounced in a dramatic voice, "I'm on a mission for God, who in his infinite wisdom, has decided that an EMT course will suffice as a medical degree in the backwaters of the Sierra Madre del Sur." He threw his juice down his throat, banged his glass down and asked for another.

"He goes on a bit, but after five years we're used to him." A playful smile spread across Sage's face as she refilled the glass and set it in front of him.

Peter spoke from the other end of the bar. "We were just telling Jessie and Neal about the Outpost. They went there for the first time this morning."

"Ah, and what are your impressions of our modest attempt at being upscale?"

"Overwhelmed, wouldn't you say Neal?"

"Yeah, I'd add unexpected, too."

Darling's eyes slid to Sage and squinted. She ducked his glance by bending into the bowels of the bar.

"You didn't say anything, did you." When she didn't respond, Darling turned back to the occupants at the bar and continued. "She loves to listen to the reactions of guests who go to the Outpost unprepared, without any preconceived ideas. Does it on purpose. Peter, you have to watch this lady of yours, she's getting a little strange."

Peter laughed and took a sip of his beer. Sage reappeared, face flushed. Jessie couldn't tell if she blushed from having her head down or if she was embarrassed.

"James, if you weren't so tired, I'd call you a pest. Maybe I'll call you one anyway."

"Now, now. Getting touchy won't change the facts."

Sage grabbed her bar towel and stomped out the door.

Darling sighed, "Oh, Peter, I think I may have overstepped my bounds." His hands went to his eyes and began rubbing; before he finished, he'd worked over his entire face.

"Don't be silly. She's embarrassed at being caught out. She'll get over it. Jessie and Neal enjoyed their experience, I think," they both nodded at Peter's comment, "and have friends who are still in Andre's clutches."

"Are you here to buy some pieces?"

"Not us, but a friend of ours is considering something for himself," said Neal. He nodded to Peter's suggestion of another beer.

"Huh . . . how did you hear about it?"

"He said someone in the States told him. He's down here visiting and convinced us we had to come."

"You live here then? Where?"

Neal briefly told him their cruising history and future plans and that they were presently anchored in Zihuatanejo.

"Zhuat, what a lovely place."

"We think so. It's convenient to everything we need, plus the market's great," said Jessie.

The door next to the bar opened and Sage emerged, carrying a plate of food. It banged as she set it on the bar in front of Darling and when she turned to leave, he caught her arm. "Will it do any good if I apologize?"

"No, you're incorrigible. And you," she nodded at Peter, "you're just as bad." She couldn't hide the smile as she eased into a turn and disappeared back through the door.

Darling turned his attention to the plate in front of him and picked up the fork.

Peter said from behind the bar, "It is wonderful."

Everyone looked at him, no one said a word.

He shuffled and repeated. "The market in Zihuatanejo, it is wonderful. If Iguala wasn't so good, we'd be tempted sometimes to head down there. They get strawberries and such because of the big American contingent that lives and vacations there."

Darling swallowed, then said, "Here I thought you were saying it was wonderful that Sage thought us incorrigible." He loaded his fork with more food. "Did Andre show you his antiquities?" He snapped the food off the fork as if he hadn't eaten for some time.

"We looked through the catalogue and didn't see any, but he had quite a few things in there not on display. Does he keep it all in that building?" Jessie took a swallow of beer.

When they had left Sonny and Sonia at the gallery, Neal remembered watching his friends disappear behind the swinging door from which Andre first emerged.

"He has pieces in vaults in the back." Peter laughed as if he thought of something. "As James suggested, Andre has a mysterious pipeline to artifacts. Course, now he's not allowed to sell them, but we know he does. I shouldn't think he'd put them into a catalogue and I'd be surprised if he kept items like that on the premises. We've never heard of him being bothered for selling them, but that might have something to do with his partner."

"You better believe it has everything to do with his partner. If you're a twig on the right branch of the Palacios family, you can move mountains. You want a gallery and you want it here, you send someone like Andre and boom . . . gallery. You ever ask Andre where he's from?"

Peter shook his head. "I thought I heard he was from Spain."

"Ask him sometime. I bet he'll say, 'Not from here.' Just ask him." The fork off-loaded again.

Peter left Darling to his food and said in his quiet, patient voice, "As I alluded to earlier, Andre circulates in that rarefied air that surrounds the people who make a place like the Outpost a success. His success makes people suspicious. We don't know him well, but he likes our food, so we see him here occasionally, and although we socialize with many of the residents from the hills, we don't often get an invitation to his gatherings. I don't think that means there's anything particularly sinister about him."

A burst of sound interrupted Darling's response to Peter's summary and Sonny blew around the corner like a gust of wind. "Oh, hello. Neal, Jessie, can I see you a minute? We won't be long."

"Sure." Neal left his bottle on the bar with promises of returning, Jessie followed suit. Sonny had disappeared again before they stepped away from the bar.

They found him outside, body bent in the car they had all abandoned. Sonia leaned over him, watching. She looked up at Jessie and Neal as they approached.

"Tomy says he can fix it. It won't be done for a couple of days, but what good news, huh?"

"Yeah, that's great." Neal walked around the car to check for any further damage. His eye caught movement on the verandah at the corner of the house. James Darling embraced Sage and then took both her hands and said something that made her laugh. As he walked away, he waved at the group by the car and disappeared down the trail. Neal waved back and completed his turn around the car just as Sonny emerged.

"It doesn't look any worse for wear, does it?" Sonny slammed the front door and stepped back for a better overall look.

"Sonny kept thinking that even if we got it back, it'd be so banged up that the guy in Zihuatanejo wouldn't want it back. Personally, coming from L.A., I thought for sure it would be stripped of everything not riveted on. I'm surprised. It doesn't even look like it spent time in a war zone. Maybe the marauders took the night off." Sonia caressed the hood with her hand, then clapped to get rid of the dust.

"You're a lucky man, my friend. If Tomy can get it to sound as good as it looks, you may get some of your money back." Neal gave Sonny a comradely slap on the back and laughed.

"So tell us, did you buy something?" Jessie slammed the back door, eyed the car one last time, then turned her attention to Sonny.

Sonia groaned. "Oh, don't get him started. I'll tell you what, my love. Buy these good people a beer and tell them all about it while I grab that nap I wanted." She reached up and they exchanged a long, lingering kiss. Her retreating step held a light bounce, and as she disappeared into the house, she tossed her blond hair over her shoulder and threw Sonny a seductive glance.

Transfixed, Sonny sighed and said, "Yeah." As soon as the door closed, he snapped out of his trance and turned to his friends. "You up for a party tonight?"

14

After Sonia left them, the three friends celebrated the car's recovery and Sonny's new art treasures by heading to the bar at Alta Linda for a round of Dos Equis. Sonny's collection now included a jaguar statue in full stride, covered in tiny, colorful, glass beads; an artist's interpretation of Quetzalcoatl, an important mythical figure in Mexican and Central American legends, done in oil on canvas; and a small, chipped jade figurine of a jaguar man. Andre volunteered to take care of shipping arrangements for the beaded jaguar and the oil painting, but the four-and-half-inch chipped jade figurine was different. That would have to be secretly tucked away in Sonny's things and carried back personally.

Once he explained it all and gave them a peek at the figurine, there was no secret about the reason for the party invitations. Their friend had just contributed a great deal to Andre's retirement fund. After initial objections, Sonny had finally persuaded them to go, but even with his reassurances, Jessie believed the dress code would surpass anything she carried in her dusty backpack.

Hours later and decked out in her newly washed and pressed sightseeing dress, she knew she had been right. The throb of mingling party guests surrounded her in a sea of sequins, silk and feathers. It didn't help that on one side of her, Sonia looked regal in a black and gold outfit miraculously unearthed somehow by Sonny. Or that he stood on the other side of her, looking tantalizingly wealthy in his wonder-suit from the Ziploc bag.

More in keeping with her own appearance, Neal looked remarkably confident in his clean shorts and cotton shirt. Any semblance of party attire he owned went with the stolen backpack. Something he said caused Sonny to shake with laughter and when that tapered off, Sonia quietly excused herself and disappeared toward the bathroom.

Jessie watched her leave, curious as to why all eyes, except Sonny's, had followed the blond all evening. It seemed something had rocked the passionate liaison, and Jessie wondered what it was.

Neal held up his empty glass and when he noticed Jessie sip the last of her drink, he volunteered to get refills at the bar.

Standing alone with Sonny, Jessie caught a glance from another guest who then turned and tucked into a tight huddle with a small group of other guests. That had been going on all night, too. She and her companions had obviously sparked interest. Andre had set up three sedately lit rooms for the evening, and wherever they wandered, smiles and nods had met them. They only had to look lost and someone came to their aid.

Voices rumbled in an even din, broken up frequently by laughter and the clink of glasses. Chords from strings, horns and piano floated above it all. It sounded so immediate that Jessie had found herself looking for the musicians until she learned it was a recording. The scent of expensive perfume, elegant attire and sculpted hors d'oeuvres on crystal platters made this one of the classier parties she had ever attended.

While she mused about her social experiences, another guest joined her and Sonny for a brief chat.

Once he'd gone, Sonny said, "That guy keeps staring at me. Has something come loose; do I look okay?" He looked down to check that everything was properly zipped, then glanced across the more than three dozen people to the other side of the room.

"Your appearance is utterly riveting, Sonny. He's probably just curious. Where is this person?" Jessie panned the room of guests. The constant motion of people standing, sitting and walking made her wonder how Sonny could know if one particular person was paying too much attention.

"His attention isn't from curiosity. There's a storm brewing on that face. He's across the room near the door. The guy in the royal blue blazer." Sonny pointed with his glass to show her where to look. "I've never seen him before, but he sure looks over here like he knows me."

"Yeah, okay, I see him. Maybe you remind him of someone. So anyway, now that Sonia's off to the ladies, what gives?"

Neal's head appeared and disappeared behind the crowd at the bar and Sonia remained out of sight. Before anyone came back, Jessie wanted to know what had chilled the other couple's amorous behavior.

"What do you mean?"

"You couldn't keep your hands off each other just a few short hours ago and now you're like aliens. You have to admit there's been a change."

"My lady, you are a good friend, but that's territory in which you have no claim."

"I know it's none of my business, but I admit I'm curious. Sonia's a part of the community we live in, just reassure me we won't regret this brief interlude."

Jessie got jostled and she turned toward the man who begged her pardon with a big, warm grin before moving on.

Sonny lingered over a pull at his drink, then raised his glass to a pretty brunette who had flashed him a smile. When his glance shot back across the room, he said, "It's no big deal. Late this afternoon we spent an hour or so in Tampu and she saw a man who reminded her of Hal. It brought her up short and blew all the fairy dust away. That party is over. Satisfied?"

He said it so crisply it felt like a spray of ice water.

"Sonny, I . . . ."

He interrupted her, "Like I said, it's no big deal." His attention had never wavered away from the other side of the room. "That gentleman is beginning to piss me off. What's your game, buddy?" he said under his breath.

The usually bright, animated face of her friend had turned stony and hard. Its darkness disturbed Jessie and she jumped as something cold brushed her arm. Neal had returned with drinks.

"Do it again, and I'm coming over to find out."

Neal said to his friend's comment, "Find out what?"

Sonny seemingly didn't hear the question and turned to speak to a group standing a few feet away. Jessie answered instead. "Sonny says that guy over by the door in the royal blue blazer seems angry or upset with him for some reason. He keeps glaring over here."

Neal easily found him. His wild gestures threw heat into the hyper conversation he was having with another guest. Without a pause, he pointed, then sneered in Sonny's direction.

"He's a local from the *pueblo,*" said Sonny when he turned back to his friends. "He's doing it again. See what I mean?" Sonny's glare sent a challenge to the man, provoking him. "Excuse me, I'll talk to you later."

Sonny's relaxed, casual party manner changed to one of rigid intensity as he pressed his way through the crowd toward the blue blazer.

"What's that all about?"

"I don't know really. Sonny just noticed him . . . ." She hesitated over the next few words.

"What?"

"Well, I think I just made him mad, but I'm not sure."

"He's pissed off at the guy across the room."

"No, before that."

"Why would he be mad at you?"

She could hear the, I don't blame him, Jessica, it's none of your business, in response to the answer she was about to give him. "I asked what happened between him and Sonia, and he got very sullen."

"I don't blame him, Jess, it's none of your business."

Well, she had *almost* known word for word. "You know, there are times when I think we've been together too long." She took a sip from her drink. "You weren't at least curious as to what happened?"

"Not especially. It wasn't going anywhere anyway, so why get worked up about it. And if you threw in that 'We've been together too long' because you knew I'd tell you it was none of your business, why did you bring it up?"

Loud voices interrupted their debate. An area surrounding Sonny and Blue Blazer cleared when the two men stood in a face-off. Jessie looked around and spotted Andre moving quickly toward the fray. Amid finger jabbing and shouts, their host wedged in between the two men, draped his arms over their shoulders and guided them through a door to a secluded verandah.

Neal grabbed Jessie's hand and led her toward the argument. "Let's get a little closer. That discussion sounds uncomfortably serious," he said.

"What could it be about? What could Sonny have done to get that guy so worked up?"

"What did Sonny do today? He bought some art and reclaimed a broken down car. Which would be the more likely reason?"

Once the three men disappeared outside, the party-goers carried on, but with occasional glances at the verandah. Jessie and Neal threaded their way toward the door.

When the crowd pushed her close to Neal's ear, she said, "Sonny didn't just buy art, he bought an artifact, too. Maybe this guy doesn't like them leaving the country."

"Maybe."

Jessie collected Sonia with a glance when she emerged from the ladies' room, and she worked her way toward them, arriving at the verandah door at the same time.

"Boy, there's quite a line for the head. Sorry it took so long."

Her long, blond hair was tied in a chignon, with soft wisps trailing down her neck. The style agreed with the loose fitting top and long, billowing trousers swirled with black and gold. More than the line caused the delay; her makeup looked fresh and perfectly applied. Sonia glanced around as if looking for someone until she caught Neal gazing out to the verandah.

Jessie told her before she asked. "We aren't sure what's going on, but Sonny was involved in a rather loud discussion about something. Andre took them outside."

The three of them fixed their attention on the verandah.

Under a canopy of foliage, the discussion continued, close and intense, but muffled. The glow from inside reached out through the doors and windows, brushing golden highlights onto the branches and the three men. Andre's glance volleyed an appeal first to Blue Blazer, then to Sonny. He spoke for several seconds.

Suddenly, Blue Blazer shouted and pointed a threatening finger at his host, then at Sonny. Andre's efforts to calm the man failed, and in his increasing irritation, Blue Blazer grabbed, then shoved the

Outpost proprietor's arm. He loudly rebuked the other two before piercing Sonny with a glare. A second later, he disappeared into the night by way of the verandah steps.

Andre and Sonny stared after him. They spoke a few quiet words, then Andre grasped his guest's shoulder in reassurance, turned, and strode toward the door. With a smile at the trio hovering around the door, he entered and rejoined his other guests.

The three of them hesitated only a moment before spilling out through the door. Jessie noticed Sonia slow and fall behind. Neal took the lead and reached Sonny first.

"Making friends with the locals?"

Sonny hiccuped a laugh. "Yeah," he said and stared at the dark, vacant steps.

"Anything you care to talk about?" Neal leaned on the verandah railing and looked out at the night.

"Ah . . . ." Sonny exhaled and let the sigh hang in the air. He looked at Sonia and then joined Neal's gaze into the darkness.

Jessie felt a tug and turned to see Sonia cock her head back toward the room. She looked back at Sonny and Neal at the railing and decided as much as she wanted to stay, Sonia might be right. The women walked back inside. As Jessie stepped through the door, she noticed Sonny had begun talking.

"I know that Sonny would rather talk to Neal without me there," said Sonia. "I hope you don't mind if I pulled you along. I just didn't want to come back in here alone. I'm sure Neal will tell you what it's all about. Do you mind?"

Jessie did mind, but interrupting the discussion now might destroy the mood, so she muzzled her comments. "No, I don't mind. Do you know what it might be about?"

Sonia's response suggested she hadn't heard. "I've been a real ditz."

A less crowded area in the corner drew Sonia, and she beckened Jessie to follow. They could talk and still watch the two men on the verandah.

"Why?"

"I shouldn't be here, I shouldn't have come. Maybe you know it already, but if not, take it from me—adultery is so much easier to commit than I thought it would be." Her emotions played out through her fingers and hands. They laced together, then pulled apart, then came together again. "I'm not sure if I'll be able to act like nothing happened. I mean, to feel so guilty that I see a resemblance to Hal in a man I see whizzing past in a car in this godforsaken place . . . what will I do . . . what will Hal do? I know he's going to find out."

Nothing about what Sonny will do.

Sonia fidgeted and continued to wring her hands. Jessie sorted through a string of responses, trying to find one that would stop the confession. In the end she waited too long. Sonia laid out the entire lamentable story of her attraction and subsequent relationship with Sonny as if Jessie had donned a priest's stole.

"Jessie, I know I've brought this on myself, but my life has just been such a jumble. Hal is so different when he's on the boat. I don't like him. I've tried to tell him he's changed, but he won't listen to me." Her glance shot out the window, she sighed, pressed her lips together, then swallowed. "I'd like to head back to Alta Linda. Would you consider going back with me?"

Jessie chewed her upper lip as she thought back to her desire to leave just before all this happened. She knew Sonia wanted company, but Jessie didn't want to leave with events still unfolding.

"I know this is asking a lot and I feel a total idiot, but I could use some company."

Jessie's eyes left Sonia's face and toured the clenched fists that hung at the blond's sides before settling on the conversation taking place on the verandah. The two men laughed. She groaned to herself, but out loud she said, "Okay, I'll tell Neal."

"Thanks, Jessie, I'm really grateful." Sonia lifted her fists and knocked her knuckles together as if her departure couldn't be soon enough.

She followed Jessie to the door, but hung back while Jessie crossed the verandah to talk to Neal. The two men erupted into laughter again.

Neal must have heard her approach because he turned and raised his arm to tuck her in close.

"I know it's still early, but Sonia and I think we'll head back to Alta Linda. I wanted to let you know. Hope I didn't interrupt anything."

Sonny pulled one of her hands up to his lips and kissed it lightly. "Never." He winked and gave her hand back. "So you think your curiosity riled this mongrel, eh?"

Jessie felt the heat of a blush and gave Neal a small push. "You ratted on me."

"Serves you right for saying we've been together too long. I'm ready to call it a night, too." He turned his gaze on his friend. "I suppose it's presumptuous to ask if you're ready?"

Sonny grinned and straightened his back. "It's early and there's still a room full of people."

"Well, we'll leave you to it. You'll take care and let Andre get you back to Alta Linda?"

"I know it's useless to tell you the best part of the night is still to come. And yes, I promise. Excuse me a sec, I want to talk to Sonia before you leave."

Neal guided Jessie to the rail where they looked out into the night. With the light streaming out from behind them, all they saw was a wall of acacias, ferns and banana palms reflecting the muted light back to them. She rested her head against his as his hand softly caressed her arm. When Sonny was out of earshot, Jessie said, "Everything must be all right, huh?"

"I don't know if it is or not. I'll tell you what he said later, but so you don't bust any buttons, you were right – the man objects to Sonny taking away a jade jaguar man."

* * *

Neal sat next to the driver. Their headlights washed the green from the foliage that whipped out of the darkness and smacked against the car. The right front tire dropped with a sickening bounce into a pothole that jarred him through the seat. Scraping metal brought back the uneasy memories of the pothole on the notorious road from Zihuatanejo. With the impact, Jessie and Sonia's quiet discussion in the back seat stopped. They didn't speak again until the headlights flooded the clearing and the big wooden door at Alta Linda.

The driver jumped out the instant the car stopped and whipped open the back door to let the women out. Neal pushed at the passenger door. Its dry hinges groaned and squealed, but finally opened wide enough to let him out into the cool night. Just as he slammed it shut, the driver laughed and called something to him that he didn't understand, then jumped back into the car with a wave and gunned it into reverse. With a growl from the transmission, the young man forced it to change gears. The tires spun, levitating a curtain of dust as the car lurched forward to the track that led to the main road, its taillights blinking with each tap of the brake.

"Man, that boy was in a hurry. We must have kept him from his lady or something. I know Andre was trying to be nice by getting us a ride back, but when we hit that bump I almost wished we had walked."

Sonia's comment brought a laugh as the three opened the big, wooden door and stepped inside. She continued, "How about a drink before we turn in? It looks like there's still light on back there. I'll buy."

Neal caught Jessie's eye, but before he could transmit no, they heard a noise behind them. They turned and saw Angel emerge and stop. It looked to Neal as if their presence startled him.

"Hi, Angel, is it too late to get something to drink at the bar?" Sonia took a couple of steps toward him.

"No, todavía está abierto," he cast his glance down and scurried through the arch at the opposite end of the room and headed toward the kitchen.

"What's with him?" Sonia watched his back and then turned back to Jessie and Neal. "What do you say?"

"Yeah . . . sure . . . why not. But it'll be a quick one, I'm really beat," said Jessie.

The two women walked together toward the lounge. Neal could have begged off, but curiosity lured him to follow.

* * *

After the laughter subsided, Jessie said, "I think you would have made a great makeup model. But that's not an unusual story for L.A., I guess. Have you ever found out where the guy went?"

"No, he took off with everything," said Sonia. "We were all so naive. I was the only model, but he left a whole staff with bills to pay. You know the kind of thing, 'Keep track of your expenses, and when we get up and running, we'll reimburse you.' Yeah, right. We all thought we'd latched onto to the tail of a comet, but as it turned out, it flashed then fizzled like a sparkler. The product line was good and he had collected good people, all the right stuff to get the company off the ground. All, that is, except enough money. Oh, well, as you say, just another story in L.A. "

"At least you can laugh about it now," said Neal.

Jessie watched the last guest exit through the wide arch, leaving only the three of them at the bar. Mareya came and went. She seemed to be involved in a dozen different things, one of which was tending the bar. Sage and Peter made no appearance.

"Hal took the sting away. He was on the board of the company my parents worked for. One of the many boards he's on. I met him at a company picnic, if you can believe it. He was older, secure and very confident, and there he was, enjoying the Arizona sunshine, and I, with my tail between my legs, was back home with Mom and Dad."

"Love at first sight?"

"Well, almost. A little L.A. shine shows up when you're in a small town in the desert. He's always said I stuck out like a diamond on a string of rocks. Even with my experiences in the big city, he blew me away." She looked at her empty glass and fell silent.

Jessie took the last swallow from her glass, and the desire to stretch out and sleep made her push the glass away.

Neal mimicked her and said, "Thanks for the drink and conversation, Sonia, but bed is calling me."

"Yeah, me too, Sonia. Thanks." Jessie slid from the stool, but stopped as Sonia spoke.

"Sonny told me to put his things just inside the door of our room, and he'd collect them when he got back. He said he wouldn't be joining me. I've been thinking maybe I should get the bus back to Zihuatanejo instead of going on with you to Mexico City."

Jessie looked at Neal, then resettled onto the stool. She felt him move in more closely, put his arm suggestively around her waist and rest his hand on her thigh. Not only was he letting her know he wanted to call it a night, but it was his way of warning her to move ahead with caution.

"Sonia, that's up to you. I think I speak for Neal, too. We have no objections to your going on with us. I don't mean to minimize what's happened, but it's a complication that affects you and Sonny, not us. If you don't want to go back, I'm sure it will be fine. We'll work something out."

"Sonny's pretty resilient," said Neal.

"He didn't sound it earlier."

Jessie said, "Well, you did slam his fingers in the door. But it's not like you've been seeing each other for long, and realistically, how far could it have gone?" Out of the corner of her eye, she saw Neal arch his eyebrow. She had stolen his line.

"I suppose, but I feel awful. It's like I've stepped in quicksand, the harder I try to get out, the worse it gets."

Mareya pushed through the door, and swept the room with a glance.

"Mareya, can I have a drink to take to my room?"

"Of course, how about you two?" She nodded toward Jessie and Neal, who shook their heads no. As she began pouring Sonia's drink, she said, "I almost forgot. Peter asked me to tell you that the *collectivo* will be here at 6:30 a.m. That will get you to the Mexico City bus in plenty of time."

"Thanks, Mareya. Could someone make sure we're awake say . . . at six?" Jessie looked at the other two and got less than enthusiastic nods of approval.

"No problem. Has Angel been through here recently?"

"We saw him a while ago, Mareya, when we first came in. He headed toward the kitchen like he had a fire under him." Sonia picked up her drink and slid off the stool.

"Oh, I think I've seen him since then. The *bribón* has been appearing and disappearing like a ghost tonight. That usually happens when he and his compadres have thought of something more interesting to do. I'm afraid we might soon lose him to the teenage years." She laughed and waved good night as she bustled back out the door.

"Thanks for listening," said Sonia. "I'll sleep on my plans. I know that Eric will need some moral support tomorrow and he's been really good to me, even with all that's happened to him. Over the last couple of days, I confess thoughts of him and Jennifer have been pushed aside and that doesn't help my mood."

Jessie had to admit that the weight of carrying the camera had lessened since they left Zihuatanejo. Sonia's mention of Eric and the reason for their trek to Mexico City underscored her feeling of fatigue. Six in the morning sounded brutal. They walked together toward their rooms, quiet with their own thoughts. At the junction they stopped. Sonia and Sonny's room was at one end of the corridor, Neal and Jessie's more than half way down the corridor in the opposite direction.

Sonia said, "Well, good night, see you in the morning." She turned and drifted down toward her room.

"Good night, Sonia." Jessie watched her retreating back and leaned against Neal when his arm went over her shoulder. "What a mess."

"Theirs, not ours." He kissed her hair, then guided her to their door and opened it.

Neal's hand lingered on her shoulder as she brushed passed him into their darkened room. She stopped just inside and turned into him. The door closed quietly and his arms encircled her. His hands caressed her back down to her buttocks and then pulled her close to him. He was already hard, and when she pushed against him, he moaned. Their lips and tongues met with a hunger that left them breathless. They separated, but only inches, as they helped each other undress. Naked, they felt the freedom of a full body press, skin against skin.

Jessie's pulse raced. A tingle spread through the core of her body as Neal pushed away and bent to brush his lips and tongue across her nipples. Her feet left the floor, and she found herself cradled in his arms as he carried her to the bed. Among the pines in the valley of Paradise, they savored its beauty by lavishing each other with the passion of lovers.

* * *

Neal groped forward toward the light, but it never got closer. He saw his hand reach out when a loud noise from behind him stopped it midair. He tried to turn toward the noise but felt paralyzed. The hair on the back of his neck prickled as he felt a presence move in behind him. The struggle to turn and face the assailant became frantic as the noise got louder. With one last monumental effort, he forced himself to move and burst into consciousness . . . .

He lay on his stomach, Jessie's head on his back. A soft but insistent rapping at the door continued.

"Neal, Jessie, wake up." In consideration of the other guests, the caller used a strained whisper, but it sounded urgent.

"God, we must have overslept. Jessie, c'mon." Neal pushed himself up with his arms and Jessie rolled off his back. She instantly awoke. "Yeah, it's okay, Sage, we're awake. Thanks."

"Neal, please come quickly. It's Sonia; something has happened."

The words took a second to process, but when they hit their mark, his feet found the floor. He made for the door and opened it slightly. "What's happened?"

"Someone's gotten into Sonny and Sonia's room. She's . . . well . . . she's been beaten up; she's unconscious. We've sent for James."

His thoughts raced with confusion, and from somewhere he heard his voice, "Jesus. Thanks, Sage. We'll get some clothes on and be right there."

15

Neal clutched Jessie's hand and worked his way through the crowd forming at the end of the corridor. He saw Mareya talking with a guest and when she noticed their approach, she excused herself and waved them through. Once they got to Sonia's door, the innkeeper eased it open and the three of them stepped inside.

The first thing to impress Neal was the smell of blood, then the flicker of a flame, the only light in the room. A shape ghosted its way toward them and from the size, he knew it was Sage.

"Oh, Neal, Jessie, we're so sorry."

"How is she?" said Jessie.

The four moved over to the bed and huddled at the foot. A candle burned on the nightstand and Neal could see Sonia's shape under the light blanket. In the dimness, he distinguished only a dark shape on the pillow. Other dark patches splattered the white sheets.

"I don't know. Peter's gone to meet James. They should be here soon," said Sage in a whisper.

Neal said, "Do you know what happened?"

"No," said Sage. "The guests in the room next door heard noises coming from here, enough to wake them up, and they came to complain. The walls in this place aren't thin . . . I knew it was Sonny and Sonia's room and with the party and all, I just thought they were . . . well, you know. Even so, I was surprised that the sound went through the walls, but with the complaint, I had to come and tell them to tone it down. I knocked and got no answer, so I knocked again. When I still didn't hear anything, I tried the door. It was unlocked, so I just gave it a little push and looked inside. It was so dark, I couldn't see anything. At first I figured that whatever they had been doing was now done and they had fallen asleep."

Sage paused and took a big breath as she folded the bloody gauze compress in her hand. Mareya patted her on the forearm, obviously Mareya knew what came next.

"It was the smell that made me stop. I knew that it was blood. I just stood there for what felt like minutes before I finally stepped through the door. The whole time I walked to the bed, I was working on an excuse for intruding on them. Even when I got there, I couldn't really see anything, so I called out and then shook the leg of the first person I felt. Nothing happened. Well, I can tell you, my heart was in my mouth. I shook the leg again, and when I still didn't get any response, I ran to the switch and turned on the light. She was just lying there. Blood all over her face and on the sheets. I have to admit that I immediately thought Sonny had done this, but then Mareya said he didn't come back with you. Whoever did it must have been looking for something, the place is a mess."

Mareya linked arms with her partner and said, "She naturally got Peter, then me. We came back with the first aid kit but decided we really needed James, so Peter went to call him and Sage went to get you. As you can see, news has spread quickly to the other guests."

"She's been unconscious the whole time. There's a cut near her eye and we've at least stopped the bleeding," said Sage. "I'm not sure what else to do until James gets here. This is all so frightening. We don't have super locks on the doors, but then, we've never had the need for them."

Mareya tightened her clutch on Sage's arm and the two women stared at their battered guest.

Neal broke away from the group and with his eyes more adjusted to the candlelight, he could see the chaos that Sage had referred to. "Have you had a look around, anything missing?"

"We haven't even looked," said Mareya.

Neal was about to go through the things sitting on a small table, when the door opened and two shadows entered the room. One tall, one short.

"A little bit of light please, Peter. I'll need to see what I'm doing. Sage, if you're up to it, I could use your help, but it would be best for me and for the lady if everyone else waited outside. We'll let you know how she is just as soon as we can."

The medic had arrived.

* * *

Sonny returned from the party shortly after James Darling took charge. When Neal told him what had happened, the fatigue from a night of socializing disappeared and he set a nervous pace along the corridor, anticipating further news. Other guests, weary from waiting, finally drifted back to bed, leaving the three friends, Peter and Mareya to keep a vigil.

The five of them turned when Sonia's door finally opened and the medic slipped out. He rubbed at his eyes, then ran his hand across his face. His hair still looked as though it had been arranged by a fan and to Neal, it seemed that James Darling hadn't yet changed the rumpled clothing they had seen him wearing earlier.

Mareya said quietly, "Well?" She pressed the fingers of one hand across her lips.

Darling sighed and explained. "Apart from a few strays, the contusions and small lacerations are concentrated on the head. Fortunately, only three stitches were needed, but they're on her face, near her right eyebrow. That area will be pretty bruised for a while."

Mareya had another question, "Any idea who would do this?"

"Sage did look around. Her wallet is there, along with her driver's license and a couple of credit cards, but whatever cash she had is gone. Don't know if anything else is missing."

"This seems more serious than someone after a few pesos," said Peter so quietly that it seemed he was speculating only to himself.

Darling heard and responded. "You know as well as I do that the increase in buyers coming in from all over has caused a few break-ins and thefts," the medic turned to the three guests, "not of art, you understand, but of the stuff these people bring with them . . . you know, cameras, laptops, jewelry. I've seen domestic violence this bad here, but I have to say, in the five years of service to God and country, no outsider has been attacked this viciously; I guess it was just a matter of time. I'll have to report this, but we haven't much in the way of police, so I wouldn't expect much action. Don't misunderstand me, this is serious and it worries me." James Darling put his hands in the pockets of his rumpled suit. The lines in his face etched deeper with concern and lack of sleep.

"Christ," said Sonny quietly, then glanced toward his room. Alta Linda wasn't meant to be brightly lit at night, so his glance didn't reach the door. The corridor fell away to darkness. "I made some art purchases today that didn't sit well with a couple of the residents. I didn't take their threats that seriously, but maybe I was wrong not to."

Neal said, "Sonny, Andre told you it wasn't serious, that he could deal with it."

"I guess he was wrong. Our stuff's been thrown all over the room; someone was looking for something. That's not random and the guy did threaten me. Not necessarily in so many words, but he went out of his way to explain cultural integrity and historical value, and that he despised Americans for stealing their land and now their heritage."

"Ah . . . you bought an artifact," said James, nodding his head. His weary stare dropped to the floor where the toe of his tattered tennis shoe tapped at a ball of dust on the brown ceramic tile. The gesture suggested his disappointment at learning another compatriot had violated a moral code of his.

Sonny's eyes followed the tennis shoe. He flexed the muscles in his face and said quietly, "Yes."

"Well, I shouldn't worry too much. It's not moral indignation that brought someone from here to do this, especially to a *gringa*. Don't get me wrong. There are those in this *pueblo* who do resent these pieces of history making off to all parts of the world, but they wouldn't resort to this level of violence. No, I think this comes from somewhere else." He brought his head up and looked at the group in front of him. "But to a more important issue: Sonia's condition. I've cleaned her up and done as much as I can, but if she doesn't regain consciousness soon, I have less than adequate facilities here to treat her."

"I don't understand," said Jessie.

"I suggest we get her to Mexico City. Mareya, Peter, if it's all right with you, I'd like to use your phone to call the university. Just in case we need it, I want to clear a way for her."

"Of course," Mareya turned to lead him away, then paused and rested a weary expression on her three guests. "I'm so sorry this has happened. With your experience on the road, it shames me to know that people from my country can do this."

Jessie's hand reached out and touched the innkeeper's shoulder. Mareya gave a slight nod then turned to lead James Darling away.

Sonny paced to the end of the corridor and back, then raked a hand through his hair, pursed his lips and walked again.

Jessie leaned against the wall, watching Sonny pace. "Why would James feel so sure this doesn't have something to do with resentment? It almost sounded like he had an idea of why it happened."

The silence stretched and then, as if on cue, the three friends turned their gaze on Peter. He cleared his throat, hoisted his huge frame and said, "It could be a while. I'll go start a fire and make us some coffee."

* * *

The wood snapped and flung sparks as it burned. The orange glow highlighted the faces of those circled around it, staring, mesmerized by the fire's dance. Jessie cupped her head in her hands; Neal and Sonny sat in the big overstuffed chairs behind her. Peter had built the fire, brought coffee, then disappeared. They all turned when they heard Darling's voice lift above the fire's crackle.

He crossed the lounge and flopped into a chair. In a big sweeping motion, one leg crossed the other and he began pulling at the hair near his temple. "Her blood pressure and breathing are normal, plus there's no sign of shock yet, and her heart beat is steady. That's all good news, but she shows no sign of regaining consciousness and I don't like that. Mexico City says to wait another hour."

"Sage said she'd bring more coffee, but there's a little more in here." Jessie lifted the pot, but he declined. In the silence that followed, Jessie couldn't resist voicing her earlier curiosity. "James, what did you mean when you said before that you didn't think this was resentment, but something else?"

He shifted his position and settled his ankle on his knee, seemingly to debate his answer. "Some residents don't want the area to change. If it gets like Taxco or some of the other small *pueblos* that have hordes of tourists all year, then they will lose their privacy. That's something many of these people can't afford, if you know what I mean." James rubbed his eyes and stifled a yawn.

"No . . . I don't," said Jessie.

His foot bounced as he began to elaborate. "Well, as you probably know, there's a real mix of people that live in the hills surrounding this *pueblo*. There are wealthy Mexicans, of course, well-connected and belonging to the powerful political parties. Then you have the artists and eccentrics who have recently moved in from all over because of the peace and quiet. And by recently, I'd say the last twelve, fifteen years. Then you have this other element, the ones who for decades have found sanctuary here from the world. Their minions circulate to make sure that their fortresses stay secure. An increase in the *pueblo's* popularity is like hot water on bare wood. It ruffles and raises the grain. To keep things smooth, you sand it down now and then. Maybe they think it's time to do a bit of sanding."

Sage joined the group with a tray of coffee and caught the last part of the missionary-medic's rundown on the local social dynamics. Once she settled the tray, her hands went to her hips and she inflated her chest to make full use of her towering height. "James Darling, you're spreading that conspiracy theory of yours again and I'll not have it in my house. These people have enough to think about without adding that to it."

"Sage, I know it's true."

"You've said that before . . . if you know it's true, tell me how you know?"

"I just know, that's all. Nobody says anything, but because of who and what I am, I get into people's homes, I notice things."

"What you see is a struggling *pueblo* that would like to carry on without hysterical people spreading ridiculous rumors of *banditos* . . . or what is it this week, the mafia? . . . hiding in the hills. This is the work of some misguided crazy, not part of an elaborate scheme. That thinking is bad for the reputation of the *pueblo* and bad for business. I've told you before, we don't believe it and I don't want you using my house to spread it . . . not tonight."

Jessie turned her attention to the fire. She glanced at Neal, but his attention stayed on the dancing flames. The exchange charged the room with discomfort. Darling rested his elbows on the arms of the overstuffed chair and stared into the fire as he created a bridge with his fingers. He flicked a glance at Jessie, twitched both eyebrows up and tapped his fingers together. With a smile he pushed himself out of his chair and glided toward Sage.

"I seem to be falling out of your good graces today, Sage. You know I'm rambling. I open my mouth and it comes out. It's just that it's easier to blame some unseen, elusive evil than to think someone from our own Tampu, the people among whom we live, could do something like this." He faced her, hands in his pockets.

Sage's brow furrowed and her hands came off her hips. "That was a very offhand apology, but under the circumstances I'll accept it. We've had this discussion before, and you know how I feel about it." She bent and began to pour coffee.

Noise from beyond the lounge drew everyone's attention. Andre emerged through the dark arch like a spirit.

"I've just heard," he said, crossing the room toward Sonny, who stood to face the newcomer. "I'm horrified that something like this has happened here. Is there any way I can be of assistance?" Neat, still in his light, linen suit from the party, Andre looked as immaculate as James Darling looked sloppy. He addressed his comments first to Sonny then to Sage.

Darling stretched his pose and stood statue still while he stared at the new arrival, his hands stuffed in his pockets. "We need transport for Ms. Sieverson to Mexico City."

Andre's attention turned to the rumpled man. Even in the dimly lit room, Jessie saw the proprietor of the Outpost sweep his eyes dismissively over the other man's appearance before he spoke. "I beg your pardon?"

"We need to get her to Mexico City, quickly. If you really want to help, maybe you could arrange that."

Andre clasped his hands in front of him and held James in his gaze. Seconds passed. "Of course, *Señor* Darling. *Señora* Weaver, if you could show me to your phone?"

Sage looked at Darling, then at Andre. "Ahh . . . yes, it's this way." They disappeared through the door by the bar.

When the door swung shut behind them, Darling laughed and slumped. "I think we just got a break."

"What do you mean?" Jessie heard Sonny's suspicion in the tone of his question. "I thought you said the hospital wanted you to wait an hour."

"My choices were either to keep her here, quiet, warm and comfortable, or put her into a truck and bounce her across the mountains to Mexico City. With one I risked that she might not improve or possibly get worse, with the other she wouldn't have a chance. I don't think it takes a medical degree to know which one of those options would be better for her."

"That may be so, but you don't have the right to make that decision. Without speaking to us, you couldn't know all the options open to you. If your reluctance to act on the urgency of her condition results in decreasing her chances . . . ."

"Now just hold on. How do you think Mr. Art Gallery found out about this?" He stared at Sonny, then leaned toward him. "I sent him a message, and I let him think it came from you. I've been here long enough to know how things work. Andre has connections, and I hoped he would do something for a client that he wouldn't necessarily do for me."

Jessie could see that Darling already had expectations of those connections. She watched as Sonny stared at the man. He started to say something, but stopped and began to laugh.

Darling shrugged. "I don't get the joke."

"It's no joke, Darling. I find you irritating, but I refuse to tangle myself up trying to understand why you felt the need to be so devious. Let's hope for Sonia's sake you've fumbled your way to a solution." Sonny ended his part of the discussion by returning to the fire and prodding it with a poker.

Darling shook his head. "We all live with demons, Mr. Jackson. You haven't come out of this unblemished."

Jessie heard Darling's comment and glanced at Sonny. He either didn't hear or chose not to hear. He prodded fiercely at the smoldering wood until sparks flew and a burst of orange flame consumed the end of one log.

Tension hung like a shroud. Neal squeezed her shoulder and, without a word, led her back to the fire to wait.

It took twenty agonizing minutes for the door to open again. Sage and Andre conferred quietly as they crossed the lounge to the group anticipating their news.

Andre made a slight bow to Sonny before he turned his attention to Darling. "It's been arranged. A helicopter should be here within the hour. We will, however, have to get *Señor*a Sieverson out to the main road where it can land."

Sage said, "There won't be that much traffic, but we'll go out there to see that it's clear. Since you all have to be in the city today anyway, Andre arranged for you to go with her. Is that all right?"

The trio exchanged glances. Jessie spoke for them. "Yes, that's great. We'll get our things together."

The plan set everyone into motion. A flurry of activity filled the stillness of the night and chased away the earlier tension. Jessie bent to collect her cup, which rested on the floor near Sonny, and saw Andre close in. She couldn't help but overhear the discreet exchange between the two men.

"*Señor* Jackson, this is regrettable. Please know that we will find out who was responsible."

"I'll be back in a few days to talk things over with you. In the meantime, I want you to keep this." The firelight played on Sonny's hand as he pulled a small figurine from his pocket and passed it to the other man. Without looking at it, Andre put it in his pocket, nodded once and walked away.

16

"Angel?" Jessie wrinkled her brow when the boy jumped.

"*¿Sí?*" Angel spun around and backed against the door to their room as he banged it shut.

"What's up, Angel?" The silence widened like a yawn, but Neal waited with hands on his hips and watched Angel fidget.

"I hear a noise. Maybe it is the thief, I think. So I go in to see. I look everywhere, but see nothing. Now I know it must only be an animal, but I want to be sure . . . with your friend . . . ." He glanced toward Sonia's room, his face pinched with concern.

The couple exchanged glances. Jessie wondered if Neal believed him; she didn't. Her husband said, "Well, thanks, Angel, but I think whoever was here is gone by now."

"Yes, but my aunt is very worried. I wanted to be sure. Please, I'm sorry if I was wrong."

"You're not wrong about wanting to check it out, Angel, but you took a big chance doing it on your own. We appreciate your concern, but I think your aunt would feel better if you had Tomy or Peter as . . . you know . . . " Jessie leaned toward him, " . . . back up." Her eyes moved over him but couldn't see any evidence that he was trying to hide something.

Like a bug released from a bottle, Angel scurried away.

Jessie watched his retreat. "Would you say he looked guilty?"

"Like a boy caught with a *Playboy.* We'd better check our stuff." Neal opened the door and flicked the light switch.

Jessie looked at the mess and felt crimson creep into her cheeks. "Gees, no wonder he scurried away, he was probably mortified. We were in such hurry to get ready for that damn party and otherwise engaged when we got back, that I forgot the place looked like this." In her tour of the room, she snapped the shower curtain back and checked under the bed. Her daypack lay there, crumpled and forgotten. She tugged it out into the light and felt Neal's eyes on her as she pulled out her billfold to check it.

"Everything still there?"

"Yeah, it's all here." She was putting her wallet back when the weight of her daypack caused her to stop. She patted it and paused again, then snatched the zipper and yanked on it until the pack fully opened.

Neal, concentrating on his own wallet, said, "We're all paranoid; he probably really did think he heard something. Well, I don't seem to be missing anything either. We'd better get a move on. The helicopter will be here soon."

Jessie only half heard him. Heat sprang from deep inside her. "Neal, the camera . . . ." She turned to him just as he shoved the camera, resting on the bed, out of his way to make room for packing.

"What about the camera?" He stopped and looked at her.

She looked back at him, then at the camera and then down at her daypack. "I could have sworn the camera was in here."

"Obviously it wasn't. You want me to carry it for awhile?"

Jessie's rubbed her forehead with her fingertips. "No, I just thought . . . oh, never mind. I can't wait for this night to end." She put her daypack aside and began packing the bigger bag that held her clothes. Fatigue from only a few hours sleep made it hard to think.

They worked in silence for a time before Jessie remembered something. "You know, you never did tell me what you and Sonny talked about on the verandah at Andre's." She glanced over at Neal as he arranged his shower stuff in his only remaining bag.

"There's really not much to tell. Sonny was more irritated than anything, he thought he'd made a discreet purchase. He's not naive. He knew exactly what he had, and I would bet he came here specifically to get it. If not a jaguar man, then something like it. The argument at the party was an embarrassing inconvenience."

"I think I saw him give it back to Andre while we were in the lounge."

Neal straightened from his packing. "Really?"

"I think so. It was small, a figurine like the jaguar man, whatever it was."

"Huh, . . . in spite of everything I'd be surprised if he gave it back."

"That disagreement with James probably didn't help."

"I don't know . . . I get the feeling those two just naturally antagonize one another. I see similarities between them, maybe that's it. At any rate, I don't think anything James could say would sway Sonny one way or the other, but maybe this attack on Sonia would."

"Could be. All I know is it got uncomfortable there for a few minutes between those two."

Neal laughed. "That's true." He looked at the small bag in his hand. "Well, that didn't take long; there are advantages to losing luggage. How are you doing?"

A quiet knock interrupted them. Neal opened the door and let Sonny in.

"We've got Sonia ready to move. While I was straightening our things, Peter and Darling put together a stretcher to get her to the helicopter landing place. I'm not sure, but we may need help. You ready?"

"Jessie?"

"In a sec. You go on ahead, I'll just finish up and give the room another check."

The two men left and Jessie finished her packing before circling the room one more time. As she glanced around the bathroom, she noticed the window ajar, pulled it shut and locked it, thinking Neal must have opened it when he showered. She lingered over the view until thoughts of the last few hours began to crowd her memory and distort the beauty of the dawn. She turned away. Other than the rumpled bed, the room looked as neat as when they moved in. She flicked off the light and closed the door.

* * *

Trees silhouetted against the orange glow of dawn lined the road where the small group huddled, anticipating the whir of helicopter blades. Birds began chirping and insects buzzed. It was chilly, but not cold, and everything felt damp from the dew. Not one car had traveled the road since they arrived.

Neal looked over at Sonia, who was still unconscious and, except for her face, was swathed in blankets on the makeshift stretcher. A deep purple and mauve bruise began on her right cheek, colored her eye and forehead, then disappeared into the hairline. In sharp contrast, a small, white, rectangular bandage covered the stitches. James hovered over her, his chalky face rough from not shaving. He seemed to Neal an unorthodox individual to have here as a missionary, and yet Sage and Peter seemed to hold some affection and respect for him, despite their earlier wrangling.

The waiting continued. Sonny pulled Andre aside and the two remained apart from the group, talking secretively. Jessie and Sage stood around Sonia, nodding occasionally as James spoke. Peter, Tomy and Mareya conversed easily among themselves. Neal hadn't seen Angel since he scurried away from their room. Each alien sound turned everyone's attention to the sky. After several false alarms, one such sound finally belonged to the helicopter.

The quiet, drowsy dawn was shattered. The blades beat the air, lifting dirt from the road and blasting it against Neal and those with him. Litter was hoisted off the ground and flung wildly on the turbulence that tore at the group's clothing. Trees thrashed and shook the birds from their limbs. Neal pressed his hands over his ears to shut out the roar of the engine and squinted his eyes against the dust.

The big, white and red whirlybird settled and reduced power. James Darling took charge.

It was obvious that the medic had done this before. Crouching under the slowed, but still rotating blades, he directed people until Sonia was firmly secured. Once that was accomplished, he went into a huddle with the pilot. Andre joined them, and the threesome gathered in closely for what looked like a serious discussion.

Sage spent the time giving each of the three friends a hug, shouting over the noise to be heard. "When you get time today, please give us a call and let us know how things went. We'll deduct the call from your room bill when you come back through." She smiled and circled Neal with her arms.

"We will," he shouted back at her. "Thanks, Sage, for everything."

"Well, I shouldn't think 'everything.' We could have done without the mugger." Before Neal protested, she went on. "It's all right, Neal. I appreciate your thanks and we all hope things go well at the university. They have an excellent reputation, and despite his misguided theories, we've come to learn James has a good instinct about this sort of thing. The university people like him and that will help once you get there. Hopefully, there's some comfort in knowing that."

"There is. We'll talk to you later."

"We'll be here. *Hasta luego*."

Neal hugged her one more time and made for the helicopter.

Andre and James shook hands with the pilot, and then said their good-byes to the three friends before backing away to the sidelines. Neal checked that all their bags were on board and then joined his wife and friend to buckle up and get ready for the liftoff.

The chopper's roar increased and the blades beat faster. The group from Tampu clutched at their clothing and backed away as the great machine lifted off the road in a cloud of dust. Friends, both on the ground and in the air, gave one last wave before they lost sight of each other. Sonny leaned close to Neal's ear and said loudly enough to be heard, "Andre heard through the grapevine that there was a *gringo* staying in the *pueblo*. Called attention to himself when he roared about the electricity going off at eight. Andre wondered if we had met the man."

They exchanged a curious glance. Sonny's eyebrows arched and Neal saw furious calculating going on behind his friend's eyes.

17

Under Mexico City's smoggy, morning sun, Dr. Alejandro Medina and his two assistants met them at the School of Medicine's helipad. The short, trim doctor dived beneath the chopper blades' gentle whirl and quickly assessed the condition of his new patient, who still lay unconscious. Turbulence disheveled his dark hair and caused his snow-white coat to flap. The three able-bodied passengers disembarked as shouted directions flew between pilot and medical men. Within seconds, the great machine lifted off in a blast of noise and wind as Medina's assistants rushed away with the gurney carrying their friend.

Medina then motioned Neal, Jessie and Sonny to follow. He led them through a maze of doors and hallways as he explained in flawless English what tests he would be performing over the next few hours. Not all of it was comprehensible. The medical man oozed confidence, but wasn't overly officious. Neal felt comfortable around him and although that was no guarantee of competence, he was relieved to know Medina was in charge of Sonia's care.

Their journey ended in front of two swinging doors. The box-like, white corridor that stretched behind them was busy with medical staff practicing their discipline. It felt to Neal like quiet, controlled panic, and although clean and modern, the center couldn't escape the reek common to all hospitals. Through the window of the swinging doors, he could see Medina's two assistants tending to Sonia.

Medina slid a pen into the breast pocket of his coat and tucked a chart under his arm. He pointed to the desk where, later, they could get Sonia's room number, then recommended a Chinese restaurant nearby where the trio could eat while they waited for news. With a touch of sensitivity, he asked them not to worry. Sonia might be incapacitated for a few days, but James Darling had worked wonders in the past with his limited resources, and Medina praised Darling's wisdom in getting her to the university so quickly. The stitch work was neat and tidy, which meant the wound would leave only a tiny scar. With that, he turned and pushed through the swinging doors.

* * *

"I think you're on shaky ground with that theory, Sonny," said Neal.

The remains of their meals sat in front of them as they lingered over green tea and tried to make sense out of recent events. The din of surrounding conversations mixed with the clink of plates and glasses as meals arrived and disappeared from nearby tables. Neal thought it would take more than one visit to get used to hearing someone of Asian descent speaking English with a Spanish accent.

"Why is it so farfetched? You didn't see the switch that came over Sonia when she thought she recognized Hal. I mean the car shot past our field of view in a second, but it was as if she had been doused with ice water. She was frantic to find the car, but it was nowhere. In the end she finally decided that it was only her conscience that had jabbed her, but the experience still turned her to stone. With all that's happened, maybe her initial impression was the right one."

"When she told me about it at the party, I got the feeling she thought it was guilt playing with her mind and not actually Hal that she saw." Jessie sipped her tea and thought back to her discussion with Sonia at Andre's.

"But you see, it would be nothing for a man with the money he's supposed to have to get here. The way I see it, Eric calls and tells him Sonia's going to Mexico City to hold his hand. Hal gets suspicious and begins to make arrangements."

"But how did he know about Tampu?"

"Eric knew about our stop in Tampu. He probably mentioned it, not knowing or even guessing the guy would go over the edge. Maybe Hal suspected Eric was getting more than sympathy from his wife and wanted to find out. Unless he saw us together, he could still think the men's clothing he bumped into in the room at Alta Linda belonged to Eric."

Jessie said, "Speaking of Eric, we have to meet him at Swainyo's in a couple of hours."

Sonny looked at his watch. "I think one of us should stay with Sonia at the hospital, don't you?"

Neal nodded. "I think that's wise."

"I'll do it," said Sonny, sliding his empty cup to the center of the table. "You two are involved with this camera thing. Leave your gear at the hospital with me. We can find a place to stay when you come back."

Jessie said, "What if the phantom mugger was Hal. Aren't you concerned about his showing up here?"

"If he's smart, he won't come anywhere near here until someone calls to let him know about the attack. Otherwise, how would he have found out? We didn't find a number anywhere in Sonia's things for him. Why take a chance? No, I think he would wait for a call. That way there are no suspicions." Sonny continued to speculate as if he were alone at the table. "He's either in contact with someone back in L.A. or he actually went back there himself to wait for a call. Since Eric may be the only person with his number, it would be a great irony if that call came from him."

Neal shook his head with a smile and turned his attention to Jessie. "So, we'll go and get this camera thing settled and then come back here. Eric will probably want to come back anyway to check on Sonia."

"I don't look forward to telling him about her. He doesn't need this to add to everything else." Jessie frowned and drank the last of her tea.

Neal smiled at her. "This time even I agree with you."

* * *

At a quick glance, the small office appeared elegant with its high ceilings edged in ornate crown moldings and its dark wood paneling set off by rich-looking, turn-of-the-century furnishings. Up close, however, the upholstery was rubbed bald on the corners of the more popular chairs, and if laid flat, the red velveteen curtains would have set up a wave of color from ruby to sun-faded dusty rose and back to ruby again. As they currently hung, only the dusty rose showed. The frayed pile in the grey carpet, plumped up by late-night vacuuming, continued to wilt throughout the day and would be flat by the time the lights went out.

In contrast, on the five desks the computers were state-of-the-art and the men and women who sat behind them wore crisp, white shirts with ties and dark trousers. For the number of people and the amount of activity taking place, the room was oddly quiet. Corbin Johnson, according to the brass plaque, greeted Jessie and Neal. Once they established that he and Jessie had already met on the phone, he invited them to sit while he informed Desi Swainyo they had arrived. Moments later, Eric joined them.

Jessie stood more quickly than Neal and gave Eric a hug. "Hello, Eric. We've just arrived, too."

Eric's floral shirt and tan couldn't put color back into his grey, ashen face.

"Hello." It was barely audible. He nodded to Neal, shook hands briefly and sat in the chair next to them.

"It's amazing that our government has offices like this. That was some security check to get in here." To Jessie, the small talk seemed necessary as sort of a prelude to her breaking the news about Sonia.

"Yeah, I guess so," said Eric.

"I was never clear about which department I was talking to, except that this Corbin Johnson told me they are with the State Department. That suggests F.B.I. to me, although I never asked and he never said. Corbin is letting Mr. Swainyo know we're here. It shouldn't be long." She didn't mean to, but she tightened her grip on the pack in her lap. It's obvious bulge arrested Eric's attention and his eyes roamed across it with a knowing glance.

Jessie began to feel warm and the silence grew uncomfortable. She rehearsed in her head what she planned to say to Eric about Sonia. If he noticed his friend's absence, he gave no indication. When the thought struck her that maybe he believed Sonny had kept Sonia from being there, she raced ahead, forgetting her script.

"Eric, on the way here we ran into a problem… it's Sonia."

Eric looked around and for the first time appeared to notice she wasn't there. "What's wrong, where is she?"

"She's at the university's School of Medicine here in Mexico City. They have a clinic there . . . ."

"What? . . . why?" Eric uncrossed his legs and leaned forward.

"She was asleep when someone broke into her room. They rifled her things and got some cash. We're not quite sure what prompted it, but she took quite a beating."

"Christ, you're serious. How is she? How's she doing?"

"We don't know yet. We're going back to the clinic when we leave here, why not come with us?"

"How did you get her here so fast?"

A buckle of wrinkles formed across Neal's forehead. He leaned forward, resting his elbows on his knees, and asked quietly. "How far did you think we had to come?"

Eric's ashen face turned forlorn. "I thought you were going to Tampu. I assume you had to come from there. I used to live here, and although I've never actually been to that *pueblo,* I know what the roads are like out there. It's hell when you're well. But why, I mean, Tampu is a small place, why would anyone . . . ?"

Neal leaned back, swept his hand over his hair and sighed. "We really don't know the reason; there's a lot of speculation. Sonny bought a few pieces of art that may have attracted some negative attention."

Jessie wondered if Eric caught the implication of a shared room and noted that Neal wasn't going to bring up the possibility of Hal's involvement.

Eric stood and began to pace. "Does Hal know . . . is he here?"

Jessie said, "We checked through Sonia's things and couldn't find a number. We know he's in L.A., but that's a big place and we had no idea where to start. We were hoping that you could help."

"We have to call him right away. Has she said anything; is she conscious yet?"

The small reception area closed in around them when Neal suddenly stood and walked over to the faded dusty rose curtains. He separated them enough to lean on the sill, folded his arms across his chest, and eyed Eric.

Neal's distrust of Eric lives on, Jessie thought as she shifted her eyes away from her husband to answer the other man's question. "No, they're doing tests right now. We left to come here before we were able to learn anything. Sonny stayed behind to stay on top of things."

"That's probably not a good idea."

"Why not, Eric?" Neal's voice sounded curt. When she turned to him, his face had hardened along with his voice.

"Mr. and Mrs. Fox?"

A greying man, about Neal's height, dressed in light corduroy trousers, casual shirt, tie and hush puppies approached them. His right hand came out of the cords pocket and extended toward Jessie. Her concern over the mounting tension between Neal and Eric retreated with the anticipation of this meeting.

"I'm Desi Swainyo. Thank you for coming."

"It seemed the best solution, Mr. Swainyo. This is Neal, my husband, and Eric Stover, Jennifer Stover's husband. I called to say that he would be here with us. I hope you got the message."

"I did, yes." The three men shook hands. "Mr. Stover, may I extend our sympathies for your loss. We will try to make this as painless as possible; unfortunately, we are bound up in procedures that have to be followed. We'll make every effort to clarify them as we go along. We can talk better in my office; it's this way."

"Mr. Swainyo? Before we do that, I need to make a call. It's long distance, but rather urgent. I have a credit card." Eric rocked on his feet like a caged animal.

Swainyo's eyes assessed the scene by quickly probing each face, then he said, "Yes, of course. Corbin, take Mr. Stover into the front office for his call, then bring him to me when he's finished." Corbin Johnson nodded and got up from his desk.

Jessie said, "You all right, Eric? Do you want any more details?"

His sickened appearance betrayed him, but he nodded. "I'm fine, I'm familiar enough with the city. I'll let Hal know what's happened and where she is." Eric dug around in his pocket as he followed the young assistant.

Mr. Swainyo led the couple through a door at the back of the reception area, down a corridor and through another door that led to his office. The grand interior decorating, which lost its gloss decades ago, appeared to carry on into the individual offices.

Swainyo sat behind his large mahogany desk as Jessie and Neal settled on the two chairs facing him. A computer, printer and keyboard were out of keeping with the rest of the decor, but were essential to the era in which the man worked. Neat piles of files lined both sides of the dinged and scratched surface with a scatter of paper in between. Swainyo scooped up the loose papers and tapped them into a tidy stack and laid them aside, then took a file off the top of one pile and spread it out in front of him.

The tidying up only took a second, but the time dragged and Jessie felt compelled to break the silence. "We have a friend who's been injured. Eric's calling her husband. He's back in the States on business." Neal shifted next to her. Nervousness made her chatter.

"I'm sorry to hear that; I hope it's nothing serious." He grabbed a quick glance at Neal's face, then retrained his eyes on Jessie. He may have been curious about Neal's raw cheek, but he didn't comment on it.

"We do, too. Do you want the camera?"

"Yes, I suppose you're anxious to be relieved of it."

"Absolutely. It's all yours. At times we've both regretted the fact that we ever recovered it." Jessie unzipped her pack, pulled it out and handed it to him.

He quickly looked it over and then laid it aside. "On the phone you mentioned it's been handled, but not opened, is that correct?"

Without hesitation Jessie said, "Yes, that's right."

"Good. When Mr. Stover joins us, I'm going to ask that you go with Corbin, whom you met outside, to an office next door. He'll record the details of how you came to possess the camera and work out how we can help with your stay here. Meanwhile, I'll go over things with Mr. Stover so he has an idea of how all this will move along."

"I don't know if this will help you in any decisions that you have to make, but Eric has really lost a lot of sleep over this." Once Jessie began to speak, she felt the anxiety that had been gathering steam during her camera-carrying days force the words out of her with a confidence and conviction she didn't know she had. "I think you would be cruel if you found some reason not to show him the tape today. He's agonized over Jennifer's death and no matter what's revealed on it, he has a right to know what it is . . . today." She almost needed to catch her breath when she finished.

Swainyo rested his elbows on the desk. Although no smile moved the muscles near his mouth, a crease near his eyes relaxed the official look to his face. "If he expresses a desire to see it, I think that could be arranged."

A light knock interrupted something Neal was about to say. The door opened immediately and Corbin Johnson ushered Eric into the room.

Swainyo stood and picked up the camera. "Corbin, can you take this back to Tinker and then take Mr. and Mrs. Fox next door while I go over a few things with Mr. Stover?"

"Yes, sir," said Johnson as he took possession of the camera and walked back to the door. He waited there for Jessie and Neal.

Jessie caught Eric's eye, and before she asked, he said, "I got through to Hal, he's on his way. I gave him the name of my hotel and where Sonia is."

"Okay, we'll talk later." She smiled at him, then glanced at Swainyo before crossing the office to the door where Neal waited with Johnson. For the first time in a long time, the pack in her hand felt miraculously light, as did her spirits.

* * *

The corridor where they waited was small, tight and unembellished. Grey linoleum covered the floor and was accented by the grey paint on the walls. Neal believed if he hiked himself up onto his toes, his hair would brush the ceiling.

Their talk with Corbin Johnson bore many similarities to another talk they had with an investigator almost eighteen months ago. Their involvement with those people snared Jessie and him into the lives and deaths of three men they didn't know and disrupted the early days of their cruise. Despite his efforts to fight it, Neal felt the tangle of this involvement tightening around him. Corbin Johnson had asked them to wait in this tunnel-like corridor for a few moments, but that became increasingly more distasteful once Eric had joined them. It might be irrational, but even though Eric shared his love of boats and the sea, Neal didn't like the man. That dislike was making him antagonistic.

Without a preamble or pleasantries, he finally questioned the widower. "What made you think Sonia was unconscious or for that matter that her attack happened in Tampu?"

Jessie shot him an irritated glance; Eric looked flustered.

"She is, isn't she?"

"Neal, stop." Jessie's tone warned him about starting an argument.

"I'm just curious. Since we didn't tell you, I wondered how you knew?"

Eric expelled a single laugh and looked around. "Oh, I get it. Now you think I had something to do with that, too?"

"I'm not sure, but I'm still curious how you knew."

"Well, I don't know . . . I guessed. You said she got beaten up, I just assumed."

"Pretty big leap."

"Not at all. You said you were going to Tampu, so I assumed it happened there. I can't remember what you said, but it made me feel she couldn't talk to you. I know what it was, the number for Hal. If she were conscious, she could have told you Hal's number. And why the hell should I have to explain myself to you, anyway?" Muscles in Eric's face and neck bunched from mounting fury and his lips stretched into a grimace. His previous pallor grew pink. "You've had it in for me since this whole thing started. I tried to understand how you felt, and I think I did pretty damn well to stay out of your way, but you keep coming at me. I've had it. You don't believe me, then fine. I'm sorry, Jessie, but your husband pisses me off."

Neal ignored Jessie's glare and jumped in before she had a chance to respond.

"Jessie has her own thoughts on all this, and you don't have to apologize to her for my behavior. She thinks I've had it in for you since the beginning, too, but I don't give a damn one way or the other now that they have the camera and we've been assured our part is over. You're right, you don't have to explain anything to me, but curiosity made me ask."

"So did my answer satisfy your . . . ," Eric narrowed the gap between them by leaning close to Neal's face, ". . . curiosity?"

"For now." Neal stood his ground and his voice held a hint of challenge. He felt a touch on his arm and knew his wife was asking him to back down.

Eric stared at Neal, then took a breath. The sneer relaxed and he once again grew pale. "Neal, in deference to Jessie I'm going to forget your hostility," he said quietly. "Without my in-laws playing these legal games, your part would never have gotten this complicated. Swainyo just told me this equipment is going back to a lab in the States and, frankly, I want to rip somebody apart. It belongs to me and when it's decided that I had nothing to do with Jennifer's death, I intend to remind my in-laws, through the courts, of the hell they put me through. Then, like you two, I'll carry on with the dream that Jennifer and I shared. Since the seas flow together, we may run into each other again and I want to remember the help you offered, not the conflict."

When Eric paused, he wiped away the perspiration that stood on his upper lip, his face grew more ashen and his voice croaked when he spoke. "Now, I know they weren't intending to let you watch the tape, but with Sonia not here, I would appreciate some moral support in there. I don't feel right pleading my case only to Jessie, so I'm appealing to both of you . . . ."

Swainyo reappeared and left the decision of who would watch the video to Eric. The widower's plea got a reluctant nod from Jessie, and Neal felt compelled by some chivalrous notion to go with her.

On the way into the projection room, Swainyo pulled Jessie and Neal aside and said, "Mr. and Mrs. Fox, maybe it slipped your minds, but can you remember at any time opening the camera even if it was just to check it?"

Neal's mind raced with possibilities, why would he ask that?

Jessie answered quickly and with a force that made the investigator blink. "Mr. Swainyo, I'll be happy to go over every detail of its journey again, from the time we fished it out of the water until now, but I guarantee that opening that camera would not have slipped our minds. Why do you ask?"

He recovered, smiled and said, "Maybe it's the handling and its journey here. Tinker seems to think it's been opened."

* * *

Neal shifted in the metal folding chair as Jessie sat next to him. He looked around and noted none of the grandeur of the offices had made it to this room either. White walls, no adornments, and five rows of folding chairs, four chairs to a row, were arranged theater-style. Long and narrow, the room felt like a converted broom closet. The blank TV at the front would soon divulge the secrets they had carried around since their initial encounter with Jennifer Stover.

Yep, Neal said to himself, the tangle was tightening and his eyes slid to Eric, who sat statue still on the other side of Jessie.

The television set sputtered to life. Pictured on the screen was the deck of a sailboat set against a dawn sky of pink and orange. Blocking a full view of the colorful horizon were the tacks of the genoa and main, seemingly grey instead of white in the dim light. The whole picture jumped as if it were being filmed on an unstable platform and showed the sails first limp, then taut as wind puffs buffeted them. A boom vang controlled the main, enabling it to take advantage of every breath of air. A light feminine voice drifted around the room, narrating the scene.

Home movies, thought Neal, but this time with a difference. He was going to see how someone actually died. Jessie stiffened next to him. Would she regret this? Would he?

"The sky is spectacular this morning. One of the few nice things experienced on a long passage. Another nice experience is the wildlife. Off to starboard, we have a big pod of dolphins. You can see them splashing, and when they notice us, no doubt they'll come and play at the bow." Even in the glassy water, the explanation was needed to distinguish the reason for the splashes. As the operator trained the camera on the water, Neal leaned forward, resting his elbows on his knees. It helped him concentrate.

"It's a beautiful morning, light winds with calm seas. Even so, we have never ending motion. Something only a foot on solid ground can cure. While we wait for the dolphins to move in, here's *Osprey.*" A jostle and bang interrupted the narration. Then an "ooh" and a light laugh. "Almost lost my balance there. Okay, back to *Osprey*, our floating home." As the camera panned the boat, Neal drank in what he saw. Light winds that barely lifted the telltale, the sails . . . .

A sudden moan came from Eric, and all eyes in the room snapped away from the screen to the grieving husband, who had clamped his hand over his mouth. Jessie leaned toward Eric, patted his forearm and whispered something to him.

Desi Swainyo stood and Eric gestured with a wave that he was all right, and the official eased back into his seat.

Everyone's attention returned to the TV screen, calm water continued to fill the frame, and the commentary turned back to the dolphins, who had moved in alongside. Unexpectedly, noise like that of a paper bag being crushed in front of a microphone issued from the television. A feminine voice cried out, "Ohhh . . . God," and the "plink," clank and bang that followed reached out into the room of riveted spectators. The picture bounced and went wild, flashing sky, then water, then sails across the screen. A loud thud turned the screen into snow and the sound to a long, unrelenting hiss.

Desi Swainyo stood and stopped the tape. He conferred with Tinker, the other man in the room, then said, "That's all that's on the tape. Do you want to see it again, Mr. Stover?"

Eric's shoulders sagged, and the remaining color in his face drained away. His eyes glazed in a stare at the blank screen as he slowly shook his head. "No, I've seen more than enough."

* * *

A heavy pall of humidity descended on them when they exited the grey, granite building where they had spent the last few hours. Sunlight muted by pollution made them pause in the shade of the portico before setting off.

Jessie stole quick glances at Eric. He looked a little better than he had inside. His pallor and trance-like demeanor after they saw the tape had alarmed her, and she had paced the corridor while he, Neal and Desi Swainyo disappeared into the men's room for several minutes. When they rejoined her, even Neal looked concerned.

While walking them to the reception area, Desi Swainyo had droned on about his regrets. Jessie had questioned him again about Tinker's belief that the camera had been opened. He went on to explain that at least until the lab reports came back, they would accept the possibility that normal handling and the jostle of the trip had cracked the corrosion. However, his eyes had been watchful of her while he talked, and he had a manner and a tone of voice that made her feel guilty even though she was telling him the truth. A rumble of defiance had stirred in her.

When they turned to leave, the investigator had handed Eric a slip of paper with the name of the lab and a contact person whom, Swainyo explained, Eric could call anytime for updates on his case.

Outside, Neal watched the cars race by on the street that ran in front of them and said, "Eric, you want to get a taco or a Dos Equis?"

"It didn't answer anything. I guess in a way that's good. I'm not sure I could have watched if she'd taped once she was in the water." Eric shuddered and fell silent.

Jessie looked at Neal then back at Eric, "Let's at least get a beer or Coke. We could find a place here, or if you want to go to the hospital, we could get something there."

The stricken husband stood mesmerized by the cars. "I really thought I'd get some answers. I've built it up so much; I counted on it to quiet my soul. I hope you two will excuse me. I think I want to be alone for a while."

"Eric, please, are you sure?" Jessie didn't feel comfortable about leaving him alone.

"Yeah, it surprises even me, but I'm sure. I'll meet you at UNAM later," he said, and like a zombie, he descended the stairs to the street.

Jessie called after him. "Where are you staying?"

Eric raised one hand and waved it in a circle. "Somewhere around here." He turned and walked backwards to look at them. "I just need some time, I'll be all right. See you at the university." He pivoted and continued his walk along the sidewalk.

"Neal, what do you think?"

"I think he wants to be alone."

They watched him until he turned the corner. Eric never looked back.

"C'mon," Neal said, "Let's go see how Sonia and Sonny are doing."

18

"I wanted there to be some official policy to prevent me from watching the tape, but when Swainyo said it was up to Eric, I knew I was doomed. I just couldn't say, 'I'd rather not.' " Jessie sat between Sonny and Neal in the waiting area on Sonia's floor.

After a pause she continued, "At least the way the tape ended, I can believe she was unconscious when she hit the water and that will save me from a lifetime of nightmares. If the camera had gotten jammed and run on, the vision of *Osprey* sailing away while Jennifer frantically tried to stay afloat, screaming in terror at the realization that Eric couldn't hear her, would have burned a permanent impression on my brain. *Psycho* cured me of ever turning my back on a bathroom door while I'm in the shower, there's no telling where this would have taken me. Since we don't plan to quit cruising any time soon, I have lots of lonely watches ahead of me."

Sonny took his eyes away from the corridor activity and looked at her. "Christ, Jessie, you've got a gruesome imagination."

"Yeah . . . well . . . it's a gruesome death."

Sonny leaned back in his chair, folded his arms and changed the subject. "So, Eric just walked off?"

"Yeah, and that was hours ago," she said.

When she and Neal had rejoined Sonny at the clinic, the report on Sonia was mixed. She had regained consciousness and Sonny had briefly talked with her. She had no memory of the events that had brought her to the clinic, and at first she didn't recognize the man with whom she'd spent the last couple of days. Her memory would filter back, Sonny had been assured, but with no exact timetable. Dr.

Medina had explained to him that with severe head trauma, rest and patience were critical.

"I'm going to check again." Neal stood, stretched and smoothed out the wrinkles in his lightweight shorts. He wandered down the hall, glanced briefly through the open doorway that led into Sonia's room, then continued to the nurse's desk.

Even though Jessie knew the staff would alert them when Sonia woke again, she understood Neal's need to check. Before they could feel free to leave the clinic, they wanted to talk with their injured friend, reassure her that Hal was on his way and that everything would be fine.

Jessie watched as Neal tested his meager Spanish on the lady who had been directing all floor activity from behind a chest-high nurse's station. In a starched, white uniform and cap, the woman worked patiently with Neal, using hand gestures and volume to get her point across. Neal nodded, then began to retrace his steps. Jessie was amused when she noticed two younger nurses huddled in conversation and stealing glances at her husband. The tanned, lean skiers' legs and abundance of sun-bleached hair made him look ruggedly handsome. Sonny may be beautiful, but her man was foxy.

"This whole thing has to be hell for Eric," said Sonny. "Don't get me wrong, I understand your motives for hanging on to the camera, but I have to tell you, I probably would have tried harder to get it back."

Sonny's comments dispelled the sexy thoughts about her husband, and Jessie turned her attention to their friend.

"It seems to me," he continued, "if I loved my wife as much as he says he did, the enormity of her death would make all this bureaucratic bullshit senseless and inane. I'd be furious. It may make sense to a lot of other people, but why should Eric understand the U.S. government's decision to act on the suspicions of Jennifer's family? I admire the guy for the way he's handling this. He's being downright civil."

"Would you have tried to steal it, Sonny? I mean, would you have resorted to sneaking onto *Dana* and going through our stuff to get it back?"

He thought about Jessie's question. "I don't know. I might

have if I couldn't get it any other way. You beginning to think he might be the one who rummaged through your boat?"

"It's one answer. The lock was on backwards when we got home that night. It could have been anyone, of course, but Eric's left-handed. If he were in a hurry, it would be an easy mistake to make, and although he's not the only person who knew, he did know where we kept the camera. If I hadn't gotten so fed up with the whole situation and thrown the damn thing into another locker, whoever came aboard that night would now have it and none of this would have happened."

"I still would have talked you into going to Tampu, Sonia still might have come with us, and someone still might have mugged her. Jessie, much of this still might have happened."

She mulled over his words for a moment, then dropped her head back until it bumped lightly against the wall. "Oh, God, I'm so sick of it all. I can't wait to get back to *Dana* and sail away."

Sonny gave her knee a gentle pat and they watched Neal's final steps.

He eased into a chair next to her and said, "There's been no change," then slouched, stretched his legs out in front of him and rested his arm on her thigh.

The three of them sat in a row and watched the subdued, steady bustle of medical life. The furrow between Jessie's eyes remained as she thought about her latest exchange with Sonny. Was Neal right in his theory that Eric was their nighttime prowler?

After several minutes, Sonny got restless. "Well, I gotta walk, you need anything?"

On one such walk-about he had come back with soft drinks and snacks, another time with the newspaper. She and Neal lifted their heads off the wall enough to shake them and he wandered away. Jessie relaxed again, closed her eyes and wondered what he would bring back this time.

The waiting dragged, and details of the room in which they sat appeared vividly in the darkness behind her lids. She saw a clear picture of the Naugahyde chairs that were lined up against the wall, spaced occasionally by a table, each with a lamp and a scatter of magazines. Most of the reading material bore the pictures of movie and rock stars in tabloid layouts - all in Spanish. She had browsed through them, making up her own stories based on the pictures.

Her thoughts turned to Eric. Would he ever show up? The impression of the waiting room vanished and was replaced by the widower's sick, haunted face as he had walked away from them earlier. That vision was then transformed into him going through her bath locker.

A loud discussion moving along the corridor roused her. Rolling her head forward, she opened her eyes and watched as two men stepped swiftly into view and strode for the nurse's station. She sat up when she recognized Eric. Although she couldn't see the other man clearly, she knew it must be Hal. She stood, and after the first few tentative steps, pushed forward to meet them.

"Eric, Hal, we're so glad you're here."

The two men turned and the white face of the man with Eric reminded her of a rabid dog. Lined, with deep-set eyes and foam in the corners of the mouth, the man looked nothing like the kind person who, over a year ago, had extended a helping hand to them in the dark water off Cabo San Lucas.

"What the hell have you done to Sonia?"

The statement hit Jessie like a strike from a rattlesnake and she dropped back a step.

With much of the earlier pallor gone, Eric's face eased when he recognized her. "Oh, Jessie, hi. I've been trying to explain to Hal that this was just a matter of being in the wrong place at the wrong time, but he's been bellowing at me ever since he arrived at my hotel. Maybe you can do a better job of it." Eric's eyes lifted to the corridor behind her.

Before she could answer, Neal's voice rolled over her shoulder.

"Hal, you made good time. Eric's right, it's an unfortunate situation, but the medical people have been great, and I think out of consideration for them and for all the other patients on this floor, maybe we could discuss your concerns outside. Unless, of course, you're interested in seeing your wife. She's regained consciousness." The two men stared at each other.

Hal broke first, stole a glance at Eric, clenched and unclenched one hand while he wiped his mouth with the other. He spun around and barked at the nurse behind the desk. "Where is she?"

The nurse looked at him, raised her chin and quietly said something.

When Hal didn't respond, Eric leaned toward him. "Hal, she said that unless you lower your voice she will call security. Please, if Sonia's conscious, we need to see how she is."

Hal blinked rapidly several times and dropped his chin to his chest. After a pause, he raised his head, raked one hand through his hair and said in a more subdued voice, "I want to see Sonia; where is she?"

Eric made a quick translation and Jessie understood a few words that explained Hal's connection to Sonia. The nurse glanced at both men and gestured that they should follow her. The men walked away, leaving Jessie and Neal by the nurse's station.

"That guy seems a little unbalanced," said Neal.

"Uh-huh. I'm glad Sonny wasn't around." They looked at each other and Jessie sensed Neal was thinking the same thing. "Maybe we should wait for him down the hall and snag him as he gets off the elevator. Just in case."

"Good idea."

They peeked into Sonia's room as they passed and heard quiet voices talking back and forth. The patient lay motionless with her eyes closed. They walked toward the elevator and recognized Sonny pacing across the corridor. He stopped abruptly when he recognized them and waited until they got close before he spoke.

"I saw them come into the clinic, but Eric was too far away, and they were in the elevator before I could grab his attention. What happened?"

Jessie jumped in to explain. "Hal nearly bit my head off. I can understand he's upset, but man, Neal's right, the guy's unbalanced."

"That's odd," said Sonny, frowning.

"You can say that again."

Neal said, "Why odd?"

"Because if someone asked me to bet on who was more angry, I would have put my money on Eric."

* * *

Sonny took a swallow of beer, smiled and stood when he saw Jessie and Neal enter the restaurant on the top floor of the hotel Desi Swainyo had recommended. Jessie looked at his clean clothes and freshly showered appearance with envy. That was her intention as soon as she had something to drink.

"You got my note. You two look as though you could use something cool. What's your pleasure?"

"I'd love a beer," said Jessie. "Thanks."

Neal held up two fingers indicating that's what he wanted, too, and Sonny gave the order when the waiter came by.

"So, what's the latest?" said Sonny.

Jessie pulled her chair in closer to the table. "You want to tell him or should I?"

"You start, I'll fill in."

She arched an eyebrow at Neal. "Yeah, right." She turned back to Sonny. "Well, after you decided to slink away, we headed back to Sonia's and our lady in white was herding Eric and Hal out of the room. Apparently Hal was close to erupting again. I think our nurse must have called the doctor because he showed up right after that. He spent quite a while explaining everything to Hal and then went in with him to see her. Eric waited with us. Hal was as twitchy as a cat in heat, and because of your idea that he had something to do with this, I couldn't help but think he was afraid she'd remember something. But he was just as twitchy when they came out and he had talked with her."

"Were you able to see her?"

"In the end, yes, but not without a hassle. Hal got noisy, claiming we had no business there and that he, as her husband, didn't want anyone interrupting her rest. Get that. In fact, he sputtered to the doctor about allowing nonfamily members anywhere near her. I'm glad we had already met and talked with Dr. Medina, and that we had an introduction from James Darling, because when we said we weren't leaving until we could see her, the good doctor shrugged off Hal's protests and took us in. The fuming husband in tow, of course. We didn't know how much Hal knew and so didn't go into too many details, but she easily remembered us and the party, but not much after that. She was still spacey, but I guess that's normal, at least for a while."

Neal said, "Eric didn't look angry, tense maybe, but not angry, so I don't know what you saw. He and Hal didn't talk much. It's possible he just got fed up with the abuse Hal had been dishing out and blew up at him."

"Maybe."

Jessie rested her elbows on the table and cupped her chin in her hands. "I'm not sure where we fit in now that Hal's here. He seemed concerned and attentive, and with Eric's full command of Spanish, they'll get more out of the staff than we did. Eric kept alive the idea that he was in Tampu with us by going along with a few things we said. He helped us call Alta Linda, too, so Sage and Peter know how the day's been going. Tomy claims the car will be finished tomorrow. What do you two want to do?"

Sonny drained his beer bottle. "I don't know about you two, but I'm ready for some sightseeing."

* * *

A day later, the familiar lady behind the nurses' station gave a smile of recognition toward Jessie and Neal as they approached. The co-worker to whom she spoke nodded then left with an armload of charts. When her attention turned back to them, the corners of her mouth turned down as she thrust her chin toward Sonia's door and shook her head. Spanish came out of her mouth, too rapidly for Neal to comprehend. When she realized he didn't understand, she laughed, then slowed and simplified her words. Hal was in Sonia's room and had apparently been a problem. He and Jessie sympathized with her as far as their limited Spanish allowed and then asked if they could see the patient.

Her uniform rustled as she led them across the corridor and through the door. Hal and Eric sat on either side of the bed and conversation stopped when the nurse ushered in the new guests. The droop to Sonia's eyes told Neal she was tired. Her pale face was marred by the deep purple and yellow bruises that surrounded the crisp, white bandage that covered Darling's stitches. After uttering a few words, the nurse left.

Eric interpreted. "She's given us five minutes and then we all have to leave. She says you seem tired, Sonia."

Her head and shoulders angled slightly higher than her feet, Sonia's voice croaked between dry, puffy lips, "I am really, plus I have a terrible headache. Babe, why don't you and Eric go back to the hotel and at least get a decent meal. I'm sure that Neal and Jessie will stand guard outside while you're gone. I'll rest easier knowing that you've had a break." She turned her bruised face to the couple and Neal noticed the eyes widen with intensity. "He's been here since yesterday without a break. Would you stay an hour or so to make sure no one gets in here?"

Neal hesitated before he said, "Of course, we don't mind at all."

Their original plan for the morning was to have been a visit to the Anthropology Museum with Sonny, but he hadn't met them for breakfast as promised. Neal had checked his friend's room and looked around the hotel, but hadn't found him. They left a note and headed off to the clinic to check there, but it was apparent that Sonny wasn't visiting Sonia either.

The nurse appeared at the door and cleared her throat.

"Go on, please, Hal. I'll be all right. I do feel pretty tired."

Neal watched as Hal's glance bounced between her and Eric. When his eyes landed on Neal, he glared and said, "I'll be gone an hour, that's all." He looked down at Sonia, relaxed the frown and bent to kiss her forehead. Everyone turned to leave and the overly protective husband followed. After closing the door, he joined the group in the corridor.

"We'll go then. Since she's so tired, I don't expect you to go in and bother her. Just sit out here and watch, we'll be back."

Neal felt the rumble of defiance at Hal's overbearing tone, but controlled the urge to challenge him. "Hal, we'll be here, but I don't understand your concern. What are we watching for?"

"I left my wife aboard our boat in a safe harbor among friends and she was fine. You come in and cause all kinds of trouble because of your high-all-mighty ideas of what's right, and she nearly gets killed. Why Eric here gives you the time of day, I don't know. I don't like what you did to him and I don't like the idea of Sonia traipsing around the mountains. How you could, on such an occasion, go off to a tourist place, an art gallery for God's sakes, to satisfy some friend of yours is irresponsible under the circumstances. It's that irresponsibility that's put Sonia in that bed and I'm angry about it. I don't like her being in a place like this. I don't trust you, but I trust these people even less. Just make sure nothing more happens to her." His voice had built during the litany and the volume brought the lady in white back to the scene.

Without touching him, she began to herd him away from the door. Her quiet voice was directed at Eric, and he helped move Hal.

Neal's heart beat with rage. The heat spread to his fists and his mouth dried up. In his ear, he could hear Jessie urging him toward the nurse's station.

Hal, with Eric talking to him, and the nurse talking to Eric, moved in the opposite direction, away from Sonia's door, past the waiting room and toward the elevator. Everyone walking in the corridor paused to see what was going on.

Neal felt his self-control filter back, but the incident had left him seething. "That man almost got me to punch him."

"I know. How are you doing?" Jessie's arm linked through his as they walked.

He took a big breath and rested his elbow on the station counter. "Better."

After delivering the disruptive element to the elevators, the nurse scurried back to her post, ignoring the couple who hung on her counter. Shaking her head as she muttered to herself, she got busy with charts until a buzz pulled her glance to a panel of lights on her desk. In a raised voice, she tossed a couple of incomprehensible comments at Neal as she stepped quickly to Sonia's room, slipped inside, and closed the door firmly behind her.

On her way to the waiting area, Jessie said over her shoulder, "Sonia probably wants to know what was going on."

Neal spent a few more minutes composing himself before turning toward the waiting room. Sonia's door opened and the nurse motioned to him and Jessie. When they got close, she opened the door wider and let them in.

Sonia still lay bruised and pale, but the eyes that looked out through the bruises were alert.

Jessie said, "Hi, Sonia, everything all right?"

"No," she said in a cracked whisper. Working the muscles in her face made her wince. "Sonny somehow got passed Hal and Eric last night, and we got a chance to talk. He wouldn't say, but I think he agrees with me. I'm almost positive Hal is the one who did this. Please, you've got to help me."

19

Sonny pocketed his hands as the three of them walked the mirror-like floor from one era of Mexico's past to the next in the *Museo Nacional De Antropologia.*

He had appeared in the clinic's waiting room after the nurse had hustled Jessie and Neal from Sonia's room. Apologizing about breakfast, he claimed he had been out checking a few things and had been delayed. Jessie and Neal relayed Sonia's fears, and they barely had a chance to discuss options when Hal, in a slightly better humor, returned with Eric. They introduced Sonny, talked for a few minutes, then left for the museum before tension among the five of them had a chance to redevelop.

The trio had spent the afternoon wandering the exhibits at the museum, going over and over Sonia's claim, sorting out how Hal might have accomplished the assault, and what they could do to follow through on their promise to help.

"Two things are beginning to worry me," said Sonny. "First, Hal showed no particular hostility toward Eric, or toward me for that matter, so he's either a very good actor, or there's nothing to act. And second, Sonia's lack of certainty. We couldn't talk long, but she kept saying she *thought* it was him. Where does the doubt come from? I assumed if she actually remembered what happened, she'd know for sure. I'm not as convinced as before."

"It was dark," said Jessie. "She probably couldn't see anything, but maybe she recognized something familiar. You know, a smell or action that she subconsciously filed away. Something she can't recall specifically, but sensed at the time."

"That's possible, I suppose, but after I talked with her, I went out to the airport and greased a few palms to find out if he came in by private or commercial plane. There's no record of his arrival, but there are hundreds of corporate names, and no doubt he's tied to one of them. The fact that he flew in from L.A. didn't help. We'd be able to find out which one eventually, just not right away. I hope she's not assuming because of their past that it has to be her husband." Sonny strolled to a painting, a large, colorful mural filled with horses and men dressed in the plumes and bright finery of the Spanish conquistadors. With menacing faces, they posed threateningly over beautiful, dark-skinned men and women wearing white robes.

"A Mexican bounding out of the night to attack a *gringo* woman is just as unbelievable to me as Hal doing it," said Neal leading them to the next painting.

"Someone did it. Maybe the whole thing was more to make a point. Nothing personal, more like business."

Neal looked at him and laughed. "Now you sound like James Darling. This isn't a scene from a mob movie."

"You weren't at the receiving end of that verbal punch and jab from of our friend wearing the royal blue blazer. I'm telling you, venom dripped off every word. He made it very clear what he thought of me and my reason for being there. Sonia was obviously there with me—how better to make a point?"

"Why do they leave Andre alone then? Get rid of the Outpost and they get rid of the problem."

"Ah, I asked that question of Darling when we were getting Sonia ready for the helicopter. He wouldn't say anything while Peter was there, but once we were alone, he could have talked all night. We have our differences, and I certainly don't subscribe to all his beliefs, but I think generally he's a decent person, and some of what he says makes sense. Apparently, Andre is connected to a powerful political family, and in Mexico that's better than a security system. It wouldn't go unnoticed or unchallenged if Andre, personally, began having problems. According to the medic, these artifact fanatics don't dare go after the gallery, so they menace the buyers and word gets out that Tampu has crime problems. It keeps the tourists away and at least stems the flow of artifacts out of the country. Darling repeated again that usually it's pain-in-the-ass stuff, like my getting hassled at the party, or having the room tossed and losing a few possessions. Up until now, Andre hasn't minded. He and his partners want serious buyers and that sort of intrigue peaks interest. Darling has seen Andre shrug his shoulders and play up the riskiness of coming to the area when a client mentions the rumors. This time, though, the violence seemed to touch a nerve. It's not the first time something's happened, but it's the most brutal, and the first against a woman. Our medic is still convinced it's thugs from some mountain mafia group, but maybe someone from the 'local historical society' broke ranks and got a little too passionate about the cause."

They leaned over a glass case and studied its contents. Sonny straightened up, pressed his lips together and stared longingly into the case. Lying on a soft cloth was a jade figurine of a jaguar man. He inhaled, sighed and walked away.

A group of German tourists passed. Jessie's high-school language lessons allowed for only scant comprehension as the guide pointed out and explained, in German, various things on display. She envied the tourists' carefree wanderings, for even after hours of drifting from one exhibit to the next, she, Neal and Sonny still had no answer to the big question that hung among them. What kind of help could they offer Sonia?

* * *

"But you're here and she's not, what happened?" Sage tucked her feet under her and took a sip of sherry. Golden bursts of light flickered across her face when Peter poked at the fire. Once the logs settled, he eased back into the chair next to his wife.

The three friends had taken the innkeepers' suggestion of riding the bus back to Tampu from Mexico City, and Peter had met them at the bus stop on the main road outside of the *pueblo.* He had arrived in Sonny's car with claims that he was testing its fitness, and except for a couple of dings, the car proved ready for the road.

Back at Alta Linda, they settled in, and after dinner Sage and Peter joined the trio around the fire to continue their conversation regarding the events in Mexico City. Muffled conversation from other guests sitting in the lounge created background noise and Peter kept a watch on the bar, occasionally disappearing to check on a guest or refill a drink.

Jessie curled up and snuggled into Neal, his arm wrapped around her. "Since Sonia wasn't in any kind of shape to move and with the staff around, she admitted to feeling safe enough in the clinic," said Jessie from her cozy position. "Her concern seemed to be what would happen after her discharge. Telling her we'd stick around Mexico City until then, and that we'd visit her every day, at least got a smile out of her. We weren't at all sure how this news would go down with Hal, but we thought we could come up with some excuse. We spent that whole afternoon at the Anthropology Museum trying to figure out how we could help."

"But Sonia solved our problem for us," said Sonny, staring at the fire. "After the museum, we went back to visit her. She seemed rested, Hal wasn't nearly as jumpy, and Eric was nowhere around. To look at them then, you'd think they were devoted to each other. The next day when we went back, she had done a complete turnaround."

Jessie said, "Hal left the room for a couple of minutes and she took that opportunity to tell us to forget her rambling of the day before. She claimed she was dazed and that made her overly dramatic. Hal had been great, she said, and to prove it she showed us a beautiful gold pin with little diamonds on it. It was a gift from Hal, a real flashy thing. According to her, guilt had made her delusional." Jessie didn't mention that the incident reminded her of the all-too-familiar battered women stories she'd read over the years.

Sonny swirled the tawny liquid in his brandy glass and said, "She apologized for leading me on . . . said she realized the whole thing was her way of getting back at him for leaving her behind. Our hanging around was no longer necessary and that Jessie and Neal should show me the sights, and she would see us back in Zihuatanejo."

"Hal came back about then," said Neal, fingering the healing gash across his cheek. "And to emphasize her point, she encouraged us to return to Alta Linda to reassure all of you that she was fine, that all this was just a fluke of circumstance. So we talked it over and decided even if Hal had done this to her, we couldn't do anything without Sonia's cooperation, which we weren't going to get. By then, we had our own doubts about his involvement and we were anxious to get back here. So, here we are."

Sage exhaled, "Not that I want a husband to abuse his wife, but it sure would have simplified things here. We'll keep asking around, but nothing has turned up so far."

Sonny stretched out his legs and crossed them at the ankles. "When I checked with Andre a while ago, he had nothing more to add to what he told me before we left in the helicopter. Maybe that's because it's true, or maybe it's because he hasn't done any more snooping around, I don't know."

"To be fair to Andre, he and James did notify the authorities, but even with Andre's connections, now that Sonia's in Mexico City, the police won't do much. By the way, James sends his regards. He's as incorrigible as ever, but honestly, I don't know what we'd do without him. Please just know that we are all concerned about this and we'll keep trying to find answers, but it takes time."

Sonny sighed. "Yeah, you're probably right."

Jessie knew her friend's decision to return the jaguar man figurine to Andre had flattened his mood, but he had told her that even though he wanted the piece, this time it wasn't worth the price.

Conversation lagged and five faces studied the flames. No one broke the silence until Peter's eye caught someone moving toward the bar and he rose to tend to his customer.

Jessie yawned. "I think it's time I went to bed. So you two will definitely come down and visit us?"

"Yes, we've cleared our calendar and look forward to it. It'll give us a chance to pick up some special things at the market. It's too big a trip for regular shopping, but Peter and I love to head down there once in a while. We'll probably stay at the Pension del Mar. Will we see you there, Sonny?"

Sonny sighed and shook his head. "No, unfortunately I have a job to get back to."

"Then maybe you'll come back here to visit us sometime?"

He looked away from the flames and smiled at Sage. "I just might."

* * *

The breeze brushed Jessie's clean body. She spread her fingers and combed them through her short hair, fluffing the wetness from it. A length of canvas, stretched tightly across *Dana's* cockpit, shielded her from the sun's intensity. Earlier, Sonny had helped them buy food, then had gone back to his bungalow to clean up. She and Neal had put the provisions away, tidied the boat and showered. Their friend would join them aboard later for a meal, and then in the morning, as the finale to his visit, they planned to sail to Isla Grande, an island only a handful of miles away. In contrast to the oily, questionable water of the harbor, the cool, clear island water was ideal for swimming, and that thought made her smile.

Dana gently rocked and the sun's heat beat through the awning. The motion and warmth made Jessie's eyelids heavy. She let her head drift back against the cabin and shut her eyes. In the distance, she could hear dinghies and *pangas* buzz as they cut paths across the harbor.

Their day had begun like it always did, listening to the morning net. She had finally made radio contact with Gail and Randy to explain the events in Mexico City. She would have to wait until they met in person to divulge Sonia's fears about Hal, their impressions of the infamous video tape, and the discreet purchase Sonny made that had turned sour. Eavesdroppers made those details ripe for gossip and she had already contributed more than enough to the grapevine. She admitted needing a couple of days to get back to a simpler, more sedate way of life, and Gail had cheered at the idea of a trip to Isla Grande. Stay the course and screw the rest was Gail's advice, and Jessie duly jotted it down in her radio log next to her friend's last jewel of wisdom, which, not surprisingly, was the same, and it had made her laugh.

Her thoughts came back to the cockpit and the heat penetrating the awning. She shifted her position so that she could feel the breeze again. Neal was below, fixing a fitting that had come loose and she could hear tools bang against each other as he rummaged through the box for the right wrench or screwdriver. When it went quiet, her thoughts turned to the night before.

She, Neal and Sonny had found themselves dining in the same restaurant as Hal, Sonia and Eric. Sitting at adjacent tables, they briefly compared notes on their return journeys and then moved on to future plans. After all that had gone on, it seemed incredible that they had talked so amiably.

It wasn't surprising to her that Hal and Sonia wanted to sail back up to the Sea of Cortez for the summer, but when Eric announced he was sailing *Osprey* to Puerto Vallarta, hauling her out of the water and heading back to the States to tackle the dispute over Jennifer's death, Jessie felt vindicated for her belief in him. She was glad he didn't appear bitter. In fact, when Neal said their plans were to head through the Panama Canal, Eric seemed enthused. And Sonny got everyone's sympathies when he said after the promised sail to Isla Grande, he had to get back to work.

The sputter of an engine close to *Dana* roused her. She swung her legs off the cockpit bench and stood, slightly stooped, under the awning. She blinked and looked again in confusion as her mind sped through the calendar. No, she was right, Sage and Peter weren't due for another week.

"Neal, I think we have visitors. Can you come out here?" She heard metal tools clank together as he tossed them back into their box.

His head popped out of the companionway hatch. "Who is it?"

Jessie didn't need to tell him. The four people in the dinghy that pulled alongside were as big as life.

"Hey, you guys, what's up? Have I lost a week somewhere?" Jessie called out as she grabbed the line to Anders Larssen's dinghy. Sonny, Sage and Peter lowered *Dana's* waterline as they boarded. The large couple had to nearly fold in half to get under the awning and balance their way to the cockpit.

"Anders, you coming aboard?" said Neal from the companionway.

"Thanks, Neal, but no. Mae is waiting on the *muella* with groceries, and we've got stuff to do. These people needed to see you, so I thought I'd drop them off. See you later."

Sonny said as he got settled, "Thanks for helping us out, Anders, we appreciate it."

"That's okay, anytime. Bye."

Jessie tossed him his painter and waved as he motored away, then she joined the group in the cockpit. "So what's this all about?"

Sonny jumped in before anyone began. "You're not going to believe this."

Sage took a breath and brushed the bangs from her face. Her long hair flowed over her shoulders and down her back, the tips nearly brushing the cockpit bench where she sat. "Well, it's Angel, do you remember him?" Her listeners nodded. "Good. He's a great kid and wouldn't knowingly do anything wrong, but we're sure he's somehow connected with Sonia's getting hurt."

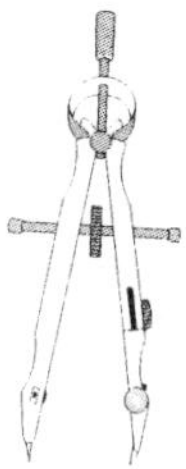

20

The news produced a long silence while everyone waded through what Sage had said. Neal was the first to speak.

"From what I've just heard, this could get involved. I'm having a beer, anyone care to join me?" After seeing nods all around, he disappeared down the companionway hatch.

Peter projected his quiet voice so Neal could hear. "Not directly responsible of course, but Mareya overheard him telling another boy about a man, a *gringo*, asking him to help play a prank on friends staying at Alta Linda. The little scamp boasted about earning some money over a video and was so relieved that he apparently hadn't spoiled the show when you two caught him coming out of your room."

"Our room?" Before the question got out of her mouth, Jessie remembered her brief panic over the unaccustomed weightlessness of her pack that night. She watched Sonny reach for the beer Neal offered him.

"What's up, Jessie?" said Sonny.

She caught Neal's eye. "We assumed he took something. It never occurred to us he could be putting something *back*. My backpack . . . I knew it wasn't right, but that would mean . . . ."

"Eric's involved." Neal said it simply without emotion or surprise.

Struggling to keep up with Neal's reasoning, Sonny said, "Wait, that's a stretch. How do you arrive at that?"

Jessie accepted the cold, perspiring bottle of Superior from Neal and took a few moments to get Peter and Sage up to speed so they could follow along. As much as she didn't want to admit it, the possibility of Eric's guilt was becoming more real. A vision of Sonia's battered body formed in her mind, but she pushed it aside to explain how they caught Angel coming out of their room, how that led them to check their few valuables and her momentary panic when she thought the camera was gone. Just as she was fighting the panic, Neal miraculously conjured it out of the jumble of belongings on the bed. For some reason, finding it hadn't made her feel better. Now she knew why.

Everyone's attention went to Sage as she spoke.

"Yes, it was a camera Angel was supposed to put in your room. Well, you can imagine Mareya, she went berserk. I think his ear still hurts from where she twisted it while he unloaded his whole story. He's young, and I don't think he connected his antics with what happened to Sonia. There's still no proof they are connected, but the coincidence made us uncomfortable. Angel was all fired up because he thought he was involved in a special assignment. Sneaking in and out of places with the sanction of an adult for a good cause would grab the imagination of any young boy. He made himself scarce that night after you let him go because he couldn't find the pack he was supposed to put the camera in, and then you caught him on the way out of your room. As far as he was concerned, he failed in his 'mission.' He waited for the ax to fall, but when nobody ever came to yell at him, he thought he had gotten away with it. And I guess he would have if he hadn't wanted to impress his friends with the story." Sage's eyes jumped between Jessie and Neal.

Peter said, "In talking to him, I think he really believed the whole thing was legitimate. That's not all, though. There are two parts to the reason we came down to see you." Peter shifted his weight and continued. "The man who dropped you off at our place . . . Fernando? He stayed with relatives in Tampu that night. They own a small hotel and were having a big birthday celebration for one of their kids. Fernando drank a little too much and started talking about his unbelievable good fortune. It seems a group of his brothers and cousins had been down the mountain for two days, working; they were on their way home when he came across you on the road. That must have been some gratuity you gave him, because he was drunk on his luck as much as the hooch. The amount impressed everyone and the story started to spread. It took a while, but it finally reached our staff and they were all talking about it, especially since you lot ended up at our place. You never mentioned anyone other than Fernando and when we asked Sonny here, he said Fernando was alone. My question is, where did all the brothers and cousins go?"

Sonny beamed and bounced his foot. Jessie could tell he was filled with possible explanations.

She rubbed her forehead. "I didn't think we gave him that much money, but let me get this straight. He started out with a truck full of brothers and cousins, but when he got to us he was alone. So the others got out of the truck for some reason before he got to us."

Sonny rushed in, "It had to be them. The sticks, the disorganization, and as soon as things fell apart, they ran. Those guys weren't highway robbers any more than you or me. And what about this *gringo*? Remember, I told you Mr. Art Gallery heard there was a *gringo* staying in the village."

Half in and half out of the companionway hatch, Neal propped one elbow on the cabin top and rested his head on his hand. "The mist is clearing. This all has to connect, we just need to figure out how."

Jessie said, "We didn't see anything on the road before Fernando arrived except a few other vehicles that passed us. There was that one white car, with the thing on the antenna that turned around. I remember telling you I thought we'd scared someone away."

Sonny snapped his head around and looked at Jessie. "Wait a minute, a white car with kind of an off-white fluffy thing at the top on the antenna?"

"Yeah, small kind of a compact car."

"That's the car Sonia and I saw in Tampu. The one she thinks Hal was in."

Everyone's voice jumped in at once; they all paused and then Sonny and Neal's voices stepped on each other again. After a laugh, Neal said with his hand that Sonny had the floor.

Sonny tripped over ideas that gushed out faster than he could form words for them. "How about this. Hal follows us. Since he knows where we're going, he doesn't have to be right behind us. When he comes around that curve and sees us broken down, he gets out of there before we can get a good look at him. He flags down Fernando, makes up some story about us and unloads a bunch of cash on these guys to rough us up and scare the pants off Sonia."

Neal said, "Okay, but that doesn't explain Angel and the camera. Plus, you heard Sonia's story of what happened – they threw her out of the truck and more or less forgot about her. And no matter how much money he has, Hal would have needed a transporter to get himself back to Mexico from L.A. so fast."

Jessie said, "It seemed those men wanted our things. Once the two guys in front got rid of Fernando and Sonia, they didn't even go for me; they reached right for Sonia's purse and my pack."

Silence followed as the volley of ideas dried up.

Neal's back went rod straight. "Even if Fernando could have fixed your car, Sonny, the plan was to get us in the truck. He fiddled around for a while to give his family time to get into place. The camera had to be the focus there, too. His family knew it would be in the front seat because that's where Fernando agreed he'd get us to put it."

The only person who would benefit from that arrangement was . . . . Instead of finishing the thought, Jessie said, "He got us in the front and you two in the back, maybe thinking that it would make the camera easier to snatch."

Sonny said, "Most of the gang went for the back of the truck, probably to keep Neal and me busy. They were confident that two of them, with Fernando not adding any resistance, could handle Sonia and Jessie. What they didn't count on was an angry woman armed with pepper spray."

Peter's voice was quiet and steady as he joined the animated discussion. "They probably didn't think anyone would really get hurt. I imagine they wanted to take you by surprise and make off with a couple of bags before you knew what was happening. If Fernando was on their side, he could be trusted to help things along a little bit. But when two of them began screaming, your driver realized he and his family had grabbed hold of a rattlesnake. He knew the plan had failed, and it was obvious you understood little Spanish, so he told them to run and got you out of there. Once again, he became your good Samaritan."

Calm returned as they listened to Peter and he continued.

"I went with Tomy to pick up your car. That road winds through the hills there. It's possible to travel miles and end up, as the crow flies, only a mile or so up and over the hill that separates the two strips of road. Given the time you said they had while Fernando tinkered with your car, they could have scrambled the distance and set up the ambush. They probably figured that would be better than just rolling up in their truck and attacking you. Even if you couldn't recognize them, you might remember the truck. I imagine they thought they could easily do the deed, deliver the camera, and then scatter to find their own way, if not home, then to some relative's place. The fact that the deal fell apart wouldn't have changed that. Seems a lot of effort to spend for a camera."

Jessie was adjusting to the idea that Eric's character wasn't blameless, but she wasn't ready yet to concede his guilt. She didn't respond to Peter's comment, and neither did anyone else.

Sonny tipped the beer bottle to his lips and drained it. "Hal has to fit in there somewhere."

"It's possible Hal and Eric are in on this together." The words came deliberately. As soon as he said it, Neal turned to Jessie and held her glance.

The cockpit remained quiet and harbor noises filled in while that thought made its way around the group.

Sonny nodded and said, "It would explain all the different aspects of what's gone on."

"It's hard for me to see Eric so brutal and conniving. He and Sonia are good friends and after what happened to Jennifer . . . no, I just can't see it."

"But Jessie, would you entertain the thought that he might connive to get hold of that camera?"

She looked at her husband. "There was nothing on the film. Why would he go to all that trouble?"

"Because he didn't know then that there was nothing on the film. Swainyo was pretty insistent when he asked us about whether we had opened it . . . ."

"But then that would mean Eric was concerned . . . about . . . what it might show." The realization evolved as she spoke. It was all happening so fast. The disjointed ideas they were throwing out began coming together. As a result, Eric's guilt loomed in Jessie's mind like a specter. The scale was rapidly tipping against him and she could no longer fight it.

"Exactly." Sonny's voice leaped in as if a thought just struck him. "Let's say the two of them are in on this. Eric calls Hal the night we were all at dinner. That gives him the whole night and more than half a day to get back into Mexico. They follow us up the mountain. The deal is Hal helps Eric get the camera. The widower doesn't necessarily have to be guilty of killing his wife to want to see it. He knows it's going into the bureaucratic mill and thinks this is his only chance to see what Jennifer recorded on her last day. Hey, I can understand that. In return, Eric helps Hal get the goods on Sonia. Only Hal goes ballistic when he finds out what's going on between her and me, loses control and beats the crap out of his wife. That also might explain why Eric was so angry at the hospital when I saw him. They had a heart-to-heart before they got to her room to get their roles straight. Hal really screwed up the whole thing by losing his head."

Neal said, "I disagree, Sonny. Eric wouldn't go to all that trouble just to see what Jennifer taped. I think he needed to know whether or not to show up at Swainyo's. While we were at the gallery party that night, Eric could have lifted the camera somehow with the intention of getting a quick view and getting it back before we returned. You said that Andre mentioned a *gringo* was staying in the pueblo that same night, and that the *gringo* freaked when the electricity went off at eight. If it was Eric, all his efforts would have been wasted, he wouldn't have been able to see . . . ."

Jessie interrupted her husband again and gave one last effort on Eric's behalf. "But if he couldn't see the tape because of the electricty, and still showed up at Swainyo's not knowing what to expect, then that must mean he had nothing to hide. Maybe Sonny's right, he knew he'd never get another chance. We weren't going to let go of the camera willingly, so he took it."

"Wait a minute," said Sonny. "He was at the hotel two nights. He would have known from the first night that the juice got cut off at eight."

"Not if he stayed at the hotel owned by Fernando's relatives," said Peter.

When the three friends and Sage turned to Peter, he elaborated. "There are a few people in the *pueblo* with their own generators. Remember, Fernando's relatives had a birthday party that first night? They would have made arrangements to have one for that. The next night things would have gone back to normal. If Eric made a lot of noise, someone would have told someone else until it got to the right person, you know how it goes, and arrangements for a generator would have been made. Of course, knowing some Spanish would be almost necessary. Most of the folks speak Nahuatl, an Indian dialect, with some Spanish words mixed in. I don't know anyone living there who could have arranged all that in English."

Another pause allowed the information to filter through everyone's mind, and Jessie coupled that with the fact that Fernando spoke virtually no English either.

That was it; the final thread of hope gave way. Eric knew before he got to Mexico City that the tape wouldn't implicate him. Finally, in her heart, she knew Neal had been right all along. No one would go to so much trouble unless the stakes were high. Jennifer's money would give Eric the freedom to pursue his passion for cruising, unencumbered. Did the man know he killed his baby, too, when he got rid of his burdensome wife? Quietly, her eyes dull with resignation, Jessie said, "He looked so stunned, so sick after he saw the tape; how do you act that? God, I can't believe it." She cupped her hand over her mouth as she came to terms with the horror this man had inflicted on an innocent woman and his unborn child.

"All these things put together have got to mean Eric's involved, at least with the events in Tampu. It all fits, I mean it's all possible." Sonny gazed out over the water and paused as a familiar sight drew his attention. "He's heading to shore."

The other four leaned to see the distinctive, curly hair on the man who piloted the inflatable dinghy toward the beach.

"I think we should have a talk with him." Sonny made a few suggestions and when everyone agreed, they prepared to go ashore. Sonny whistled to a passing *panga* and negotiated a lift to shore for himself, Peter and Sage. Jessie and Neal closed up *Dana* and followed them a few minutes later in *Pointer.*

* * *

"With all that went on in Mexico City, I never got to thank you for remaining discreet about Sonia and me."

"That's okay, Sonny; you know my reasons."

"Yeah, I think I do."

Eric paused as he lifted the beer bottle to his lips and released a light chuckle. "What's that supposed to mean?"

"Well, it's just that Tampu is a nice, quiet place. Attacks like the one on Sonia are very unusual there." Sonny took a swallow of beer. He set the bottle down on its napkin, then lifted it again and began to make a design out of the wet rings left behind on the paper. When he looked up and saw his friends, he met Eric's eyes. "You don't mind if Jessie and Neal join us, do you? Thanks." He didn't give Eric the opportunity to respond before he waved the couple over.

"Hi, Eric, Sonny. Hope we're not interrupting anything," said Jessie.

"Not at all. I just told Eric, again, how stunned Tampu was about Sonia's attack, and then I thought I'd bring him up to speed on everything we couldn't talk about at dinner when Hal was around. You can help fill in the parts I forget."

Eric's eyes darted from the new arrivals back to Sonny. "What are you getting at?"

"Apart from what happened to Sonia, we had the most interesting time in Tampu. I thought you might like to hear about it."

Three sets of eyes watched him. Eric shrugged. "Sure, why not. You said you were buying."

"So I did, so I did." Sonny gave a wave to the man behind the bar to bring four more Coronas.

Sonny began at the beginning. Eric stared with interest as Sonny told the story about Fernando and the attack on the mountain road. Angel's story followed and at the mention of a *gringo* taking advantage of the naiveté of the young boy, a tuck began to appear between Eric's eyes as his brows pulled together. His glance slid around the table and rested, in turn, on each of the three who shared the table with him. When Sonny wound down the narration with Sage and Peter's unexpected visit to town and the news they had brought, Eric leaned back in his chair and, with his left hand, pulled a coin from the change on the table and began to tap.

Sonny finished and the tapping stopped. Silence yawned and held for several seconds. Eric's frown deepened, his eyes fixed on the coin. More seconds passed until in slow motion he leaned forward, put the coin down and rested his elbows on the table. He took a breath and focused on Sonny. Neal felt the heat of Eric's rage radiate out toward Sonny, but his friend seemed unaffected.

"You set me up. This was never intended to be a friendly chat, and with the company you keep, I shouldn't be surprised. The way you've explained it, though, someone has gone to a lot of trouble to make it look like I had something to do with what happened in Tampu. I'm curious to know who that might be." He stopped talking and the furrows in his face softened, but only for a second. "I play 'what if' a thousand times a day and this game of yours is nothing compared to that." He hurled a pointed stare at the people sharing the table and, with deliberation, stood. The corner of his chair caught the back of his leg and tipped over, crashing to the floor. He ignored it and the attention it drew as he walked slowly out to the street.

The stares from the other patrons lingered as Neal righted the chair. "That went down well, don't you think?"

Jessie stared at the door through which Eric had disappeared and said nothing.

Sonny rested his elbows on the table and propped his chin on a double fist. "He didn't flinch. If he's involved, he's good."

"That's the thing isn't it . . . 'if'? I don't trust the guy," said Neal. "I don't like him, but I wouldn't hang him on that performance; he gave nothing away."

Jessie looked at the two men and shrugged. "He certainly slapped us in the face. I've struggled so long with 'is he guilty or is he not' that I don't trust myself anymore. Do you guys think there is a 'who' and a 'why' to the idea that someone's framing him?"

They both mumbled, "I don't know," and sipped at their bottles of warming Corona. After the last sip and mulling over a few more ideas, they paid the bill and walked out into the blast of heat and humidity. Sage and Peter waited under a tree at the main *zocolo,* watching a basketball game. The group sat in the shade and talked until they were weary of hearing about Eric, Jennifer and all the related issues. A change in shirt colors on the players indicated an end to one basketball game and the start of another.

Neal had an idea. "Sage, Peter, it'll be tight, but in this weather, we'd spend most of the time on deck anyway. Why not come to Isla Grande with us tomorrow? All we were going to do is sail over and anchor for the night. Last year we didn't eat at any of the *palapa* restaurants, and their food is supposed to be pretty good, we thought we'd check it out. We wanted to laze on the beach, have a nice meal and sail back the next morning. How does that sound?" His suggestion brought enthusiastic urging from Jessie and Sonny.

The couple looked at each other, then Sage said, "If you think we'll fit, it sounds like fun."

"You can have our bunk, we'll sleep in the cockpit. It's only for one night, we'll manage." Neal's mind worked on the arrangements as they strolled back toward the Pension del Mar. It would be tight, but there was an ease of friendship developing among the five of them that made the prospect an adventure rather than a battle of logistics.

21

Dana frolicked when she escaped the crowded harbor for the freedom of a light sea breeze. With the heat of civilization behind her, and under billowed sails, she cruised easily toward the tiny island that would tuck her into its protected bay. Reflections of sunlight burst on the cobalt blue water like a barrage of popping flashbulbs.

During their stints at the helm, Sage, Peter and Sonny couldn't suppress smiles each time the wind, sea and vessel harmonized and transmitted power from the rudder's bite up to the tiller in their hands. They felt the surge and glowed as they crossed the distance to Isla Grande in a few hours.

Once there, *Dana's* anchor and chain clanked as it tumbled to the sea bottom.

"I love the sound of an anchor dropping. It's reassuring somehow, I don't know why." Sage brushed aside her bangs and adjusted her cap. Her sigh made Jessie smile.

Off to one side was the vast expanse of mainland Mexico, to the other, Isla Grande. Aft lay an unobstructed view of the rocky rubble at the end of the island and beyond that, open ocean.

On a signal from Neal, Jessie tightened her hand around the tiller and put the engine in reverse. They drifted back. Neal kept his hand on the chain until he felt the pull that told him the anchor had caught and gripped the seabed. With *Dana* still in reverse, he slowly released more links until he saw the two nylon ties that marked one-hundred-feet pass through the deck plate and descend toward the water. He stopped the chain when the two ties dipped beneath the surface. He secured the windlass and gave Jessie the signal to goose the engine in hard reverse. The anchor felt set, and he relayed that to his wife with a wave. She slipped the throttle into neutral. After attaching the snubber, he looked around. Their floating home settled into position on the outside edge of the flotilla.

The three guests watched the choreographed routine of tidying up after a sail and helped when asked, but they discovered their biggest contribution was in finding a place out of the way.

After everything was stowed, *Dana's* crew settled in the cockpit to sip cold bottles of Superior and eat ham sandwiches while they observed the endless antics of the throng on the beach. Shipped over from Ixtapa's high-rise hotels, the droves spent the day playing and splashing. Small power boats or *pangas* pulled long, bright, lemon-yellow inflated tubes around the bay. Known as banana boats, the tubes were fixed with handholds and were mounted by people who rode for the thrill of speed and staying on. Jet skies circled like gnats. The bay water bounced from all the activity and slapped against *Dana's* hull, making her rock.

"Looks kind of . . . busy . . . doesn't it?"

Neal laughed at Jessie's comment. In spite of the frenzy of tourism, he felt a freedom away from town and from all the complications that existed there.

"I'm going to get my suit on and swim to shore. You guys coming?" Sonny leapt down the first couple of companionway steps before turning to see the response to his suggestion.

"I'll tell you what. Put the stuff you want ashore in *Pointer* and I'll meet you there," said Neal as he made his way forward to check their position. He could hear talking and laughing below as the other four juggled the space to don bathing suits. For their size, Sage and Peter had done well in adapting to *Dana's* dimensions.

Jessie tripped down the side deck toward him, wearing his favorite of her swimsuits, a black one piece that showed off her tan and her figure. His eyes always lingered where the high French cut of the suit rode over her hips; he thought it looked very sexy. Her smile cut right through him and he felt a lucky man, not only to be living out the dream of his life, but also to have such a willing partner. He wrapped his arm around her and kissed her lightly on the lips through her smile.

"The stuff we want ashore is in the cockpit; I'll help load *Pointer,*" she said as they pressed their foreheads together.

"You go ahead, I'll do it. Just grab Sonny and meet me when I get to shore."

She leaned back to get a look at his face. Apparently satisfied that his volunteering for the job wasn't a sign of stress, irritation or illness, she said, "Okay, see you there," and she stepped toward the cockpit to join the others.

One by one, his wife and guests jumped into the sea, sending a gush of water skyward. Once in, they laughed and splashed all the way to shore. Several familiar boats dotted the anchorage, but he had met few of their crews. Mae and Anders must have been below; their boat with its dinghy stretched out back was on the other side of the bay. No one sat in the cockpit.

But someone was in the shaded cockpit of another boat that caught his eye. He saw a woman in a multicolored, pastel bathing suit remove her reading glasses and give a lazy wave. He smiled and waved back at Claire as the vision of her painted nails wrapping flyaway hair around her ear drifted through his thoughts.

A half hour later he was ashore, enjoying the life of a tourist. Eventually, Mae and Anders joined them. Sonny cajoled them all into riding on the bright yellow banana boat. They laughed and bounced around the bay behind a buzzing speedboat. As a tourist this was fun; as a cruiser trying to enjoy the peaceful surroundings on your boat, it was a pain in the neck. Neal drew the line when Sonny suggested a turn on a jet ski.

The sun's angle to the horizon diminished and with it, the multitude from Ixtapa. Boat after boat departed with a load of sunburned tourists bound for the mainland hotels. Anders and Mae left in their dinghy after admitting they wanted a shower, food and an early night. The bay grew as quiet as an amusement park after hours. The five friends lounged on the sand, slicked down with repeated applications of suntan lotion and crusty from dried saltwater. When the topic of dinner came up, Sonny had a proposal.

"I was talking to someone at the end *palapa,* and they're staying open for a special party tonight. A group from one of the hotels is coming here for a special barbeque. They said we could join them.

Shrimp, lobster, the works."

Price tags fluttered in front of Neal. He had in mind a more modest meal, to quickly grab something, as they were, before everything closed for the day. But, this was Sonny's last fling.

His next thought went to Sage and Peter, but they apparently had no reservations because Peter said without hesitation, "It's just what we need to wrap up an absolutely delightful day." Peter stroked Sage's knee and she smiled as if they were courting.

Jessie wrapped her arms around Neal's neck and kissed his ear when he said, "Why not."

The relay back to *Dana,* the shuffle for deck showers and then the relay back to shore took them until after dark.

Their bare feet scrunched the warm sand and a light, cool breeze ruffled the bay's corral of water. A string of brightly lit bulbs gently swayed overhead, powered by the generator that putted somewhere behind the *palapa*. The five friends settled at a table especially set up for them by the man Sonny had spoken to earlier. The other tables and the rest of the staff waited expectantly for the crowd from Ixtapa.

"Peter, if we ever get tired of the mountains, I wouldn't mind a small place on a quiet beach somewhere. If it was like this, it would be perfect."

The moonless night hid most of the boats, but the glow from shore reflected off the nearest hulls, making them look like swans. Tiny lights winked and bobbed in the darkness, giving away their positions. One of them belonged to *Dana*.

"Can you tell which one of those is yours?"

Neal leaned out over the table to scan the anchorage, then answered Sage's question. "No, I can't tell for sure from here. I'd have to get away from these lights, but she's one of those in that cluster there toward the outside edge." Sage followed his point.

As they all studied the water, dark, ghostly shadows moved into the arc of light thrown from shore. The boats from Ixtapa had arrived. Once they nudged the sand, their cargo of party-goers spilled out, laughing and shouting all the way up the beach.

"There goes tranquility," said Neal.

Music and laughter erupted in the once quiet restaurant. Dressed in fluorescent shorts, shirts and sundresses wildly designed with parrots, palms and boats, the newcomers danced and cruised the crowd while waiters hustled drinks and food through the bar at the back.

Once the five joined in the festivities, they lost their outsider stigma. Plates vanished to clear the tables and a patch of sand to one side became a huddle of people bouncing and gyrating to the endless recordings of rock and roll music. No one seemed concerned about the neighbors, for the new arrivals had no idea there were neighbors. Neal's thoughts turned with some guilt to the few people he knew on those boats trying to enjoy the evening.

Almost at the same moment, Jessie danced in close and yelled over the music, "This noise is probably going down well out in the anchorage." Since there was nothing they could do about it, they shrugged at each other and continued dancing.

For Neal, the night passed in a swirl of pleasure. Good atmosphere, good company and good food made him feel like he'd been given an unexpected bonus. He enjoyed and savored it until the water taxi drivers began preparations to leave.

Envy spread across several faces when the troop from Ixtapa assembled their belongings. The fact that some among them belonged to a boat that floated just outside the arc of light fascinated them. Neal felt more than just the glow of beer as he pointed in the general direction of *Dana.* I'd envy me, too, he thought.

With his wife and friends, Neal stood on the beach and waved good-bye to the crowd that boarded the boats, almost as if he were saying good-bye to guests. The boats picked their way through the anchorage, and quiet returned to Isla Grande as if someone had flicked a switch.

In bare feet, the five trudged up the beach to say thank you and good-bye to the men and women who had kept the night well oiled, then found *Pointer* and shuttled home.

* * *

"Beep, beep, beep . . . ."

The continuous, shrill screech yanked Neal from his dream. He sat upright and blinked in the darkness, wishing more than anything to shut the noise off. Where was it coming from?

Two additional sounds reached his ears simultaneously.

One, an agonizing thud and scrape of contact which vibrated through the hull, the other, a scream from Jessie.

"The depth alarm. Neal, we're on the rocks!"

"Beep, Beep, Beep. . . ."

Another scrape and Neal, launched from his makeshift bed, pounded up *Dana's* deck, yelling, "Start the engine," over his shoulder at Jessie, who was already hunched over the key.

He spun a 360-degree turn and swept a glance across the anchor lights of the other boats, now a good distance away. Finally realizing this wasn't a dream and that he wouldn't wake up, he dropped to his knees at the windlass and tried to control the shake in his hands as he grabbed the anchor chain and pulled. Hand over hand the chain clanked aboard, sliding in all directions as it hit the deck. Again the scrape of rock contacting fiberglass reached him and he murmured again and again, "We'll be fine . . . calm down . . . we'll be fine . . . ." Another scrape. His heart beat so loudly it blocked all other sounds except *Dana's* cry when she made contact with the rocky shore. He couldn't hear whether or not Jessie got the engine going. *Dana* shrieked again. He heaved at the chain and nearly pulled himself overboard when the anchor broke the surface and chipped *Dana's* bow as it swung into her with a crash.

Neal had heard of overwhelming strength released in times of crisis, but there was no way he could have already pulled in all the chain he'd let out when they anchored. Another thought dawned on him right then. The nylon snubber line, used to soften the jolt on the anchor system when *Dana* stretched her leash, was swinging free instead of being clipped to the chain, where it belonged. Another scrape forced him to pigeonhole those thoughts for later; he had more urgent things to think about.

Sonny appeared at his elbow, "What do you want me to do?"

Neal couldn't think. "Is the engine going?"

"Yes."

"Stay here and make sure this stays put; it wouldn't be good if the anchor went down again just now." He finished securing the chain around the sampson post as a cry went up from the cockpit. "Oh, and I don't want any more chain to go down that hole on the deck."

"Neal!" Another cry from the cockpit.

The shudder and desperate clang came from the stern this time, not through the hull. Neal's heels thudded on the deck as he moved amidship and checked around. At least the weather's calm, he thought, grasping for anything positive. Every neural circuit in his body hummed from sensory overload and he didn't trust his legs. Leaning into the rigging, he wrapped his arms around the wire with what strength he had left. He saw Jessie bobbing up and down to work the tiller and throttle. The incoming swell lifted *Dana* then dropped her with a crunch, pushing the wind steering gear that hung off the stern into solid rock. Their home of eighteen months shuddered. His wife yelled.

"Jessie, forward gear."

"I'm in forward gear." She shouted as if Neal were on the other side of the globe.

"Then give it more fuel."

"We're stuck."

"Give us more, we'll be all right." He wasn't sure why he said that, he certainly didn't believe it.

He heard the engine's rumble increase and saw another swell begin to lift *Dana.* "Jessie, give us all we've got . . . ," he waited until the swell crested, then shouted, "Now!"

To Neal, the scrape felt like a knife tip had pierced the skin at his throat and sliced all the way down to his toes. *Dana* screamed and his knuckles went white around the rigging. When it was over, he watched the dark, menacing shapes of the rocks disappear and blend into the beautiful tropical isle of a few hours ago. Weakness descended. He shivered and realized his T-shirt was soaked. They had found a stinger in paradise, he thought, then turned his efforts to what lay ahead. They weren't free and clear yet.

His own, unrecognizable voice called out over his shoulder, "Jessie, we're doing fine. Do you see the anchor lights?"

Her voice, raspy and broken, reached out to him. "Yes."

"Slow down and aim for them."

Like an infant on wobbly legs, he moved to the bow where Sonny still sat, watching the chain. They exchanged a glance and Neal put his hand up to stop his friend from speaking. He didn't want to talk. Normally he would take time to properly secure the chain and anchor, but there was something he wanted to check first. Reassured that the wrap of chain around the sampson post would do for now, he made his way back to the cockpit and the rest of his crew.

Sage and Peter peered out of the companionway hatch. The alarm was silent. Jessie stared at him and said nothing.

"Babe, if you're doing okay, I'd like you to circle outside the anchorage until we check to see if we have any water coming aboard."

"I'm fine," she managed to say before she bit down on her lip.

When he saw her swipe a hand across her face, he felt a wash of tears flood his own eyes. He stretched a hand toward hers; they laced fingers and gripped for a moment. He blinked, cleared his throat and turned toward the other two.

"Peter, if you could go to the bow with Sonny and keep watch up there, I'd appreciate it. Sage, I'll need your help below. You both okay with that?"

He heard the muffled assent, after which Peter emerged from the cabin and pulled himself to the bow.

Neal grabbed a flashlight and with Sage's help pulled line, bottles of Superior and El Presidente out of the bilge and checked the hull. When he wiped his hand along the inside wall, it was dry. Next they pulled cans and plastic boxes of spare parts from lockers in the engine area and lastly they checked the lockers in the bow. It took twenty minutes, but he found nothing breached. They needed to examine the hull from the outside, but that would have to wait until daylight when he could hop over the side with mask and fins.

When he pulled his head out of the last area, the chain locker, he stared at the cavity and thought. His findings confirmed what he had suspected earlier. He made his way back to the cabin where Sage sat waiting for him. His eyes took in the mess their search had made.

"Well, Sage, I can't see anything in this light. At least we don't have water pouring in anywhere. We'll anchor and have a better look in the morning. How are you doing?"

"Apart from the initial fright of that alarm, we're doing okay. We're sorry about the boat, though; there's bound to be damage."

He nodded and stood.

She stood with him. Neal saw her hesitate, but when she spoke, the quiet warmth he felt from her concern eased the doubt that had begun to creep in.

"Neal, what happened? It seemed you both went to a lot of trouble earlier to make sure the anchor was all right."

"That's a good question, and since we're not sinking, we have time to think about it. Right now, though, let's re-anchor."

He climbed topside and allayed Jessie's fear with the news that they were not taking on water. They cruised the bay, picked a new spot and went through the anchoring process again, just as they had done earlier and just as they had done hundreds of times before.

Their guests watched the ritual for the second time in a little more than twelve hours, and after they were satisfied with their position, Jessie brought out the El Presidente and glasses. They all sat in the cockpit and silently sipped the golden elixir. The drama that had gripped and twisted their well-being went unheeded by the rest of the anchorage. It slept on as if nothing had happened.

Even with the brandy, Neal felt tension build. If he explained what he believed to be true, would they think it merely an excuse for a bad job of anchoring? He cleared his throat.

"Jessie, how much chain did I tell you we had out after we anchored this afternoon?"

"We were in twenty-five feet of water, so you told me we had a hundred feet of chain out."

He nodded.

"What I pulled in was only a fraction of that. As I pulled, some of it went into the locker, but I was pulling so fast most of it skidded around on deck. What I saw and felt was maybe just enough for the anchor to touch bottom. Sort of like standing in water where your toes barely touch without your nose submerging. The snubber wasn't attached either."

"You always attach the snubber."

"I know; I can't remember ever forgetting to do it and would you say we've ever had a problem with it coming detached?" She shook her head.

Sonny followed the logic. "That's easy then, someone diddled with the chain."

"It seems so bizarre, but the only other choice is bad anchoring. Call me arrogant, but I'd bet what we own on that not being the reason for what happened tonight." Neal's glance swept across the silhouettes of a dozen or more hulls sharing the anchorage. A single white light hovered above half of the hulls, the rest were dark. Out of habit, his eyes went to *Dana's* anchor light. Its white beacon danced in time with the wavelets that struck her hull.

Jessie said, "We've been ashore almost since we arrived. Whoever did this wouldn't need a lot of time, but I know subconsciously I looked out here now and then just to make sure the boat was okay. I never saw anyone near *Dana.* What do you think, that they pulled the whole thing up and then just dropped enough to touch the anchor on the bottom?"

"The bag of laundry we threw in the chain locker is wet; I felt it. When we left town this morning, you moved it out of the way and replaced it once we got settled this afternoon. I doubt it was wet then, right?"

"Right."

"Most of the chain I hauled in stayed on the deck and Sonny made sure none of that fell through the deck plate. Since I wasn't sure just how much had fallen through initially, I couldn't tell by looking at the locker how much chain I'd pulled in. But those clothes were damp through, as if something wet had been sitting on them for a while, so . . . ." He shrugged. "I checked our position when we got back from the party and we were still all right. If someone did get on board, whoever did it knew enough about anchoring to make the move toward the point a slow one. With the new moon, we've got spring tides, and I bet if we check, low tide was sometime after dark. The change isn't big, but big enough for the anchor to lose its grip. If the wind came up, all the better for them." Neal stood, put his hands on his hips and bounced his glance around the anchorage again. "Which one of you did it?"

Jessie threaded her arm through his and said, "It won't do us any good to stamp our feet about it because with the exception of one person, everyone will think we did a poor job of anchoring. You know how it is."

"Well, who out there is a good friend of Eric's?" Peter's voice rose from the quietest corner of the cockpit where he and Sage sat holding hands. Above, a blanket of stars lit the night.

A vision of pastel nails curling hair around her ear brought Claire's face into focus. Neal thought of Satch, but knew he couldn't do it without Claire knowing, and she's on our side. Neal dismissed it. Who else? Mae and Anders? He wouldn't believe it.

"It seems hard to believe that someone would go to this length, even if they sided with Eric. The damage to *Dana* is bad enough, but one of us could have gotten hurt." She scanned the anchorage, too. "Maybe it would help if we wrote down the names of the boats that are here. I recognized some of them."

"Jessie, let's go for a row. You're right, we should get all the names. Maybe someone will eventually look guilty, even if not now, sometime down the road. I want to remember who was here tonight. Sonny, you usually don't need much sleep, can you keep watch until we get back?"

"You bet, I'm not tired at all. Tell me what you want me to do."

Neal briefly explained how to monitor *Dana's* position, and while he pulled *Pointer* alongside, Jessie grabbed pen and paper. Their guests watched as they climbed into the dinghy, a routine as common to Jessie and Neal as taking the car for a spin. With a rhythm of dip and pull, Neal swung the oars and *Pointer* melted into the black shadows in search of an enemy.

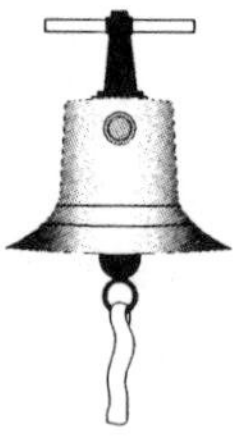

22

"I can't very well say no." Sonny pulled the sunglasses off his face and slid them into the breast pocket of a brightly colored shirt.

Jessie said, "What made her change her mind?"

Neal watched the waiter deposit three more bottles of beer on their table. A breeze caressed them from the open window, but didn't chase away the limp, clammy feeling he had. He looked at his watch. Sage and Peter were well on their way home, and in a few hours Sonny would climb into a taxi that would take him to the airport. It appeared he wouldn't be going back alone.

"How should I know? She can't pin it down . . . describes it as just a feeling she has. The thought of leaving Zhuat on the boat with him terrifies her. For all I know, Hal's on board still thinking they're taking off day after tomorrow."

In spite of the serious circumstances, Neal smiled. "Well, my friend, you've got some interesting times ahead of you."

Jessie said, "When do you see Sonia again?"

"She's at the *pension* now . . . waiting . . . bag in hand. She knew we were all off today and arrived ready to go. I haven't had much time to talk to her, but she brought a picture of Hal and gave it to Sage and Peter to see if Angel recognizes him. I noticed it was a group photo that included Eric, which she, either on purpose or not, didn't point out. They promised to call me at home after they talked with Angel."

"Should be interesting. We'll expect an update when you hear. Is she on the same flight?"

"As far as I know, yes. The lady at the *pension* helped her call the airline and make a reservation."

"What's she going to do once she gets back to the States?"

"She hasn't said, but I get the feeling she hopes she can stay with me for a while. I suppose it's all right. There's plenty of room, as long as she doesn't expect anything else, which she assures me is the case."

Jessie shook her head. "The important thing is whether or not you want to deal with this."

"I suppose it's like you and the camera. Damned if you do and damned if you don't. Even if Hal didn't hit on her this one time, he obviously has before. I don't think she'll leave him on her own, and if for some reason grabbing hold of me gives her the courage to do it, how can I refuse? Who knows, she may get home and change her mind again, but at least I know I did my bit."

The conversation paused.

"We wish you weren't leaving," said Jessie.

Sonny laughed. "Me, too. You guys really know how to spice up a vacation. Even I feel the need to go home and rest. You have some interesting times of your own ahead. Lots of unanswered questions, and I expect answers when you find them."

"If we find them." Neal popped a tortilla chip in his mouth.

Sonny lowered his voice. "We still keeping the anchor incident to ourselves?"

Neal nodded. "At least for now. So far all we've gotten are innocent conversations and smiles from the people who were on those boats at Isla Grande. I don't know if we'll ever find out who came aboard *Dana* that night."

"So the boat will be all right until you get to Acapulco?"

"I think so. The biggest gouges are at the bottom of the keel. There will be fiberglass work to do, but we can pull her out of the water there and get that fixed up. I'm just glad the wind vane wasn't seriously damaged. The part we need to replace is already on its way to Acapulco. It should be there when we arrive. We were lucky the weather was calm; any worse and the repairs wouldn't be so straightforward."

Jessie rested her elbow on the table and cupped her chin in one hand. "I hope this is all over now. I've had enough conflict and antagonism. Never again."

Neal teased her. "I'll remember you said that next time we come across a body."

She laughed. "Yeah, right. Agreed."

"If it's any consolation, the pressure might be off in a couple of days. Eric had planned to leave with Hal and Sonia. She said they were going to travel together up to Puerto Vallarta. That's where Eric's leaving the boat while he goes back to the States. Of course, Sonia's leaving could derail Hal's plans, which might affect Eric."

The Larrsens, laden down with market bags, walked past the open window and Mae looked in. She smiled and called out to her husband to get his attention. Jessie motioned them in and they came off the hot, bright road and moved toward the threesome's table. Sonny pulled in two more chairs, and the older couple settled their packages, pulled their sunglasses off and let them drop on their lanyards.

Jessie stood while she slid the chairs in place. "Sit, you two, and join us for a Corona. Sonny's leaving this afternoon and we're having one last salute to him before he goes."

"Sounds great. I could use a beer. I always get so hot schlepping those bags around." Mae wiped the bridge of her nose where her sunglasses left a dent. They also left a racoon-like white mask around her eyes from months of living in the sun.

"So, how did you enjoy your visit?" Anders crinkled his tanned face into a smile.

"I'd have to say it's been interesting and very memorable."

"I'll bet. Give my regards to L.A. when you get back. It has its faults, but it's my home, and there are times when I miss it. Not enough to go back, mind you. Say, you know night before last when we all stayed at Isla Grande?"

Neal swallowed his sip of beer. "Sure."

"I heard a boat went up onto the rocks. Did you see it?"

The table went quiet, all movement hesitated for a moment.

"I really wish I weren't flying off; I'll miss all this," said Sonny.

Anders and Mae exchanged a glance as if asking each other what they said. Mae turned wide eyes back toward the table, "What's happened?"

"Who mentioned this to you?" said Neal.

Anders rested his elbows on the table and looked at the beer in front of him. "Well, no one actually mentioned it. We overheard it this morning at the market."

"Who was mentioning it at the market this morning?" Neal's heart picked up its pace. Any cruiser that saw another boat on the rocks would have come to help. Since no one had come, he assumed everyone had slept through it. Everyone, that is, except maybe . . . .

Anders looked at his wife and shook his head. "That's why he slunk away from us like a dog caught on the good sofa. It explains a lot." The older couple's eyes continued their silent communication.

Neal pulled his glance away from them and looked around the table; everyone sat mesmerized. He shifted in his chair and leaned toward them. "Who was mentioning it at the market?"

Anders' eyes let go of his wife and turned toward Neal. "Let me ask first if you know who went up on the rocks."

The pause hung like a hawk, suspended in air, eyeing the ground.

"We did," Neal said with more control than he felt.

Like the hawk spying his prey, Anders swooped down on the truth. He recoiled in distaste and threw himself against the back of his chair. "The bastard!"

Mae's fingers covered her mouth. "Anders, I can't believe he'd do such a thing. He's a good friend of ours."

Neal could hear the impatience in Jessie's voice. "Who?"

Mae turned toward her and in a voice just above a whisper said, "Satch."

23

"Neal, wait up." She watched as her husband's determined step pulled away from her. She couldn't remember when she had seen him so angry. Sonny strode next to him, her husband's unwavering ally and comrade in arms. The backs of both their shirts billowed from the power of their stride. Somewhere behind her, Mae and Anders followed.

The older couple had stumbled through their story. Around the corner from the vegetable stall in which they were shopping, they had recognized Satch's voice in a conversation with someone about a boat that had floundered at Isla Grande two nights before. Since Mae and Anders were in the throes of haggling produce prices, they hadn't announced their presence nor paid too much attention to what was said. It was only when the other male voice in the conversation seemed to get angry, and Satch's voice got more defensive, that they had begun to take an interest. Anders was handing *pesos* over to the vender when the two men rounded the corner.

Anders had said, "Satch looked as though he'd been caught stealing state secrets, and Eric was so red we could have barbequed hot dogs on his forehead. The two of them squirmed around a piss-poor excuse for pleasantries and slunk away. It was obvious Eric was fuming. Satch had done something to piss him off and he looked guilty as hell. Since they had been talking about the boat that floundered, I assumed one had to do with the other, but didn't think much about why or how until just now."

As soon as the story was out, Neal had tossed enough *pesos* on the table to cover the cost of the beer and announced he was going to find Satch. The hesitation of everyone else at the table lasted only long enough for Neal to reach the street. Sonny had caught up to him, with Jessie a few steps behind, and Anders and Mae dropping out of sight at the back of the pack. It didn't really matter. They were headed to the beach where everyone put their dinghies. They'd collect each other there.

Jessie felt events spin out of control and careen toward a precipice. It reminded her of the wild ride up the mountain road to Tampu. She knew there was no way to avoid the pothole that loomed in front of them. Sweat ran down her face and she panted from the exertion to keep up. The question that ran through her head was why and how Satch had gotten involved in all this? Jessie thought Claire was a bit eccentric, but Satch, even if upset, seemed so . . . normal.

Neal and Sonny were almost on the beach. A shout stopped them, and Jessie slowed as she saw Eric close in. By the time she caught up with her husband and his friend, Eric was already part way through his speech. Beside her, Neal and Sonny's chest heaved in time with her own, they all glistened with sweat.

" . . . obviously heard. I can't tell you how sorry I am about this. I had no idea things had gone so far," said Eric. His apologetic tone did little to dispel Neal's anger.

"Where is he?" Neal's heavy breathing surrounded the question. He stood on the balls of his feet, prepared for action if needed.

"I want you to know, I just found out about it myself. It was no secret that you were headed over there, but I can't believe he'd do this."

Neal clenched his teeth and with more volume said again, "Where . . . is he?"

Eric hesitated and slowly spoke. "Claire is waiting for him at the basketball court. He's late."

Neal brushed past his adversary and walked away. His determined step kicked sand up as he ground his heels into the beach. His comrade paused a moment in front of Eric and studied him. From Sonny's half smile and the creases around his eyes, Jessie wondered what he saw in the other's face. The two men exchanged no words and in seconds Sonny followed Neal.

Eric took a step closer to Jessie. His voice was quiet and sounded sincere. "Jessie, I don't know what to say, except I'm sorry."

She watched the billowing backs of Neal and Sonny's shirts as they strode away from her, then turned and faced Eric. "That's charitable, but you don't need to apologize. I'm beyond caring." Her chest squeezed tight with anger, but she pushed herself to say more. "It's taken a while, and I fought it every step of the way, but you're guilty as hell. Every time something happened, we'd turn around and there you were. That can't be a coincidence. There's no way to prove you killed Jennifer and . . . ," she faltered, but couldn't bring herself to say, 'the baby.' It wasn't a topic she wanted to raise with him. "Or that you were involved with what happened to Sonia or to us at Isla Grande, but the fact that we can't prove it doesn't change the truth. You've been a big disappointment, Eric." She didn't wait for a response. Her words and the pace from her forced march caused her heart to beat so loudly she wouldn't have heard anything anyway.

She took long strides down the beach and fought the temptation to look back. After their ordeal at Isla Grande, she decided she really didn't care what happened to Eric.

* * *

She was wearing the same peach dress she had worn on the day she snagged Jessie at the postcard stand. On a bench in the shade watching the players bound up and down the court, she sat looking cool with one slender, tan leg crossed over the other, her back straight and her hands folded in her lap. Sunglasses hid her eyes. No one normal sits like that in this heat, Neal thought.

She must have caught his movement out of the corner of her eye because she turned toward him. The corners of her mouth lifted. A big smile for her, he thought.

He stopped square in front of her. "Where's Satch?" Even with his attempt to soften the inquiry, she picked up on it.

The smile disappeared, but her voice was casual, unhurried. "Why?"

"I'd like to talk with him."

"What about?"

"Are you waiting for him?"

She dropped her gaze to the court and watched for several seconds. When she turned to him again, her voice remained steady. "We could go back and forth this way for a very long time. So, let me say this: unless you tell me why and for what you want him, I see no reason to talk to you." Her gaze dropped again to the mix of colors finessing up and down the court

Neal wanted to shake her, but instead he sat down next to her. Her sunglasses were so dark, he couldn't see her eyes. Sonny moved toward Jessie and they huddled in quiet conversation. Mae and Anders had not caught up with them.

"During the night we all spent at Isla Grande, *Dana* drifted onto the rocks. Not because Jessie and I anchored poorly, but because someone tampered with our gear. I think Satch may know something about it and I'd like to ask him."

Her gaze remained fixed on the action taking place on the court. The slight movement of her head told Neal that her eyes were following the ball. After a moment and a cheer from the crowd, she adjusted her sunglasses and said, "I see."

"Are you meeting him here, Claire?"

She hesitated, then pulled the delicate leather band on her watch around her wrist to see its face. Her voice didn't change; it was like he'd asked her the time. "I was. But I'm not any longer." She rose and began to walk along the beach from which the trio came.

The peach dress undulated as the breeze picked at it. Neal stood to watch her go. "Claire?"

She ignored him.

"What did she say?" Jessie had joined him.

"What a strange woman." Neal looked around before he sat on the bench. "They were meeting here. If she knows anything, or guessed anything, she didn't say. Eric's probably right. He's late and she's now tired of waiting. That was all I got."

Both Sonny and Jessie stood with their hands in their pockets, rotating around to search the streets and sidewalks in all directions for the familiar face. Sonny pulled one hand out of his pocket, checked his watch, then put it back.

A moment later he said, "Just what we need."

From his position on the bench, Neal looked up at his friend and said, "What's that?"

Sonny nodded his head to indicate the direction Neal should look.

With a determined stride and arms swinging wide, Hal crossed the square toward them. Neal stood and the trio faced the approaching storm. The closer he got, the faster Hal's fists pumped in and out of a clench. He stopped a few feet in front of them.

"You know where Sonia is, now tell me." Hal's directive was aimed at Jessie.

Sonny remained in a casual stance, his hands in his pockets. "No, I don't think so."

Hal's head jerked back slightly with surprise when Sonny answered and like a nail gun, he spat out the words. "Stay out of this, it's none of your business."

"I disagree. You see, Sonia is going back to the States . . . with me . . . today."

Neal knew Sonny had strung out the statement to give it more impact. He wasn't sure, in Hal's state of mind, if it was such a good idea, but he had to admit the effect was curious. Instead of anger, the man who faced them creased his forehead in confusion.

"What the hell are you talking about?"

Sonny explained, discreetly leaving out his brief affair with the man's wife. Hal stood with feet apart and fists balanced on his hips. He listened, until he caught the accusation that it was he, Hal Sieverson, whom everyone assumed had put Sonia in the hospital.

The movement was a blur and before Neal could react, Hal's hands had found Sonny's throat. The two struggled upright until Sonny recovered enough to jab his attacker in the ribs. Hal let go, but then lunged again and the two of them fell onto the bricks, punching and kicking at each other as they rolled around.

Once Neal saw what was happening, he dived in and tried to pull the two apart. His hands gripped a shirt, but the brawl nearly pulled him down on top of the struggling pair.

A crowd began to gather.

Neal was ready to let go when Anders' voice boomed loudly in his ear. "You're acting like damn fools. Now stop it."

Working together, Anders and Neal were both able to seize Hal and yank him to a stand. In one final effort, Sonny slammed a fist into his attacker's chest and the two fighters separated. Hal squirmed futilely against his captors as they tightened their grip and dragged him clear. Jessie helped Sonny to his feet.

Blood trickled from Hal's nose and mixed with the spit that flew when he bellowed, "How dare you accuse me of . . . of . . . doing that to Sonia."

"You bastard. She's the one who thinks you did it. She's terrified. That's why she's leaving." Sonny rubbed his neck, then slapped at his clothes to get the dirt off. Blood ran down his forearm where his elbow had scraped the paving stones.

Hal's struggling eased as Anders spoke quietly to him, encouraging him to control himself. Neal added a word now and then, but let Anders take charge; the other man's words seemed more effective.

The basketball game had carried on without interruption and the crowd drifted back to it when they realized the fight was over. People still glanced across the square, but once convinced the action wouldn't start again, they turned their full attention back to the court.

Finally released from his captors, Hal sat on the bench, propped his elbows on his knees and cradled his forehead in his hands. Anders and Mae sat on either side of him.

Sonny looked at his watch again. "It's time for me to go. I have to clean up and get my things." He stopped in front of the bent head. "Just so you don't get any ideas, there's nothing going on between Sonia and me. I happen to be going her way. She knows you call your office regularly. I don't know why, but she plans to give them a telephone number where you can reach her. You want me to take her a message?" He waited, but when he got no response, he shrugged and turned to leave.

A muffled response came from the buried head. "Tell her . . . it wasn't me."

* * *

"That's what they all say, isn't it?" Sonny inspected his wound when they stopped to let a car pass before crossing to the *pension.*

"Probably," Jessie said as she stepped into the street with the other two. They reached the shade of the *pension's* verandah and passed through the arch that led to a central courtyard. She felt an instant drop in the temperature.

Sonny stopped. "I'll tell Sonia what happened at the *zocolo* once we're in the air. I'm not sure how fair that is, but I think his bravado over this might make her feel guilty about leaving. If she wants to turn right around and come back, then that's fine, but I'm going to give her a few hours to think about it."

"Sounds good to us."

"My stuff is all packed. Wait here. I'll change and wash up. We'll join you in a sec."

"Fine," said Jessie.

She and Neal sat on cane chairs among the ferns and banana palms that shaded most of the courtyard. It was small, but pretty, Jessie thought. It reminded her of the little garden at her mother's place. Other than her mom, the only thing missing was the iced tea.

"Wonder how Anders is doing with Hal?"

Neal grunted, but didn't speak.

Mae and Anders had volunteered to sit with Hal. Jessie would check with them later to find out how it went. Sitting in the green courtyard, she thought about the older couple and realized that from the beginning, Mae and Anders had struck a good balance between the conflicting sides. Eric respected them, as did she and Neal. Hal might be miserable, but he was in good hands.

Voices and footsteps sounded from between the buildings, and Jessie turned as Sonia and Sonny emerged with their bags. Sonia, dressed in the black and gold outfit that Sonny bought her at Tampu, offered them a tentative smile. The purple and mauve bruises were turning yellow, and a thin scribble of a scar under her right brow was pink, but, as always, the makeup looked fresh and expertly applied.

"Hi, you guys. I've really done it this time, haven't I?" Sonia bent to place her bag on the ground and pulled at the outfit to straighten nonexistent wrinkles.

Jessie fought against saying, "It'll be all right." The phrase sounded so trite and hollow. All she could think to do was reach out and touch Sonia's arm. The other woman's smile reappeared briefly.

"Cab's here," said Sonny as he grabbed luggage and moved out through the arch to the street and the waiting car.

The other three laughed as they tussled over the rest of the bags and joined him.

Jessie watched Sonia's glance dart along the street in both directions. Her shoulders slumped as if she were trying to make herself smaller and she scooted rather than walked the few steps to the taxi.

Neal shook Sonny's hand and as Jessie moved in to give Sonia a brief, good-bye hug, the woman tensed, then inhaled sharply. The, "Oh, no," boomed into Jessie's ear.

They all followed her stare. Eric jogged up the street toward them.

"Sonia, if you don't want to talk with him, get in the cab and we'll go." Sonny moved in beside her.

"I can't just leave. He's been a good friend, it wouldn't be right. I'll have to say something."

Eric slowed to a brisk walk and crossed the street. His clothes looked limp and damp from the exertion, and large beads of sweat worked their way down his face. A swipe from his sleeve wiped them away, but he was sweating again before he reached the group standing by the taxi.

He nodded and said, "Hello, everyone. In case you're wondering, no one told me, but I figured you'd be here. Sonia, I wanted to say good-bye."

Sonia nodded at him, but made no move toward him. "Thanks, Eric."

Jessie could see his eyes probing Sonia's face. He looked around, then gathered up both her hands in his. "Whew, can we get out of this sun?"

He pulled her into the shade of the courtyard and Jessie watched as they sat in the cane chairs. Still holding both her hands, Eric leaned toward Sonia to speak.

"*Un momento, Señor,*" said Sonny to the taxi driver. The old man shrugged and wandered across the street to stand in the shadow of a tree.

The three friends faced each other next to the taxi. Jessie turned her head to gaze at the pair in the courtyard. "You may have a rough ride home, Sonny. Regardless of how right she thinks this is, she's going to be miserable."

"Yeah, well, I've thought of that. I only have to get her to L.A. From there, I know some people I can call. People who know about support groups, that sort of thing. From what you and others have said, this is just one in a long string of incidents. She needs someone with experience in handling what she's going through."

"Well, good luck, and let us know how things go. I was going to ask you to call anyway, to let us know you got back okay." Jessie passed him the slip of paper she had intended to give him at the *cantina*, before everything fell apart. "Here's the telephone number of a Ham radio operator who comes up every day on the net we listen to. Call him and tell him who you are and what's going on. I've written our names, call signs and boat name so he can pass the message to us. It's the easiest and fastest way to contact us. Will you do that?"

"Sure. You'll do the same?"

She nodded. "He's got equipment that can patch us through to you on the phone, so we'll try that. We call home that way, but we haven't done it before with you because it's a collect call. Now that you've been warned, just send us the bill." Jessie smiled at him and reached up to wrap her arms around his neck. "It's been great to see you. Take it easy."

As the friends said their good-byes, Jessie watched Eric and Sonia come back out to the street. Sonia wore a puzzled frown and looked at Eric as if he'd just said something confusing. It eased in a flurry of farewells as the moment finally arrived. The travelers ducked into the taxi, closed the door and left. The dirt lifted by the taxi's tires filled the air and obscured the turn that took them out of sight.

An uneasy silence grew before the dust settled on the threesome left behind.

Eric cleared his throat and wiped the sweat from his forehead. "I might as well say good-bye, too. I'm provisioned and off tomorrow. I was just talking with Hal down at . . . well, you know." He took a deep breath and continued as if he were reciting a prepared speech. "We see no reason to delay. We're both going to make a straight shot to Puerto Vallarta, haul the boats and head back to the U.S. . . . take care of business. All this hasn't been pleasant, but I still wish you good luck with your cruising plans."

Jessie couldn't believe it when he thrust out his hand. Neal looked down at it. The moment dragged as if it were mired in a bog. Neal looked at the man opposite him, lifted his hand and held it there.

Eric laughed and reached the few extra inches to grip the hand and briefly shook it. "I have no hard feelings. I just hope someday you realize the truth about all this, that would really please me. You never know, we may meet again."

"Yeah, maybe." Neal sidestepped Eric and crossed the street.

Jessie had begun to follow Neal when Eric stepped in front of her. His sweaty arms wrapped around her and his lips quickly landed on hers. He hugged her tightly, his head of curls brushing her eyes and before she had time to think about pushing him away, he let go. "I'm sorry you lost faith in me along the way, Jessie. It's what kept me going for a while, you know. I appreciated it. Well, good-bye." He turned and walked away.

His curls bounced as the heels to his thongs hit the road. The damp T-shirt clung to his back and his brown legs pumped. He never looked back as he increased the distance between them.

Jessie wiped her mouth, she wanted a shower.

Neal called out to her from across the road, "You all right?"

"Maybe now I finally will be."

24

"Hey, Jessie, can you bring me the needlenose pliers?"

Her assent sailed out of a porthole near where Neal's body draped over *Dana's* side. His fingers rested from laboring unsuccessfully to free a hard-to-reach cotter ring and his body relaxed. Without the work distracting him, he became conscious of something, other than the bulwark, pressing into his side, and when the pressure mounted to pain, he shifted. To his annoyance, so did the pressure point. To divert his attention from whatever was jabbing him, he gazed up the mast and rigging to the cloudless sky. For the first time, he noticed that the rich, deep blue at the zenith washed to almost white near the horizon. A length of bright pink yarn, used as a wind telltale, fluttered on a shroud several feet above his head. He watched the breeze lift and drop it as puffs blew through. In the moments he waited for the pliers, the aggravation of the last couple of days returned.

After Sonny and Sonia had left for the airport, he and Jessie waited until dark for Satch to return. When they finally pulled *Pointer* into the water and motored home, the man's dinghy was still on the beach. By then, the news had reached a few key people, and next morning the radio nets buzzed.

What had made it worse, Anders came over before the nets started to tell them Satch and Claire had hauled anchor and left during the night. Since the errant couple's original plan was to return to the Sea of Cortez for the summer, everyone assumed they were headed north. But, a day later, it was confirmed that their boat had turned up in Acapulco. Their dinghy sat deflated and secured on deck; the boat was locked up tight. No one had seen or talked to its crew.

Once the news got around the anchorage, he and Jessie again

found themselves besieged by visitors. The cruising community was not divided this time. After the flurry of speculation over *Dana's* adventure with the rocks, Satch and Claire's ghostly nighttime departure had confirmed their guilt as much as any hard evidence. Neal still questioned Claire's knowledge or involvement, but that was something they might never find out.

Discomfort brought his thoughts back to *Dana* and the stubborn cotter ring. His side burned and forced him to shift again. The pain relief matched the relief he felt at hearing Jessie on the companionway steps. He swore at the cotter ring and grabbed at the pain to knead it away. A puff of air lifted the bright pink telltale and cooled his face. Then he heard the unmistakable "plink" of something banging hard into the aluminum boom, followed by a screech.

The cotter ring and pain forgotten, he battled out of his awkward position and worked his way back on deck to ensure his mate was all right. Jessie had pulled the billed cap off her head and was rubbing the wounded area. Her curses reached him and he relaxed, but the echo of the impact rebounded through his thoughts until the sound connected with a memory. He had to close his eyes to concentrate. When he opened them, Jessie's eyes met his a heartbeat later. They stared at each other.

"You heard it, too," he said.

"God, all this time. It's so distinctive, why didn't we realize it before?"

"I don't know. I remember the water looked glassy and with a boom vang . . . maybe it didn't seem logical so we dismissed it. We need to let Swainyo know. It'll be a day or two before Eric gets to Puerto Vallarta. That should give them enough time to check it again, and if it's true, get ready for him."

Jessie hurried down the companionway steps first and called back over her shoulder. "We don't tell anyone else, agreed? It'll get out over the radio and he'll find out someone's made the connection."

Fifteen minutes later, Neal pulled the cord to *Pointer's* engine and they headed for shore and a phone. In his head, he played and replayed as much of the tape as he could remember. The shuffle of the camera made it hard to hear, but now that the connection was made, it seemed impossible that they had missed it. Eric must have watched Jennifer and timed his move for when she was most vulnerable. Maybe when she said, 'Oh God,' she saw the boom swinging over and knew she couldn't stop it. Or worse, she saw Eric and realized what he had done. The sound they all mistook as her unsuccessful attempts at grabbing something as she lost her balance was the boom hitting her head. By then, her finger was slipping off the taping button. Neal blinked and studied his own wife to knock the vision from his thoughts.

They beached *Pointer* and nodded at another couple who pulled a dinghy loaded with bags into the water. The couple smiled in return and got ready to launch. In the last few weeks, Jessie and Neal had become increasingly more sensitive to anyone who wouldn't meet their glance. Never before had a smile and a nod in response to their greeting meant so much.

Once at the phone, they went over what details needed to be relayed. Jessie lifted the receiver, inhaled deeply and dialed.

It took a few minutes for her to outline their speculations.

"What did he say?" Neal laced her arm through his and they turned away from the phone.

"He's going to call the lab and tell them to check. If we want, we can call back tomorrow and find out what happened."

"Good."

They stopped to look out at the harbor. Boats bobbed under the bright, warm sunshine, and dinghies moved back and forth like shuttles. Neal had thought the anchorage was more pleasant, more peaceful since Hal and Eric had hoisted their anchors and sailed off. He remembered feeling glad to see them go. Not any longer. His recent realization made him hot with anger and he wanted to witness Eric's crash. The man had very likely killed his own wife and unborn baby, plus was involved in beating up a good friend. That should be enough to want justice, but it got personal for Neal when he thought of how he had allowed Eric to mess with his own life. He and Jessie had been teased and used from the moment they had met the greedy son of a bitch. What a victory it would have been to see Eric plucked off his boat by harbor officials and led away to some dark and obscure Mexican jail to agonize over his fate. Even so, Neal felt some satisfaction in knowing the man had made a mistake. A mistake that would cost him. Neal was sure the lab would find it. After the indignity of Satch's escape, he wanted someone to get caught for something.

Again the tape played in his head. *Osprey's* telltale barely fluttered in the calm conditions as Jennifer Stover's camera panned the boat. Seeing it again in his mind, he was positive the boom vang had secured the main. With the direction of the wind and a secured main, the boom couldn't travel across the boat without assistance. Jennifer had taped continuously. She couldn't have released the vang without the whole audience knowing it. Someone else had been on deck with her. Neal shook his head at the obvious conclusion. He looked at Jessie and instinctively wrapped his arm around her shoulder, tucking her securely next to him. How could Eric have done it? Neal now believed that at the screening this killer had deliberately swooned with grief to distract everyone, especially the two most likely to catch any nautical discrepancies. The incriminating seconds passed unnoticed. Would those seconds reveal an unfettered main?

"You okay?"

Unsure of how to answer her question, Neal said, "I suppose so, but it's hard for me to understand what drives a person like that."

"You know he's been playing with us, me especially. I must have given him hours of entertainment."

"Oh, he got to both of us at one time or another."

"I feel awful."

Neal pulled her closer and kissed her hair. "Want an ice cream?"

Jed Caldwell's comfortable, familiar voice coordinated the calls that raced across the radio waves. *Dana's* cabin danced with sunlight while Jessie and Neal hugged their morning coffee and listened to the chatter. Comments passed back and forth between them when a location of someone they knew was confirmed. Their good friends, Randy and Gail, planned to arrive the next day. Their sail to Zihuatanejo had not been as eventful as Jessie and Neal's.

Jed read out the call sign of the next person on his list. Jessie's mind wandered until she heard, ". . . KC6 Charlie Bravo Quebec."

A pause of dead air hissed.

"CBQ, are you aboard this morning?"

Jessie slopped coffee on the table as she set down her cup and scrambled for the microphone. The cord got caught around a retaining bolt and she nearly yanked the equipment apart before getting it close enough to her mouth to press the transmit button.

In a rush she said, "Roger, KC6-CBQ here; I didn't catch the sign of the caller."

The repeated letters and numbers were familiar; she recognized it as the net's relay back in the States. It was the man who helped them call home, the man both their families used as a contact in case of emergencies. Her heart began to pound more loudly as he suggested another frequency on which to meet. She agreed and spun the dial and waited for him to call her again. When the familiar voice reached out to her, the face that materialized in her mind was one she had invented. She had never seen this man, but his voice conjured up a picture of him. Her success rate of building a face to match a voice was abysmal, but it didn't stop her from doing it.

"I got a call from your friend Sonny again, and he wanted to talk to you. Said it was important, so stand by while I get him on the phone."

Jessie and Neal exchanged glances, at least it wasn't a family emergency. They had heard from Sonny the day after he left, just to let them know he and Sonia had arrived safely. They weren't expecting another call from him so soon.

"Okay, CBQ, go ahead."

"Sonny, good morning. What's up?" She said it lightly, but when she handed the transmission to Sonny by saying "over," she knew this call was anything but a light, casual hello.

"Good morning, you two. Hope I didn't alarm you, but I thought you might be interested in a call I got from Sage and Peter last night. Over."

"Yes, of course, you've got our attention. Over."

"Angel didn't recognize anyone in the picture that Sonia gave them, but . . . *Andre* did. Sage told me he doesn't like talking about his background; in fact, he perpetuates the notion that he's from Spain.

But apparently when he saw this picture and recognized someone, he knew the implications and decided to confide in her. He really comes from a large town not far from Mexico City. He was the second son of a modest family with an ambitious father who made all his kids go to school. While in school, Andre got involved in athletics and one year the . . . I can't remember what she called it, but it's like a sport conference where teams compete . . . well, one of the schools had an American foreign exchange student. Andre remembered him because he was the first American he had ever met . . . to talk to, I mean, and this American had a woolly head of hair. When he recognized him in the picture with Sonia, he got curious and decided to take the picture and show it around. Sure enough, the man who runs the hotel in Tampu recognized Eric. A couple of other things. Eric did borrow a generator from the hotel owner's brother and . . . he wasn't alone. The hotel owner didn't know anyone else in the picture, so the other man wasn't Hal."

Jessie had begun to untangle the cord as Sonny spoke, but half-way through she had paused, trying to take it all in. She grabbed a quick glance at Neal, who sat staring at nothing in particular. He must have sensed her glance because he snapped out of his trance to look at her. She heard Sonny's "over" and then the hiss of dead air. It was her turn; she was supposed to speak.

She lifted the microphone and pressed the transmit button. "Ah . . . that's very interesting, Sonny. You've taken us off guard a little here. If we can just think for a second, we'll come up with something to say." Her "over" limped out of her mouth and she cringed at how all that must sound at the other end. If they had radio lurkers, this part of the story was out. Neal picked up a pencil and scribbled on a piece of paper, then passed it over to her.

"While you think, I've got more. Eric recognized Sonia's outfit the day we left Zhuat. He made a couple of comments about it as if he'd seen her in it before. At the time, she felt strange about it, but didn't understand why. It wasn't until this picture thing clicked into place that the implication crystallized. I bought that for her in Tampu; the only other time she wore it was for Andre's party. Eric had to have been watching Alta Linda or Andre's to see her in it."

He forgot the "over," but Jessie knew her U.S. relay had instinctively picked up the cadence of the conversation and flipped the switch for her transmission.

"Yeah, that's right, I remember. Neal wants to know if there was a description of the other man?"

"No, but then we may already have an idea who it could be, don't you think?"

"You might be right. Well, Sonny, this is quite a lot to take in. Thanks for letting us know. How's it going otherwise?"

"Funny you should ask. Sonia called Hal's office and gave them my number. As she predicted, Hal called her via High Seas Operator, but not to plead his innocence, which she now knows is likely, at least in this one instance. Apparently he and Eric had set up radio schedules for their trip up to Puerto Vallarta. Hal lost contact with him two nights ago."

* * *

They sat, half watching the perpetual game of basketball and discussed the latest events. The bench was the same one Claire had occupied the day they came looking for Satch.

"His radio could have died." Neal scooped pistachio ice cream on a small plastic spoon and put it in his mouth.

"Maybe, but then he would have used the VHF. I guess he could have tried and still not connected with Hal. We'll just have to wait a few days until he shows up. Since Swainyo has gotten cooperation from all the Mexican authorities around Puerto Vallarta, they should know as soon as he pulls in."

Shouts from children playing on the beach competed with the sounds from the court. Lost in their own thoughts, they savored each mouthful of ice cream. Something occurred to Jessie; she slowly straightened and sat back. Plunging her spoon into the melting scoop, she stirred Neal from his reverie when she said, "He's not ever going to arrive in Puerto Vallarta, is he?"

Her husband paused, stared into his cup, then turned to her. "No, I don't think so."

She slowly loaded her spoon, placed it on her tongue and

wrapped her lips around it. Her mouth cooled and filled with the nutty taste. What she really wanted to do was scream and throw something. The man might actually get away with murder. An overpowering feeling of indignation consumed her. It was unpleasant enough to be the victim of a scam, but to realize that Eric wouldn't pay for his twisted crimes was intolerable.

"What can we do?" she heard herself say.

"Apart from telling Swainyo our thoughts, nothing. We certainly aren't going out to look for him. I'm just glad the lab was able to find and document what we were talking about." In the pause, he slipped in another mouthful of ice cream. "He must have felt so sure of himself. To have both of us sitting there watching. He took a chance that we wouldn't raise the alarm right then. There's no excuse, I should have seen it."

"Neal, we were there under duress, you more than I, and at the time, I was still sympathetic. Besides he did a terrific job of acting. He looked and acted so distraught, there was no way you could have convinced me he wasn't a distraught husband who had just seen the nightmare of his life."

"Yeah, no doubt about that, he was convincing."

They both scooped another spoon of ice cream into their mouths.

Neal said, "He knew exactly what he was doing. It was all very calculated. If he could make it through the screening with two sailors watching, then only if there were a sailor in the investigating team would he need to worry. I think the odds would favor him in that gamble and those few seconds would have gone unnoticed forever. You have to admit he's had his share of luck in all this."

She scraped out the last of her ice cream. "You can say that again . . . maybe with all we've learned recently, his luck has finally run out," she said, popping the final spoonful of green pistacio in her mouth.

For the next few days they waited for news. Randy and Gail arrived and supplied them with enough distractions to occupy them between listening to radio nets and calling Swainyo.

The investigator told them during one conversation that a search for Eric had been instigated. He also had other news. It seemed Eric had been busy while he was in Zihuatanejo, which meant few on

Swainyo's team believed his disappearance was accidental. Most of Jennifer's money had been protected by a prenuptial agreement, but the couple did have joint accounts, which had been closed and the assets transferred.

Swainyo had laughed when he said, "Which, by the way, would provide my wife and me with a very comfortable retirement."

He had gone on to say that Hal Sieverson had arrived safely in Puerto Vallarta and, when asked, admitted to having a phone conversation with Stover about banking. This had been shortly after Jennifer's death when Sieverson was back in the States on business. Under the circumstances, Sieverson didn't think it unusual that Stover had concerns about his accounts and gave his friend the name of a lawyer. The follow-up showed that the lawyer had helped with the transfers, but that was the end of his involvement. The money was then traced to Grand Cayman, where the trail went cold.

The news was disappointing, but not surprising, and brought Eric no closer to justice. Jessie and Neal continued working toward their own departure. Each day they awoke thinking they would learn something; each day disappointed them. After ten days of waiting, with the sea search long since suspended, they called Desi Swainyo and said good-bye. Over the course of events a mutual respect, even friendship, had developed, and after wishing them well, Desi promised to write if he learned anything more.

Finally the departure day came and after farewell hugs to Gail, Randy, Mae and Anders, the Foxes hauled anchor and headed south to Costa Rica. The anxiety of waiting had felt like an itch that no amount of scratching would satisfy, but once the wind filled *Dana's* sails, the itch eased.

"Nothing puts things into perspective better than time at sea." They clinked wine glasses to Neal's toast and bit into the cheese and crackers that filled the small tray between them. From the wind off her aft starboard quarter, *Dana* coasted across the sea with an easy tension in her sails. The hazy dusk disqualified it as a Green Flash sunset, but still they settled in to watch the panorama of reds, oranges and pinks blaze across the unobstructed sky. They had begun another journey.

* * *

Naked under a wall-to-wall blue sky, he picked up *Osprey's* log and turned to the right page. Under the date, he began to write.

"Just woke from a two-hour nap. The water is glassy, the sky clear, but hazy. Every now and then I see the telltale hump of a turtle's back on which rests a sea bird of some kind. So far, they are the only company I have. The radio's been off for days. As I look out across the oil-slick water, it reminds me of the day I lost Jennifer."

Eric's pen lifted off the page, but the passage prompted a scrolling of events, and the imaginary interviewer, who had replaced the company of the radio, again became an attentive listener as he spoke out loud.

"Man, it's hard to describe this feeling. There's no one else to worry about but me. I feel so free."

After putting aside the log and pen, he propped his elbows on his knees and leaned closer to the phantom interviewer.

"I did want Jennifer here, but no matter how much I tried to make her comfortable, it was never enough. She got so set on going back, she refused to see how great all this is. Her money, if we had used it wisely, could have kept us going for the rest of our lives." He sighed and rubbed his face. "But . . . she wanted to go back and if she went back, her money went with her. Unfortunately, she misjudged me. She thought I would choose fatherhood, and all that goes with it, over the freedom to roam the globe. God, what a mistake.

It became a matter of survival, really. The thought of going back to that life we had before gave me claustrophobia. If I were a candle, returning would snuff me out. She sat right there, right where you are, and listened as I explained all this to her. She answered me by saying, 'Eric, you can't raise a child properly on a boat. They need stability, an education and family around. You'll get over it, you'll see. Having this son or daughter to care for will change your perspective.'

I'll never forgive her for that."

He exhaled sharply with a "hmph" and stood. After one look around, his gaze settled on the water ahead.

"Hal should be in PuertoVallarta by now and it won't take long for people to wonder why I haven't shown. In the end he helped give me a good head start, and thanks to Mae and Anders, he changed his mind about taking the next plane out of Zhuat to follow Sonia."

He dropped to a sit and imitated Anders and Mae's voices for his imagined listener.

" 'Give her some time,' they said. 'Go with Eric up to PuertoVallarta, secure the boat so you can forget about it. Then go home and deal with the situation.'

I admit it was a relief when he finally said yes. I knew then that I could easily get away from Zihuatenajo and have at least two, maybe three days to put some distance between me and Mexico."

He paused and then another thought occurred to him.

"I just wish Sonia hadn't been in that room. She was supposed to still be at the party. Her lover was. She scared the shit out of me. I know, I know . . . I got carried away, but there was a lot at stake and all I thought about was how to stop her from seeing me. It was dark and it all happened so fast. I just followed my instincts . . . all of a sudden I was on top of her. Jesus Christ, I just wanted to make sure she didn't know it was me."

He stuffed a cushion behind him and leaned back. Curls bobbed as he shook his head and a crease formed across his forehead. He looked troubled.

"Everything seemed so simple. While everyone was at the party, all I wanted to do was take the camera, watch it to see what I was up against, and then put it back before anyone knew it was gone. No complications, no panic, no need for diversions. Damned electricity. But even with that, I thought my plan was simple. That guy from the party who came huffing into the hotel, fuming about his fight with an American over artifacts gave it to me. I knew if I could get into Sonny's room, make some noise and throw a few things around, the Foxes and their team would have been so busy being mortified at a crazed local, and making sure everything was all right, that Satch and the kid could have slipped the camera back. It could have been so easy. But you see, she was there . . . in the room."

He propped his elbows on his knees again and rubbed his face as if erasing the image.

"I was nervous the first time I saw her after that, but she seemed fine around me. When we talked at the university, I began to realize she thought it was Hal . . . what a bonus. He may be rich, but sometimes he's not too smart. As usual, he was too wrapped up in his own concerns to sense anything and I certainly wasn't going to enlighten him. Since then, I've thought a lot about it and as I see it, she's the one that screwed everything up. Everything would have been fine if she hadn't been in that room."

He sighed and leaned back, folding his arms across his chest.

"It seemed luck had left me, but then, I still had Satch. He was so certain I was innocent that he believed everything I said. It struck me that I might find that loyalty valuable and I was right. When the speculations about Tampu began to fly, I knew his time had come and that Isla Grande was the perfect place for his fall. He's still probably trying to figure out what happened. Thanks to him and my wife's, now my, abundant resources, Lady Luck found her way back to my corner."

A bird swooped in close to the mast and then flew away. He grinned.

"Everyone was so serious while we watched the video. A couple of bites on a shrimp and I didn't even need to act; I had them all thinking I was losing it. Not one of them even entertained the idea that it might be something I ate.

The best laugh, though, was waving good-bye to the Foxes, knowing they had blown the only opportunity to stop me. It was just those few seconds. I knew when I first saw it, if I could just get past those few seconds, I'd never have to worry. I could have messed up the tape, made it unwatchable, but then doubts would have lingered. This way, it was all out in the open and backed up by the king and queen of cruising. When I managed to get Satch through the damning seconds, I knew I could do it, and the Foxes waltzed right through, too. Yeah, I know I manipulated that, but so what? It worked. That tape will get hung up in some lab forever."

Eric yawned and stretched. The sun was hot on his skin; time to put up the small awning. He pulled it out of the lazarette and began getting the lines ready. His safety harness sat next to him. Normally attached while on deck, he just hadn't bothered yet to slip into it. Since it was easier to move around without it and the lines to the awning took him only a couple of steps out of the cockpit, he'd put it on once he had the awning up.

He gazed about him at the expanse of sea and sky. The feeling of space made his spirit fly. Dots on the chart that represented his progress marched ever closer to Ecuador. The "miles remaining" window in his GPS continued to decrease. Everything was perfect. With no proof, only Jennifer's family would carry the torch of suspicion. Overworked officials would eventually tire of them and, uncertain of the cause of his disappearance, their attention on him would fade. He could wait; he planned to be away for long time.

It was the jackline that caught his toe as he stepped out of the cockpit. To right himself he leaned into the lifeline, but the lock on the gate's pelican hook had come free. The pressure he put on it released it and he fell through.

The water felt cool against his hot skin and it took a second for the enormity of his situation to click. When it did, the realization slammed home and banished all normal, rational thinking. His heart pumped so fast he felt it would explode in his chest. Suddenly he needed air, but with each gulp he sucked water. Pressure on his chest made it harder and harder to breathe. He lost the composure he needed to survive and uncontrollable panic set in. He spun around, flailing his arms, splashing like a bird taking a bath. His voice still strong, grunted and whined as his eyes searched. Water beaded up on his sunglasses and made it impossible for him to see. He ripped them off and relief renewed his spirits when there, just beyond his reach, the word *Osprey* spanned the white transom.

Gurgling, he uttered words of encouragement. "Swim, I've got to swim."

It felt like his arms wore sand bags. They lifted, reached and pulled, while his feet kicked. To get more streamlined, he lowered his head into the water. A second later he dropped his feet and clawed to the surface, sputtering, coughing, gasping.

Air, need air.

His arms pumped and his feet kicked. Too afraid to put his head in the water again, he focused his eyes on the word *Osprey.* His chest heaved and he sucked, but his lungs went unsatisfied.

Air, need air.

He flipped onto his back as the thought occurred to him it might be easier to breathe that way. A wavelet flooded his face; water ran into his nose and mouth. He bolted upright and coughed, gasped in and coughed some more. It felt as if something were squeezing him around the chest; he couldn't fully expand his lungs.

Air, need air.

Grunting and whining more loudly, he paddled on his stomach again. Even though his arms felt heavier and no longer cleared the water, the word *Osprey* looked bigger. He kicked harder and pulled harder. His grunting got louder and louder, and the word grew bigger and bigger.

With a wail and groan that lifted a bird off the back of a nearby turtle, he touched the boat. He scrambled around, searching for something to grip, something to take the weight of his body. His arms and legs were so tired, he needed rest.

Air, need air.

The expanse of fiberglass under the word was smooth. His hand touched it and felt around. Nothing. He pumped and kicked around the stern and worked along the hull. A wail escaped with each breath.

Air, need air.

Grunting down the side, he lifted his arm up to feel for something to grip. His head went under water. He dropped his arm and sputtered to the surface.

Air, need air.

He coughed, choked and retched. Treading along the hull, his eyes caught the gleam. Not far from the water's surface glinted the metal fitting where the boarding ladder attached while at anchor. A renewed surge of power came over his arms and legs and he paddled toward it. Toward his salvation.

The lesson he learned before about raising his arm out of the water made him pause under the fitting and eye it for a moment.

He struggled for a breath, kicked double time and with a scream, he surged out of the water. One hand flung out and latched onto the fitting. Using it as a stepping stone, he hiked his other hand to a stanchion on the deck. After he wrapped both hands around the stanchion, he hung there, whimpering. His chest heaved and his heart thumped so loudly he could hear nothing else.

His lungs relished the abundance of air and he sucked until he could fully inflate them.

A laugh escaped and he yelled.

"You thought you had me, you son of a bitch." The laugh weakened to a chuckle and he wailed more quietly. "You son of a bitch."

Hanging there gave him time to think, collect himself, catch his breath. Moving at less than a knot, the boat's lazy amble made it possible for him to hold on. Once rested, he would pull himself up.

But when the time came, he couldn't. He tried again and again, shifting his hands from the stanchion to the lifeline and back to the stanchion, trying to improve his position. With each effort he felt strength flow out of his arms until they shook. His thoughts grew as sluggish as his limbs, so he stopped. He focused on relaxing and conserving energy. In his efforts, each time he was able to get his eyes above the deck, he caught sight of the unfettered windward jib sheet that ran the length of the deck. If he could get hold of it, he'd be able to tie himself to the boat, maybe eventually find a way to use it to get back on deck. To grab that line, though, meant the arms that stretched over his head and gripped the stanchion would have to pull his body up far enough to make the reach. To make the reach, one hand would have to let go of the stanchion. In his weakened state, if he missed . . . .

He had one chance. The muscles in his jaw rippled as he thought it through, then went slack. With a calm resolve, he took three deep breaths and force-fed his limbs with determination. His wail sailed across the sea as he hiked himself up, let go of the stanchion and reached for his life.

EPILOGUE

four months later

Ceiling fans whirled in an effort to keep the tavern cool. Long eaves on the corrugated iron roof extended out beyond the walls to provide shade and prevent rain from blowing inside. Large, open gaps without glass served as windows and allowed the breeze free and easy access throughout. In the corner, two men drank beer and smoked as they chalked up their pool cues. A moment later, balls clicked as they rolled across the green felt table and bumped into one another.

A bright, hot sun shone from a sky filled with big, white, puffy clouds. The kind of clouds that later in the day would darken and bring the usual afternoon rains to the Costa Rican countryside. Thick, green foliage crowded about the tavern except for one wall. That wall, supported by stilts set into the rocky shore, extended out over the brown, bay water.

Jessie and Neal sat at a table with two sweating bottles of Imperial beer and a pile of paper litter they usually created when going through a welcomed and much-awaited mail package. *Dana* bobbed on her anchor just out from their vantage point.

Neal lounged, enjoying his letter. Something he read straightened his back. "My kids are coming."

Jessie looked up from the envelope she was about to open. "Really? When?"

"It doesn't say. They want us to decide when would be best and they give school vacation dates. I'll be damned, I didn't think they'd really do it."

"Such little faith you have," said Jessie and returned to her envelope. Added, in pen, to the formal government address in the upper left-hand corner was, 'D. Swainyo.'

Once the realization sank in, she ripped it open as she said, "Neal, this is from Desi. Desi Swainyo, you know, our cop friend in Mexico City who handled that mess with Eric."

Pulled away from his own bit of good news, Neal said, "What does he have to say?"

Her eyes scanned down the page. "Mm . . . it seems Satch, of anchor fame, has turned up. Do you want me to read it out loud?"

"You go ahead. I'll read it when you're done," he said and went on to another letter.

Jessie took a sip of Imperial and leaned back into her chair to read. When she finished, Neal was ready. A little dazed, she passed Swainyo's letter across to him.

One look at her and he said, "Everything all right?"

"Judge for yourself."

Neal settled in to read.

Dear Jessie and Neal,

I hope this letter finds you well. As I said to you before, I think you lead an interesting life, and from what I remember of your plans, you should be in Costa Rica, one of my favorite Central American countries. Enjoy, and if I can do anything for you while you're there, just let me know.

I'm sending you an update on the case concerning the disappearance and presumed death of Jennifer Stover. I believe you'll find what I have enclosed interesting.

A few weeks after you departed Mexico, Satch Jurgeon introduced himself to the Talbert (Jennifer's) family. When he told them he was there with information regarding Eric Stover, the family called in their lawyers and got a deposition. The report was long, so bear with me.

Many of the speculations that we all discussed before saying goodbye have been confirmed. I should say here, too, that Mr. Jurgeon spent several minutes explaining how, until the incident at Isla Grande, he believed Stover was being unfairly harassed over his wife's death. He was sympathetic and wanted to help, which is why he ended up in Tampu.

Mr. Jurgeon freely admitted to bribing Angel and confirmed, after thinking about it, that Angel never actually met Stover, which is why the boy didn't recognize him in the photo.

It appears the two men had watched you leave for the art gallery party; then, while Stover kept a lookout, Angel unlatched your bathroom window and passed the camera out to Mr. Jurgeon. One of the mistakes Mr. Jurgeon believed he made was in telling Angel they would be back in an hour, and to be at the window.

When they got the camera back to their hotel, they made the discovery about the electricity and Stover went into a rage until the hotelier promised to find a generator. Once everything got set up, Stover announced he wanted to view the tape alone. This news disappointed Mr. Jurgeon, but at least his friend would see it, which, after all, was the reason for all the clandestine activity. A few minutes later, Stover reappeared saying it wasn't as bad as he had feared and was going to run it again if Mr. Jurgeon wanted to join him. About halfway through, Stover broke down, but managed to compose himself quickly. Sort of brings back memories, doesn't it?

The problem with the electricity meant they were delayed longer than the hour promised, and when they returned, Angel was nowhere around. It took another hour for Mr. Jurgeon to finally find the youngster, but by then the kid was sputtering that the prank was wrecked because you had already come back. Jurgeon told Angel to hold tight, and he went to tell Stover what had happened. The two mulled over their problem until Stover came up with an idea. He would create a diversion that would pull you two out of your room so that Mr. Jurgeon could replace the camera, with Angel's help.

Stover left to carry out his part of the plan and his accomplice left to brief Angel. After dispensing instructions, Mr. Jurgeon waited near Alta Linda, expecting his young accomplice to appear at the window, but instead, the boy showed up at his elbow, very upset. Alta Linda had erupted with the news of Mrs. Sieverson's attack and with so many people around, the boy couldn't get near any of the rooms without being seen. This alarmed Mr. Jurgeon, but he made light of it and sent the boy back into the hotel.

When the two men reunited, Stover was agitated and said he'd seen a Mexican man go into Mrs. Sieverson's room. He had heard noises, but didn't know what had happened. At the time, Mr. Jurgeon had no reason to question him and it seemed only natural to relay Angel's news.

Stover went nuts and lit into Mr. Jurgeon about not taking advantage of the assault to return the camera. As more time passed, Stover got more agitated, and Mr. Jurgeon grew afraid that his friend's behavior might attract attention. He finally convinced Stover to go back to their village hotel, and as you know, Mr. Jurgeon and Angel eventually succeeded in making the delivery.

That was beginning of the end. Confidence in Stover began to erode and at the time he gave his deposition, Mr. Jurgeon was convinced Stover was the man behind the attack.

Your names also appeared in his details of the incident on Isla Grande. Mr. Jurgeon alleged he spent one whole day trying to get to the bottom of allegations that he tampered with your boat. Since he knew he hadn't touched it, he went in search of a way to clear his name. When Stover seemed bent on blaming him for the incident, Mr. Jurgeon grew suspicious. After all, it had been Stover who had encouraged him to get away and enjoy the island for a few days. Through an interpreter, he finally found a *panga* driver who had ferried a *gringo* to Isla Grande in search of some rare bird.

Apparently this *gringo* spent a lot of time looking through binoculars and studying a book. Just after dark, he told the driver to detour into the anchorage. He claimed he had promised to check on a boat for a friend touring inland. The detour didn't take long and they returned to Ixtapa.

Mr. Jurgeon described Stover to the driver and got a positive response. That's when he became concerned not only for his physical safety, but also his wife's, and rather than take his chances with authorities in Mexico, Mr. Jurgeon left to return to the United States. He understood the Talbert family had suspicions about Jennifer's death and although there were eyebrows raised as to his reason for delaying a month to contact them, the information he had brought renewed officials' interest. That brings us up-to-date on him.

Now on to Mr. Stover. Less than a week before the date of this letter, his boat was brought into Panama by a small freighter. On board we found his passport, boat papers and other personal effects. His log was there, and although sunbleached, his last entry was readable and referred to his wife's death. Given the growth of mold and the deterioration of equipment, we think the boat had been floating around alone for a couple of months. Speculations as to what happened to Mr. Stover are as varied as the people doing the speculating, but it's unlikely that he's still alive.

Hopefully, my account answers many of the questions we all had when we last spoke. Since there was no body, the case is still on the books, but little more will be done. The Talbert family is still active in searching for the money, but I have no details.

Well, that's about it. All else goes well here. Enjoy the riches of Costa Rica and whatever port comes next. Take care of yourselves and best regards,

Desi

"So, they think he's dead," said Neal as he looked up from the page.

"Yeah,"

He scanned the letter again. "It all seems so bizarre when it's written out like this."

"The letter acts like a reminder to me on how gullible I was," said Jessie. "To find out that all that was going on behind the scenes amazes me. I never would have believed it at the time. At least you knew something was wrong."

"Yeah, but I wasn't all that sure either."

"Thanks, babe, for trying to make me feel better." He smiled at her as he handed the letter back. She looked it over again, then tossed it onto the table. "Do you think he's dead?"

"My first instinct is to say yes, but would I dismiss the possibility that he hitched a ride on a passing freighter, intentionally leaving everything behind to make the impression that he's dead? No. Stranger things have happened." He took a swallow of beer as he considered the suggestion. "I wondered sometimes where he ended up, whether he found a place to hole up or whether the sea took payment for what he did. I admit it's much more satisfying to think he's not sitting on a beach, sipping the local brew with a lady who keeps asking him what's so funny."

Their eyes went back to the letter. Jessie almost stopped him, but thought better of it and watched Neal rip the letter into bits, then add them to their pile of debris. She had Swainyo's address in their book and she would thank him for the update. As tragic as it was, the idea that Eric wouldn't reappear in their future gave her a sense of peace.

A burst of laughter and a shout drew their attention to the area around the pool table. Jessie and Neal watched the two men shake hands, slap each other on the back and set up for another game. The outburst brought the couple back from the past. They smiled at each other and knew without words that so much lay in front of them, they didn't have time to look back. Neal picked up the letter from his offspring, read it out loud, and over a fresh round of *cervesas,* he and his wife planned a family reunion.

GLOSSARY

aft at or toward the back of a vessel; used as a position or motion

amidship the middle of a vessel; can be used when referring either to the length or the width of the vessel

block a revolving wheel or wheels encased in wood, metal or a composite through which a line is passed; used to increase the mechanical power applied to a rope or line or to guide them to convenient positions

boathook a long pole made of wood or metal with a hook on the end; used to aid in fending off, picking up mooring lines and generally extend the reach of a sailor

boom a horizontal, metal or wooden pole, usually hollow, used to keep taut the foot, or bottom edge, of a sail. On *Dana* and *Osprey* it is attached to the mast and used to keep taut the foot of the mainsail

boomgallows a horizonal bar, supported by two vertical posts on which rests the boom when not in use

boom vang holds the boom down when necessary; often on cruising boats it doubles as a boom brake and restrains the boom from swinging back and forth from port to starboard

bow the front or forward portion of a vessel

bridle a network of lines used to center an attachment point for an object that needs to be pulled or lifted; this bridle affords the object better balance during the pulling or lifting

brightwork all the woodwork on the boat that is coated with gloss varnish so that it shines

bulkhead an upright partition dividing a boat into compartments

bulwark the wall built around the edge of a ship's deck. Depending on the ship's design and size, it can be a few inches to a few feet high

cabin sole the floor of the cabin

chocks wooden mounts, usually situated on deck, upon which a dinghy can be secured while the vessel is underway

cockpit the command center, typically where the helm and most instruments are located

companionway ladder or stairway which leads from one deck to the another. On *Dana* and *Osprey*, it leads from the cock pit to the cabin below

cotter ring a ring of stiff wire, coiled nearly twice around; threaded through a hole or opening to secure some thing or to hold parts together

deck plate a metal plate, usually of bronze or stainless steel, and found on the deck. The many uses can include: re inforcing necessary holes, covering necessary holes or reinforcing high stress areas

dinghy a small boat used as a shuttle or hauler for a larger vessel; made of wood, fiberglass, heavy-duty rubber and then inflated, or a combination of these

drop boards two or three boards, fitted to easily slide into place to act as a door for the companionway hatch

flotilla a grouping or fleet of vessels

flotsam the wreckage of a vessel found floating at sea

forestay a wire or rope that is used to prevent the mast from falling back. Located at the very front of the vessel and is a part of the rigging.

genoa a large foresail, one that's attached in the bow and hung from the forestay; provides significant driving power for a yacht

GPS Global Positioning System. A network of satellites that orbits earth, transmitting signals; it enables people with the proper receiving unit to determine their location

grommet a reinforcement ring of metal or thread placed or sewn around a hole in fabric

gunwale (Pronounced gunnal) the top plank—the top edge of a boat's sides

halyard the rope or line used to raise and lower a sail

hatch an opening in the deck which leads to the spaces below, usually covered by a hatch cover

head a ship's lavatory

helm the wheel or tiller of a vessel

hull refers to the body of a vessel. Included: deck, sides and bottom. Excluded: mast, boom and rigging

jackline a secured line or wire on deck running fore and aft onto which safety harnesses can be attached

jetsam objects deliberately thrown overboard

jib a foresail, smaller than the genoa

keel located on the very bottom of a vessel and referred to as its "backbone." It provides stability, and in certain conditions provides resistance to the sideways force of wind and water

knot used as the international nautical unit of speed equivalent to 6,080 feet per hour. Correctly used — "we're traveling at two knots," not "we're traveling at two knots per hour.

lanyard a cord or tether used to secure one thing to another

latitude a measure of distance due north or south of the earth's equator. It is represented by a series of parallel lines and expressed in degrees

lazarette a storage place or locker usually found near the rear of a vessel

lifeline lines or wire, usually two to four feet high, which run the length of a vessel and parallel to the deck. They add a measure of safety for the crew, who can grip them or clip their safety harness to them when ever moving around on deck

longitude a means of measuring an east or west position from Greenwich, England. It is represented by lines running north - south and measured in degrees, with

Greenwich, England being the starting point. Zihuatanejo is approximately 102 degrees west of Greenwich or 102 W

main term used for the mainsail on a yacht. It is the principal sail with one edge, the luff, attached to the mast, and the bottom edge, the foot, attached to the boom

mast a vertical pole, usually hollow, made of metal, wood or composite, and from which sails, booms, and rigging are attached

painter a short rope or line used to tether a small boat to a dock or to another boat

panga term used in Mexico for an open boat typically made of wood or aluminum; used for fishing and ferrying goods and people

pelican hook a metal fitting with a hinged clip used to connect two lines or rigging wire together; typically found on the lifelines of a sailboat to allow for an opening or gate; usually has a locking mechanism to prevent accidental "unclipping."

port the left half of a vessel, or off to the left; used for either position or direction

rigging wire, rod or line used to support the mast; more specifically known as the standing rigging

rudder a flat board or piece of fiberglass attached to the back of a vessel. When moved, it steers the vessel

sampson post a post used to secure chain, rope or line. Typically positioned near the anchor windlass and used, if necessary, when raising or lowering the anchor

sheet a line or rope that is attached to the loose corner, or clew, of a sail, and controls the sail's position to the wind

shroud refers to that part of the standing rigging used to laterally support the mast

snapshackle a metal fitting which connects lines or ropes to other things around the vessel. A ring is at one end through which the line passes and is tied; a clip is at the other end with a spring loaded mechanism to secure it shut. On *Dana* it's used to attach halyards to sails and to attach the main halyard to *Pointer's* launching bridle

snubber a length of line or rubber used as a shock absorber

spinnaker a large, light air sail used when the wind is blowing from behind

spinnaker pole a long, lightweight pole used to extend one of the bottom corners of the spinnaker; it allows the sail to take better advantage of the wind

spreader light lights found on the spreaders, which are horizontal struts high up on the mast and which aid the lateral support of the mast

stanchion an upright support, typically made of stainless steel, and strategically spaced and affixed around the perimeter of a sailboat's deck; they carry the lifelines

starboard the right half of a vessel, or off to the right; used for either position or direction

stay refers to that part of the standing rigging that supports the fore and aft position of the mast

staysail	strictly used, it refers to any sail attached to a stay, but in more contemporary use, the term refers to a smaller sail located aft of the jib or genoa; aids in sail trim and driving force
stern	the back portion of a vessel
tack	two common meanings: 1: The forward most corner of the sail that is closest to the deck and attached to the vessel. 2: While under sail, the act of changing the vessel's relationship to the wind by momentarily passing the bow into the wind
teak	a hard East Indian timber commonly used on boats
telltale	a length of lightweight material attached to the | rigging, enabling the crew to know the direction of the wind
tender	a small boat used as a shuttle or hauler for a larger vessel
tiller	a horizontal bar typically made of wood and attached to the rudder; it enables the sailor to steer the vessel
wake	a track of disturbance that a ship makes as it moves through the water
winch	a ratcheted drum around which, in contemporary sailing terms, sheets are passed in order to secure and trim the sails.
windvane	a mechanism designed to use the wind's power to steer a vessel
windlass	a ratcheted drum around or over which, in contem porary sailing terms, line or chain is passed to hoist an anchor; can be mechanical or electric; *Dana's* is mechanical

windward the direction from which the wind is blowing. The side of the boat onto which the wind is blowing is known as the windward side